THE NOBLEST SHARE OF EARTH

ALSO BY NANCY BLANTON

The Prince of Glencurragh

The Earl in Black Armor

When Starlings Fly as One

The Snow Path to Dingle
(also published under the title *Sharavogue)*

Brand Yourself Royally in 8 Simple Steps

The Curious Adventure of Roodle Jones

THE NOBLEST SHARE OF EARTH

A Novel

NANCY BLANTON

ELLYS-DAUGHTREY BOOKS
JACKSONVILLE, FLORIDA

Ellys-Daughtrey Books
4600 Middleton Park Cir. E., A227, Jacksonville, FL 32224

THE NOBLEST SHARE OF EARTH

Disclaimer:
Certain characters in this book are historical figures, however, they may participate
in events and interact with characters who are fictional, products of the author's
imagination. Any resemblance of fictional characters to individuals living
or dead is coincidental.

Published by Ellys-Daughtrey Books
http://ellys-daughtrey.blogspot.com

ISBN: hard cover 978-1-7335928-5-7
ISBN: soft cover 978-1-7335928-6-4
ISBN: e-book 978-1-7335928-7-1

Library of Congress Control Number: 2024917146

Cover design includes a portion of a 17th century painting in the public domain from
https://jenikirbyhistory.getarchive.net. The identities of those in the painting are
unknown. The back cover includes part of a digital map of the
Province of Ulster in 17th century Ireland, from mapsofthepast.com.
Design by the author.

For my father

Edward A. Blanton

1925 - 1997

*Thank you for enriching my life
and the lives of my sisters with the
tenacity and pride of the Irish*

Author's Note

Thank you for choosing to read *The Noblest Share of Earth*. First and foremost, this is a work of fiction based on factual accounts. It is a heroine's journey, a story of love, war, struggle, rebellion, loss, and redemption.

I have respectfully used the names of real people to help the reader connect the story with the history. However, any descriptions of individuals, their speech, mannerisms, relationships, or their interactions, are entirely imagined. I couldn't know what the individuals were truly like, what they thought, or how they behaved, but have relied on information gleaned from historical documents and research.

Any resemblance of these characters to living individuals is purely coincidental and not by intention.

ACKNOWLEDGEMENTS

For the accomplishment of this book, I am grateful and indebted to many, the first of whom is my husband, Karl Shaffer, who supported me, tolerated my moods and frustrations, and welcomed me home to the present day when at last the manuscript was completed.

I may never have started this work at all if not for the encouragement of my sister and traveling partner, Daphne Berry, and the grand tour of Donegal led by novelist, musician, and retired teacher David A. Dunlop and his lovely wife Mary. While in Donegal I also gained much valuable information from Raphoe Heritage Officer Edward Harnett. From the tour of the Titanic Museum in Belfast, I gained stimulating and unexpected inspiration.

Most of the chapters are informed by the work of others, the dedicated and thorough Irish historians, particularly Brian Bonner and James O'Neill, but also Ruth Canning, Hiram Morgan, John McCavitt, F.W. Harris, Hugh Allingham, Robert M. Chapple, Francis Martin O'Donnell, James Mooney, Seán ÓDomhnaill, and others.

The manuscript was much improved by the expertise of my editor in London, Kelly Urgan, and the thoughtful and sharp eyes of beta readers Gail Vivian and Daphne Berry. For these and other helps I thank Andrea Patten, my co-founder of Amelia Indie Authors writers' co-op.

For my introduction and addiction to the fascinating, magical, and resplendent world that is Ireland, I thank my father, Edward A. Blanton, to whom this book is dedicated, and to my dear friend Eddie MacEoin, who introduced me to his family and hometown of Skibbereen, County Cork, and shared with me an unforgettable adventure exploring the island. If you wonder why an American writer should become so entangled in Irish history, you can blame them.

LIST OF CHARACTERS

[R = real person, I = imagined person]

Primary Point-of-View Characters

GEEP: The storyteller of Buncrana Castle, I

CAHIR O'DOHERTY: The O'Doherty, Clan Chieftain, R

MAIRE O'DOHERTY: Lady Maire O'Doherty, wife of Cahir, R

STOAT O'DOHERTY: Trusted friend and protector of Cahir, I

Secondary Characters, Last Name Alphabetical

Charles Blount: 8th Lord Mountjoy, Lord Deputy of Ireland, R

Arthur Chichester: Lord Deputy of Ireland after Blount, R

Rita Coyle: Baker for Gormanston Castle, I

Henry Docwra: First Commander of Derry Garrison, R

James Kintor: Captain of ship, Eimher, I

Nonie MacCarthy: Cook and maid servant to Lady Maire, I

Felim MacDavitt: Younger brother of Hugh, Advisor, Warrior, R

Hugh MacDavitt: The MacDavitt, Clan leader, Cahir's mentor, R

Finn MacTyre: Irish warrior, O'Doherty Clan, I

Lady Finola O'Donnell: Red Hugh O'Donnell's mother, R

Red Hugh O'Donnell: The O'Donnell, Clan Chieftain, R

Niall Garbh O'Donnell: Cousin to Red Hugh, R

Peg O'Hanlon: Cahir's sister, married to Eochy O'Hanlon, R

Hugh O'Neill: Leader of Ulster Rebellion, Earl of Tyrone, R

George Paulet: Second Commander of Derry Garrison, R

Catherine Preston: Maire's mother, R

Cat Preston: Maire's younger sister, R

Christopher Preston: Maire's father, 4th Viscount Gormanston, R

Jenico Preston: Son of Christopher, Maire's younger brother, R

Christopher St. Lawrence: Baron Howth, County Meath, informer, R

King James VI & I: King of England, Stuart Dynasty beginning in 1603, R

Henry Vaughn: English army captain, rewarded with Inishowen land, R

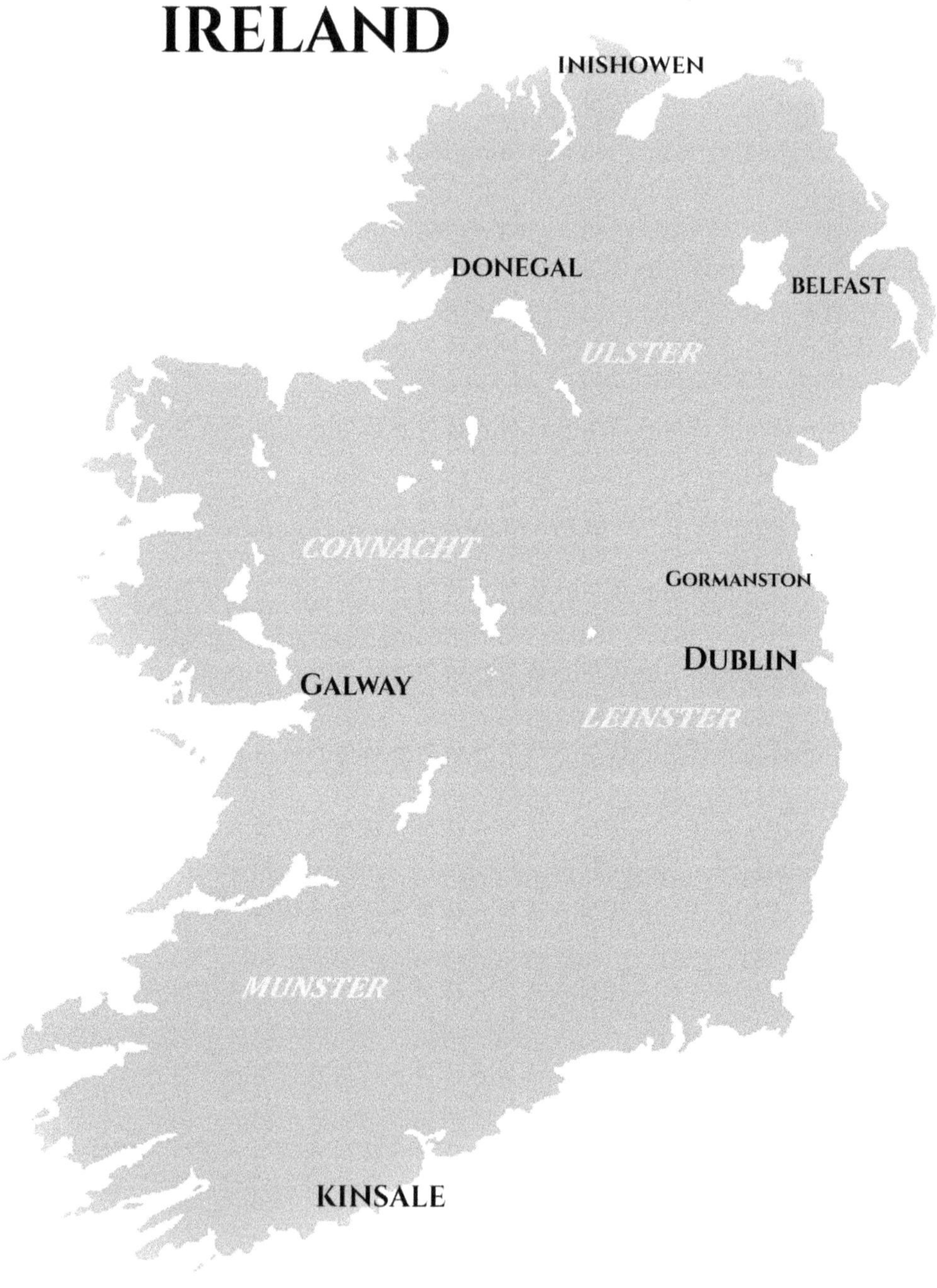

IRELAND

INISHOWEN
DONEGAL
BELFAST
ULSTER
CONNACHT
GORMANSTON
DUBLIN
GALWAY
LEINSTER
MUNSTER
KINSALE

ULSTER PROVINCE

TIMELINE

1600
Sir Henry Docwra arrives as Commander,
Culmore and Derry garrisons
Province of Ulster

Cahir O'Doherty and Maire Preston
are married

1601
Following his father's death,
Cahir assumes leadership of O'Doherty Clan

1602
The English defeat the Spanish and Irish
at the Battle of Kinsale

1603
Queen Elizabeth I dies

Treaty of Melifont
Irish surrender, leaders O'Neill and
O'Donnell pardoned

1604
Cahir comes of age,
claims his patrimony, Inishowen

1605

Sir Arthur Chichester named
Lord Deputy of Ireland

1606

The Gunpowder Plot
Discovered in London

Catholic persecution escalates

1607

The Flight of the Earls
O'Neill and O'Donnell abandon Ireland

Sir George Paulet replaces Docwra,
Commander of Culmore and Derry

1608

Sir Cahir O'Doherty launches clan
rebellion against the English

Plantation of Ulster escalates

The noblest share of earth
is the far western world
Whose name is written Scotia
in the ancient books:
Rich in goods, in silver, jewels,
cloth, and gold,
Benign to the body in air
and mellow soil.
With honey and with milk
flow Ireland's lovely plains,
With silk and arms,
abundant fruit, with art and men.

Worthy are the Irish to dwell in this their land,
A race of men renowned in war,
in peace, in faith.

*— Donatus, Bishop of Fiesole, mid-ninth century.
Translated by Liam de Paor.*

From *Treasures of Early Irish Art*,
published by The Metropolitan Museum of Art

1

GEEP

1616

Inishowen Peninsula, County Donegal, Ireland

I said to young Fia, "In all of Ireland, from jagged mountain to crashing sea, you'll find the most fierce and valiant warriors, and the most brilliant, silver-tongued schemers. The trouble is, to have the both in a single soul is worse than rare. It's been the death of us, searching for such a being, but once…sure we had it for a time."

She sighed and dropped her bony young shoulders. "That's rubbish. My Uncle Henry is a soldier and a gentleman. The one goes along with the other."

"That's as may be in Captain Henry Vaughn's case, but I tell you: a man may call himself a soldier while having no notion of gentility, and a gentleman may wield his sword and lead men into battle without the slightest whim of cunning. Only fate can piece together a person of such worth." I gave her a sly wink.

"Oh, Geep! What does it matter? You're stalling again!" She stamped her foot like the petulant eleven-year-old she was. She'd named me 'Geep' in her early years when she couldn't say a name like Gearalt—passed down to me from my fabled chieftain ancestor. I gladly buried my pride just to hear her call me. As light and lithe as the swiftest deer of the forest, she was a ward of Captain Vaughn who leased Inishowen, the finest, most beautiful, and most fertile land in all of Ireland, stolen from our broken clan.

Fia plopped down upon the weeds clustered between the old flagstones, her frock too fine for such treatment, especially with the morning dew still lingering. She'd begged to hear the story of the great Clan O'Doherty that once owned the land, and the Lord and Lady who ruled. I regretted having promised her. Better she should dance among the yellow furze, untroubled by tragedies and the empty pile of stones overlooking Lough Swilly. Once a formidable castle, now it were as battered and useless as I.

Each day I watched the captain's workers dismantle the keep's outer wall, stone by stone, and cart the pile across the field to enlarge his own modern castle—a monstrosity meant to boast his English favor and wealth. The sight of it burned at the core of my heart. If I be a seer as my Ma always said, why did I never see the truth of what was to coom?

"I was the one to first bring you here, didja know that, lass? I spent many a year around this castle, but on the day I delivered you to Captain Henry and his wife, I sat myself down where you've always found me, knowing I were to die wi' me spine against the last cold stones of Buncrana Castle. We'll be bound forever, this crumbling tower and I, both having failed in our only duty. You mustn't waste your sunny days on me."

"Of course you won't die! And what duty? Is that part of the story? I must know it all before I go. Today the carriage comes for me, and I may never see the castle again." Fia's voice trilled with urgency.

"Ah, yes, I nearly forgot you're off to Dublin today. Think of all you'll learn about the ways of a fine lady. And, won't you be glad to meet your betrothed? I pray he's a good and honorable lad. Sure he is fortunate."

"You'll come, too, won't you?"

"Oh! They'll have no wish to see this cross old fella, and the lad's eyes'll never find a sight more lovely than your own fine self. Why d'ye wish to hear a sad tale when you're to be carried off to your happiness?"

Fia shook her head impatiently. "You promised, that's all. Begin with that girl you mentioned. The lady of the castle. Begin with herself, and then tell about the boy."

I sighed and shifted my bones to sit taller. My spine protested as if already it had bonded with the old castle wall. "The lady, you say. All right, so," and I gave my stubbly beard a thoughtful scratch—a necessary pause before starting. "Her name was Maire, a young lass like you, soon to be wed; and the lad, her husband-to-be, was named Cahir."

"Care?"

"Exactly right, my girl. And you'll need ta know about a fella named Stoat, as well."

"Stoat? You haven't mentioned that name before."

"Aye, 'tis the name he were given. We'll come to him naturally," I said, tapping my fingers together in a point as I pondered. "But first, as you asked—the lady, Maire. She were a few years older than yourself when she first met her betrothed, but she had no joy for it. In fact, 'twas a near disaster. Now then, so."

2

MAIRE

First Encounter

December 1600

I heard them before I saw them, their heaving war horses thundering up our carriageway, the songbirds scattering as they neared our castle. Three abreast they were with a few guards behind, their shoulders dusted with snow dislodged from the trees. There was no mistaking himself, my betrothed, front and center and sitting tall, his eyes wide, his ginger hair stiff as a patch of buckthorn. I hurried from my bedchamber and down the stairs as they approached the great hall entrance.

The guards stayed outside while my father welcomed the three men into our great hall. The tall boy, my betrothed, stood before me. He was dressed in what I'd later learn was traditional for the northern edge of Ireland: a saffron shirt with long draping sleeves and a brown jerkin over it embroidered with geometric markings. I'd never seen a man anywhere near Dublin who dressed in such a way. Dublin was a city of modern people, with sophisticated fashion brought in by the English and French. In my own County Meath, even the shepherds looked smart, but it seemed such notions never reached the far north. I was not having it, no, not for a minute. How dare he think I'd be courted by a buffoon.

In that instant his eyes met mine. My face must have shown my displeasure and he clearly read my thoughts. He glanced down at his vest and his shoes and seemed to freeze where he stood. The others looked surprised. "What is it, lad? Are you right?" one of the men asked. He gave no reply but stared at me until I had to step back, then he turned on his heel and left the hall. He called for his horse and then cantered off the way he'd come, the others trailing behind.

Well enough then, I was glad to see the back of him. Because I won't. I'll not have some Irish boy come in like a peacock and me supposed to curtsy and titter about him like a besotted fool. Not to even mention the idea that I was to wed him. I'd sooner hurl myself from the corner tower. Then my father slammed the door. "Up to your room," he shouted, and there was no mistaking the sound of his boots coming fast on the stairs behind me, my mother on his heels. So many times those sounds had come, my father to swear at me, mother to beg and stay his hand. If I was resistant and rebellious, it was only because he had a demand for every moment and every act. I feared him, yes. And I loved him. But I couldn't bear to always give him his way as mother did. I'd rather take the beating.

The door swung wide and hit the wall behind it. "What have you done, Maire?" he thundered. "What did you do to send them away even before they'd fully arrived?"

"I was only looking at them. I've no power over what they…"

"You're my firstborn daughter. Don't dare to think I don't know you well and the things you do to have your own way. Hear me. If I don't see them return, and soon, you'll have shamed our house and defied your father, leaving little hope that even the convent will take you after."

"Convent? Father, he was dressed like a character in a masque! You'd have done the same in a different circumstance, and I…"

"Daughter," his voice rose, and his hands began to tremble. "I care not if he arrived naked as a newly hatched robin, he's your betrothed and you will marry Cahir O'Doherty. You will."

He stepped back a bit, calming himself, though my mother still pressed her fingers against her lips. "Maire, let us be honest," he said. "Your poor mother has taught you everything she knows, preparing you exactly for this day. You've had the finest tutors, the best clothes, the advice of our best parish priest. The time has come, in fact it's overdue. You must marry and allow your sister Catherine to marry behind you. You've met the lad's father, Sir Sean Og O'Doherty, a wise man, a good Catholic, and ruler of one of the most fertile and beautiful bits of land in all of Ireland. He also commands an army of men who would fight God himself if he asked them to. You'll have a good life."

"I have a good life now. I'm 17. I can live on my own. Why must I marry at all?" My mother closed her eyes and sighed.

Father stomped his heavy boot. "Because it's what is done," he thundered, "and it's your duty to your family and our religion! Your duty, I said! You will marry this boy, you will birth an heir, and we will have a strong alliance to our north. It's settled, and by God it's paid for!"

"I…I can't," I said, though my lower lip trembled.

His eyes bulged. His cheeks turned crimson. He grabbed my shoulders and swung me around toward the window. He spoke harshly and slowly as if to an idiot. "Look toward those hills whereupon the ancient kings once prayed. Look at the cattle and sheep that give us sustenance. These lands have carried us through four generations in which a Preston has served as Viscount Gormanston. Your brother Jenico will be fifth. We have survived and prospered only because each one of us understood duty, and the great bond of family. Despite any hardship they faced, no Preston has ever said the word "can't."

He stormed out of the room. My mother, Lady Catherine Gormanston, took my hand. Would I be a 'lady' one day? Would I ever have the grace and hospitality she has? I couldn't see it.

"Listen to me, my lovely little girl." She stroked my hair, blonde, like hers, and tears rimmed her eyes, like mine. "I know full well what it's like to have your life changed without your consent or even knowledge of what has been planned for you. I'm sad that you must endure it, just as I did. But you'll not be terribly far from home. You can visit, and often. You're a clever girl. You will see over time that you can create your own way, even on the path your father has given you. Have faith in God, that what you long for in your heart awaits, though you may not even know what it is yet. Remember, paths are meant for discovery, are they not?"

"Yes, mother."

"And anyway, you can surely convince a man to improve his clothing, yes?"

"Yes," I nodded.

"That will only be the beginning, my sweet. He will likely be chief of his clan one day, and then you will live like a queen. You'll be admired and influential all across the land. Wouldn't you like that?"

She kissed my forehead and left me alone to repair my tear-stained face and come to terms with my situation. Was it really about his clothing? Or had the flash of yellow fabric been just enough to awaken my deepest fears? I sat on the edge of my bed and ran my fingers along the carved oak frame. I stroked the blue silk bed curtains my grandmother had purchased in Lancaster. Could I expect such comforts in a wild place like Donegal?

If Cahir O'Doherty would be chieftain of the most fertile lands there, wouldn't I become just a farmer's wife, and not a lady? Or would he be a constant warrior, leaving me alone and trapped in a strange and bellicose place? His attire had only alerted me that I was to enter a peculiar and uncertain world. Of course, I resisted. I was afraid. But could I manage it?

3

CAHIR

Changes

The alehouse at the edge of Gormanston village was dark even on a bright day, and smelled of piss, vomit, and stale drink—perfect for my mood. Felim sloshed a pitcher of ale upon the scratched and marred wooden table and we drank without words. I was glad my voice had dropped the year before to a fine low tenor, and my stature made everyone forget I was but 14 years old. I was to marry like a man, so I damned well ought to be able to drink so. Good that my father was not with us to disapprove.

"What ails you, lad?" MacDavitt asked. He'd been my favorite uncle since I'd learned to crawl, and I'd lived as his younger brother since I was seven. The MacDavitts had fostered me well, according to tradition so that my father's attentions could be focused on the needs of our clan. Because he was the eldest, I called him MacDavitt or The MacDavitt. The English called him 'Hugh Boy,' a gross alteration of his given name that seemed to disrespect his maturity and the decade of proud service in the Spanish army. From him I'd learned how to walk like a man, how to speak with confidence, how to read situations and weigh my choices of action. He ought to have figured out what troubled me, but he was handsome and vain. Sometimes, when his mind was more on hisself or his schemes, his vision reached no further than the tip of his nose.

"Didja not see?" I asked. "The way she looked at me? She thinks I'm a dumb peasant from the far north who deserves neither her time nor respect. It's been a long span since someone's dismissed me as a child, but

I remember what it looks like, and how it feels!"

"Well now, she knows your father as a good friend to her own. She knows many of his stories. To her, he's like a legend. Surely that level of respect will carry over once she gets ta know you," MacDavitt said.

"Right," Felim confirmed. MacDavitt's younger brother had been my tutor as well as my foster uncle. He was quiet with his thoughts but most observant. "The marriage has been arranged for some time. She must have always known what to expect. You've done no wrong, lad. Likely she's just scared, is all."

"Scared, you say. She's three year older and wiser," I snapped. The drink was settling into my shoulders, soothing away some of what felt like iron straps across my back and neck, but it hardly eased the queasiness gnawing in my gut. What a tremendous fool I was and ever would be. What would me Da say when he learned his careful arrangement for an English Catholic alliance had failed? He'd not want to hear it, having far more on his mind, with Sir Henry Docwra and four thousand English soldiers camped on the doorstep of Inishowen, breathin' the Queen's fire down his neck.

More than ever I yearned for the peace of my birthplace, the quiet hills just beyond my father's castle, Elagh. But The O'Donnell had forced us to move ourselves and our cattle from our own lands to his. He'd have us all beyond the reach of the English, in hope that those invaders would just starve and die. They were takin' their bitter time of it.

"So," MacDavitt asked with a bit of mirth on his tone. "She didn't like the look o' you, is that it?"

I scoffed and nodded. Isn't that what I'd been saying? He smiled and whacked my knee with the back of his hand, then tipped his head to direct my attention toward the alehouse door. "God does provide," he said.

Here was a sight to behold: a man well bearded, thin and tall, his eyes sagging weary, his hands shaky, his gait weak. A city dweller for sure from the look of his clothes. His clothes! His shirt was white, and over that came a fine quilted doublet of black, and over the doublet a short jerkin of good leather with patterns of holes punched to let bits of white show through. His breeks were long and as flawless as his black leather boots. A finer suit of clothing I'd never seen, and though my Da's best suit of slashed sleeves and knee-length breeks were of good quality, this man's attire was something truly modern and fierce. For him to wear it while lookin' so discouraged, I couldna imagine the cause.

"Looks like a man of the gaming tables. Likely he owes a debt," MacDavitt said. "It'll be no surprise if he's of a mind to sell. Wait, while I conjure some magic." He gave me a wink, then approached the man and handed him a fresh tankard of ale. They sat at a table near, and MacDavitt talked on with his persuasive ways while Felim and I observed. Soon the man walked out, and MacDavitt waved for us to follow.

Behind the brewing shed the man pulled out of his clothes and my uncle pressed a purse full of coin into his palm. The man waited then, and I realized 'twas my own clothes he was expecting. I halted for a spell. Was I to hand over traditional Irish clothing to a man unlikely to be Irish at all, and quite likely to be of ill repute? My father would have my hide! But MacDavitt nodded, and across my mind flashed the hoped-for look of the lass at Gormanston Castle. I skimmed out of my saffron shirt, jerkin and breeks in a single breath's time, and the next thing I knew the man was back at his ale, and I was looking like the finely clothed gentleman instead. Every piece was fitted to my frame, and though I knew it was cow hide, it felt like the seal skin—thick, protective, impenetrable even by water. Let her try casting her scorching glance at me this time.

MacDavitt flicked a finger at my ear. "That's just the first part, Cahir. It's time now to find a good barber who can fix you up smartly. I know a man just down the road. He'll know what to do. Come along, Felim."

The barber conducted his business in the front of his house. He sat me on a short wooden stool and worked for a bit, his scissors scraping. Then he combed a few drops of oil through my hair. When he held a wavy mirror to my face, my wild, bushy, orange spikes had become smooth locks of auburn color. He combed back from my brow and let the curls find their place at my ears and nape. I looked well-groomed and appointed, like a man in a master's oil painting. I was lighter, taller, my shoulders giving enviable form to my new leather jerkin. Suddenly, I was a man to be well regarded and not dismissed. Such a man could surely gain the good and proper attention of a woman.

"Aye," MacDavitt said. "Now we're ready." Felim nodded approval.

"Let's go," I said.

4

MAIRE

Portraits

I prayed for the men to return, even though my heart trembled at the thought of it. I couldn't shame my father, nor could I run from what had been arranged. I repeated to myself, over and over, my mother's words: Paths are meant for discovery. I will create my own way. I will live like a queen.

As the sun descended over the icy Delvin River, I heard their horses coming up the road. My prayers had been answered, though my heart fluttered with anxiety. I had to face these men, bear the embarrassment of having turned them away, and change my behavior against my own wishes. I must pretend to admire them even if it galls me. I must accept my future, a prison though it might be. I must accept, accept, accept.

I crept to the bottom of the stairs where I waited until we heard them pound the door. Father welcomed them back to Gormanston. After a moment I approached the point where I'd first seen them. No yellow sleeves stung my eyes, no strange colors or shapes offended me. Between two men stood a tall, handsome boy with groomed hair and a striking appearance, all in black. He stepped closer, his face still but for one brow slowly lifting. His eyes seemed to burn with a dare. My breath stopped for an instant and then I knew it was a dare I was ready to take.

Repenting once again that I'd even for a moment doubted God's watch over me, I gave thanks that I still wore the fine gown I'd donned for Cahir's first arrival. I wondered at how simple and petty I must seem, of no more depth than an infant's bath, to be so moved simply by the change of his clothes. What it meant to me was far more than garments. It meant that he was shrewd enough to read the look on my face; that he would bend for me, not be harsh and rigid like my father; and, that he would be willing to please me as a loved one and a partner, instead of insisting I be a slave to his demands. I would not be forced to become something I was never raised to be. In this joining, we'd stand on even ground. Should we face each other in quarrel, I welcomed the challenge.

"It's a fine horse you have," I said, desperate for something to say to Cahir while my father greeted the MacDavitt brothers.

"Oh, aye. Asher." He turned toward the window facing the stables. "Swift and steady, him. One of our best." I looked up in time to see the corner of his lip curl upward in a way I found charming. Up close, his youth was more apparent, his jaw smooth but for a few light whiskers, but his height and dark clothing gave him a manly aspect. His gaze crossed my face and then drifted down to my breast. Now I was the one with the wry smile. Despite the new clothing I could still smell the horse on him, and the pungent tanning fluid from the fine leather garments.

"This is my daughter, Lady Maire," my mother said, though I'd forgotten she was behind me. "My darling, these fellows have had such a long journey. Perhaps Cahir would like something to drink, a cider to warm him. A fire burns in the parlor."

"Of course," I nodded. This would allow the elder men to withdraw to the library, have their whiskey and settle the business at hand. The dowry had been paid but Father said there was always something more to be done. I curtseyed to my guest and led him through the great hall and into the parlor, an intimate space intended for conversation. My heart raced, the two of us alone except for a footman stationed at the door. We knew nothing of each other. What could we talk about?

"Nonie!" I called, with more urgency than intended. Our maid stepped through the kitchen door that was disguised as part of the paneled wall. "Bring us some hot cider, will you? And cakes?"

"Yes, Missy Maire. Straight away."

I chose the damask slipper chair by the window because it would allow me to drape my skirt in an appealing way, but mostly because it prevented him from sitting beside me. He warmed himself by the hearth.

Snow had banked against the diamond-shaped windowpanes, robbing the view of color. It was just as well, since the oak branches had been stripped of greenery and the stone path blanketed white. If mother had been there, she'd have chattered the whole time trying to put us both at ease, but I couldn't think of a single word to say. Why was Nonie taking so long? I turned toward him and realized for the first time why we had so many paintings fixed on the walls. Behind him was exactly what I needed in that moment.

"Let me show you our portraits," I said. Our eyes met and he nodded politely. Truly, he was tall, his shoulders broad, his mouth rather wide. But those eyes! Brown, yes, but a light shade of it, and bright around the edge as if ringed by fire. I was a little startled, if I'm honest, and pleased to feel my green silk gown flutter behind me as I moved. I knew the gown was flattering. The green acknowledged Ireland itself and my place as the betrothed of an Irish clansman. The lace on my sleeves had come from France, the embroidered slippers from Spain, all to symbolize our kinship with Catholic nations. The meaning was carefully planned but never mentioned—just expected and understood.

The nearest painting featured a young man wearing a jeweled crown, his dour face framed within a broad, stiff collar. "My father is most proud of this acquisition. It's a copy of a portrait of King James VI of Scotland. One day he will be king of England."

The corners of Cahir's lips lowered. "He is Protestant, aye?"

"He...well he is, yes. But it's rumored his wife Anne favors the Catholic. She was just fourteen when they married." I felt my cheeks flush hotly with the blood of my embarrassment. How could I have said that, when he was the same age? He merely nodded. I moved on quickly to the next portrait. "This one is my grandmother, Catherine, daughter of Gerald Fitzgerald, the ninth Earl and Countess of Kildare."

Cahir grinned. "I s'pose you'll not get more Irish than that." He pondered for a moment. "She is lovely, though her nose is quite long. Was she brave?"

I started. What an odd question. "I never knew her. I suppose she was. We Prestons do tend toward long noses."

"Yours is not long, but proportional."

Was that a compliment? I could hardly tell. "I...uh...I wonder, are O'Doherty women brave?"

"By necessity. Inishowen is a distinctive land, fertile, full of mountains as well as vast meadows and lowlands, and fat beeves, I mean cattle, in the fields. It has on three sides the finest fishing waters in Ireland. It's nearly a nation unto itself. At each turn you'll find something more beautiful than you've found before. Though a lamb trot across it, or a deer, or a herd o' beeves crushing every sprout and stem, it is no less pleasing than a thousand roses blooming. Our land is desired by many, but we know what we have and we protect it. Our women will give no ground."

"They…they are warriors?" He tilted his head, watched me, his eyes narrowing and that eyebrow rising again. What exactly was he looking for? "I'm not meant for battle, if that's what you're wondering, but I'm no weakling either. Pick a fight with me and you'll see."

He laughed, not a boy's playful laugh, but a man's mirthful one with a layer of wisdom beneath it. "No, they're not warriors but they'll not shrink from a fight either, if that's what's called for. I can see you will fit in well."

Nonie brought the cups of cider, and we sat on a bench near the low hearth fire. He took a long drink and swallowed hard, his Adam's apple jumping.

"This painting over the mantel is given special importance. What is it?" he asked.

The pastoral scene had been there since before I was born, so familiar I hardly ever looked at it. "Supposedly it's our namesake town in England. Preston, in Lancashire, but I've never visited, so I couldn't say what it is like. Paintings tend to improve things above what they are."

His eyes widened. "Well then, I shall have a portrait made of you, and it will cost me nothing. I'll tell the lad I'll only pay his fee if he can improve on what he sees. He'll never manage it, not in a thousand years."

Stupid girl that I am, my jaw dropped, didn't it? I never expected such a comment. Perhaps he felt as awkward as I, having no words in response. After too long of a delay, I merely scoffed. We began to move around the room to look at other paintings, then something else caught his eye and the playfulness was gone. I followed his gaze to a small sketch that leaned against the wall from a sideboard—a gift to my father from one of his tenants. I'd only given it a glance, but Cahir was completely taken by it. He picked it up to admire it closely.

"Do you like it?" I asked. He heard me, I know, but seemed caught in his own thoughts and was slow to respond, and then spoke in a low, reverent tone.

"You wouldn't know who this person is. Even your father may not know. But I know, as if the man himself stands before me. It is Red Hugh O'Donnell, leader of the O'Donnell clan, and the greatest warrior of our time. The sketch may be crude, yet the artist has captured him, and even his essence of power. Some believe he is a prophesy fulfilled and may one day rule all of Ireland. I am to learn at his feet."

He set the sketch as it was. "There are few in the Pale who'd be pleased to see this in your father's possession. They might question his loyalty."

I thought about the people from Dublin who had enjoyed my father's hospitality over the years, gulping his wine, gobbling his beef, and babbling about one thing or another. No one had ever paid the slightest attention to pictures on the wall unless they were somewhat forced to, as I had done to Cahir. I shrugged. "They may not care for the art, but I doubt they would recognize the man."

It was his turn to scoff. "So they wouldn't!" His face suddenly brightened, his cheekbones and strong chin revealing the man that was emerging.

"I meant to ask earlier, as I'd noticed your family crest on a plaster patch near the door, a running fox upon it. I've not seen that before. Has it special meaning?" he asked.

"Well, yes. I suppose it's because there are a lot of foxes around our woodlands, but also it comes from Preston family lore. When one of our ancestors lay dying, the foxes gathered near the castle and began a chorus of barking and howling that continued until the end. Supposedly they will do the same whenever a Preston faces death."

"'Tis an honor then, to be so revered," he said. "The wily fox can always find a way to to outwit his enemies, and he would ever be a friend held dear."

I nodded, a bit embarrassed at my swelling pride, and again at a loss for words.

He grabbed a log from the wood box by the hearth. "I'll build up the fire for you, will I?"

I nodded sweetly, a tiny surrender. "I have no doubt of it."

By the month's end, Father still hadn't forgiven my disobedience, but he beamed with pride and satisfaction when he walked me toward the altar in the Gormanston family chapel. Mother had dressed me to perfection in a taffeta gown glowing with silver threads to symbolize purity. I hardly remember the ceremony except that I was trembling. Mother wept, and Father—now that his arrangement was sealed—glowed with more pride and arrogance than I'd ever witnessed. It almost made me sad that the consummation of my marriage to Cahir was to be postponed until he came of age. Only then would I join his household. On the day after the wedding, he left for Inishowen with the MacDavitts at his side.

I didn't mourn his leaving. I found it quite pleasant to be married, to have the status of it, and yet not be married. I was changed, and yet I was not. I had hours to myself, alone in my room, ignored by Father, neglected by Mother, reviled by my younger sister who wished I had married and left Gormanston much sooner. Day upon day I contented myself with my prayer book, thoughts for my future and how I would manage my own house, and romantic daydreams of dances, banquets, a castle garden of my own, and entertaining guests as the lady of the house. Three weeks later I would learn how foolish I truly was.

Mother's scream alerted me to the hallway where Father had collapsed. The footman and butler helped him to his bed, but he died before our physician could arrive. It seemed impossible. How could a man of my father's power ever truly die? How could such a man at one moment be vibrant, alive, and in the next, dead, with no disease or pain or hint of any trouble that could take him?

We gathered at his bedside, Mother, me, Cat, and the boys. The servants all stood behind us, weeping and moaning for the loss. I gazed upon Father's face, absolutely certain he was only sleeping. At any second he would rise, stomp across the room, and shout at me to leave him to his business. My mother wailed and wept, and I could not console her. "Wake up!" William demanded, and he shook Father's shoulder to stir him to life. But he could not make it so. No one could, and the foxes did not come.

Three days later we buried him at the Preston Chapel of St. Patrick's, at Stamullen. My sister Catherine cried the entire time, while brother William, sickly as he was, swayed in the wind without comprehension of what had occurred. My brother Jenico, heir to my father's title, stood tall and quiet, aware of the responsibilities that would overtake him. Mother, who might have found joy in a new-found freedom, instantly began to fade. Her blue eyes lost their brightness. Her graying hair began to sag and dullen. She cared not for food or drink, nor any consolation.

My letter to Cahir informing him of my father's death couldn't have reached him before the burial, and if it had, Cahir could never have arrived in County Meath in time to stand at my father's grave. I was helpless, and worse than that, useless. I no longer had a role in the Gormanston household. Cat had assumed my daily chores, while Jenico investigated his new responsibilities. I felt like a ghost my own home. But it wasn't my home now. Soon, after the mourning period, I must go to my husband.

20

5

CAHIR

Fields of Frost

Maire's messenger had been delayed, first by having to locate me, and then by having to cross vast fields made deadly by the slick black frost. I was not in my own home, Elagh, but miles west of it, at Ballyshannon—the castle of Red Hugh. Yet, the fellow arrived with urgency, perhaps having some knowledge of what would be conveyed. I could not open the letter even so. Not for hours. My own dear father had just died before my eyes.

Was it a fever that claimed him? A pox of some kind? The great Sean Og O'Doherty had taken to his bed, extreme in his weariness. The next day he fared no better but waved me away from his bedside. O'Donnell's physicians arrived on the third day of his illness, and though I was excluded from his presence I could hear my father's groans and angry shouts as they tortured him with useless cures. They improved him not, but made a bloody hell of his final hours. Amid O'Donnell's furious demands, the physicians begged forgiveness and retreated from my father's bedchamber like rats from a flood.

I ran through the door, grasped my father's shoulders that were still warm, still muscled and firm, but his head lolled back and his eyes could not see. His lips did not move and his chest did not rise.

"Away!" Red Hugh shouted and jerked my arm. "Lest you contract whatever illness took him. Out!"

I tumbled into a state of brutal, thundering grief. I roared at him, no words but the guttural animal sounds that sprang from my belly. My hand instinctively reached for the skean at my belt.

Hugh's mother, Finola O'Donnell, stayed my hand. She was called 'the dark daughter' for her long black hair, which fell across her shoulder as she drew me to the doorway and settled me on the top stair. She she stroked my head and rubbed my back with motherly kindness.

"Ciunaigh, ciunaigh, quiet down, my sweet, dear boy. How strong you are. How proud your father was of the fine lad he had raised. Your father Sean Og has struggled, and he has shown us all his grand leadership and his masterful diplomacy. We shall never forget him. But he is at peace. He is quiet. He is in God's hands." She remained at my side until my breathing had slowed and my tears of anguish finally stopped. My face was hot and swollen, my belly in knots, my mind still grasping for anything that could make his death untrue.

"He stands with God. You must allow him that, and show him you are brave," she said. "Summon all his love and all his teachings. Lift your face to the heavens and show your father that you will carry on, just as he raised you to do. Everything he did was for you and the future of the clan."

"It was. I know that. I am just…not prepared to take his place."

She took my hand and squeezed it. "The fact that this has happened is proof that you are ready. I see it. My son sees it. All of the O'Doherty Clan will see it: God's intention. And the moment you yourself see it, your life will change, you'll find your powers. Your world will open up to you."

Her words brought comfort, yes. Members of the clan began to arrive as they heard the news, to acknowledge my loss and share their sorrow. It forced me to wear my warrior face and be strong, though I wanted only to run, and run, and run.

When I remembered Maire's letter, I tore into it, expecting words of love, hoping she would beg to leave her father's house and join me in mine. But her script suggested a shaking hand, the letters slanted with force across the page: Her own father, Christopher Preston, Viscount Gormanston, had died suddenly and mysteriously just a few days earlier, at the age of sixty-three.

"He simply fell away," she had written. "Mother is in pieces. She will not be consoled, will not eat or drink, nor speak. Father will be buried in three days but I dare not leave her side until I'm sure she is well."

The coincidence of these deaths confirmed Finola's words, that I was ready; that Maire was ready. The loss of our beloved fathers forced us to accept our new status. It was time. The message was delivered.

6

STOAT

Clear as the Stars

MacDavitt sent for me. It could mean one thing only, that Sean Og O'Doherty was dead. The chief of Inishowen had been a brilliant man of reasoning and generosity. I was fortunate to have served him in many ways after my father. I was several years older than Cahir, and he'd treated me nearly as if I were his first born. Sure I would miss his strong presence. I hoped I had stored some of his wisdom in my head, because I would now assume even greater responsibility. I, Stoat, was to serve at the side of his son, the new lord, in a life-long bond.

Did Cahir thirst, I was to bring his ale. Did he shiver, I must fetch his mantle and fuel the fire. Did he wish to send a message to the next castle, I was to run it there, nae matter the weather or distance. And did he face danger, my sword would be the first blooded for his protection. An honor it was, and I was proud for it, sure enough.

"It's no wonder Sean Og called you Stoat—you favor a weasel by my reckoning," MacDavitt said. "Always dartin' about, left and right, up and down, rounding corners as quick as you please. It's no fault, only from here on all the weaselin' you'll do is on behalf of your lord Cahir, and there's the end to it. Just one wee little flaw that ought be fixed by the time our lad comes of age, and that's your temper. You're peevish, always complainin' about the folk in the castle getting in your way, teasing you, or speaking of your master in ways you don't approve. You rear up, pawin' like a horse on hind legs, and the other lads make a joke of it. It distracts you from your duties."

"It's the truth, sir. By Almighty God, I swear to make things better." But I kept to myself what often affected my ways, something MacDavitt could never know.

The night before Sean Og died, I rested uneasily on my pallet, the roasted pork supper heavy on my gut. My legs twitched of their own accord beneath my old woolen blanket. I sat up to give 'em a stretch, and before my eyes the old man stood, looking down upon me kindly. 'Twas not the man himself, but a vision, the kind that had plagued me for much of my life. "My Lord? What shall I do for you?" Sean Og gave a crooked smile, as he did when his thoughts were divided. He looked weary, lifted a hand toward the stair and the first room at the top where Cahir lay sleeping. I rubbed my eyes, and when I looked again the master was gone. I ran up the stairs to check on the boy, but Cahir slumbered peacefully.

Why had Sean Og coom? What value was such a ghostly visit, when he offered no words of advice? He must have feared greatly for his boy, for what else could stir a spirit to rise even before the body has died. Of course I'd look after the lad, if that was what he were meaning. Could it be something else? Something more troubling?

Queen Elizabeth's armies were spreading, intending to clear the way for Protestant English families to replace of what she imagined were savage and untrustworthy Catholic Irish. Sean Og had invented his clever delay tactics to manage these armies, to soothe them and confuse them, often keeping them at bay, but behind the soldiers were coming the soulless, ambitious English adventurers with their dubious business deals, intending to gorge on the most fertile properties. Without Sean Og to stand in their way, the greedy rogues would close in on Inishowen.

Fear stirred in my belly that we might be overpowered, and then I realized I hadn't fully understood the meaning of my vision: Sean Og meant to warn me of the coming crisis Cahir faced, and the courage required to oppose it. I was a seasoned warrior, but this would demand from me more than ever before. I'd been given a rare gift, a glance into the future. Clear as the stars over Kinnegoe, came a vision of Cahir's grieving eyes, and I knew without question what was meant. Already I'd accepted the honor to serve at his side, but now I would devote my very breath, and yea, my life's blood to the protection and survival of this cherished son.

Cahir stood by the hearth in the main hall of Ballyshannon Castle, the seat of Hugh O'Donnell's power but only one of the fortresses guarding Donegal's rolling fields, mountains and rocky ledges. Here we'd been given temporary residence since the first spring rains. The castle overlooked the River Erne as it pooled, twisted, and finally spilled into the great Atlantic.

O'Donnell housed his foot soldiers and cavalry, some within the castle and others camped within the bawn, guarding the fords along the river. O'Doherty soldiers camped along the outer walls that stretched from the north shore of the Erne to the south and minded the sheep and cattle that grazed in stone enclosures.

In younger years, the Erne had been our playground, and I'd learned at Cahir's side how to sail a boat across the rippling river, to heave the fat salmon from its murky depths, and to suffer bravely when we shed our clothes to swim the icy waters to the sacred Inis Saimer Island. We shared those pleasures and challenges as brothers, but now we were to face a massive change.

Sean Og's body lay still upon the wide trestle table in the center of the hall, shrouded in white linen, his head to the west, feet to the east, barring the evil spirits from the north and allowing his soul to walk toward the judgment bar of God. Twelve candles lit the table, to burn for two days until burial on the third. The corpse would never be left unguarded until then. I took my place and assumed my sworn purpose to stand by Cahir, to learn as Cahir learned, to be not as good as he but better, so that I could protect him. If I could have spared him his grief, I would have done.

O'Donnell approached and clapped the boy on his shoulder. "Sad I am for such a loss, lad. He were a fine leader, Sean Og, a brother and a friend. Clever, he was. There be none to match the workings of such a mind."

Anyone could see the startling difference between the two. The great chieftain was not so tall, but he raged with muscle like a wild bull, his shoulders impassable as a stone wall. His russet hair hung in ropes to a chest so thick beneath his tunic surely no spear could ever penetrate, and his dense beard was so red it looked as if it were stained with blood. His legs were thick as pillars, and yet he was quick, agile, and could make a fool out of any man who dared to try him.

Next to this giant oak, Cahir was but a twig, tall and thin, and any growing muscle needed to stretch across longer bones. His ginger hair was untamed, and his beard was barely a wisp, his chin jutting with pride and challenge. Over his saffron shirt, Sean Og's mantle hung flat despite the lad's broad shoulders, taking little more shape than a calf skin draped over the back of a chair. Cahir scanned the room, his gaze piercing as a dagger. If he held anything in common with O'Donnell it was this, and no man dared approach him without first receiving the permissive nod.

Having spoken his sorrow to Cahir, O'Donnell ignored me and moved on with his characteristic sway, the result of two big toes lost to frostbite during his legendary escape from the Dublin Castle prison. Cahir seemed to settle then. "Stoat, get me drink," he said.

I waited just behind him. He knew I was there, would always be there, it was simply understood. Still, I felt the smallest sting from the lack of even a friendly nod from either of them. How status does go to men's heads. My ancestors had held Inishowen long before either of them were born. I went to the table where food and drink had been set in great abundance. Whiskey—uisce beatha—the water of life, was the right and only choice. I darted around those who blocked my way and filled a weighty cup for Cahir.

Near the shrouded corpse, mourners left tokens, coins, and gifts on a linen cloth as the wake carried on and the drinking increased. Cahir's mother, Lady Elizabeth, trembled and wept as she looked upon the collection of items. She avoided the shroud until her son came to her side, her thin fingers grasping his wrist as together they paid their last respects. Through the linen, the shape of Sean Og's face could be seen, and the steel gray of his short, spiky hair, the width of his shoulders, and the bony hands crossed over his breast. Cahir looked away. Already taller than his mother, he leaned forward to kiss her temple. She closed her eyes, and after a moment turned to usher forth the line of younger children waiting to look upon their father one by one.

Cahir barely had time to sip his drink before Lady Finola slipped past the other mourners and came up beside him. Sure there was a purpose on her mind. Red Hugh's mother was revered as a woman who would have her own way. Marriage to this Scottish princess had been a triumph for Red Hugh's father, but the man was no match for her determination and persuasive charms.

Above anything else, she was fiercely devoted to her eldest son. She'd proved so by her scheming and plotting, hiring Scottish gallowglass to assassinate her own nephew, and to kill in battle her stepson, all to ensure Red Hugh's position as the O'Donnell Clan leader. She cupped her palm upon Cahir's cheek, her visage kind as if she were a raven-haired angel. The back of my neck bristled.

"Your father was bright and gifted, aye. He will be missed by us all, and he leaves a legacy of peace and prosperity for beautiful Inishowen and her people," she said. "'Tis a steep climb for a young lad to follow, but sure you are mightier than you know. My son and I support you and understand your pain and sorrow. We stand together always, do we not?"

Cahir was surprisingly steadfast. "My father strived for peace, that the folk of Inishowen could grow their crops and raise the stock that feeds us all. Never did he think of his own power or enrichment," he said.

"Wise as the serpent and gentle as the dove, was he," she replied.

I moved closer. I'd served long enough beside my father and Sean Og to be ever alert and suspicious, even of a lady. This one would like to wipe Cahir off the earth if her son could gain more power from it, and for certain Red Hugh would love nothin' better than to claim Inishowen as his. In truty, he was our overlord, but by ancient traditions and Irish law, the land belonged to O'Doherty. My beard stiffened like spikes along my jaw. I would step between them and turn her away should she weave any further her sticky web. I was no Romeo, but I'd been told my gold-flecked eyes could be quite a distraction to a lady. I started to intervene, but Mac-Davitt and his brother Felim were well ahead of me.

"Ah, 'tis the siren, Lady Finola. I must have you to myself for a wee taste of wine," MacDavitt said. "Sad the day, of course, but it is ever so powerless to diminish your beauty." She gave him a half-grin. He took her hand and led her to the wine table.

Felim approached Cahir. "Will ya not come away? Have somethin' to eat and then get a bit of rest?"

"I wish to stay as I am," Cahir said. "I will see every face and know the intentions of all who have come. I'll know who loved my father, who are my friends, and who cannot be trusted. Has our cousin Niall Garbh been seen?"

"My brother," Felim said. "Niall defected to the English, so angry and resentful was he toward Red Hugh for claiming the O'Donnell leadership. Still he insists he ought to be chief himself, but Heaven help us if that mongrel traitor ever succeeds. We'll see little of him here, God willing. But you mus' listen to me. There are friends and enemies everywhere. You find yourself in a position few would envy, so. Let us watch for you, and give you time to grieve your Da. If you doona rest you'll surely fall. You trust me, aye? And MacDavitt? And good Stoat?" Felim grabbed at my sleeve and jerked me closer. Cahir saw my startled face, huffed and grinned. His stiff posture softened.

"You look like a mongrel, Stoat! Who can fight such a tide? Come on then. We'll have a rest," Cahir said, but before we could leave Felim's side, harsh voices sounded at the far end of the hall. Red Hugh was arguing with MacDavitt. Lady Finola watched calmly from the wine table where he'd left her.

"It's to be Felim Og! It canna be otherwise. This one's too young, and the times too perilous!" Red Hugh shouted. He spoke not of Felim MacDavitt, Cahir's trusted foster brother, but of Sean Og's half-brother, an aging man—more farmer than warrior—whose allegiance rested firmly beneath Red Hugh's wing.

MacDavitt countered, "It's his right. His father's legacy must be honored and we…"

Sure he spoke in Cahir's defense, but he was cut off. Red Hugh swept a dismissive hand, just missing MacDavitt's face. "You're a fool. I'll not allow it."

Red Hugh stormed out of the hall and after a stunned moment of silence, MacDavitt followed, but turned in the opposite direction.

To my eyes, the argument was clear: O'Donnell would have an older man and one he could control to lead Clan O'Doherty, rather than Cahir who would fight to maintain the independence Sean Og had built, and had yet to come of age.

Cahir was ready to charge after both of them but Felim stopped him, his body blocking the way like a solid stone wall. "Settle, lad," he said. "It means nothing. Trust us."

7

CAHIR

The O'Donnell

Until my father's death, I believed I was a welcome and treasured guest in O'Donnell's household.

I, my father, and all my family came to open doors at Ballyshannon Castle. Red Hugh offered hospitality, abundant food and refreshment, warm and spacious bedchambers, and every freedom, so it seemed. MacDavitt decided it was time I learned the ways of the Irish warrior, there being no better time nor quality of instruction than at the side of The O'Donnell himself, leader of the great clan, who also took a keen interest.

With O'Donnell I studied the art of leadership—how to speak to men, inspire them, incite their bravery and win their hearts and minds to victory. I learned war tactics by listening at the table when his war councils strategized and planned. By day I learned weaponry when we practiced with swords and muskets, acting out the skills of the skirmish. By night I heard the battle stories passed down through the centuries, all the way back to the first legendary ancestor in Ireland, Niall of the Nine Hostages. The tales told each night by the fireside could fill a man with purpose, and I absorbed it all as the earth soaks up the rain.

"Tell it again," I would beg Red Hugh when we gathered after a meal. "Tell of your escape from Dublin Castle! Yes! And then tell of the victory at Curlew Pass!" The fire crackled in the hearth and the men in the hall pressed in closer to hear each word though they may have fought such battles themselves and had heard the story before.

"You canna wish ta hear all that again," Red Hugh said, but the men urged him on, pounding their scarred and calloused fists on the massive oak table. The noble leader stood, shoved his chair back behind him. "Curlew Pass was a grand victory indeed. We lost good men, our brothers, and their families yet grieve, but we paid a wee price compared to the English who lost more than half their force. More than half, I say!" Shouts exploded and the hall thundered as men stomped their boots on the stone floor.

Red Hugh raised a hand for quiet. "Victory in the pass came from wise planning, well-trained warriors perfectly positioned; men disciplined to maintain the fight though they took vicious fire and resistance. The English retreat and the head of Conyers Clifford were our well-earned rewards." More shouts rose but he silenced them again. "You wish to hear of battle? Stories of true bravery? Follow me."

We all pushed together and charged out the main door after him like wild horses. He stopped by the outer wall of the northwest tower that guarded the mouth of the River Erne.

"Place a hand into the holes in our Ballyshannon, here and there to the north. Holes and divots and scars. You can sink your fist inside—the scars of cannon fire against our blessed home and the seat of our clan. Clifford, the Governor of Connacht, was just another greed-driven Englishman with more bollocks than brains. He convinced O'Connor and Murragh to join forces wi' him and sneak upon us by way of our own river, and our monastery of Assaroe, the pride of our own lands. They dared to camp on our south shore, and in the morning landed their cannons. Huge guns, and monstrous they were!

"They thought to take us all, but no cannon has yet been built that can take Ballyshannon. Am I right, lads! Her walls are five feet thick, standing ten feet high. And as our boastful Murragh led his men against us, we shot him off his horse, aye?" Shouts rang out that could have shattered the windows, but our men carried on.

"They brought their ships from Galway, and they marched on Ballyshannon, fired on her for three days wi' no relief. But our brave warriors held the castle though the guns did roar, and showered the enemy with shot and stones, never suffering without ale or water, nay nor their meats, and returned the heavy fire until the English could do no more. And when at last of the enemy retreated—tails between their legs—our fighting men chased after them, all the way to Sligo. What a grand display of courage and power it was! What a marvelous victory!"

"Ballyshannon! Praise God for Ballyshannon!" the men shouted. And the shouts roared louder than any guns until someone brought out a fiddle and began to play. The men shouted more, heaved the fiddler to their shoulders, and he didn't miss a note as they carried him back into the hall for more drinking.

I stayed beside Red Hugh until the noise had passed enough that I might speak. The great man still brushed his palm along the side of the tower, feeling as he went the dents and holes left from the great battle.

"Sir," I said. "The men fought so hard to protect Ballyshannon. It was important, as if to protect the castle was to protect the clan itself, isn't that so?"

"So it is," he said. "And glory be to them. It could ha' been a terrible loss to us."

"Yes sir. Well then, sir. The O'Doherty Clan. My father's castle Elagh was the seat of our clan. It has been abandoned to the English. We must go and take it back, isn't it so? Isn't it every bit as important as Ballyshannon is to O'Donnell?"

Red Hugh turned and glared at me, his visage fierce. "You're to go nowhere. You're to remain. That was the agreement with your father, and you were meant to ensure it. Elagh was sacrificed to the English, and they've made their garrison. Let them stay and may they all soon die. There's to be no battle and you're not to speak of it again."

"But, sir, I love Elagh as you love Ballyshannon. I must at least go and see if she still stands. It is my true home."

"I said you're not to leave. You're not in command, not of age, and if I must put you in irons to keep you, so I will."

"I am a prisoner?"

"A hostage, to be sure of my commands. Have I not said? Go, and do nah trouble me again. You've no understanding of this." He turned away and stomped around the side of the tower and away. And with those steps a fire flared within my chest. Was he intending to just take over the O'Doherty Clan? We were not to be allowed to fight for our own? For what we were born to? If that should be so, O'Donnell'd be facin' a bloodier battle than he'd ever seen. I could not allow it, on my father's soul. I'd no idea how I would manage it, but I'd not wear the shame of losing the independence of our clan, not for a moment.

I wrote to Maire, intending to pour out all of my troubles. She of all people would understand, as it would change her future as well as mine. She'd married the heir of the O'Doherty Clan and the owner of Inishowen, not a prisoner of the O'Donnells. O'Doherty Clan would fully support Red Hugh's scheme to starve out the English invaders. But, instead of starving, the English were terrorizing the poor farming families of Inishowen, raiding, robbing, and murdering in a desperate and vicious quest for food. My father's spies had learned that Sir Henry Docwra sent for reinforcements from England, so to overpower and take full possession of Inishowen. Before more soldiers arrived, would it not be best to negotiate? Offer sheep and cattle to feed his men in exchange for the safety of our people?

Days passed and I did not send my letter. My anger festered and I did not want her to know. It seemed the MacDavitts, my strong allies, could do nothing to secure my father's honor and stand against Red Hugh. MacDavitt didn't return to attend the burial. The keeners wailed over the grave so loud and disturbing it removed my own need for mournful cries and drowned out the sounds from my weeping brothers and sisters.

Within a few days, the news reached Ballyshannon that parties from O'Donnell's country had converged on a sacred hill south of the Inishowen border, and there before witnesses had inaugurated my uncle, Felim Og O'Doherty as the new leader of Clan O'Doherty and the lands of Inishowen. Him, when it was meant for me.

Had I been abandoned? Made a *bodach*, useless as a tick? Who was I, and what was I now?

My mother wept. My brothers and sisters romped around the inner bailey as if their lives had not forever changed. I distracted myself, combing through books from my father's private library, especially those he'd passed by, like the works of Ovid and Cicero, saying I was yet too young. Later I returned to books I'd read before: the histories of England, Scotland, and Ireland, but nothing eased my darkening mood.

Stoat walked beside me as I scoured the edges of our castle prison, past the guards who were all on notice that I was not to escape. We took the measure of each man, Stoat and I, to determine which we could best and the times of day we might slip unnoticed through the gates to make our way back to Elagh. It comforted me to imagine such a thing, but in truth I was not prepared for the journey, and I had no place to go as long as the English held my castle.

Two weeks later MacDavitt returned to Ballyshannon. He collected his brother Felim, and the two rode off into the woodland, leaving me with nothing but a promise to return. Hours later I saw them again, though it seemed like days.

"So ye're a tick, is it?" MacDavitt asked, grinning. I scowled.

"Aye, he's a tick on Red Hugh's arse, there be no doubt," Felim said with a hearty laugh.

I started pacing, unable to stand still, frustration getting the better of me. "And you lads just left me to it. Walked out, leaving me and Stoat with no word at all, my father barely in his grave, and me a prisoner for I don't know what," I said. "Where've you been? And do you know what Red Hugh has done?"

"Cahir, of course we know. Are we not always workin' on your behalf?" MacDavitt said. He looked to his brother, who gave him a nod, and then he continued. "I've come up with a solution. Daring, of course, or it would be no plan o' mine."

"Quit your braggin' and jus' tell him," his brother said.

"I've been to the English garrison at Derry. Met with the commander."

"Docwra?" I asked, completely surprised.

"Sir Henry Docwra, yes indeed. Despite being an English invader, he seems to be a fine and reasonable fellow."

"You're lucky he didna murder you both on the spot!" Stoat said.

"Quiet, Stoat. Let him talk," Cahir said.

MacDavitt continued. "It all comes down to bein' reasonable ourselves. Negotiation is about discovering what each fella truly needs and wants, even if it's never clearly spoken. Docwra needs to please his queen and show her he's making progress. And he needs to feed his men. He doesn't want them robbing and murdering folk, but he can't stop a starving mob. So, we give him a bit of food, aye, and a supply he can depend on. When his letters back to London seem friendly enough to calm the queen, Docwra will open to a bit more negotiation, and then we'll gain peace for Inishowen."

"It sounds wise," I said, "but what about Red Hugh? He is still wanting to starve them out or slaughter them. His men are bored and itching for a fight. Besides all that, it won't change the fact that he has made me his hostage."

MacDavitt nodded. "I've never known Red Hugh to lack for something or someone to fight. He's a warrior who leads an army. It's like breathin' to 'im. But let them fight some other battle." He grinned, giving a show of his fine teeth. "This is where the beauty and daring of my plan flowers into a rose of many petals."

Felim rolled his eyes. "Brother, come on now!"

"Alright, so here it is, and it all revolves around you, Cahir. You will leave Ballyshannon and go to Docwra's garrison. You will be at his side, learn from him, support him as if you are of his own ranks—for a few months, mebbe a year."

"A *year*!" My face must have shot red, for a furious gush burned in my cheeks.

MacDavitt raised his hand. "Hear me. You will befriend him. Discover all of his ways, learn how the garrison is run, when the soldiers work and when they rest, who guards the gates and how are they managed. You'll learn their battle tactics and how they practice and prepare, where they store their guns and ammunition, how much they have, how it is all guarded and accessed. D'you see?"

"I'm to be a spy?" I asked.

"Cahir, you're to learn, of course, but be yourself! You are The O'Doherty! The right and true leader of O'Doherty Clan! Docwra wants to know you as much as you want to know him. He'll want to know how you think, what your values are, what your skills are. Let him learn what he might. I believe it will only build his respect for you."

I sighed, releasing some tension at the chance for a way out, but I was far from any ease. "It does indeed seem a good plan, except for the great and glaring issue of Red Hugh O'Donnell. He's already inaugurated Felim Og as The O'Doherty and cast me aside. He'll never stand for me going to Docwra, and Docwra will have no use for me if I hold no leadership.

"And there's the truth of it," MacDavitt said, "but you must trust me. I will convince Red Hugh that this is by far the better plan than keeping Felim Og in place. Felim is older, but you are stronger and brighter. Felim would rather be mindin' his farm anyways. My brother and I have the full support of our clan. I must only convince Red Hugh that this all works to his benefit. Felim Og must step aside, and you must take your rightful place as the intended leader of Clan O'Doherty."

I paused. The idea that I might still assume my father's role—it was my life's expectation and what I truly wanted: to return to my home, to live with my wife, and to look after Inishowen as my father had. "What will it take to convince Red Hugh?"

"I've thought much about this." MacDavitt said. "The man wants to have control. He sees himself a king, aye? As things stand, Docwra is a potent threat to that vision, and a concern of unknown depth. The things you discover at Docwra's side will change the unknown to known. Red Hugh will be satisfied because he can find many ways to get the better of Sir Henry. It's a tremendous gift that Felim Og could never have given him. You will be released, free to return to Inishowen and to learn at Docwra's side." MacDavitt tugged on the points of his fine fitted jerkin. "Do you see?" he said, "Everyone gets what he wants."

I should never have doubted my good uncle. By May, Felim Og had stepped down as chief and I was inaugurated as The O'Doherty, head of the clan, to the shouts and joy of Inishowen's people. The MacDavitts would serve as regents for the next three years until I came of age, and I would soon enter the garrison at Derry, a new and eager student at Sir Henry Docwra's side.

8

MAIRE

Gormanston Castle

Jenico had only just turned fifteen, but after the shock of our father's death, he quickly cast off the fears he'd exhibited at the funeral. He not only embraced the idea of becoming the Fifth Viscount Gormanston, but seemed to bask in it, as if the cold, wintery sky had suddenly parted, allowing the brilliant sun to shine upon him, and him alone.

Within days, he came upon a big idea, and revealed it to me across the breakfast table. "I shall not only take up the hereditary title," he claimed, "but also realize my true destiny. Having been named for our grandfather, I shall embrace my ancestry and leave my own indelible mark on it."

"My goodness, such ambition. What are you planning?" I asked.

"Quite simply, I shall elevate the family's position from viscount to earl, just as our ancestor Robert Preston in 1478 raised our title from baron to viscount. It is recognition long overdue, clearly."

I'm sure my face flushed as he finished speaking, for he looked startled. "That's more than a century past," I reminded him. "The way titles are created has changed."

He jutted his chin. "Yes, and that is precisely why it must be now. To have served the crown for centuries, it is time our family is fully credited for our loyalty and good standing."

"Perhaps, but you'll have to go through our new Lord Deputy, Baron Mountjoy, to get that kind of recognition. You must have heard, he has sent an army north to Derry," I said. "They've built a garrison on the edge of Inishowen, my husband's homeland, his birthright."

Jenico scoffed. "It's just a strategic location, so they might guard against enemy ships approaching through Lough Foyle. Spanish ships have entered there," he said.

"The Spaniards were all killed. It is hardly a threat. The garrison's just an excuse to claim another man's land, and you know they'll set their eyes on Inishowen. You can't possibly support that, though it will be expected. What kind of life will I have if our lands are taken for plantation? And besides, Baron Mountjoy is not likely to elevate a Catholic family."

"Who knows what he would do, if I deliver good service."

For a second my breath caught in my throat. "Jenico! I pray you'll never be forced to choose, but you'll do well to decide where your loyalty lies, and it had better be with the family."

"Don't you see that an earldom is for the benefit of our family?"

"Well, yes, you could have more income and greater powers, but please do not take in one hand what destroys us in the other."

My brother heaved an exasperated sigh. "I'll hear your advice when I ask for it, sister."

As cruel as my father could sometimes be, I'd wished a thousand times that he still lived. His presence had always meant our home and family were safe. Now I was was exposed to the elements, to all the dangers of the world, and to the arrogant and inconsiderate decisions of others. Terrible battles were being fought in the south and far north. County Meath remained shielded, but such violence cast a wide veil of fear. And Mother, God protect her, had stopped caring for what would become of us.

The house needed repairs, but our caretaker wasn't to be found. My younger siblings William and Catherine behaved atrociously, being idle, arguing, ignoring their lessons and chores. The servants neglected their duties as well, with no one to mind how they prepared our meals and managed our supplies. The cook had served us plates of only soft vegetables, and no meat! My father would have dismissed her and all in a roaring rage.

While he lived, never was the house without visitors, the clink of his whiskey glasses a most common and comforting sound to my ears. For months, we'd not entertained guests, nor had we been invited anywhere. Letters were few because Mother wouldn't answer them. And though young Catherine begged for her marriage to be arranged, Mother declined every offer and suggestion. Each day she seemed frailer and more distracted. The order my father had constructed was falling away.

I never thought I would long to leave Gormanston, but the situation was making it easier to let go. I began to grow curious in favor of the new life that awaited. When the messenger arrived with Cahir's letter I was filled with joy and hope that he would send for me, even beg for me with words of sweet love. I was beginning to recognize his hand, the long and narrow letters leaping forward like a herd of wild horses. But no, he wrote of his own joy at being inaugurated as leader of O'Doherty Clan, of spending the spring under Red Hugh O'Donnell's guidance, and now to learn at the side of the English commander. He was filled with his own importance, and rightly so I supposed, but for me it meant more days of lonely misery before I would get to be a part of it.

"I have promises to keep for MacDavitt," he wrote, "who captains me with wisdom and proficiency. Yet, I'll find a way to come to you soon. I have not had the pleasure to dance you in my arms, and I long to see if I can draw out your bright smile. If there be a gathering, I'll try not to embarrass you with unbeseeming garments." This made me laugh and also sparked an idea.

"Mother?" I found her in the solar, where she was reading her prayer book. She still wore her mourning clothes, but at last had fixed her hair, and opened a window allowing the jasmine to send in its perfume. I sat on the stool beside her.

"I am wondering if we might have a late spring supper," I said, "inviting guests to help bring some cheer back into our household. Months have passed since…well, you understand. Dear Cat is so woeful she cries herself to sleep each night."

"Oh no, Maire. It's much too soon. I should wait at least a year, perhaps two. It would be unseemly and certainly would cause our reputation to suffer. People will think we hardly cared for your father."

I lay my hand across hers so that she would look into my eyes. "Such a mourning period is old fashioned. Everyone's life has become so complicated that no one can afford to spend a year in grief. Cat is blooming like the wild violets. It is such a wonderful time in a girl's life, and so brief. Shouldn't she at least get to wear a pretty gown, to have a handsome boy take her hand in a dance? I'd keep our guest list small, but it would mean so much to her, and our Jenico would be recognized in his new position."

"But…what about William? He is older than Cat, and shouldn't he be first to…"

I shook my head. "Mother, he shows no interest in anything but the horses. He pets them, grooms them, and feeds them our apples. Sometimes he even sleeps with them. He is sweet and childlike, but he couldn't hold a position, or manage his own wealth if needs be. He'd never make a soldier, and in truth he makes poor marriage material. It's the reason Father chose young Jenico as the successor."

Tears sprang to her eyes. She looked away. I was sorry I had pointed out the obvious, though it had to be done.

"Mother. Please. Will you allow it?"

She sighed. "I am just not up to it, my sweet. But if you will arrange it…and see to the food and settings…Oh I'm just not sure it's proper…but you're a married woman and should be managing these things. Bring me the guest list when you've written it."

My first step was to tell Cat, who hugged and kissed me, and leapt around her bedchamber like a masque dancer. I brought her the green gown I'd worn for my first meeting with Cahir so that she could alter it and make it her own. Next I informed Jenico. Together we chose the last Saturday in May, for 16 guests. He began at once on his guest list, and I to the kitchen to inform the cook and maids of what was to come.

I sent an invitation to Cahir, though I knew he couldn't attend. Bound as he was to the side of the English commander, I might be lucky to see him by autumn.

Jenico invited two of the boys at Malahide, friends from his earliest years, and they would bring along a cousin. We invited our closest neighbors, relatives from Castleton and their daughters, and then of course the aunts and uncles, particularly Uncle Martin who would bring his bodhran drum and join the fiddler from Delvin town. By the time our list was finished, the table of sixteen had grown to twenty.

The menu would be simple but rich: lamb pie, roasted beef with brown sauce, baked salmon and capon. Mother selected wines from Father's collection, though I knew she'd cry when we opened them.

On the day before the supper, a messenger arrived with a letter and package from Cahir. I tore into the letter. Yet I hardly knew him, but I was beginning to feel love for him, and a sense of emptiness without him. The letter was brief: "Sweet Maire, I regret to my soul that I cannot be at your side and thank you for the invitation to your supper. May the gift accompanying this letter please and assure you that ever you are deeply in my thoughts." The package contained a tiny box holding a beautiful gold ring finely engraved with a twining rose and set with an emerald cabochon. A warmth surged within my breast and to my shoulders as I slipped it upon my finger where a wedding band was meant to be.

41

42

9

MAIRE

The Supper

Jenico sat at the head of the table with our uncles and their wives on either side of him. Mother was at the opposite end with a Baron and Baroness Delvin, and I made sure Cat was at mid-table with the Malahide boys on each side. At my right was their cousin, Mister Anthony Warren, who was fresh from studying law in London and hoped for admission to Dublin's Kings Inns.

With each dish brought to the table, I shuddered a little. The lamb was well spiced, but the pie crust was ill-shapen and fragile, allowing portions to fall to a heap. The beef was overcooked. The salmon was too salty, the capon appearing more murdered than prepared. Thank the heavens our fruit was fresh and the custard sweet. Mother's wines would help our guests overlook the shortcomings.

Talk at the table was cautious at first, no one wishing to disturb any recent wounds, nor stir up political differences. Changes in Dublin seemed to be the safest topic, the city stretching ever closer, and more houses seeming to appear each day on fashionable Dame Street.

The barons fumed that Ireland was growing more dangerous than ever. "Thieves abound and skirmishes are everywhere, and yet people have a notion that land is free and it's all a short leap to wealth," one of them said. "Just yesterday I heard the lands of Cork are scorched and wasted. The new opportunities lay at Monaghan, Tyrone and Donegal."

"Should they leave County Meath less disturbed," my brother said, "I favor it."

The others laughed, but I felt a jab into my gut, that again Jenico would sacrifice my future if it better suited his own.

"What news have you of Donegal, Lady Maire?" Mister Warren asked.

"How kind of you to ask, sir." I shot Jenico an icy glare. "My husband assists Commander Henry Docwra in an effort for peace and compromise. He has fought in skirmishes against the O'Cahans, who clan violently opposes the garrison because of its interference with their fishing rights."

He nodded, as did the other men. "Such conflicts must be quite concerning. I'm afraid the situation is all too common across the land."

"Ah!" Lord Dunsany raised his hand to cough into his sleeve, then continued on. "Speaking of the O'Cahan's, I've a fine story I'll wager you've none heard. Will I?" Everyone urged him on, even the young ones, for we all loved a story.

"One of the Queen's favorites—for she's had quite a few—" he gave us all a crooked grin, "was the tall and handsome Lord Chancellor, Christopher Hatton, famous as one of the judges against Mary, Queen of Scots. He became extremely wealthy—by way of Elizabeth's gratitude. Before he passed away, some nine or ten years ago, the Earl of Tyrone, The O'Neill, befriended him and visited him in London.

All the guests seated around the table leaned forward, and the room was utterly quiet but for the wheeze through Uncle Martin's nose hairs.

"The English generals sent Sir Henry Bagenal north to relieve the garrison at Monaghan," Lord Dunsany began. "But the Irish were numerous and fierce. They attacked his men and sent Sir Henry running back toward Dublin, tail between his legs. When he reached Newry, O'Neill was waiting, and quickly had Bagenal and his men all but surrounded."

"Were the O'Cahan's there, as well?" brother William asked.

"Well, yes, but wait, I'm coming to it." Lord Dunsany scratched his head. "Let me see. Yes. Oh, yes. O'Neill's men weren't the wild, disorderly Irish the English had come to expect. They were disciplined and organized. The fighting went on for three hours until a bold cavalry officer charged O'Neill with such force that both he and the earl were struck from their mounts. The officer stabbed and stabbed at Tyrone's chest in murderous rage, but he couldn't pierce the earl's heart, and then—here it is, William—an O'Cahan swung his sword and struck off the attacker's arm! O'Neill jumped free and finished his attacker with a brutal stab to his groin."

Everyone at the table gasped. Mother's face went pale. "How could it be?" Jenico asked. "How could O'Neill have survived?"

Ah, now we return to the beginning of our story. Before he died, Christopher Hatton gave O'Neill a priceless gift: a canvas doublet with overlapping steel plates sewn inside. Likely the queen herself had commissioned it for her favorite, so that he would never be mortally harmed. That day at Newry, O'Neill wore the doublet. The plates blocked the officer's blade, saving the life of the great Irish earl. And the moral of this story? Treasure your friends, and the many gifts they may bring to you!"

We all laughed and clapped hands for the clever story. Then, when the last piece of silverware rested on the table, our fiddler started a soft tune—the signal that we should rise and move into the hall. The music quickened as Nonie cleared the dining table, and the boys and young girls were already dancing. Mother quietly retired to her chambers.

My aunts and cousins admired my new emerald ring, and I wished I'd kept the green gown for myself to wear with it, but Cat positively glowed and I was happy for her. She danced with her uncles and each of the boys who attended. I noticed she took particular interest in the tallest fellow, but he seemed to offer Cat little more than politeness. I prayed he would not break her young and fragile heart.

I remained standing as the dance continued, and soon Mister Warren approached. He was richly dressed, his dark hair cut short, and his blue eyes kind. "Lady Maire, it seems you're enjoying the evening. Might I join you for a while?"

"Of course," I said. "What an interesting story from our Lord Dunsany. I shall remember the moral of it."

"As will I," he said. "I've already found it to be true in business dealings." He stepped a respectable bit closer. "Might I ask, is it so that your new husband has been named the O'Doherty chief?"

"Oh yes, sir. He was inaugurated just recently. He's advised by the MacDavitts until he comes of age."

"Then congratulations are in order. It interests me because I have relatives in Donegal, at Culmore and near Raphoe. My father sometimes has business there."

"I hope I should meet them all someday. I've not been to the north yet, but wish to join my husband and see his homelands of Inishowen."

"He is wise to keep you safe at Gormanston, at least until the violence settles."

I nodded again, as if I knew all about it, but his words disturbed me. The fiddler's pace grew faster, the boys spinning the girls as they laughed and squealed with delight. I gestured toward the wall, that we might distance from the music. "What have you heard about violence?"

"I am sorry to alarm you, my lady. I don't go in for rumors, but I do try to stay aware of the situation. There was an event at Donegal town while the chief, Red Hugh O'Donnell, was away. His cousin marched troops upon Donegal Castle. It was not heavily guarded, and the soldiers took the castle in quick work, but they also ruined the abbey nearby."

The fiddler's strings seemed to scream at the highest chords, and yet he carried on and the dancing boys and girls ducked and turned in a swirling motion. My fingers felt cold as if I held them in ice, and my stomach seized. I tried to hide my concern, clasping my hands. "It sounds quite bad. I'm…I'm afraid I have little understanding of where things are in that region. Is Donegal near Derry? Would my husband or his family be in danger?"

Mister Warren shook his head. "Donegal town is miles from Derry, in the southwest corner by the bay. It wouldn't have endangered him, but it bodes poorly for peace in the region."

"Oh, dear. And why is that?" I asked, not sure I wanted to know.

"The, uh, the cousin, Niall Garbh O'Donnell. You may know of him. He's committed himself and his men to the Queen's army. His reputation is of malcontent, in that he believes he should be chief of the O'Donnell Clan, rather than Red Hugh. But also…"

The fiddler began to play in short bursts of frantic sound. His chin jerked upward and his elbow back as he whipped his bow across the strings. The boys leapt high, and then bowed low to impress the blushing girls. I watched them, pretending only mild interest in what Mister Warren was saying. "But also?"

"He claims he should also rule O'Doherty Clan."

I was stunned for an instant, but then something came over me. I stepped back and stomped my right foot like an undisciplined child. Where did I collect such a foolish reaction? And when, oh when, would I shed it? My voice pitched higher and louder than intended. "The English garrison, the land-hungry adventurers, the O'Donnell, and now this Niall

Garbh. Is there anyone, anyone at all, who does not covet my husband's lands?"

At this outburst, Mister Warren reddened and apologized, but the music had stopped, the dancers halted, and all in the room turned to stare.

"Oh heavens, please forgive me, I just took a bit of surprise. Please carry on," I begged.

People soon began to breathe and speak again, though Jenico glared at me with disgust. The fiddler resumed with a softer and slower tune, but the dancers had lost their mood and turned away, and then Lord Dunsany and his family called for their coach. The fellows from Malahide did the same.

Though Mister Warren touched my hand with kind understanding, and perhaps some regret, the evening was over. All the guests were going home. It was time anyway, but I would have preferred it to end on a happier tone. Jenico paid Mr. O'Keane and retired without a word; my sister, who had enjoyed the most exciting night of her life, turned her back on me and stomped off to her bedchamber.

I ached with shame for my disturbance, but worse I feared for my husband and for myself. Would Inishowen be the next property to come under siege? When the time came to join my husband, would we still have a home? My hands trembled. My feet turned cold, and the chill claimed all of me as if I'd been cast upon a rocky shore, the tide rushing in.

48

10

CAHIR

Elagh

By late August, I prepared to leave Sir Henry and the garrison at Derry. He had treated me well, had kept me beside him, and had taken to me as a nephew or even a son. Once he told me of his childhood.

"I understand what it's like to be born in a fine castle, to love it, even to be promised it for your future, but then to be prevented from making it your own," he said. "My home in Berkshire, Chamberhouse Castle, was built in the 13th century. It had an enclosed hunting park that was rich with game, and it fed us well. Many times, I had the entire park to myself, and those were grand days I'll never forget. But there were men in the region who disliked the enclosure. It prevented them from hunting the best game, as it was intended to do, but it also barred them from the ready means of feeding their families.

"Eventually, raiders came and broke down parts of the wall. The enclosure was fatally breached, and soon our castle itself was threatened. Before long, my father was forced to sell. I miss that home even now. But you are more fortunate than most. Though Elagh is no longer a home for you, other properties await your coming of age."

That, my 18th year, seemed so distant as to never arrive, while my want of it burned ever deeper. I left the garrison on the finest of terms, comfortable that I had truly made a friend in Sir Henry. Having accomplished my mission, I could return in good spirits to the MacDavitts and Inishowen. But if any of them presumed Elagh was no longer my home, they were vastly mistaken. Elagh was the ancient seat of our clan, and I planned to oust the English at the first opportunity, then restore and improve it to the grand palace it was always meant to be. Elagh's towers would stand in warning against any challengers who might dare come for it. I'd see them depart one and all on their knees.

Stoat joined me along the last stretch from Buncrana to Felim's castle, Carrickabraghy, on the western edge of Inishowen, far from Derry and safe from enemy ears. He welcomed me with a hearty grasp and when we approached the castle bawn I was comforted by the roaring current of Lough Swilly rushing through the inlet and to the strand.

"'Tis a fine castle, aye?" Stoat said. "My own ancestor built it. Gearalt, you know."

"Yes, I know. It has guarded the mouth of the river for many decades. It's of great importance to us." Stoat was silent for a moment, but then spoke what I assumed was coming.

"Begging your pardon sir. I have always hoped mebbe one day, when things are settled, when you assume all of your powers, when Elagh is repaired, and we are at peace…"

"Ah, Stoat, I know you'd wish to have Carrickbraghy, and who would not? It is as fine a castle as any. But it comes with great responsibility, with great pressures as well. It needs a fearsome commander and overseer. These men regard Felim as such and obey him. You are an equally fearsome warrior, but I think your destiny lies elsewhere, at least for now. I need such a warrior at my side, aye? Is that not your duty? Is that not an equal responsibility, to mind your clan's chief?"

"Nay, sir, it is no responsibility, but the greatest honor. Forgive me if I should forget that even for a single breath."

I clapped him on the shoulder. We crossed the muddy bawn and pushed through the castle's great doors.

There in the hall I delivered to the MacDavitt brothers and Red Hugh himself all that I had learned, heard, observed and discovered. My head was full of details, and I was pleased to be the hero bringing such valued information. I drew maps of the region, and outposts the English had constructed. I marked out the lines of every section and corner inside the garrison, provided numbers and estimates of all provisions and weapons. I'd met and spoken with every soldier in Docwra's command and gave my perception and regarding the strength and prowess of each man.

When I had finished, I stepped away while Stoat joined the others to study the information and consider the opportunities it might reveal. I'd grown tired of living a soldier's life when I had other responsibilities to build and confirm my position as The O'Doherty. Lands and livestock needed tending, and clansmen needed reassurance of good and stable leadership. I had not seen my wife for several months. I wished to begin that relationship, to introduce her to the wonders Ulster and Inishowen itself.

The first time Maire saw our county, she would love the emerald hills, the proud forests, the roaring, tumbling ocean. She'd see the fields, and the great numbers of beeves grazing upon them. And then, the people. It might take time for her to accept the kindness, the hospitality, the lack of formality among families, for we were all family and all committed to the care of Inishowen.

Then, when she first gazed upon Elagh's walls, she'd see the disrepair, but soon she'd see how every villager and neighbor helped to make the castle our home, and before too long I'd have colorful gardens designed for her, and a library with—no! That would be wrong. I shall ask Maire to design our gardens and ask her preferences for the furnishing and portraits for a parlor like Gormanston's. I will keep our castle safe, but she is the one who will make it a palace. And one day, I'll have a large portrait made of her, like a queen, perhaps with our first child by her side. Oh, and we will have many children, Maire and me.

I spoke to MacDavitt, interrupting him and pulling him from the others gathered around the table strewn with my maps. "I must go and collect Lady Maire. It's been far too long, almost a year since we were wed, and yet she's not seen her new home."

MacDavitt turned and looked at me doubtfully. "This year could not be more complicated, nor the ways of travel any worse," he warned. "You've been shielded from much of the bloodshed across Ireland these past years. O'Neill and O'Donnell had nearly succeeded in crushing the spread of English rule. But now the English come in great numbers and with bigger guns. Worse even than the guns, are their merciless tactics. East of Burt Castle, and south near Strabane, our Lord Deputy Mountjoy has chased O'Neill deep into Tyrone territory. He's unleashed a new commander by the name of Chichester who favors the scorched earth tactics. He burns the crops and cares not who burns with them, or who starves and dies in the dirt, be it man, woman, or child. He's after terror and famine to force O'Neill's surrender.

"All of Tyrone has been in bloody strife, at every fort and ford along the River Blackwater as O'Neill holds the line, pray God's mercy for his protection. I should not be surprised that Docwra has withheld this information from you. Had you known, you might have attempted to leave his company much sooner, before he could be sure of your allegiance. He is satisfied now that you are under his wing, and that is as we like it. We should do nothing to stir the fire.

"There is good news though, lad. O'Donnell says the Spanish are coming, sure and swift. Where they shall land we scarce know. Let us pray it is not Inishowen, because into that place the English will send their greatest defensive force. But if it shall be so, let them come, because all of Ireland will unite like never before, and rise with the Spanish to rain down our terror upon the dirty English. It will be the rebirth of Ireland, loved by God, his powers invincible!"

MacDavitt's excitement infused us all, but there had been rumor after rumor about Spanish ships. Until I saw the sails and masts for myself, I'd focus on my own needs.

I learned that Docwra was withdrawing men from Elagh to make ready for a march to wherever the Spanish would land. He must have learned something that was more than a rumor, but I had heard nothing further. I took advantage of the withdrawal and scoured Elagh castle and its grounds.

The timbers from the garrison would be repurposed. The same great stones that had been cast into the courtyard would be used to restore the ten-foot towers facing Lough Foyle. The roofing had to be replaced, but that was expected. Most troubling was how the trampled grounds could be remedied with autumn approaching. There were massive holes and filthy latrines, sections of the surrounding forest massacred for firewood, and dead animals partially buried and rotting. It was far worse than I might have imagined and the time to work drew short.

Still, the north view into the great cone of Inishowen, reaching all the way to the ocean at Malin Head, remained as beautiful as God could have made it. The sight of it lifted my courage to begin.

In a letter to Maire I ignored the threats of danger, and described Elagh in its best form. I told her my plans to make it ready. Soon, I wrote, she would see for herself, embrace its beauty, and love it as much as I. Despite McDavitt's warnings, I prayed we would not have long to wait.

11

CAHIR

Burt Castle

When Docwra withdrew the last of his remaining soldiers from Elagh I knew the castle could be cleared and restoration could begin. That day I was crossing the bawn toward the north wall and saw a rider rushing toward me as if the Devil was hot on his tail. I seized up, cautious of anyone approaching. Then I heard a shout, and realized it was only my good man Stoat. I ran to greet him. His horse thundered toward me and reared up at the hard stop and nearly cast him off. Stoat's boots thudded on the ground. "We've had word! They've arrived!"

"Who has arrived?"

"The Spanish! They've coom!" He grabbed my arms and shook them as if shaking the leaves from the trees.

"Settle! Ya barmy lad. What are you talking of?"

"The ships are in harbor at Kinsale, near Cork. It's just as hoped for, and thanks be to God. They are plenty late, but at last the weather's allowed them in—twenty-eight ships, Cahir! Thousands of men! And they're already building forts. Tyrone and McDonnell march south with every warrior, and doubt you not, the English are marching as well. There's to be a battle like none have ever seen!"

"Ah! So at last the rumors are true! And it was no generosity, Docwra recalling his guards from Elagh. We're free of them and pray us all that the favor is ours at Kinsale. By God himself, it could free us of the English for good." The seed of excitement burst into a ball of fire within my belly. I ran this way and that, suddenly needing to act but not knowing where to begin.

"Coom! Let's get your horse, man. MacDavitt calls for you. We're all ta meet at Burt."

Stoat had me by the sleeve and then we were both running for the stable. I mounted Asher with naught but a blanket across his back, and we galloped across eight miles of hard ground toward Burt Castle, skirting marshland and bog, picking through the last bit of rocky ground. Only then did our mighty Burt Castle rise before my eyes, her twin towers black against the sky—guarding Inishowen since that blasted King Henry had claimed to own all.

The sight of it swelled my chest, and also my head. This was my castle now. These were my lands to oversee and protect. The men of my clan trusted me to lead them and believed in the rightness of my position. At once I understood my father's ways, always to put Inishowen first, and all else second to the larger, God-given responsibility. I needed no telling of what was to be done. It was time to collect Maire from Gormanston Castle. The Irish and English forces were speeding southward, clearing the way for us. And no matter which side succeeded in this bloody war—God willing it must be Irish—I'd have her with me to take her rightful position as Lady O'Doherty.

Felim ran to the bawn to greet us and summoned some young lads to mind our horses. We smelled the food even before he pushed open the big oak doors. MacDavitt stood over a table steaming with meats, breads, corn and the like. Our cups were filled with ale even before we could sit, and then it was no talking but fierce eating for a while, especially for those among us who'd suffered losses under the English raids. MacDavitt smiled. I knew it was part of his strategy, for he won't have a man's ears before he's satisfied his belly.

I sat at his right hand, and before I could reach for the first bit of bread, I swore it was the noisiest feast ever I'd witnessed: men shouting greetings up and down the long trestle table, throwing chicken bones at each other, trading insults, sloshing ale, belching, teasing, growling, farting, laughing, fists slamming the table, shouts for more drink, the fire roaring and crackling in the hearth as if it had come alive to join the jesting and joking. I ate sparingly, the excitement stealing my appetite, but not to waste, for Stoat made sure to finish his share and mine as well. Before long, men began to push back from the table, stand, move about the hall, stoke the fire and rub their swollen bellies.

When MacDavitt himself pushed back, voices softened, and when he stood to face the gathering, a hush settled until only whispering could be heard. It was not the first time I'd seen such respect, having been around MacDavitt for most of my life. Within a few years I'd be of age to take my place as the true and only chief of the clan, and MacDavitt would step to my side. I saw him with different eyes, recognizing his clever ways of managing the crowd, his implicit control, and the way men watched him without appearing to. These were the men who noticed, interpreted, and responded to MacDavitt's cues, leaders themselves whose actions trickled down to their subordinates. All eyes were on MacDavitt, and every tongue still.

"Good men. My brothers and cousins, and all who hold dear the great Clan O'Doherty!"

Shouts shook the hall but were quickly silenced, for every man in the room—there being no women among us— knew the importance of what was to come.

"Tonight we honor our inaugurated chief, Cahir O'Doherty." He pulled me up to stand beside him. "Son of our beloved Sean Og, who was son of Sean Mor, who was son of Felim, son of Conor Carrach, son of Brian Dubh. Our glorious history tells the story of our strength, fortitude, and undeniable love and patronage to the fair and fruitful Land of Inishowen—a land once called by the great Bishop Donatus, the noblest share of earth.

Indeed, all of Ireland he said, was rich in goods, in silver, in jewels, cloth, and gold, benign to the body in air and mellow soil. With honey and with milk flow Ireland's lovely plains, with silk and arms, abundant fruit, with art and men. Worthy are we to dwell here, men renowned in war, in peace, in faith.

Again, the men shouted, but all went silent as I stood tall before them, allowing each man to take my measure. I gazed across the faces I knew, the faces I had yet to know. I summoned every shred of warrior within me to give them confidence, to show strength. Then the shouts again burst forth, this time perhaps with a softer sound of reverence and murmured prayers that quieted gradually to allow MacDavitt to continue, for every soul was eager to hear the news and of the Spanish landing.

"You've all heard…" MacDavitt held up his hands to hold back shouts and cheers until he'd finished what he needed to say, "…that the Spanish have landed at our southern shore, Kinsale, in County Cork." It was impossible to remain quiet at such a momentous event, so MacDavitt waited, took a swallow of ale, and then continued.

We've learned that more Spanish war ships are sailing to support the existing force. High winds have delayed them and sent some ships back to Spain, but in a matter of weeks the mighty force shall take our side to terrify and crush the invading English!" He climbed upon a chair to be sure he would be heard, "O'Neill and O'Donnell have formed a solid alliance, and thousands of men march south to support the Spanish. If any of you feel you must join them, then by all means, we should not stand in the way of God's will for any man. Search your own soul for what guides you."

He looked at the men's faces from left to right and back again. "But," he continued, "We have before us a critical mission. The O'Doherty Clan must rise, that is to stand as rear guard, to protect and defend our Inishowen and the lands of our cousins fighting at Kinsale. We can never leave our homelands unprotected against those who would gladly sweep in at our moment of weakness and steal it all away. Ours is the most vital and noble of responsibilities. Our beloved Inishowen, Donegal, and Tyrone—these lands are what our armies are fighting for. Our lands, our heritage, and our freedom!"

Voices fluttered up like the beating wings of great birds rushing to the heavens, then settling again to the ground.

"Tonight, having drunk our fill and so to have celebrated, let us continue our joy and reverie. At dawn, we commence serious talk. I will meet with the commanders and I, Felim, and Cahir will prepare and execute our strategy. The rest of you stay close, to be ready when you are summoned, and believe me all of you will be called forth to receive instructions. Together as one we conquer!"

A clamor of talk among men ended with hands clapping and gestures of solidarity. MacDavitt stepped down from the chair and grasped me and Felim by the shoulders. "Our motto, together!" he shouted. Chairs and benches scraped the stone floor as men pushed back to stand with their brothers. "Ár nDuthchas! Our heritage! Ár nDuthchas!"

The shouts in Irish sounded much like the English words, unto us, but even so the meaning remained. I surged with pride for every man in the hall, and men anywhere who called themselves O'Doherty. I swore I would lead this clan with the same love, wisdom, and independence my father had maintained throughout his life.

Ale splashed as we shouted again and again, the walls returning every hearty voice as we drank, and then slowly the noise quieted as the elders looked to their beds. MacDavitt used the moment to pull me toward two wooden chairs in a shadowed corner.

"I know what's in your heart, lad, and it isna war and battle. 'Tis Lady Maire! You wish to bring her to safety, aye?"

I steeled my spine, sat taller, no longer his young foster brother but a mate. A comrade. A man carrying the weight of responsibility. "As I said before. Now the circumstance has shifted. There may be no better time."

"Right you are," he nodded and clapped me upon the shoulder. "If we Irish fail at Kinsale, the whole country may be overrun by lawless English rovers. And if we succeed, as grand as it will be, the Spaniards will flood into Ireland with the idea of conquering England in a bloody rage. The best we can do is to fortify and protect what we have and hold strong as our ancestors have always done. We have a moment, and only that, to prepare ourselves for whatever will come. You must go to her and bring her home, but let us find the safest, fastest way."

"Aye, I should spare no time."

"Stoat!" MacDavitt shouted, but I already knew my man was no more than three paces away. He was at my side in an instant.

"Ah, here you are," MacDavitt said. "Keep those ears open. Your master is preparing for a journey. A romantic one, sure to sweep his bride into his arms, bring her to safety, and settle her in the ancestral home. Heading out to Gormanston will be no easy journey. The soldiers will have gone before ye, but there will be stragglers, deserters, desperate men most like. So, I suggest you be discreet. Look like any other man eager to join the battle. Stay on friendly ground as best you can. You'll need two more men to serve as guards. Anyone asks, say they're cousins. Stoat, you'll get the men, aye?"

"I will, my lord."

"And some good, fast horses for the way down, but not Asher, not the best, for you may have to leave 'em behind on the return."

"I'll choose them," I said.

"And if at any point you run into trouble wi' the English, claim the protection of Viscount Gormanston."

"As it should be. What else?"

MacDavitt rubbed his eyes and leaned a bit closer. "Remember, she is a new bride, daughter of a nobleman. You won't be able to just jump on the horses and ride back. She's been learning and preparing for years to establish her household. She'll have her maid with her, at least one anaways, and she'll have a lot of things."

"Things? What things?" I asked.

"Your own mother should have taught you better. She'll have heaps of clothing, boxes of dishes, and linens for your bed. She'll have gifts from the family that she'll not part with, things her mother has given her for the first grandchild, and what all else I can hardly tell you. But if you'd be a happy husband you must be ready and make space for it."

"But that would require a great carriage and a train of wagons behind it," I said. "We can't possibly. We'd be attacked and robbed before we even left the county and…"

MacDavitt held up his hand as a calming gesture. "Wise you are, but still…you'll have a better go of it if you bring what she wants. I've arranged, if you'll have it, for a trusted friend to collect you and bring you home by sea."

"By sea? But it could take much longer, we could be ruined by weather, or we'd be taken up by the English patrollers!"

"My friend, and you'll be pleased to know him, captains a Highland galley. It is large enough to carry cattle, but small enough and with a shallow draft that it can maneuver faster and better than any ship the English have ever built. If you can bring Lady Maire and her things the five miles to the inlet at River Nanny, he'll see you home in two or three days' time. He'll bring you in at Torr Head, and we'll collect you there." MacDavitt tapped a finger to his nose and gave me a wink.

"Who is this man? Did my father know him?"

"I don't believe he did. Our man is James Kintor, of the Highlanders' fleet. I know him well and trust him without question. He makes his living this way and you'll pay him generously for his service. So then, glad will your young wife be."

"He'll be Seamus, to us," Stoat said.

"So he will," MacDavitt said. "Now lad, as to your wife. You've not asked for advice, but if you'll no' mind I'll give my experience to use as you may."

I nodded. It seemed a common understanding that MacDavitt had more experience with women than anyone, yet he'd never spoken of it before. I'd seen him admiring them at times, and always treated women with respect, but sure there was more to his ways than that. I'd be wise to listen.

12

STOAT

Forever Bound

I pulled my stool a bit closer to Cahir's chair where I wouldn't miss a word of MacDavitt's. What man does not need to know better about women, and what man knows best of what he speaks?

"Once," MacDavitt began, brushing a blond lock from his forehead, "when I was nearabouts your age, I approached a bonny woman wi' my feathers fluffed, if ye get my meaning—all proud and beamin' like I was a gift from the heavens. She put me in my place right quick, she did. So grand ye are, go out an' slaughter me a swine, she says. I learned—eventually—to set myself aside, to be respectful as I'd have her be to me. With one of fine upbringing like Lady Maire you mus' set yourself aside and then some. She's no just your wife, aye? She's a goddess."

I scoffed. I couldna help it! What man beyond MacDavitt would call a woman 'goddess' when she walks the same ground as he?

"Nay, Stoat. Doona laugh if you wish to avoid the hell holes men have all stepped into before you were even born. For you and Cahir both, I'd advise this way of thinking. You've been on a long, tiring journey, aye? Make no complaint. Do not drop your muddy cloak upon the floor and send her off to fetch your supper. You'll be lucky to get cold gruel if you do. More like you'll be sleepin' wi' the sheep. Say something nice about her first. Tell her you've missed her. Notice something she's done to make your life better. Say something sure to make her smile. And, you've a long journey ahead? Tell her you need her, because it's so. Look to her to organize,

59

make sure you'll have food to eat and water to drink on the way. Trust her with the task, thank her, and let her feel the importance of it.

"Next thing, unless you've already been married a decade or so, you canna bring a woman to a broken-down castle and tell her to make it a home. Ye must give her a clean and comfortable place to rest and put her things. Bring her to Burt. We'll have it all brushed up for her, an' we'll set the lads to work on Elagh while you're away. When we've made some progress, you bring her to her new palace, and she'll decide then how she'll make it her own."

I sighed. It would be a longer piece of travel to get to Burt Castle from Torr, but Cahir nodded. So be it.

"It makes good sense," Cahir said. "Anathin' else?"

"Yes. One more thing I've learned. Lady Maire will be the lady of your house, trained to manage it. You must let her and never interfere. It is the one thing that gives her purpose and pride. Look at your own mother, Lady Elizabeth, aye? Kind and beautiful as she is, your father—God rest his soul—was broad in his leadership, and tended to advise not only his men, but also Elizabeth in the work she was born to do. She lost her confidence, I would say. She seemed to fade into the shadows instead of hosting her table with good cheer."

I found myself looking at my shoes. It seemed wrong to criticize Cahir's father, who could never fail in my eyes. But now as I thought of his mother, it was as MacDavitt described.

"When I was just a few years old," Cahir said, "she danced me about the garden. She made sweet cakes just for me, and sometimes at night she sang songs or we'd play word games. Now she's worn down by eight children. When we were at Ballyshannon, she rarely left her bedchamber, and at Elagh she left the meal planning to the cook. The past couple of years, she barely responded when my Da spoke to her. I can't remember when I last heard her sing. But, if truth be told, it was more than Da's leadership, as you call it, that drew her down. It happened after he took that mistress."

It was MacDavitt's turn to gaze at his shoes and sigh. He shook his head. "We canna know Sean Og's needs or his thinking, and so cannot judge him for it. He's not the first man to seek comfort from one who holds no grudges. But there are others who have mated and loved for life, forever bound, and I hope such joy will be yours."

Cahir set his arm on his knee and leaned closer to MacDavitt's. "I feel I have a mountain before me that I must climb, but I'm strapped to a rock and cannot move," he said. "I'm yet a boy but I wish—no, I am called to be a man and a husband."

MacDavitt scoffed. "You've come upon the toughest lesson all of us must learn, and that is patience. Especially if you're to succeed and do a job well; if you're to frame a strategy and see it satisfied, it canna be forced but unfolds in its own time. You pray for guidance, do what you must, and then no matter what you want or think, you must steady your eagerness… and wait."

Cahir sent a message ahead of us to Lady Maire and her brother the viscount, that we were coming to Gormanston and she should be packed and ready in five days' time. We would be four riders: Cahir, myself, two guards, and two pack horses.

The guards I chose not so much for their prowess as fighters, though both were fair enough in that regard. They ought also be sons or brothers who could look after a lady and hold their tongue at times. That said, I liked a travel companion who brought a bit of humor to the mix. I thought first of my friend MacTyre. He was blond-headed like MacDavitt but shorter and wiry, quick with a blade or a joke, whichever the occasion required, and he was not prone to laziness.

Second was Rudd, a black-haired, long-faced son of the McGonigles of Killybegs. Sensitive, alert, and quick, I could count on him to do whatever was called for, never miss his target, his loyalty true; and by God he never laughed at MacTyre's jokes. Under the worst teasing, he'd either lift one corner of his lip, or else slam MacTyre to the ground. MacTyre gave up fast, and I liked the balance of the two.

We left at dawn the following day, traveling through forest and farmland along the River Foyle to Strabane. From there, the river pushed eastward through Newtown and Knock into boggy, low-lying ground, then through Tyrone's country. We crossed the pass along the Sperrin mountains where the heather and gorse had turned the moors rust colored. We reached the Blackwater River with wary eyes, knowing the vicious battles not long past. The O'Neill's defense against English forces had left the ground barren and burnt. The forts and wooden towers along the river banks were all but abandoned, and we crossed at dusk unnoticed.

We had 80 miles yet to travel, keeping to the shadows when possible. Before we reached Dundalk we were pounded by heavy rains and huddled in a wood, adding a full day to our journey. From there the way was muddy, but our clothes had mostly dried by the time we saw the spires of Gormanston. Sure, by then we had a stink on us, needing a good wash-up, but you'd not know it from the behavior of Lady Maire. When at last we approached the castle, she burst from the doors and threw herself into Cahir's arms. It gave us all a spark of joy, and if we didn't know or love our lady before, 'twas certain we all loved her now.

13

MAIRE

Lady O'Doherty

After supper with my mother, brothers and sister, I led our guests to their beds for the night. MacTyre and Rudd to the grooms' quarters to keep watch and tend the horses; Stoat to a small room at the bottom of the stairs, never to be far from his master. And Cahir? We would spend our first night together. Never have I felt more eagerness, and never was I more hindered by awkward fear.

Mother had told me a little of what to do. First, make him feel at ease. Help him to remove his cloak, his jerkin beneath. If they be filthy, have Nonie brush them clean. Take his shirt and hang it in the fresh air. Help him remove his boots if not too muddy. And when finished, allow him to help me with my gown and underclothes. "You may be a little shy, after all it's your first night together," she said, "but do not worry. Trust him, as you are bound by marriage to love and cherish each other. Feelings tend to sort themselves out and you'll find comfort."

She didn't tell me about the queasiness in my stomach, the twitch of my hands, or the way my skin would tingle from my scalp to my toes. I trembled like a little bird when at first he touched the back of my neck to unfasten my lacings. I cursed myself. I was older than he! I knew what was to happen. I'd even longed for it. In my solitude I'd explored the regions beneath my skirt enough to know what was what and where things ought to go in the event, but it was altogether different when his fingers warmed my skin, and when his kiss on my cheek drew the hot blush to my face.

We faced each other in my bedchamber. Cahir took my hand and rubbed his thumb across the emerald ring he'd sent me. "It is far more beautiful now that it's where it belongs. When we arrived today and you came to greet us, sure I thought I was the most fortunate man alive. You looked like an angel to me, sweet Maire. The other lads are mad with envy." He pressed his lips to my forehead.

"Oh goodness, I…well…it's lovely to meet them."

"And then, you provided a most amazing feast. Everything tasted so delightful, I had to restrain myself from eating like a pig! The meat was rich and juicy, and the pies! Wasn't I proud for the other lads to enjoy such a marvelous meal. They'll never see the like."

"Thank you. I wanted it to be a special welcome for you." I tried to help him with his doublet. He pulled free of it and tossed it to the floor, then sat on a chair to remove his boots. When he stood, I started unbuttoning his shirt. He hugged me to his chest, his breath warm against my neck. "Is this all right?" he asked.

"Yes, of course. We'll be used to each other soon, and you'll never have to ask."

"You are sweet, Maire. I have thought about our getting used to each other. We shouldn't have to use formal names with each other. We ought to have something special between us. Something private, like an expression that only we understand. Nicknames, mebbe, used only for each other."

"That could be fun. Do you have something in mind?"

"Well, I do. For you I was thinking Sionnach."

"Shon-nock?"

"Aye, it's the Irish word for fox. Like the foxes at Gormanston. I believe it suits you—as a symbol of where you're from, I mean."

"Truly? So, you are thinking I'm a wild animal?" He laughed and shrugged.

"Aye, you might be, but I was thinking more that you are clever like the fox. Foxes are admired mostly and considered friendly to the Irish."

I nodded. "So, it is a compliment. Thank you. Then, if I'm to be a Sionnach, what animal would stand for you?"

He grinned most disarmingly. "Ah, my mother always said I'm just a badger—a broc—soft and bright on top, but dark and fierce underneath. Also clever, and rather relentless for getting my own way."

"Oh dear. I'm afraid we might have that inclination in common,"

I said. "Nonetheless, it shall be Broc."

He nodded in agreement.

"You must be so tired. You'll need your rest tonight."

"Sionnach," he said with a grin. "Tomorrow may be long and diffi-cult. I'll need your help to see us through. But may I never, in all my days to come, be too tired for a bit of congress with you."

I giggled, nervous while he finished my lacings and my gown fell open in the back. He turned away while I stepped out of it, sparing me the embarrassment of facing him in my shift.

"Do you have a gown to wear?"

"Yes," I nodded. "there on the bed." He fetched it and looked away as I stepped from my shift and slipped the soft linen over my body like a mild summer breeze. He set his palms upon my shoulders. We stared into each other's eyes—another frozen moment. Was it cold in the room? How I shivered! "I have a nightshirt for you. It's richly soft," I said like an idiot. I gestured toward the bench at the footboard. He shed his breeks while my back was turned and slipped the shirt over his head.

"Let's to bed then," I said, though I could just as easily have run down the stairs and out into the woods.

I snuffed the candle, and we climbed beneath the sheets. Almost immediately, Cahir struggled this way and that. So tall was he, that he barely fit the mattress. His night shirt tangled among the bed linens, and he could not pull his legs free. Yet he didn't curse or growl. He kept a gentle tongue.

"'Tis a fine garment you've given me, and I'm pleased for it. It's just that, at home, we lads tend ta sleep without a stitch on, and just let the cover keep us warm. Would you mind terribly?"

"Of course not, you should sleep as makes you comfortable," I said, and he sent the nightshirt to the floor beside him. Beneath the covers his long feet made a steep peak at the footboard. "Better?" I asked.

"Aye. Much so."

"Help me pull mine off then?" My voice was so high. How did it get so high? I squeaked like a mouse, but he didn't seem to notice, and gently pulled my night gown up from my ankles, across my hips, and over my head. He stopped then, to gaze at my bare skin, my neck, my breasts. He touched one of them with no more force than the brush of a cat's tail, and then his hand drifted down to my belly. I lay still and allowed it, being his right as my husband. My skin tingled, the sensation surging such that I might swell to bursting. I tried not to writhe but the unusual pleasure was so insistent I could hardly lay still.

Then in a thin ray of moonlight from the window, I saw my Cahir, the muscles of his chest flexed above me, and a swelling of his own with a need too great to hinder. I must have stopped breathing, for I wanted and feared the next. We joined in sudden, irresistible bliss, becoming closer than I imagined two people could be, so astounding, and then unbearable, a searing pain spreading from my belly to my fingertips and toes. I feared even to move, the pain radiating across my center in waves. But we did move, my body burning as if with fever and the pleasure it brings before delirium.

He comforted me in his firm arms. Soon he lay sleeping in the dark beside me, a soft snore heralding every breath. I could only stare at the bed curtains, hoping I would not die while the ache in my belly throbbed on for hours. It was done, and I was no longer a maid, but truly a married woman.

Sleep did eventually come for me though I remained sore when I woke. Nonie brought warm water for my ablution, and as I dressed, I began to feel better. Cahir had risen well before me to prepare for the day's journey. Five miles of riding, and then to a ship, he'd told me, but of this I was certain: I had no intention of riding a horse all day. It seemed an impossibility after such a night, and so over breakfast I assured him I'd be far more comfortable in a coach, or in the wagon with my things.

"Oh, I think it may not be so very comfortable, but anaways there'll be no coach or wagon, Maire. We must be swift and discreet. We shouldna call attention to ourselves. Most of the soldiers have rushed off to Kinsale, but still there are stragglers about, and thieves. We should appear to be common and travel fast."

I remained quiet, for Nonie and I had spent hours packing, wrapping, and strapping my belongings into the wagon that waited in the stables, and my brother Jenico planned to accompany us as far as the river.

"Coom now, let's see to the horses," Cahir said.

We walked to the stables, Stoat following just behind. As we neared the doors, Rudd opened the left door wide, and then MacTyre opened the right. Stoat ran to help, but he started backing out to make way. Through opening came Jenico, dressed in his full viscount regalia except for his coronet. He was firmly seated on the back of his favorite white horse that was equally groomed and adorned. Behind him came the coach and driver he'd borrowed from the Baron of Delvin, and then came our stable boy in livery, driving the horse team and pulling behind them my wagon full of goods.

The domed lid of the wedding chest my mother had given to me was visible above the wagon's side. I recalled the feeling when I first drew my fingers across the studded leather adornments, forming floral shapes on the top and sides. Inside, the chest was lined with the most gorgeous blue velvet, and I'd filled it with my best clothes and undergarments, my linens and dishes, a few books and pieces of jewelry from my mother's own collection, especially her silver Tudor Rose pendant—things I'd been gathering for years, things that I treasured. Next to it were the stacked crates of food supplies, blankets, lanterns, baskets of fruits, extra tackle, and much more, under canvas coverings for the trip. The wagon creaked and wobbled under the weight.

Cahir was clearly stunned, his mouth partly open, eyes blinking. He turned toward me, his face growing as red as the Heleniums still blooming in the garden. "Maire," he said. He took a deep breath and spoke again. "Maire, we can't possibly bring so much with us. The weight, the space… we…"

Stoat was suddenly behind him and touched his elbow. Cahir looked at him, both of their eyes wide, somehow communicating something without words. After a moment Cahir came to me, lifted my hand and kissed it. "Excuse me, my love, I shall speak briefly with Jenico."

"Of course," I said, watching closely. This could be interesting.

My brother nodded politely to my husband, but refused to dismount. Cahir had to look up at him to converse. He spoke softly, for I couldn't hear what was said, but Jenico's reaction was quite audible.

"Brother-in-law, I am a nobleman of the Pale escorting my elder sister to the port from which she departs to her new life as Lady O'Doherty. I may not see her again for some time, and I will not shame the memory of my father by delivering her unto that life without the most noble ceremony as possibly I can provide. I will not, under any circumstance, reduce her encumbrances. Nor will I cower and hide from any criminal who might dare to approach us. By God and by my sword, I'll have the head of any who would try."

My heart thumped and swelled! My dear, difficult, wonderful, prideful brother was standing up for me. Or perhaps for himself, but either way I was thrilled. What in the world could Cahir do?

He glanced back toward the house, where my mother, sister, second brother, and all the servants were watching. He turned to Stoat and nodded toward the stables. "Proceed," he said.

Stoat brought Cahir's horse which looked like a mule next to Jenico's finery. Then he mounted and ordered Rudd and MacTyre to bring up the rear of our train. I climbed into the coach unassisted, and Nonie joined me. I stretched my spine straight and tall as if I were Queen Elizabeth herself—a most delicious and absolutely lovely moment, especially after noticing the envy on Cat's face.

A quarter hour into our journey, as the coach swayed, clattered, bucked, banged, and bounced us across the wheel ruts, rocks, roots, mud, and every other possible obstruction, I realized the coach was more of an idea of safety and comfort, and far less an actual representation of such. Never would I admit so to Cahir, and never would be far too soon to admit the same to Cat.

14

STOAT

Captain Seamus

From Gormanston, the way north was fair, there being frequent travelers between Dublin and Drogheda and a well-defined lane for most of the way. We turned east for the last mile to the river, where farmlands had been churned to muck by an English garrison camp. The narrow wheels of the horse-drawn coach were quickly overcome, the stokes fully clogged. Lady Maire and her maid would have to abandon it, ruining their shoes, while leaving the young driver to dig the coach free or fetch help from the town. I looked to Cahir, who frowned and shrugged. There was no help for it, but I had to collect the ladies.

I stood ankle deep in the mud. The driver and I folded a blanket, creating a seat between us for Lady Maire, and she rested her arms across our shoulders. Before we could take a step, Viscount Jenico rode back to where the coach was stuck and leaning dangerously.

"Sister! My Lady O'Doherty!" he shouted. "It seems appropriate that I bid you good-bye at this time." He rode closer, the horse's hooves splattering mud upon our breeks and Lady Maire's skirt. "You are near to your place of departure, and thus my purpose is complete." He reached for her hand which she offered to him with some difficulty. He kissed it and straightened his back. "'Tis a fine day to travel. I bid you good fortune, and the most joyful arrival to your new home and position," he said.

Lady Maire shook her head at him in disgust. I could guess at her thoughts, the way her brother was speaking, as if she was some noble stranger. "The rat doth abandon ship," she said.

"Lord O'Doherty," the viscount shouted to Cahir where he waited on dry ground to receive his wife. "To you the same, and may your home soon be blessed with the gift of many beautiful children. Fare well!"

Maire scoffed. Cahir replied flatly, "Your escort is appreciated, brother, and we bid you safe return." And so, without a spot of mud on his boots, Lord Gormanston did trot away, deftly navigating his horse from the field back to the roadway, where he soon disappeared from view.

Cahir lifted Lady Maire upon his own horse and walked beside her toward the riverbank. I returned to the tilted coach to collect her maid. "Miss?" I asked, "I do apologize, we have not been introduced. I'm called Stoat. I'll carry you out to your mistress, will I?"

"Yes, please. I am Nonie, Mister Stoat. You saw me last night, serving the dinner. Remember?"

"Ah, I do, yes. Please forgive a forgetful lad. And, 'tis just Stoat for a fella like me, no mister." She nodded and put her arm around my neck and the driver's. She was brown haired and brown eyed, with a charming, crooked smile, and she smelled like fresh baked bread. I found her quite agreeable. We carried her on the blanket to the sturdier supply wagon.

We'd lost time and I had to calm Cahir. "What if the captain sees an English gunship? He'll not wait. He couldna risk being being trapped."

"There's no ship at all to be seen," I said, "but you can be sure our ship will be smaller and faster than anathing the English could bring." We approached the wooded cove where the Nanny River lapped against the white strand and a stream of blue water curved around a shoal shaped like the back of a giant sea turtle. "Clever of our captain to choose such a meeting place. No English ship could navigate here, and the cove is large enough to hide a birlinn or a Scottish Galley."

"I s'pose," Cahir said, still searching the horizon.

While Maire and Nonie inspected the goods in the wagon, Cahir and I walked the strand, searching the horizon for signs of our ship. It was not long before we spotted a mast coming 'round the shoal. We ran back to where it was headed. In minutes the bow of the galley appeared, such as it was, the name Eimher crudely painted on it—a tribute to the wife of the legendary hero, Cu Chulainn. Eimher was known for having all the gifts of womanhood, and all Ireland's young lasses were to learn these gifts and demonstrate them. What were they, now? I could not remember. The vessel skimmed quickly toward the strand. Cahir called to Maire, who came to see the approaching vessel for herself.

"That…that is our ship?" she asked Cahir.

"I believe so. I've not seen it before. MacDavitt arranged the meeting. Who else would come up this river at this time?"

"But, it is so small. I thought you said it was a galley. It looks hardly larger than a fishing currach."

Cahir shook his head. "Oh no, Maire. Look down into it. There be at least a dozen or more oars and men to pull 'em."

"Yes, but the sides are so low. Won't it sink when we all climb in?"

Cahir laughed. "Only if we wobble it so badly as to flood it ourselves. These vessels are made to carry goods and especially beeves. Cattle, I mean. We'll be fine, sweet. You'll see. Will she not, Stoat?"

He looked to me, his eyes wide, surely wondering himself whether we were in for a bit of trouble. The galley had overlapping panels of wood forming a sturdy body with a wide deck, a high bow and stern. There was a single mast suitable for one square sail, and 16 or 18 oars, but only two men per oar where three were wanted. There'd be no carrying space below deck, and all had to be fitted between the oarsmen, the horses and the passengers. I couldna say it, but with all the things to be loaded, I wondered if we looked upon the end of a wee short marriage. Just then I remembered something important from MacDavitt's advice and whispered in Cahir's ear: *Let her.*

Cahir's brows lifted, and the beginnings of a grin crossed his cheek. Two men climbed out of the galley to hold the ropes, and two others leapt over the bow and scrambled across the strand. "Lord O'Doherty, sir?" the first lad asked.

"Aye, 'tis me, my wife, Lady O'Doherty, and our escort. Who sent you?" he asked cautiously.

"Our ship's captain, James Kintor, and it were Lord MacDavitt what sent 'im. Cap'n awaits you onboard, an' we're ta load your goods, aye."

"Aye, it is well. Let's to it," Cahir said.

I brought the lads to the pack horses to be loaded first. Later we could relieve the animals of the heavy bundles and bags. Some fellas onboard were setting the ramps that formed the loading platform, and Cahir was first to cross. He shook the captain's hand—a wiry fellow nearly as tall as Cahir, his hair a brighter ginger, tied back with a leather thong. His eyes were sharp and hooded by thick copper brows. It seemed his mouth formed a constant frown, his lips shaped like an overturned boat, and yet I realized he was smiling.

Cahir returned to the strand and waved the lads to continue with our mounts. Next, I helped the stableboy unhitch the wagon and we pulled it to the strand, Lady Maire and Nonie walking behind.

"Sweet Maire," Cahir said, kissing her hand. "I'm sorry, truly, but the wagon—with the horses onboard, we've not the space to load it. We'll have to gather our belongings piece by piece, those things that can fit, and the rest we'll stay in the wagon back to Gormanston."

"But, without the wagon, how will we carry the belongings to our home, once we're landed in the north?" she asked.

"We will rent, borrow, or buy another. Wagons can be had, not to worry. These are your precious things, and you know best what is packed and where. Do you wish to mind the lads yourself, as for how things are placed?"

"Most certainly, I would! Thank you. May I board the boat first, to see what spaces we have?"

"Of course. Coom." Cahir held her elbow as they crossed the ramps. The boat rocked with the flow of the tide, and I watched Cahir with admiration, along with some amusement. Lady Maire struggled at first to find her balance. Then she curtseyed to the captain as she was introduced. He bowed deeply, perhaps mockingly in return. As she explored the deck, sure she'd be forced to see she must leave her things behind. Already the galley was loaded to bursting. But she showed no distress, and if anyone learned a lesson that day it were me, meself.

Cahir walked her back down the platform to the strand. "Stoat," he called. I stood before him without delay. "Please accompany Lady O'Doherty as she sends her items aboard the ship. See that she has the help she requires, and her every wish heeded."

I was startled! I had reminded 'im of MacDavitt's lesson. I'd given 'im the idea, and now he'd tossed me into the fire? But soon I thought better of it. 'Twas not for him to be the cause of her disappointment. Let him always be her hero, and me her servant. Best yet, should blame be assigned, I'd see to it the captain was the one who caught it, and not Cahir or myself. Suddenly light on my feet, I was at my lady's side and ready to work. But her first request was a tall one.

"Let us start with the largest casket, shall we? Have it placed near the bow," Lady Maire said.

I was doubtful. "My lady, with all the horses already onboard, it will be a trial to get the casket past them to the bow."

"Well, Mr. Stoat, you've offered the solution yourself. Let it be passed, by dozens of men at the oars who have naught to do at present."

"As you wish, my lady." I shrugged and sent MacTyre and Rudd to the ship with the unwieldy thing. They put it toward the first pair of oarsmen, and the shouts broke out like the squawk of fighting crows.

The captain came leaping from bench to bench over the scrapping oarsmen. "Wat's 'iss? Wat ye doin' heer?" he roared.

I couldna hear our lads' reply, but Captain James turned to Lady Maire and roared even louder. "Wat's 'iss, wi' yer heavin' a load upon me oarsmen? Et's no' their job fer such! Your own mus' heave your own!"

My lord Cahir started to her rescue, but she raised her hand that he'd stop. Instead, she approached the captain herself. "Captain Seamus," she said sweetly, using the Irish form of his name, "may I apologize to your oarsmen, please?"

"Yeh, o' course ye can and quick," the captain replied, and stepped back for her to say what was due.

She crossed the platform with hardly a sound and nodded to the oarsmen. "Please forgive me for not asking first for your help. It was poor manners indeed. May I try again?"

The oarsmen looked at each other in confusion, and Captain Seamus crossed his arms over his broad chest. "Go on!" he said to my lady.

"Dear sirs, this casket is quite large, I agree, but within it are things of great importance to me, gifts from my poor departed father and my dear ailing mother. You all look so strong and capable. Could you please grant me this wish, and pass it back to where it may rest out of your way?"

The first oarsman just grabbed the casket and heaved it to the next row without a word, and the others passed it quick as you please all the way forward to the bridge. I was reminded just then about those qualities that made the Goddess Eimher a legend. One of them was about the voice. A gentle voice! Hadn't our lady just demonstrated its proper use?

The captain reared back, his face as if he'd been splashed with red wine. He blubbered, dumb-stricken, but then he swung his chin high, and grinned. "Aye, then! Yes, indeed. Bring et! Bring et all. We'll find a plez for every spec, won' we lads?"

"Aye, sir!" the men replied, and the loading commenced, each basket, bin and bundle was stowed, under benches, around the horses where they wouldn't get pissed, in any open space along the gunwale, in the empty seat where a third oarsmen should have been, and wherever else I could not see. The last piece to come was my lady's precious wedding chest. MacTyre and Rudd brought it most unsteadily up the ramp, but Captain Seamus stopped them before they reached the top.

"My lady, you canna be serious wi' such a rig. Look at et! 'Tis monstrous in size when we've hardly space for a wee flea. There be seven passengers yet ta load. You must tek this burden back."

Lady Maire shook her head. "Captain Seamus, this piece is most precious of all, and we must take it, or I will stay behind myself. If your vessel is meant for transporting cattle, surely this is smaller and lighter than any cow, and it needs no feeding or care. If your men won't load it, you may as well start taking everything off the ship because I won't leave without it. If they will load it, Nonie and I will sit upon it until we reach the north. It shall cause you no worries."

Captain Seamus looked to Cahir, who was certainly as red-faced as the captain, but nodded his consent. The captain took a deep breath and turned to Lady Maire. "Aye, well ye've got your way here," he said, "but know this, I'll decide where it will or it won't go on my ship, and if the weather gives us a toss, we're no to blame fer what goes overboard. Agreed?"

"Yes, Captain," Lady Maire acknowledged.

"'T'will go against the loading ramp, and if you'll set upon it, so be it. Now, everyone onboard." All but the stable boy boarded, he needing to return the team and wagon to Gormanston. The captain waved the men forward with the chest and saw it lashed down on the boarding ramp. Sure it would soon be drenched in sea water and broken to pieces. The ship was then secured for the departure, and Lady Maire stood firm beside her precious chest.

Captain Seamus turned toward the bridge and then turned back toward Lady Maire with a sly grin. "Tis a fine piece, that there. Ye might remember, my lady, that anathin' on this ship when she launches to sea belongs to the captain until he should say otherwise. 'Tis only maritime law, and if not that, then it be me own law."

As the ship pushed off and the great oars sliced the water and heaved away, my lady was left to her thoughts. I didna believe she was brooding. Scheming, more like, and I admired her all the more.

15

STOAT

Dark Clouds

There was no joy traveling in a vessel such as the Eimher, cramped and uncomfortable as we were, wet most of the time, and the oarsmen increasingly vexed by the horses and manure crowding the deck, and a devil for a captain barking foul words and insults. To his credit, Captain Seamus was ever watchful for the English ships that might stop us and take all we had. Our best protection was that most of Her Majesty's ships were supplying and defending her soldiers at Kinsale.

Our first day had been sunny, the waters clear enough to see the white jellyfish with their long tails trailing. We slept beneath the stars with Lady Maire's warm blankets upon us. The second day brought quickened current, dark clouds streaming toward us from the horizon, and then the rain as sure as the thunder, our captain tossing out tarpaulins for shelter. The bow lifted and fell with the white-capped waves. MacTyre and Rudd took up oars with the other lads to keep us steady, but soon Nonie was heaving o'er the gunnels. Then, as quick as the squall had found us, so it fell away.

By the third day, the current rushed us northward. The very power of it stirred my blood and shifted me about like a plaything. Before us, the Straits of Moyle led to the North Sea. The tossing waves foamed, peaked, and rose like the mouth of a serpent yawning wide to swallow us whole. Our destination lay just before the straits and it were a fine bit of maneuvering to get us to shore. Cahir held Maire close as the captain demanded more strength from his oarsmen. I now understood the wisdom of completing our journey by land, though 50 miles lay between us and Burt Castle. If we had to cross those straits to the sea we would surely be swallowed and drowned.

We found safety in the cove at Torr Head, and no one was more eager to leave the ship than Nonie who was greenish-gray with sickness. The captain took no heed of her but smiled, his job done ahead of schedule and his fee to be paid.

Just as they had at the Nanny, two of the oarsmen jumped from the ship and held the ropes tight as the others unfastened the wedding chest from the loading ramp. The greatest urgency was to offload the horses that saw and smelled land and struggled against their harnesses. Then they quickly passed our goods from man to man and set them on the strand.

The wind whipped around our legs as we worked, and Cahir met the captain at the stern to pay his fee. They shook hands and Cahir offered a hefty sack of coin. Captain Seamus held it, tossed it upward and then grabbed it as it fell.

"'Tis no' enough," he said.

"It is what was agreed, Captain." Cahir stepped back a bit, as if offended.

"Aye, that agreement covered four horses and seven passengers. There's a wee bit more, wouldna you say?"

"It was for six horses. Perhaps your vessel was not fit for the task. Besides, I canna pay more, sir. I've given you all I have save a few coin to see us fed on the journey home."

"I'll have them," the captain said, and then he grinned. "An' I'll have that as well." He pointed toward Lady Maire's wedding chest and gestured to the men on the strand. "Bring et!" he shouted. They lifted it at once though Maire screamed and cried.

"No! It is on the strand, not your ship! It is mine," she shouted.

"Now et's mine," the captain said as the men heaved it aboard.

Cahir dug into his pockets for every last coin he could find. "Have it all, but please don't take my wife's belongings. You see how it pains her, and it means nothing to you."

"Et mus' have gret value for her to covet it so. Mebbe I'll sell it for a bounty. Anawez, I've no doubt you'll buy another one day. You're the new taoiseach, a chief soon to become wealthy. For this day, I'll take my due."

"You are no honorable captain, nor even a pirate. A thief, that's all you are. MacDavitt called you friend, but he shall hear of your treachery. Expect no more from him."

"Make ready!" Captain Seamus shouted, and the crew on the strand leapt aboard the Eimher and pushed off.

Cahir trembled with anger but what could we do short of battle, and us badly outnumbered? He turned to Maire who sat helpless on the strand, her reddened face streaked with tears. I never saw eyes more pained and sorrowful than hers in that moment. It was grief, aye. Betrayal, most certainly. But worse by far was her shattered look of disappointment. From this, a man might never recover.

"Maire," Cahir said, in a soft, firm voice. "I swear to you, on my life, one day I will return the chest to you. I will. And be it full or empty I will lavish it with treasure upon treasure, to restore your tender heart."

She closed her eyes, lips pursed, and allowed a faint nod.

At Cahir's command, I climbed the high bluff above the cove to find our way out, and our nearest opportunity for shelter and food. From there, the land was green and thick with brush and bramble, but barren of life or sustenance. A low mountain ridge blocked any view of what might lay beyond.

We'll have to leave everything on the strand then," Cahir said. "We'll find a wagon soon enough and come back for it. It's not possible to carry. I'm sorry, but we've no choice."

Lady Maire, her crying finished, stood and faced Cahir without expression. "I have lost already what was dearest to me, and nothing to be done. No choice. I have heard those words more times than anyone should in a lifetime. No choice but to wed. No choice but to mourn. No choice but to go to a new home. No choice but to sail off with a thieving pirate. No choice but to leave all our belongings on the strand, to be stolen or ruined by the elements. Cahir, promise me I shall never hear you say those words again."

"I promise," he said, though I doubted, not his desire to keep such a promise, but his means to control the constant potential for troubles and limitations.

Poor Nonie was in no condition to creep through tangled vines and over steep hills. I wrapped her in a blanket, set her on our gentlest horse, and held the reins myself. We packed the rest of the horses as best we could. MacTyre and Rudd walked them up and over the bluff as the rest of our party climbed through waist-high grasses. From there, Cahir led us northward along the line of the ridge.

For a time, no one dared to speak. We trudged more than an hour, seeing no humans, no beasts, no houses. Where had we landed? How would we get out? My own temper started to flare, wondering whose idea it had been that we should land in such a barren place. Why were we sent to a man like Captain Seamus, who would steal from a woman? Who had left us to such a grim fate, unsheltered, starving, and spent?

"MacDavitt did this, Cahir. Why?" I asked.

"Nay, Stoat, do not lose your senses. MacDavitt did right by us. We're bringing my wife home under impossible circumstances. That there is no one about? It would suit us perfectly if we still had our wagon and food—no one to threaten or trouble us. That things didna go exactly as planned, and that his friend was not true? MacDavitt couldn't have known. He found a solution for what I asked, called on those he had trusted. Made all the arrangements and paid for it as well. And in the end, we are here just as planned. And we are together, and we are safe, aye?"

I heaved a great sigh. "Right. And there's the reason you're ta lead and I'm ta follow."

Lady Maire walked beside us and must have heard Cahir's words. I dared a glance at her, sure she must have some thoughts for it, but she showed no response. MacTyre broke the silence.

"Move yersel off me path. D'yo no see I'm walkin' here?" MacTyre shouted, and shoved Rudd on the shoulder. Rudd stumbled and yanked the bridle of the horse he led behind him. The horse reared his head, grunted, and blew.

"Gobdaw! Ye t'ink yer the only one tryin' to get through this tangled bush? Mind the horse, too!" Rudd shouted.

"Shut your mouth!"

"Shut yours, ye bleedin' …."

"All right, there's a lady present. Calm yourselves," I said.

"Calm yourself, Stoat!"

"Wait just a wee minute, MacTyre! You'd not be on this job at all but for me."

"Aye, and leave me behind next time, and Rudd as well, so!"

"Shut it!" Rudd shouted. "Speak fer yourself, you venomous toad! Ye rutting, good for nothing…!"

Cahir stopped suddenly and with one fierce look halted all of us where we stood. He raised a hand, listening. After a moment I heard it as well. Horses, coming closer. Cahir looked at me, questioning, and I read his thoughts. What do you think? I held up my pointing finger. Wait. He turned back toward the sound, holding still as a stone. Lady Maire lifted her chin.

16

MAIRE

Torr

The sound of horses slowed, and then the first of them came around a bend to face us. MacDavitt! And behind him, a band of twenty or more men, thanks be to God.

MacDavitt swung down from his horse and embraced Cahir heartily, then hugged me though it had been nearly a year since I'd met him. I was stiff and cold and surely he felt it. I'd have to know him better before I'd decide whether to trust. Behind him, five mounted soldiers watched, while the foot soldiers stood at rest or dropped to one knee. They were tired, sweaty, filthy, undoubtedly hungry, and miserable. I knew exactly how they felt.

I wanted to nurture my growing anger, and I wanted someone to blame. This was not the experience I expected when my husband would take me to his home, but one look at Cahir told me he was equally far from his intended plan. I couldn't blame him for anything more until he'd had the chance to sort things out with MacDavitt, but MacDavitt looked similarly troubled, his face lined with worry, his blue eyes dark and sunken.

"We've been two days to reach you," MacDavitt said, "but it is well timed thanks to the Viscount Gormanston, who sent a fast rider to ensure we'd collect you at Torr upon landing. We are late, and the way has been difficult, but at last we meet."

"Thanks be to God, for I'd quite run out of the means to keep this traveling party in good form," Cahir said. "Captain Seamus took the last of my coin and left us without sustenance, and we've no wagon to move my wife's belongings. They sit on the beach unprotected."

MacDavitt looked surprised, but then nodded. "I know you're eager to go on, Cahir, but we'll have to pitch camp for the night, it being already late in the day. You may rest and eat while we find a place to hire a wagon and collect the rest of your things. You won't mind waiting, Lady Maire?"

I minded enormously but summoned a brave face. "I'll be grateful if we won't have to leave anything behind," I said. "Cahir will have a story to tell later, about your Captain Seamus."

MacDavitt shifted on his feet as if he hardly had time to hear my response. He scratched the back of his neck again and again. It became clear this was no joyful homecoming. Something was afoot. "Lord Mac-Davitt…is there something else? The concern on your face…" I asked.

Cahir looked from me to MacDavitt and back again. Perhaps he was too tired to see the man's discomfort, but his shoulders started to rise.

"Aye, we'll get to all of that," MacDavitt said. "Only know you are both needed. Inishowen suffers a difficult time." He started toward his men but Cahir grabbed his arm.

"Wait! Wait my friend. You cannot say my homeland is troubled and then walk away. Tell me now. What do we face?" he said.

MacDavitt sighed deeply and turned to the mounted soldier nearest. "Brannan, take three others and see can you find a suitable wagon for Lady O'Doherty, and victuals for the men—anything you find." He pressed coins into Brannan's fist and turned back to Cahir. "Sit on the grass just there and I'll tell it."

We tucked our legs beneath us on the cold, damp grass, my own fear spiking as if soon we'd lay our heads upon a chopping block. I braced against the news, my empty stomach curling in a knot.

"In the past few days, I've learned there are schemes spreading among those who stayed behind after the march to Kinsale. Sir Henry Docwra's activity, for one."

"Docwra? I've barely left his presence! What is it?" Cahir asked.

"Niall Garbh," MacDavitt said. "Traitor that he is, he'll never give up until he gets what he wants. He joins with Docwra in planning to take Ballyshannon."

I shook my head. "Please! Who is Niall Garbh?"

"I apologize, Lady Maire. Thoughtless of me. Of course you

wouldn't know of him. He is the cousin of Red Hugh O'Donnell, leader of the great O'Donnell Clan, and the O'Doherty overlord.

"Remember, Maire? That portrait of Red Hugh in your father's parlor?" Cahir said.

"Oh yes. And you admired him. But I didn't know he was your overlord."

"A good man, he is, my lady," MacDavitt continued. "Niall Garbh believed he should've been made clan leader instead of Red Hugh, and he holds a bitter grudge. When Red Hugh is away, Niall takes advantage. He claims he built Ballyshannon Castle, and will take it back now while both the armies of Red Hugh and O'Neill are headed for Kinsale.

"Never!" Cahir blurted. "He can never have it. Red Hugh will not allow it."

"Niall would never attempt such a plan if Red Hugh was within a hundred miles. But what can we do against him and Docwra beside, those of us who remained behind? We haven't the men to fight an English siege. And even if we did, well, we have even greater difficulties to face."

"What could be greater than…"

"Greater than Niall Garbh? It would be Lord Deputy Mountjoy." MacDavitt shook his head. "He relies on his burning tactics to weaken us, Cahir, and his man Chichester carries them out. He sees to the complete destruction of cornfields, cattle, sheep, grasslands, orchards. Everything, and now, just before the harvest. They've burned most of Tyrone, and south near Armagh, then parts along the southern fringe of Inishowen. Those who've not been killed by fire itself suffer the aftermath, trying to feed their families when there is nothing but ash. People have lost their homes, and all that they owned. Many have died. Refugees are coming to us for help but we're nearly helpless. We're facing a famine that could take years to heal."

"My God!" I said, clasping my cold fingers to my face. "I never expected such troubles. We are stuck here, helpless, and people are dying? There must be something we can do?"

Cahir and MacDavitt looked at me as if suddenly remembering I was there.

"It will be all right," Cahir said. "We will take care of our own, won't we, MacDavitt?"

"I am working every angle I can think of, and it's why I need you. I'm thinking, what's best for Inishowen is to let the English take Ballyshannon without interference."

"No!" Cahir said. "Ballyshannon is an anchor for the entire region. As long as Ballyshannon stands, we are safe among our own, isn't that so?"

"It always was so, lad, but now, the further we can push the English from Inishowen, the better we will be. You can see that, can't you?"

"I can," I said. "Get rid of them quickly so that we can tend to the families, the children who have no place to go and nothing to eat. Oh, I don't know if I can bear even to see it!"

"I wish you'd never have to, my lady," MacDavitt said, "but we cannot get to Burt Castle without passing the evidence of what's been done. The only good to come from it is our drive to save and protect what remains."

Cahir left my side and started to pace across the grass. "If the English march into O'Donnell country, it doesn't mean they leave Inishowen. They do not move, but spread. You are right, we must focus on our own. But Ballyshannon? Is it just to be abandoned?" Cahir asked.

MacDavitt shrugged. "'Twas always a risk, to drain the strength of Donegal in favor of Kinsale, but hope is more powerful than fear. O'Donnell and O'Neill believe with Spanish support they cannot fail. I pray they are right. In the meantime, I've sent word to Red Hugh, if it's even possible to get a message through. Ballyshannon is his seat of power, and it's for him to decide what to do—a bitter choice, in any case."

I'd been grasping my own hands so tightly they began to ache. And no wonder? What sort of life awaited us? How can they value a distant castle when people around us are starving? Of a sudden I longed for the safety and comfort I'd had in my parents' house at Gormanston. Never did I know a time of fear or lack. Never did I go hungry. I'd struggled beneath my father's tyranny, all the while enjoying the benefits of such a privileged life, not knowing any alternative. Soon I'd see tyranny beyond my imagining. I had fumed over a lost wedding chest, but if I had it now I would tear it open and give what I had to the suffering families, the starving children. And had I a butcher's knife from that chest, I'd slash it across the throats of that Mountjoy and his Chichester.

17

CAHIR

Inishowen

As soon as we passed the hills from Torr to open land, I started to feel close to home. In little time we encountered barren farmlands, glens, and bogs until we reached O'Cahan country and the town of Coleraine. My back bristled, for I'd fought against these warring folk at Docwra's side. I had tried to prove my loyalty while gathering as many English secrets as I could. Thanks to MacDavitt and his many contacts, if any local men recalled my stand against them, all was forgotten. At an inn we ate frugal meals of barley with bits of beef, and slept on uncomfortable pallets, grateful for a roof over our heads.

At dawn we crossed the River Bann and followed a rugged path all the way to Derry. As we neared the English garrison, the lands were scraped and beaten, but passage was easier. Along the River Foyle, the road narrowed, and recent rains had swelled the bogs. The horses struggled, we had to walk them rather than ride, and the old wagon we'd found to carry Maire's goods finally broke. We were so close to Elagh, I had Stoat's men drag what was left to store within the castle. I assured Maire her things would be safe and we'd return for them, but the look on her face was truly painful to see. In truth, I knew not myself the condition at Elagh, but we were just a few hours from Burt Castle where our troublesome journey could end, and that became my primary goal. I prayed this last bit would pass quickly, but between Elagh and Burt, we began to see what MacDavitt had foretold.

For miles we saw nothing but ravaged lands without crops, without livestock, without life. Even the poor birds searched elsewhere for their pickings. An eerie sight, if I'm honest, but I dared not speak it to Maire lest her fears be further confirmed. Later we came upon the burnt ruins of two houses, where brothers and their wives had lived. After we passed, the air freshened, as did the surroundings, but in truth what we'd seen and experienced could not be swept away. The scents of smoke and decay clung to my nostrils.

Halfway to Burt, the road turned west, and we followed a veiled sun past farmlands, fresh graves mounded with dirt, a partially burned house abandoned. One mile further, a family huddled together against the stones piled beside their ruined farm. The parents were gray-faced and shivering. The children clung to their mother's torn skirt, their frail legs like the twigs of a dying tree. Maire called for us to stop, and with Nonie's help she gathered all the blankets we had bundled on the horses, and gave them to the family, along with all the food we had remaining.

She cried as we continued on. I should never have brought her into such a situation. She deserved far better, and sure she must have expected so. I ought to have waited for the outcome at Kinsale, to bring her home on a great wave of victory and joy. If only I'd been more patient, she wouldn't have had to see such tragedy. I stopped looking back at her so I wouldn't have to see those tears. Instead, I searched ahead for the crowns of the towers at Burt. When at last they peeked above the hills, my spine seemed to grow an inch and I lifted my head. "Maire!" I called out. "Do you see? We are almost home!"

A wan smile was my reward. I tried to imagine her perspective, having passed such destruction, loss, and hunger. A horror to her—to me as well—and yet we were arriving at Burt, sturdy and sound, guarded, protected, furnished with many comforts, and seated at the gateway to beautiful, beloved, abundant Inishowen. How would I get her to release what lay behind her and embrace all that was before her?

The castle grew before my eyes, larger and taller, the turrets at alternate corners like giant clubs to thunder down upon our enemies, and on the walls around the castle, bastions where soldiers would blast the same away from our moat and bridge. A great cannon on its platform held its deadly aim east toward the English garrisons. The vaulted roof protected three floors from rain and snow, and upon seeing it I could imagine myself within, warming my bones by a hissing fire. It was not a beautiful castle, nor was it the largest, but it was strong, and it was mine.

Thanks be to God, as we approached the outer wall my mother, Lady Elizabeth, stepped out into the bawn. She was first to embrace each of us as we arrived. She took Maire into her arms as if she were a beloved daughter and held her tightly as we all moved toward the castle. I still smelled smoke, but this time it came from a cooking fire. Even the smallest meal would be a feast to us, and as we ate, my mother's harpist played soft tunes to lift our hearts.

That night Maire and I slept on the second floor in the largest bedchamber reserved for the taioseach—for me, not yet of age but still recognized as the lord of the castle, and his lady. I swelled with pride as I drew Maire close to me beneath the warmed bedding.

"Sweet Sionnach," I said. "I know you are tired. Your arrival has not been fit to your imaginings. You have sacrificed much and must deeply miss your family. Tomorrow we will do what's possible to make you truly comfortable and restore your things. But tonight, before you sleep, I'll tell you one thing. I promise, on my heart, I will show you the Inishowen you will love and cherish. When we wake, you'll see the four corners of the earth from the highest tower at Burt. I will be the smallest beginning."

In the dimness of our room, I couldn't see her expression but assumed it was not a frown. I held her until I heard her rhythmic breathing, then allowed my body to drift into a needed sleep. Within my slumber the soldiers still marched, the starving children cried, and the oatfields burned faster than the horses could run. I dreamt though I was aware, my mind whispering…you are responsible…your father would not fail…*you are not your father…*

By morning, I awoke full of fire, my dreams nearly forgotten, my skin alive and burning next to the cool, smooth silk of her own. I couldn't bear it but to have her even before she fully woke. She moaned, and though I thought she might push me away, she embraced me. She might have harbored anger toward me for all of her loss and struggles, but somehow, she accepted my love. And when my strength gave way, I fell across her, my breathing as if I'd just run a mile. She stroked my shoulders and my head until I could speak. "God bless my father for choosing you," I said. "You are magnificent in every way."

She kissed me gently, stretched and sighed. "It is marvelous to sleep so, when I thought we might not lay in a true bed again."

"Rest a while longer, love. Soon the sun climbs and we shall climb the east turret to greet it together." I started then to rise without her, but the excitement overwhelmed me. "Oh blast, please come now. I can't wait until you see it!" We wrapped ourselves in robes and I gripped her hand, leading her up the cold stone steps to the top of the east tower.

"Here is your glimpse, your first true introduction to Inishowen."

She stepped close to the wall, placing her hand on the tower's edge. The wind lifted a lock of hair to her eyes. She swept it away and spoke not at all. A bright edge of light stretched across the horizon.

"The sun rises first over Elagh, my father's home. I haven't lived there since I was seven, being fostered with the MacDavitts. The English garrison nearly destroyed it, but soon it shall be ours and we will restore it to the most beautiful of all our castles, as it was meant to be. I'd started repairs just before I came for you."

"Yes, you did tell me."

I wrapped my arms around her and turned her toward the south. "You can't see it from here, but as a boy I could run beyond those hills to the ruins of an ancient cashel, a great mound where people once worshipped pagan gods and crowned their kings. When I'm there I hear the ancients speaking to me, but I strain to understand their words."

I held her even closer and turned her again. "To the northwest, can you see it? Inch Island. It was my own island, my secret place where I'd pretend to slay all my enemies with my oak twig sword. I practiced daily to prepare against attack. Here we graze beeves, and there's a castle at the north end to defend it. Lough Swilly's just beyond, its waters deep enough for any ship off the North Sea, and in the middle there at Rathmullen? Well, the wharves are always lively."

Once more I turned her, now to the north. "On the riverbank just a bit further is the village of Buncrana, and our castle of that name is in the care of my cousin Connor. A surprise waits for you in the old churchyard: a magical wishing stone set into the wall."

"A wishing stone?"

"The wall has a cup-like hole carved into its middle. The legend is that you stand a few paces away, reach out your arm toward it, close your eyes and make your wish. Then, with eyes still closed, you walk toward it and if your hand fills the cup, you'll get your wish. And if you miss, well…" I shrugged.

"Oh, I must try it."

"We shall, one day soon. There are other places to see. The Great Gap that passes through the mountains. You climb one side and run down the other toward the sea. Some say you're a changed person when you've done. And in the summer, we'll ride horses to Felim's castle at Carrickabraghy. It's grand and strong with seven towers instead of two. It sits on a promontory, the waters around it sometimes bright turquoise, sometimes dark as indigo, and sometimes, both at once, in startling, sparkling swirls."

"I must see it! How will I wait until summer?"

I jumped up on the tower's ledge and reached down to her. "Take my hand. In my arms you'll be safe." I lifted her to the ledge beside me, holding her tightly. "Together we are like the birds, ready to soar into the sky, and you are my Lady O'Doherty. We can see almost everything that surrounds us, all of our lands, the massive cattle herds that fill our purses as well as our bellies, for they are the source of all our wealth and sustenance. Beyond them, the rich fields will soon be heavy with fruit and grain. Is it not grand and wonderful?"

"It is. This land is you, your heritage. One day our children will know it and love it as you do."

"How could they not?"

The sun was halfway above the horizon, high enough to turn her tears into liquid gold.

For the next two months we worked together to keep people fed with what little we had; to clear the fields so that crops could revive; to comfort our people with kindness if that's all we had, and to try and restore a peaceful life to Inishowen. Some families had traveled on foot to nearby counties where relatives would take them in. Others scoured the shoreline for crabs, anemones, seaweed, and snails. There were few berries to be found, and the hunger drove folk to eat anything, even the clovers and grasses.

For years the O'Donnells were celebrated for their trade of salted fish for Spanish wines, but no one remained to pull the nets, and no Spanish ships entered our harbors. Anything stored was shared, and so in December Maire and I acknowledged our first wedding anniversary with a thin fish soup meant to feed every person who lived and worked at Burt Castle. Together we dropped to our knees and prayed for all our people, and for our beloved fathers, both gone from us for nearly a year.

In the far north of Inishowen, there remained cattle and grain that could support our surviving families. The trick was to distribute to our people without the English garrison getting wind of it, for they'd surely take it all. We had done well.

The third week of January brought news that pulled from beneath us what solid ground we'd restored.

18

MAIRE

1602

Lost

Kinsale was lost—a battle meant to wrest Ireland once and for all from the spreading English grip.

We learned the bitter truth of what had caused our downfall when Sir Henry Docwra's letter arrived. Cahir tore into the pages, but after a brief glance he shook his head and handed it to MacDavitt.

"Sir Henry remains kind, though he stands victorious," MacDavitt said. "He writes that the Spanish were ill prepared for such a battle. They arrived shaken by bad weather. They had failed to communicate effectively with the Irish armies, the example being that their ships were loaded with saddles when no horses were forthcoming.

"He says our Irish troops were slow to arrive at the battle site, because O'Neill and O'Donnell pillaged the towns as they traveled south to their supposed victory. As the result, the combined Spanish and Irish army—meant to overpower and vanquish the English forever—never fully formed. Lord Mounjoy laid siege to defensive forts the Spanish had built, and pounded the buildings of Kinsale with heavy artillery, forcing the Spanish underground.

"And this next is perhaps worst of all," MacDavitt said. "A sudden retreat of the Irish Cavalry through our own infantry lines scattered those men from their positions and exposed them to the murderous English cavalry. Because of this, at least 1,200 Irish soldiers shall never be marching home. Remember now, Cahir, this comes from an English pen. It sounds disastrous, but when our men return, we'll hear a different tone and learn the truth of their heroics."

Cahir cast him a doubtful glare.

"Here is the last," MacDavitt said. "Docwra informs us that Her Majesty is so pleased over Mountjoy's victory, she will have him return to London, to be rewarded and elevated to the Privy Council. Upon Mountjoy's departure, Sir Arthur Chichester shall be named Ireland's new Lord Deputy, and he to reside at Dublin Castle.

"Docwra's garrison will resume occupancy of Elagh Castle, to prevent any trouble brought by enemy soldiers returning from that front. It is only a precaution. He expects there will be few."

MacDavitt dropped the letter on the table. Cahir pounded his fist upon it and turned his face to the wall, his spine stiff, his hands trembling with rage. He didn't storm out of the hall as I expected, as he might have done a year ago. In truth it's what I wished to do. The desire for scraping together another weak meal to feed far too many people had escaped me. What did it matter when it seemed the world was ending? What hope remained for the families of Inishowen if the English victors came for our lands? What will happen to my brother if the English discover he'd supported the Irish? And worse still, what will remain for Cahir when he comes of age to claim his patrimony? I fretted over these things just as the men did, but the most I could do was to pray God's help, keep doing the work that is before me, and listen at the doors whenever possible.

Cahir sent men to collect our belongings stored at Elagh while the news trickled in about who had been killed and who returned on foot from the battlefield. The Spanish ships had gone, yes, and Red Hugh O'Donnell with them. Red Hugh O'Donnell! Had he abandoned Ireland? MacDavitt said O'Donnell would return with an even greater Spanish force that would overpower and sweep away the English completely. Could that be true? Hadn't that scheme already failed?

Cahir and MacDavitt would not admit it, nor even discuss it, at least not in the company of a woman, but I did feel abandoned. I had never even met Red Hugh, but I recalled his portrait, and the reverence Cahir and MacDavitt had for him. He was a leader who could draw others to him, inspire them, rouse them to fight. He was admired and feared, but I was certain if he didn't soon return, the fire and fame of the O'Donnell Clan would dwindle down to nothing.

After suffering such unbearable news, the weeks passed as slowly as the drip of tar, the men writing letters to distant supporters, begging for support and supply. Clan leaders from all parts of Donegal gathered to argue and strategize over what could be done next, and to sort out bits of hope from the latest missives. Nothing had come of it so far and by my observation, nothing was expected.

When a letter arrived from Jenico, my heart lifted. I was starved for news from home and eager for any word about what was occurring in Dublin. Burt Castle had become a dark and brooding place, crowded with people both homeless and hopeless. How I'd longed to hear about Gormanston, my family, and any news—especially regarding a weakness among the English authorities. Wouldn't it be grand to see the faces of the men in Cahir's company if I could bring some valuable information to their private discussion.

I opened the letter, only to have my heart cast down, and every remaining bit of hope shattered into a thousand shards of glass.

My beautiful, brilliant, beloved mother had died. She had weakened further after I left home, and just slowly faded away. Cat had found her in the solar, her chair turned toward the garden, her chin upon her chest as if she'd been napping. "Cat," Jenico wrote, "is truly inconsolable."

The back of my neck tightened as if pressed in a vise. Cat. I could just spit. She'd never loved Mother as I had and never understood her the way I had. To my knowledge she'd never even had a serious conversation with Mother, while I had learned everything at her side, and had known her tenderness well. How I wished to wrap my arms around her once more and hear her sweet, loving voice. How could it be possible that I would never, ever hear it again?

This, on top of all that had happened, drove me to despair. I couldn't eat nor speak to anyone, not even Cahir. I cried until I had no more tears, and when they returned to me, I cried them all out again. Mother was gone, and here was I, helpless and lonely in a land of burnt ground, destroyed homes, starving families, and defeated soldiers. Mother would have been able to comfort and guide me, but I was forever lost. I should remain alone in my bedchamber until I followed her to the grave.

Days later Cahir came to me, Nonie behind him. "You must dress, Maire. Someone's come to see you. Someone special. I've brought Nonie to help."

"Who is it?" I asked, "I'll speak to no one." He turned and hurried down the stairs. "Nonie?"

"I do not know who it is, my lady, but she must be important. She's created a stir among the men. I brought the water so you may wash."

I scrubbed the tear streaks from my face, and Nonie brushed my hair. I was unsteady, going without food, and pressed my hands against the wall to keep from falling. She was still pulling the laces of my bodice when the visitor entered the bedchamber.

The lady took up the laces and nodded for Nonie to leave. I was embarrassed to be in such a state with a stranger, and fearful of who she was and what she wanted from me. She finished with my dress and took my hands in hers. We faced each other, and though we'd never met I seemed to know her. She was thin, her hands bony, a crimson shawl around her head and shoulders. Her eyes were brown as a wren, alert and penetrating, but also motherly. She pushed back her shawl to reveal thick dark hair streaked with silver. "You may call me Finola."

I had heard of her as if she was legend, not real. She was, after all, the mother of Red Hugh O'Donnell himself. How could I call her Finola when I couldn't even speak? Through my tears she seemed an apparition.

"Poor lass. Come, let's sit." She led me to the bench at the foot of the bed where Cahir liked to pull on his boots. "Your mother has passed, and it's only a year since you lost your father. I'm so sorry for your sadness. You've just arrived at Inishowen, hardly having your feet on the ground. 'Tis not fair. Not at all."

She cupped my cheek with her warm, soft palm. If this was the woman everyone feared, the fierce mother who summoned Scottish warriors to kill for her son, then all were badly mistaken. This was a woman of compassion. I wondered of a sudden who I should believe among the voices at Burt Castle.

"I have come because I'm also sad," she told me. "And sadness that is shared is halved."

"You have lost someone?"

"My son has sailed for Spain now that his war has failed so terribly. He is my heart and my light, and I fear he may not come home for a long time, if at all. Worse still, he has left me with no grandchildren to cherish in his absence. And so, I wondered, might we struggle through our sorrow together?"

I gazed at her, wiping away my tears, grateful for her company but also a bit ashamed I was not more composed before a person of such nobility. "You are exceedingly kind, my lady."

She scoffed. "I'm sure no one's ever said that to me before, but thank you. Nonie?" she called, apparently aware that my maid listened outside the door. "Please bring us wine and sweets. And tell Cahir we will not be down for some time."

We drank red wine until our tongues turned purple. She asked about my mother, what I wished to remember most about her. Everything, I said at first, but if it could not be that, then I'd choose the sound of her voice, and especially those words she offered when first I met Cahir. "She said I could mold my life to suit my heart, and that paths are meant for discovery."

"She was wise. I've found those truths in my own life. It doesn't mean we won't suffer, but that powers within remain, even if we feel weak and empty. It means we have choices."

I shrugged and shook my head. "Nothing that has happened to me has been of my choosing."

She nodded. "Could it be that God chose for you, and once he has you on the proper path you'll be free to make your own choices?"

I was startled, not having thought of it in quite that way. "I don't know," I said. "Do you believe so?"

She sighed. "I've known great victories in life. And joy. I've learned to bear the sorrows as well. If I'd had God's powers I'd have brought my good son Hugh back home to his lands, and sent to Spain my guileful and traitorous stepson, Niall Garbh. Nevertheless, I remain, survive, and over time I can see a higher purpose in events that have occurred. When I see God's work, I take a little sprinkle of comfort from it. Sometimes, when things are not to my liking, I simply have to wait for the plan to unfold."

The strength showed in her face, along with the compassion. How terribly foolish had I been to judge God's choices because weren't my own. If I could never recognize what higher purpose was being answered, it was because I closed my eyes and railed against it. Mother would have told me to be patient and trust God, but I had to have my fuming. Perhaps the wine and lack of food had taken over and muddled my thinking. "What is the word to use when you are so angry it becomes laughable?"

She half-smiled. "Mocking, I suppose."

"Well then. I must certainly beg forgiveness in my prayers tonight for mocking God. I trust it is not the first time for him. Thank you, Lady Finola, for showing me another side to things. Now, another sprinkle of comfort for you," and I poured more wine into her cup. She giggled a little, and soon we were both outright laughing, and then laughter settled back into tears. Nonie pushed open the door to see if all was well. We waved her off and finished the bottle of wine.

"Finola, won't you stay the night with us? You've had much to drink, and few daylight hours remain. You're nearly twenty miles from your home."

"You are generous to ask, but I cannot. I have yet another visit to make. And you needn't worry. I've the most charming escorts to see me safely wherever I wish to go."

We said our goodbyes and I watched from the bedchamber window as she stood on the cobbles below, arranging her shawl. A man brought forth her gorgeous black mare and helped her to mount. When she rode out of Burt Castle, four brawny guards minded her safety.

I couldn't travel to County Meath for my mother's funeral. Though the Lord Deputy was in full control for keeping the peace, the journey was too far, too arduous, and exceedingly dangerous. Those who returned from the failed battlefields in the south were all penniless, desperately hungry, as ruined as the roads beneath their broken, battered shoes.

Each morning, I still cried for Mother. I'd settle, go about my day, and then something would remind me of her walk, her laughter, her words, and I'd sink into tears once again. I was learning how to accept my dreams of her as visits and not haunts; how to beg forgiveness for the poor daughter I had been; and how be a better wife. Nothing was as I'd expected as a girl.

With Docwra's men inhabiting Elagh, Cahir also was forced to wait, collect supplies for the work he wished to do, and send his men to help other clansmen to restore their battered homes. One evening in early spring, Stoat returned from supervising just such a job, and visiting his aging auntie near Raphoe. He burst through the wooden door of Burt and dropped himself on a bench at our supper table. He was not keen on good manners, our Stoat.

"I've seen 'em, Cahir. Clear as the day, I have," he said, his breath nearly failing him.

"Seen who?" Cahir asked.

"Why, the English, o' course!" Stoat said. "'Tis wha' we been watchin' for, aye? Passed before my eyes, all in step, mebbe hundreds of 'em, towin' crates and likely guns in them. All heading west."

Cahir looked at me, and I back at him. It was a new disaster marching toward us.

"Follow them, Stoat," Cahir said. "I think I know their intent, but follow and learn their destination. Do not get caught, aye? I canna afford to lose you. Take Rudd, not MacTyre, he talks too much. I'll get word to MacDavitt."

"Ye might set MacTyre to training the young lads—keep 'im busy that he won't coom lookin' fer us." Stoat bolted out of the door and into the darkness. Cahir braced his hands on the table.

"Now it begins. The closing in."

"What? What will happen?" I asked, though a discomforting tingle crept up my spine.

The English will take what is Red Hugh's while he is away and cannot fight them: Ballyshannon Castle. When they are done with The O'Donnell they'll take The O'Neill, and his castle Dungannon. Next, they'll come for The O'Doherty. Inishowen. It is inevitable, because we'll not have the power of the other clans to protect us."

"Are you sure this is true?" I asked just to give myself time. I had known we were at risk, but trouble could be closer than expected.

"I've no doubt their plan is already drawn. Our steps from this day must be cunning, fully defined, utterly secret, and perfectly executed if we—Clan O'Doherty—will survive." He took my hands in his, larger and longer than my own and beautiful in a way, like the hand of a Roman soldier sculpted in stone.

"Your help will be crucial, Maire. Beautiful wife, daughter of a viscount. Your standing helps us greatly, and your brother can help in other ways. MacDavitt is already studying our options. I wish my father still lived. My youth makes men assume I am foolish and weak. Perhaps I am. But with you beside me I am ever stronger.

"I think the best course of action is that I become titled, like your brother. An English title, a viscount or perhaps even an earl. Sir Randall MacDonnell of Antrim is seeking the same. Once a man is thus titled, he is treated like a brother of a sort, and other noblemen are reluctant to trouble him or lust for his lands for fear it brings trouble back upon themselves."

"That's very wise…Broc," I said, glad the badger in him was emerging. My heart started to race, partly from fear of our situation, but more from the realization that I could truly help. I could have a higher purpose, like Finola. Could this be my path?

19

STOAT

The Siege

Ours was not a journey for horses. To escape notice by the English, we'd have to melt silently into the surroundings. That meant traveling swiftly, entirely on foot, and with the lightest gear—an ability we'd mastered since childhood. If we wished, we'd vanish among the trees and never be found.

Rudd was exactly where I expected, at his cousin's tavern outside the walls of Burt. I'd warned him to stay near after our return to the castle, not because I'd had another vision or visit from the dead—I had no voice of instruction, but instead a strong urging, somewhere on the edge of a fever—that I must be prepared to act. Even if Cahir's journey had ended at Burt, mine had only slowed and there was something more I must do. After the difficulties of our trip from Gormanston, Rudd was not so inspired for the task.

"We're ta walk all the way to Ballyshannon? 'Tis just spring, the land cold and wet. I'm only now feelin' my toes again. Can we not take a wee break, then?"

"If The O'Doherty says we go, we go, no matter where they be headed. He called your name specifically," I said.

"Did he." Rudd was on his feet and pulling his doublet about his shoulders. No more need be said.

The English soldiers had two days lead on us, but they were a large group confined to an organized march, while we could be clever and swift. The first twelve miles to Letterkenny was done in two segments, a brief rest between, after which we set down for the night on cots at the back of an inn. We gave the filthy canvas a good shake in case of lice left by another weary traveler.

"Letterkenny once belonged to kings," I said, making a bit of conversation as I sat down. "It were the O'Cannons centuries before the O'Donnells." Rudd wiped the sweat from his brow though the air was cold enough to frost.

"I should care, should I?" Rudd muttered, as he struggled to pull off his mud-caked boots.

"Aye! We must all have a care for our history, and where our blood comes from. Else why would we be here for O'Doherty? Why not just let the blasted English tek over? No! They're not our kind, not our blood, they doona understand our religion, and they've not worked this land for centuries. It's to spit on your own father's grave not to remember who he was, what he did ta keep you alive, and what ye owe to the clan."

Rudd heaved an exasperated sigh. "You're after givin' me a history lesson, is it? Can ye not let me have a moment o' sleep? I'd serve Lord O'Doherty just the same in any case."

"Oh, aye, you're right, lad. Rest yourself." I lay a while, my tired legs settling but my mind carrying on, a vision of the O'Cannons marching with the first of such guns, mebbe 300 years gone, pounding their enemies from the hillside above us.

We slept but three hours and then were back on our task. The trail left by the English told their story. They'd be two companies, a hundred men, mebbe a score more, all foot soldiers, no cavalry. Only two sets of hoofprints, likely mounts of the commanding officers, and no heavy artillery. We moved off the trail and kept to the woods, lest we be discovered.

If Ballyshannon were the true destination, the English would likely head for An Bearnas Mór, the great gap in the mountains toward Donegal Castle. We followed well behind, skirting Donegal along the lake spilling into the River Erne. So many memories had I, of a peaceful summer with Cahir. What would become of the castle?

At the lake's northwest curve I realized my mistake, for the English had stopped short, inhabiting the ancient abbey of Assaroe, pitching camp on the hillside facing the castle. They were not going to Ballyshannon. At least not yet. We backtracked through the forest and crawled like crabs until we found a stand of trees west of the abbey. In our search for good cover, I stumbled over a great rock draped by thick, leafy vines. I rubbed my wounded knee, then realized the rock was not natural, but a broken piece of a wall, part of a ruin, placed as a marker of some sort. Something urged me to take a closer look.

Behind the stone and some low hanging branches, I discovered a cave, its opening disguised by vines. Within was a flat, cleared floor well packed, its stone vault solid and secure, and a ledge carved around its inner wall where pilgrims might sit for a secret meeting or ceremony. Dust and spider webs told us the cave had been abandoned for some time, making it the perfect shelter from which we'd watch over our enemies.

We settled in, grateful for such a grand discovery, and then the English started their cookfires and began to roast their meats. The scents slowly crept into our cave, skimming the walls, lingering above our heads in a ring of thick vapor as if the English had discovered a new means of torture.

"Hell's bacon!" Rudd complained.

"Aye, and your mother's ears are burnt from your swearin'."

"As if you're no sayin' the same and worse. We'll have to set here and drool or find a way to steal a bit o' meat. We canna chance it, in truth." Rudd said.

"Speak for yourself. The time's coom I lived up to my name." I ducked low to creep out of the cave and then slither like a reptile toward the scent of meat.

Thick smoke curled above their fires. Sure the meat had come from beeves they'd already stolen from Inishowen. So then, it wasn't stealing if I took a bit for Rudd and me, just takin' back what were ourn. I swung a wide arc to the north but well away from the encampment. 'Round the back side of the abbey were two outbuildings. I found a butcher's stained leather apron hanging on one of them and I tied it on. Emboldened by that stroke of luck, I went straight for the roasting spit. Several soldiers were lying fat and sated on their sides near the fire. I strode up bold as you please and putting on my best English accent. "Just a taste for my poor daughter and child?" I didna wait for a response but pulled off a dangling rib and darted into the darkness.

"Don' let Cap'n Digges catch ye," one of the men drawled, but I was already well around the corner and out of the apron. I passed a stone arch leading into the abbey and glanced at the heads of the men bent over a supper table, not in prayer but in ravenous eating. One fellow looked like Niall Garbh O'Donnell hisself, by the shape of his head and the wiry nature of his hair. Cahir knew he'd wanted Ballyshannon, and he'd be the best man to guide the English there. Beside Niall, another traitor, Henry

O'Neill, a cousin to the great clan leader. Next to him were four others I recognized vaguely, more traitors from among the hundreds Niall Garbh had impressed to his army when he defected to the English. And traitors they were, not just to their clans but to all of Ireland. I clenched my teeth, for they all needed lashing, but I couldna linger long enough to be sure who they were, and certainly I were outnumbered. I dared not linger but darted from shadow to shadow and back through the dark of the woods. If someone came after me they'd find only dust.

By the time I got back to Rudd, the meat was cold and the cow's rib I'd grabbed was already well used, yet we had enough to keep our bellies from growling.

"You stink of blood, Stoat. Ye'll have the wolves comin' after us."

"Well then, keep your skean sharp and ready, so you can cut the mongrel's throat, aye? Now listen. One o' the English mentioned a Captain Digges. Have you heard the name?"

"Aye," Rudd said. "One of Docwra's."

"God's bones!" I shook my head. "On the one hand we be friends, cooperate with the English. On the other hand, here they are to besiege Ballyshannon. 'Tis a war between who can deceive the other faster and better."

"As ever it's been," Rudd said. "But these lads don't seem eager to mek a move, no one's packin' anathin' nor breakin' down a hut. They could attack the castle any time, but it seems they be settled, mebbe waitin' fer something. Shall we breakfast wi' the lads in the castle? See what they know?"

Our mouths watered for a cooked meal in the castle, but we dared not risk exposure in the daylight. We waited and watched. Our patience was rewarded the following day when another company arrived at the English camp. This one brought with it a mounted cannon. We knew now what they'd waited for, and within an hour the activity increased tenfold in every quarter of the abbey.

By dawn the winds howled their warnings to herders and travelers. The English took no heed and surrounded the walls of Ballyshannon. The siege had begun. First, a call to surrender. The small guard left by Red Hugh could hardly resist such a force, but having no permission to surrender, and possibly on a point of valor, they refused. In response, the English aimed the cannon and fired, the blast sure to split our ears apart and shatter our skulls! They blew a great hole in one of the tower walls. The guard returned gunfire, making a weak show of it and having no effect. Then the cannon fire continued, and the flame volleys lit up the castle's woodworks.

After two days of such punishment, the guardsmen surrendered and escaped. The castle walls were pocked by cannon blasts, stone walls tumbled, and the rooms and floors burnt. So damaged was our fine castle that Digges sent his men back to Assaroe, there being no part remaining that was fit to house them.

The next morning, Rudd and I saw the smoke still spiraling from the castle, though we were nearly a mile away. 'Twas my job to bring the truth home to Cahir, but I dreaded it, and more with each step closer to Burt.

20

MAIRE

Be Thou a Knight

Stoat and Rudd arrived at Burt while we were at our breakfast.

"Sit, lads," Cahir said, "and tell me nothing until you've eaten, in case I'm for casting the both of you out, aye? No one wants bad news before breakfast."

"Nonie!" I called. "Something warm to drink for these poor lads?"

She brought out a pitcher of warm, watered wine. They took their seats and ate bread, bacon, and clabber in silence. When they'd finished, Cahir gave them a stoic nod.

"Sure you're expectin' bad news, Cahir," Stoat said, "and bad enough it is, but know this first. The soldiers left by Red Hugh to guard the castle were few and poorly armed. Having no instructions, and no permission to surrender if they came under fire, they made a brave stand."

Rudd nodded. "They did, sir."

Stoat continued. "It were two days, mebbe some men were injured but none killed. The English fired their cannon, blasting holes in the towers. Jaysus, ye never heard such a thunder! Then they set the interior afire. The lads surrendered and escaped with their lives. The worst is that surrender were not enough for Docwra's man, Captain Digges, who blew things to bits though no one was fightin' back, as if it were just a game for him. He ruined the castle thoroughly, leavin' no shelter even for his own men. He sent them back to Assaroe. I've no more ta tell you than that."

"A terrible shame, sir, for our Ballyshannon" Rudd added.

Their sorrow brought tears to my eyes though I'd never even seen Ballyshannon. I was sad for Cahir, knowing how important it had been to him, it being place where his father had died. Most troubling to my mind was knowing we now had English garrisons on our east and west flanks.

"Anything more?" Cahir asked.

"I happened upon a hall at Assaroe where men were dining," Stoat said. "I recognized Niall Garbh. And Henry O'Neill. Several others that I could not be quite sure of."

Cahir sighed. "Well then. Traitors they are." He looked at the table's surface, turned his knife this way and that. He gazed out the window that faced Inch Island. He poured more wine and sighed again.

"You've done well, both of you," Cahir said. He handed Rudd a stack of coins. "Get yourself some rest, or whatever you need. Stoat, stay with me for a bit, will you."

Stoat followed Cahir into his closet where they often went for private discussion. The room was spacious enough for a resting couch, a few chairs, and his desk. MacDavitt was expected soon, and they could be in there for hours. What would they say behind that door that the rest of us in the castle did not or should not know? Perhaps it allowed them to feel powerful. Secrets had power even if they lacked importance. I was accustomed to such exclusion from my father and brother. I was meant to know my place as a woman, and they were sure to keep me there, but from Cahir it felt especially cold.

I shrugged it away, for my mind was troubled by other things. I searched in our bedchamber for Cahir's writing papers. My own papers, and all my expensive inks, had been packed in my wedding chest. For all I knew, they'd been sent to the bottom of the sea. My brow creased at the thought of all I'd lost to that greedy, selfish, crude Captain Seamus. And so, until writing materials could be found, I distracted myself by composing in my head a letter to my brother.

Jenico's position as a viscount was inherited immediately upon Father's death. Cahir's father, Sean Og, and his grandfather before him, had been knighted, but it seemed the honor of leadership and title had to be earned, by more than a victory in battle. Would Jenico have contact with other nobles who could suggest a means for Cahir to acquire an English title? Or even a position leading to one? He could be an administrator, a steward of some kind, and he would be a marvelous master of the horse. Ultimately, he should be made earl to acknowledge his lordship over Inishowen. As the wife of an earl, I'd be a countess. I'd have access to all the information, because I'd have meaningful responsibilities that would help us maintain our position and service to the king. How interesting that could be!

But I needn't have bothered with all my musing, for MacDavitt burst into the castle full of energy and purpose. I rushed into the hall, not to be caught with my ear to the door. He greeted me with a kiss to my hand, and then joined the others. It would be like him to already have a plan that would elevate Cahir from knight to nobleman, to protect both him and Inishowen against the English. MacDavitt was smart, and charming to the highest degree—that I could not deny. Handsome, he certainly was. And shrewd. But it seemed to me that whenever MacDavitt arrived, I had less of a voice in Cahir's matters. As it was, I could only listen through the door as he advised Cahir about things that affected us both.

In hushed tones they spoke of the tremendous loss of Ballyshannon, though they'd known it was coming. They chattered about Niall Garbh being knighted for this betrayal, vowing his allegiance and that of his army to the English. He called himself The O'Donnell, though he wasn't recognized as such by most of the clansmen awaiting Red Hugh's return.

MacDavitt carried on. "By our reckoning, Lord Mountjoy lost more than 6,000 men at Kinsale. Sure if the Spanish had not surrendered the Queen would've had him hanged! Instead, he feeds his lust for O'Neill's prized castle, Dungannon, and no blood will be spared. He's so desirous to clip O'Neill's wings it has made him ill. He suffers in bed at Trim Castle, not far from Lady Maire's beloved Gormanston. If he recovers, he'll be coming for O'Neill, full force.

"Even so, I don't fear for O'Neill. He's wise, wily, and has barriers of protection wider than any of us know," MacDavitt said. "He remains at Dungannon but I believe his time there will be short. He'll fight them, but his loss of control over the Blackwater River was severe. It may send him into hiding, at least until the odds are better. The English will never take him unless he delivers himself to their hands.

"What this means for you, Cahir, is an opportunity for the knighthood you seek. Think of this: while Mountjoy recovers, he's losing precious time that allows his enemy to gather strength. He'll want someone else to worry O'Neill, aye? To distract him, weaken his resistance until the English field army can return? Wouldna that someone be Sir Henry Docwra?"

"I believe it would," Cahir replied.

"And…that would mean…"

"Docwra will need more men. And he'll need guides to scour the places where our man might make his camp. If you're suggesting I and my men should assist, I could not. I'd be a fool to become an enemy to O'Neill."

"Yes, it would appear so," MacDavitt said, "but O'Neill's smart enough to know what you're about. He himself used every advantage to gain his position, and you'd be able to mislead the English wherever possible. Should you come upon O'Neill's rear guard, you might stage a valiant skirmish, just enough to convince Docwra of your worthiness, and him then to request that knighthood from the Lord Deputy."

I nearly kicked the door at MacDavitt's suggestion, it so sparked disgust in my belly. Of course, I wanted Cahir to have his knighting, but to plan and lead a false skirmish against this most powerful man in Ireland? It was all a game to them. Didn't they see the risk, or realize or care that men—Irish men—would have to be killed to prove Cahir's bravery? And what if Cahir were killed instead? Perhaps the role of women as cooks, servants, and child bearers was right after all, for I'd just as soon not even know of the foolish schemes of men. Then my Broc began to resist.

"Look now, MacDavitt, I've never even met O'Neill, whether because of my youth, the battles and skirmishes that have separated Inishowen from Tyrone, or for some other reason, but I'd be a fool to anger the man. He'd come at me somehow. I don't know if he is beloved by his people or only feared, but I've heard the stories. How he hanged his own cousin with bare hands to strike him from the line of succession. How he paid for the other cousin to be killed after escaping Dublin Castle, while O'Donnell miraculously survived. Everyone knows he is ruthless, with fists of iron and allies everywhere. My father would never have crossed him."

MacDavitt scoffed. "Exactly so, but he didn't face the same constraints that burden you. And no one understands better than O'Neill what a leader must do to secure his lands and his power. He'll not be alarmed by you. To him such a skirmish is merely a fly on a stag's neck. I will speak to him if I can, but you've no cause to worry. And anyways, it's time to renew our battle training before the Lord Deputy's army arrives. They are coming, to be sure."

I backed away from the door. How little I knew about the region where I lived. And even less of the ferocity of its leaders. The more I learned, the less I understood, the smaller I felt, and the weaker my sense of being. Where were all these maneuverings going to lead?

Cahir began training each day with his core group of soldiers. He knew much already, having trained with the English, but his own soldiers drew him in, showed their techniques and skills with pikes and skeans. From the tower I watched him stand beside each man, getting to know him, each one pleased to demonstrate his mastery. Then they gathered up and practiced the famed art of the Gaelic skirmish: attack and withdraw, attack and withdraw, each time disappearing into the wood to confound even the best of the enemy's soldiers. It was marvelous to see, their quickness, their power, their ability to melt into the brush like the spotted fawn.

They loved and admired Cahir, these men. They clapped his shoulders and tried to make him laugh. Many of them treated him like a son: young, strong, worthy, willing to learn from their experiences. They had loved and trusted Sean Og, and had fought beside him whenever such was called for because they all had a stake in Inishowen, and Sean Og made sure of it. The same men would willingly fight for my husband as long his priority remained the same.

The spring rains and cool breeze carried away the sorrows from earlier months, at least for a while, and new growth signified renewal that was more than welcomed after so much grief and hunger. Grief for my mother's death troubled me less when I remembered her love of a garden, her joy when the bluebells bloomed and filled the grassy valleys beside the walking paths. The air remained cold around Burt Castle, but I enjoyed so much the tingle of warmth each time the sunlight touched my skin.

How much like my mother I truly was. Would I be so fortunate as she to die as she had, asleep by a garden in a comfortable chair? But there was so much I wanted to do before dying. I wanted most of all to be a mother just like she had been. I imagined what it would be like to have a little girl that I could hold and hug. I could bathe her and comb the tangles from her fine hair, and as she grew older we'd sing songs together and I'd teach her all things my dear mother had taught me.

In spite of the many times Cahir and I had coupled, months had passed and I had yet to feel any tingling in my belly, any disruption of my courses, any indication that a child might be on the way. We were both still young. I had turned 19, and Cahir was not yet 16 years, yet I'd noticed the glances at my belly by other castle dwellers and had my own moment of disappointment each time the blood appeared. Cahir had not asked nor made mention of it, well engaged with other duties as he was, but I longed for the moment when I would first feel a movement and could tell my husband that I'd fulfilled my duty as well.

By late May, MacDavitt returned to Burt with news. This time he didn't bother with secrecy, but joined us at the hall trestle table and called others near.

"You all may as well hear what I've to say, for it will be common knowledge quite soon. Lord Mountjoy has sent an English regiment to Newry. That's just thirty miles south of Dungannon. They're well supplied with guns, ammunition, and heavy artillery. I'm quite sure the O'Neill is their primary target, but Inishowen is rarely spared when the soldiers grow hungry. We must prepare for what the summer holds."

Two weeks later, as I collected fruits from the castle garden, a great spiral of smoke climbed to the heavens before my eyes. The view from Burt was broad and clear across the meadows, yet I saw no source of a fire. I must have seen a distant flock of birds swirling. But wasn't there the scent of smoke upon the air? Faint but growing stronger. I ran to the castle's kitchen, my skin starting to tingle, but no fire burned. Outside in the bawn, men were working, training, sharpening their blades, and brushing down the war horses. No fire burned, though the ash from their night fires scattered upon the wind. Suddenly Stoat was beside me.

"Do you smell it, my lady?" he asked.

"I smell smoke but see no fire. What is it?"

"It's O'Neill. The wily old wolf burns his beloved Dungannon just so Lord Mountjoy won't have it. You canna see it, nor can I for it is 15 miles away, but sure that's what it must be. I know it. It rides across the wind. When Mountjoy marches north from Dublin, he'll have nothin' ta to show for his victory at Kinsale but a smoking, ruined pile. O'Neill himself will disappear."

"He'll be after O'Neill, then?" I asked.

"His war has cost the Queen dearly. She'll want to see proof there's an end to it. The castle would have been a grand prize, but now Mountjoy must be after O'Neill's head. Things are going to change, and it could get rough."

"Will it? What will happen?" she asked.

"I canna be sure, but something stirs as if the ground itself quakes. Something has…"

"Yes," I said, the tingling beneath my skin spreading, and my ears hearing only the wail of high-pitched bells. "I feel it, too. *Something*."

21

STOAT

Glenconkeyne Forest

The something began with the arrival of families, servants, and lone stragglers who streamed into Dunalonge, Strabane, and the village at Burt. Lady Maire summoned all of her servants to help in comforting them, at least with a place to rest, a bit of food and water. I followed her about with a wagon full of supplies to offer these troubled folk. They reeked of smoke and filth and were all too eager to blurt out their stories condemning the The O'Neill of Tyrone.

"They loved and trusted him," I told my lady. "He was like a father to them, even if a bad tempered one."

"Yes, I know something about that," she said. "But how cruel? How could he have burned Dungannon when so many of their homes were built against its walls?"

"I s'pose he wanted nothing left standing that the English could use. All that remains, so I'm told, are the two decorative towers of red brick that were never intended for battle anyways. He'd never need them for defense because, up until Kinsale, who would have dared to strike O'Neill's at his seat o' power?"

"Oh dear. The consequences of things do often seem worse than we imagine," she said.

To a family with four small children, we delivered woolen blankets, bread, and milk. I wondered how long they would manage, gathered upon the ground without a proper shelter over their heads. I talked to Lady

Maire as we worked, telling her more than I probably should have, but it seemed to settle both of us when so much was uncertain.

"MacDavitt thinks O'Neill will lead his army to the Glenconkeyne, nine miles distant. If ye've not seen it, 'tis the most enormous, dense, and proud forest in all of Ireland. The oaks be taller than any, and 10 men couldna with arms fully stretched close a ring around their mighty trunks. And around every tree, thick networks of vines and brush keep all but the smallest and most agile creatures from passing.

"Worse yet for common folk, the forest is dotted with boglands, wet and odorous, thick with decayed plants, dead animals, and earth. Seven or more of these bogs run so deep as to easily swallow an entire horse or beeve leaving no sign at all of its doing. Many who have entered Glenconkeyne were never to be seen again."

Lady Maire sighed heavily. "Stoat, do please tell me Cahir is not to go after him."

"It is my hope, dear Lady, but if he goes, I'll be at his side."

Only a few days passed before a letter arrived from Sir Henry Docwra, just as MacDavitt had predicted. Cahir read the instructions to all at the dining table.

"The Lord Deputy has ordered Sir Henry Docwra to seek out O'Neill and corner him until the larger English army can arrive," Cahir said. "If there should be a surrender, a capture, or a killing, Mountjoy demands to be present. Docwra writes that having accepted my vow of service, he now calls for my presence as part of the search party to capture O'Neill." He looked to MacDavitt who was shaking his head in dismay.

"If Docwra wants to scour Glenconkeyne," MacDavitt said, "You dare not. Only the wisest and most experienced men can survive it, those who understand that the bogs themselves are the key. They know how to read the bogs like a map, study the patterns where firm lands lay and where rocks or thick roots offer a solid step for safe passage. Yet, even these wise lads can be lost after heavy rains altered the expected course.

"The English will require guides to manage any search within these forests, and guides, if there are any, are sure to be in O'Neill's employ, or dead if they refused him. I'll go back to what I suggested before, that you find a way to stage a skirmish on the edge of the forest, but never to go in."

The next morning, Cahir chose 15 foot soldiers, myself included, to complement Docwra's company of 40. We'd march to join Docwra's troops in two days.

It being Docwra's expedition, Cahir made sure to remain in a supporting role, riding Asher on Docwra's left, along with Captain Henry Hart on Docwra's right. Thus, he had a respectable position and could watch for an opportunity to demonstrate his valor.

Docwra decided to approach the Glenconkeyne from its south end, assuming O'Neill would seek shelter close to his homelands to mind Dungannon and watch for the English army's return. After several days searching without sight of anyone nor any movement, Cahir suggested a different tactic.

"Might it be possible, Sir Henry, that O'Neill left only a few men behind to report activity around Dungannon, and moved his family and the larger part of his army to greater safety?"

"Quite," Sir Henry replied.

"I wonder that they might head farther north to rely on the village of Kilrea for sustenance. Between Kilrea and the River Clady, three known bogs make a dangerous and uncertain entry to the forest. Were I to go into hiding, the bogs would provide the perfect barriers against an enemy."

"I should say. That seems a strong possibility. What do you propose, then?"

"Sir, we cross the Clady and turn northward, combing the forest's outer edge. We search for a trail, tracks, or other signs of our quarry, and try to draw them out."

"A wise choice, O'Doherty. You shall lead us."

"Sir." Cahir nodded. I knew this was not quite what Cahir was hoping for, but he was in a dangerous position, for his life and for his standing if he should fail. It was my place to make sure he didn't.

We prepared the muskets, fastened our iron helmets, and pulled the skeans from our belts to be ready for any surprises. Cahir guided Asher forward, sending me ahead with three men to scour the earth around the nearest trees and hunt, or appear to hunt, for any sign of ingress by foot soldier or horse. We hunted three days to no avail, and Docwra grew impatient until we reached the Clady. We found the ford and crossed without incident. Within hours we came upon signs of scraped ground, a heel print perhaps, and some broken vines cleverly replaced to hide a possible opening. There was no way of confirming a connection to O'Neill, but Cahir signaled to Docwra, who brought his men close, weapons ready.

Sure it seemed only seconds to me when I heard a crash, and then a roaring rush like an ocean wave coming down from overhead. Eight men, or mebbe ten, came at us from the rear. Some shook great leafy branches, their faces smeared with mud to disguise themselves and confuse us, while others brandished half pikes and skeans, surrounding and attacking Docwra's rear soldiers. Two men fell even before I and mine could counter, but Cahir wasted not a breath. He jerked Asher in a swift arc toward the attackers, his sword drawn, glinting with light. We fell in behind him as his sword swung down on one of the men and then he turned on another. Captain Hart protected Docwra while Cahir fought, and I beside him to fell the others. But no more would die that day, for the attackers retreated into the brush and disappeared in an instant. Attack and withdraw, and none used the tactic better than the soldiers of O'Neill. We searched the edge of the wood, tracking them slowly and as far as we dared, and soon lost the trail. Docwra hailed us back.

"We have accomplished our mission and determined the general location of these rogues," he said. "We must look after our wounded and return to the garrison. O'Doherty, your quick response was exemplary. The Lord Deputy shall be pleased."

True to his word, Docwra sent his report to Mountjoy, reminding the Lord Deputy Cahir was the son of a knight, Sir Sean Og O'Doherty, and requesting a knighthood recognizing Cahir's performance, loyalty, and service to the crown. The much-desired honor was soon granted, but Mountjoy still being too ill to travel, asked Docwra to formally bestow the honor. The ceremony would take place at Derry two weeks hence, and all of Cahir's family could attend.

On that glorious day, we dressed in our finest clothing and assembled in the garrison's court. Sir Henry approached, a young assistant following just behind him. Sir Henry wore his military coat studded with pins and decorations denoting his status. Tucked within his gold-colored sash was a long scabbard, the silver hilt of his sword bright and ready.

After a brief welcome Docwra, glowing with a fatherly pride, called Cahir forward to kneel upon the blue matt that had been placed for him.

I was growing more excited by the minute, for I'd never actually seen a knighting before, and just in front of me, Lady Maire trembled as a leaf in the wind.

The lad removed Docwra's sash, and Docwra drew his sword, its smooth silver surface gleaming in the midday sunlight. Gently he placed the flat of it upon Cahir's right shoulder, then upon the left. I wanted to jump, did I.

"On behalf of Her Majesty Queen Elizabeth, and our Lord Deputy Mountjoy," Docwra said, "I dub thee, Sir Cahir O'Doherty, a knight of our realm." Cahir remained kneeling as Docwra sheathed the sword and we all waited in reverent silence.

"Sir Cahir," Docwra said, his voice louder so that all could plainly hear, "You shall know and adopt these rules of knighthood: When seeking wisdom, find solitude. Never announce you are a knight, behave like one. You're better than no one, and none are better than you. Show others respect by offering the best of yourself. Allow that each of us walk our own road. Forgive. Look for the best in others. Fight for justice. Always remember, truth is the water, light, and soil from which we rise. And lastly, fear not death, for the work one knight begins may be finished by others."

Docwra bid us farewell, and with that it was time for celebration. We retired to nearby Elagh where Lady Maire, Lady Elizabeth, Felim, Mac-Davitt, myself, and all could congratulate Sir Cahir. More wine was spilled than swallowed, and a great deal was swallowed, to a staggering degree. We believed the ceremony marked a new level of status and authority for Cahir that others would have to recognize. But the honor of knighthood came with its price.

After a few days a missive arrived from Docwra that Cahir should report to the garrison at Derry, bringing to his service 100 men. Mountjoy had sent word that he was yet unable to come north to collect O'Neill, and as the general area of his hiding had been discovered, Docwra was to gather forces and take the earl into custody. Mountjoy could not understand, nor would he care about the complexities of such an order. He simply expected it done, and Cahir was duty bound to respond.

Lady Maire cried when she learned of it. "Isn't it enough to gather men and prepare them for battle? But now we must send them into dangerous and uncertain ground against a foe as deadly as O'Neill? The mission seems nothing short of impossible."

"Perhaps you are right, Lady Maire." MacDavitt nodded. "Impossible as it may seem, if Cahir doesn't do as Docwra commands, he'll lose the man's trust and confidence. It will be a long road to gain it back, and there's a risk that he never could. Should he see you as a traitor, Cahir, you might become a target."

Cahir thought in silence for a few moments, then drummed his fingers on the table. "I think I must go, Maire. Docwra will think I'm a traitor, or a coward. Either way it does us no service."

Cahir set me to work gathering the men to answer Docwra's call. I took MacTyre with me in case we encountered reluctance. A man would volunteer for almost anything if it could remove such a violent and nagging rodent from his presence. Rather he should bathe in a patch of stinging nettles than listen to MacTyre's unceasing demands. As it turned out, assembling troops was not as difficult as I expected, for the men wished to serve their new chief and show their fealty. They also hoped to be fed regularly, and perhaps to take a bit of plunder that would feed their families.

And so the men came, and the men marched. When we reached the outer ridge of the Glenconkeyne, Cahir stood by as Docwra climbed upon a stone and informed the rows of soldiers of their mission and who would be their prisoner.

"I send you forth in arms to surround and secure a mighty enemy who opposes the crown and has caused great concern and difficulty to the Queen. He must be stopped, he and all the rebels who follow him. We would have him alive to face his trial, but we will if needs must, have his head. Hugh O'Neill of Tyrone shall terrorize these lands no longer."

While Docwra's company stood by, a rumble of discontent erupted among Cahir's troops. It began in one corner, and then blistered in a rapid pace across every man we'd assembled. Loyalty and obedience melted into one grotesque roar of hate. At the front of their formation, men threw down their weapons and raised their fists.

"We shall never hunt down for the English the great Tyrone. We shall never betray him nor our birthrights!" And before my eyes the soldiers' formation crumbled at its edges and then shattered as the men left their positions and walked away.

Docwra commanded them to halt, but his words were lost in bold refusals and the stomping and cursing of their bitter retreat. Cahir was stunned, unprepared for such an event, and said nothing for he would never be heard.

I understood what had happened. I should have expected it and warned Cahir. I wished I'd had a vision of it, but none had come.

Though his rebellion had so far failed, O'Neill remained the closest thing to an anointed king of Ireland than any had seen, even stronger than Red Hugh O'Donnell. Many believed he was the answer to a long-held prophesy that a true king would come, rid the island of all intruders, and restore Ireland's sovereignty. That was reason enough to refuse Docwra's command. Their mutiny was immutable and complete. They deserted the field, and Cahir's reputation and leadership took a crippling blow.

We returned to Burt in utter gloom. Lady Maire met Cahir in the bawn as we arrived. Having already heard of the mutiny from returning soldiers, she reached for him, surely to offer comfort and sympathy, but my lord would not have it. He brushed past her and into the castle, seeking the darkest corner of the hall. We followed him there, though I stayed a few paces away. Lady Maire sat beside him, only waiting, for words seemed unwanted. After a while, he turned to her.

"They were right, Maire," my lord said. "They were right, and I was so wrong, blinded by what I could get from it, what advancement I could gain from the English. I should have known the minds of my men before we marched. I should have done more to support O'Neill. As brutal as he can be, he represents the best of us. He fights for our religion. For freedom from English tyranny. He stands for our hope, and these men love him for it. I only wish I could be more like him. Respected. Admired. A man who inspires loyalty, rather than demanding it. The men were right, and they are teaching me. I must become a better leader."

118

22

MAIRE

Bread and Butter

My husband set himself a task that every day he would—one by one—rebuild his relationships with the men of O'Doherty Clan.

"I shall talk with them. Confess my error of judgement. I never should have sent them. I'll ask their forgiveness, their advice, and their loyalty. I must show them that I care for them as I'd have them care for me," he declared. "I will ask them if they knew my father, if they loved him, and if they had stories to share about him. I hope it will help to restore that bond. And soon, I'll speak with Henry Docwra. There must be limits to his expectations, and limits to my response. I will make him understand that. MacDavitt can help me plan that conversation. 'Tis his greatest strength. But most of all, I will shift my tactics to be more like my father's: promise, promise, delay, delay, delay."

He continued to suffer great pain and shame. I felt for him, but I had to disguise my joy over it. I loved when he shared his thinking with me, his plans, and especially his feelings. The older he grew, the more guarded he became, which I supposed was natural as boys become men, and I had so loved the gentle honesty of the boy. He was getting stronger, less in need of support and advice from others, and led more by his own beliefs and intention. This reaction by his men would only elevate him to his rightful position, well earned.

I turned to my daily tasks, which mostly concerned our meals. Finola had sent us a new cook named Rita, who loved to bake things in the stone oven. I found her mixing milk into cornmeal for bread, while Nonie mashed tomatoes for a soup. We'd harvested all our sweet peas in July, devoured most of them, and put some to dry that we'd have vegetables to eat over winter. Roasted pork would be our main course for supper, along with some pigeon pies, and greens for salad. It was hardly lavish but nourishing and well flavored.

When my own tasks were done and I had my leisure, I trailed my husband from bedchamber window to tower, to kitchen door, to the main door, and back again to see with whom did he speak. I watched the way he walked, each day with greater confidence, and I realized most happily I'd become more than his arranged wife. I truly loved him and knew that he loved me. It filled me with a warmth as lovely as the sunbreaks that drew me out into the courtyard. I wandered carelessly, pulling the weeds from between the cobblestones. Once I allowed myself to rest in the tall grass, absently rubbing my palm across my belly. After a few minutes I sat upright in surprise. It was no habitual gesture, in fact one I would not want others to observe, but it stirred wonder. Could something at long last be happening there? Oh, how I needed my mother!

Instead, I sought out Cahir's mother. Cahir was Lady Elizabeth's first child, but she'd birthed four more after him and would certainly know all I needed to learn. I climbed the creaky stairs to her chamber, just above ours in the castle. She spent most of her time there, and I hoped it did not mean she was ill.

"Lady Elizabeth," I called. "Are you fit? May I enter?"

"Please come in," she replied in a gravelly voice. "Yes, there you are, sweet lass. Come sit beside me and tell me what troubles you."

She'd been reading a prayer book. I sat on a stool by her knee, for there was no other choice. I must see about getting her a chair. "How do you know something troubles me, my lady?"

"Because you've never come to me before. Let me help."

I sighed, a bit perplexed. "I am longing, perhaps too deeply, to feel the growth of a babe within my womb. Some women are with child almost immediately after they wed."

"If not before." She smiled. "You've no call to worry, you are both young, and children will come even if not right away. Do you feel unwell?"

"No, I just…"

"Your courses?"

"Perhaps a little late but it's too soon to be sure. I…well I thought

I felt something."

She smirked. "If you're with child, what you'll feel first is not movement, but a dreadful need to vomit."

I shook my head, allowed my shoulders to settle. "Knowing that, I ought not be so eager, but I shouldn't want to disappoint Cahir either."

She touched my hand. "The little ones always come in their own time. When the world is not at ease, when there is violence, unrest, famine, all the things we have seen, I believe God's angels whisper in the infant's ear, *wait*. Better to arrive in a time of peace and plenty. Have faith that the angels watch over your child, that it will come to a world of safety and it will know love.

"And know this as well: Some men need a child in their lady's womb to prove their virility and their worthiness under God. They brag and strut about as if they have great power, when it really has little to do with them at all. Cahir is not like that. He is concerned only with doing what's right, and being a good man, to honor his father and secure his future—all of our futures. He'd have himself remembered as a great leader. When your time comes, he'll be stronger in his position. Your child will benefit from that. And if you wish it, I will be at your side every moment through the birth."

Tears welled in my eyes. "I wish it, Lady Elizabeth."

"Oh dear. Call me Eliza."

I hugged instead of thanking her because I could not speak.

When I reached the bottom stairstep, brown leaves had scattered across the floor, the last of spring foliage blown in beneath the hall door. I opened it wide to sweep them out when I saw just over the hill MacDavitt coming on horseback, and five others with him. I ran to the kitchen to warn Nonie and Rita we'd be feeding at least five more for supper, and then I returned to greet them. Cahir stepped in front of the door, not realizing I was just behind him under the arch. I slipped my hand into his.

MacDavitt swung from his mount, his boots clapping the stones where he landed while the others led the horses to the stables. His eyes were merry and he clenched a white clay pipe in his jaw. "What say you, Sir O'Doherty?" He spoke only to Cahir but nodded in my direction.

"I say welcome, ye wily old dog!" They grabbed each other's shoulders and ended with a hearty grasp of the forearms. Where ha' you been?"

"Goodness, let him come inside first," I said. "Nonie will bring some ale, and your men are welcome at our table."

MacDavitt settled in a chair, reared back and pressed one of his boots against the table's edge. Let Eliza or Rita chastise him this time. I'd keep my lips closed, more interested to hear the news he might bring.

"Well timed," Cahir said. "You always arrive at the perfect moment, when the wine is poured or the beef is carved."

"'Tis an art, so I'll admit." He laughed, never releasing the pipe from his teeth. "I've been to see Niall Garbh. Good to keep an eye on 'im even when he's doing nothing. He's taken to bragging o'er his knighthood after Ballyshannon. I knew he was involved in that somehow. Now he says he wants naught to do with Docwra, nor his garrison, even though he claims the men there prefer him over Docwra."

"Is that so?" Cahir asked.

"I believe it's true. They admire his extraordinary prowess in a skirmish. I canna argue that wi' them, he is better than good. If only he were trustworthy. Anyways, I heard he quarreled with Docwra over pay and plunder."

"Should I be concerned?" Cahir asked. "He's made no secret of his belief that Inishowen should be his, along with every other part of Ulster."

"Niall is greedy by nature, sure enough. But I'd say, one of his greatest strengths is that he waits for opportunities—he's not so likely to create them—and he has no opportunity for Inishowen. We are strong, defended by Docwra should we need him, and the Lord Deputy comes. It's no time to go pillaging. He'd be a fool to draw attention, or to forget that Red Hugh could return with a Spanish army on any day. No, there is nothing you must do but continue the good work with your men. I hear rumors you are turning them to your side, gaining their respect. You could not do better. And like Niall Garbh, you must wait, and trust that things are coming into position for you. By the time you come of age, just a bit more than two years, your power will be cemented."

MacDavitt's five riders joined us at table. They were all MacDavitts or MacSweeneys. Nonie brought bread and butter to the table, *aran agus im*, as they called it, and a lively supper began with hands reaching this way and that, tearing bread, spilling soup, cutting pork and gnawing the meat from the tips of their knives. The experience was far from what it would have been at Gormanston, but the rich scent of roasted pork filled the hall, bringing with it a sense of well-being.

"And so, MacDavitt, you'll stay the night, and mebbe a few more? Sure your advice on a few things would set my mind at ease," Cahir said.

"Och, we must be off just after dawn. I've a business meeting at the village of Omagh, possibly an import of tobacco that I…"

"Ah, so that is why the tobacco pipe?" I asked.

"Aye, my lady, did I raise your curiosity?"

"Quite so." I grinned. "Isn't tobacco smoking harmful? Does it not make you cough?

"At first, I suppose, but you mustn't let the criers and screamers get the better of you. Tobacco is credited with many virtues. Good for the fingernails, for instance."

"Fingernails?"

"Of course."

He held up his hands which I'd hardly noticed before. The skin was smooth and clean without so much as a freckle, his nails were longer than mine, and well-shaped. These could not be the hands of a man who had led companies of soldiers in the Spanish army. Yet I could not imagine tobacco having anything to do with them. More likely a lady friend had given them special care.

"Tobacco prevents worms as well, cleans an odorous breath, soothes toothaches, and can even cure cancer. The smoke has been used to clear away bad air in times of plague. Quite remarkable, I'd say. A high-quality leaf is what you look for, golden brown, without mold or spots."

"I see," I replied, still doubtful.

"A planter is considering import and storage in Omagh, a most splendid crossing point for trade, from which he'll need a trusted agent and distributor. Indeed, I anticipate a profitable result from this, and work for our folk. But not to worry, Cahir, I'll return in a week or so to tell you all about it, and we'll have the time we need for plans and strategies, and mebbe a plot or two."

He cocked his head back and laughed. Cahir laughed with him though I thought there was disappointment in his eyes. If only MacDavitt realized the place he held in Cahir's heart and his life.

124

23

STOAT

Omagh

"Stoat! Wake up. You must wake!"

My lord Cahir shook my shoulder, though there was yet no daylight or sounds about.

"Wake and help me. MacDavitt just left Burt with his men, headed to Omagh. I wanted him to bring back tobacco samples I could gift to Docwra, but he took to the road before I could ask. Go after him, will you? Or send MacTyre? It means much to me, to restore favor with Docwra."

I blinked to clear my eyes. Cahir's hair nearly stood on end, reminding me what it was like to awaken with the energy of a squirrel. I had since outgrown it; I could still move fast, but I needed more time to get started. "Aye, aye. Wat's 'is about tobacco so early?"

"Get up please! Send MacTyre to bring me some hogsheads of tobacco? I canna go myself."

I hurried down the stairs, though finding MacTyre was generally easy. For a small fella, he had the snore of a giant, and therefore if he didn't sleep in the village, he camped against the outer castle wall, away from the other lads. I didn't have that far to go this morning, for he was wide awake and chattering with the stable boys roused by MacDavitt's departure. Annoying as he might be, MacTyre was dependable. He needed only to know Cahir requested his service. He chose a fast horse and was on his way in minutes.

If he couldn't catch up with MacDavitt, he'd have a full day's travel to Omagh, a walled village south of Derry and west of Dungannon. It benefitted from the confluence of the two rivers that fed the north-flowing River Strule. The rivers teemed with salmon and trout, but also offered a ready means to move goods by boat. MacDavitt was right; it would serve well for distributing hogsheads packed with tobacco.

I assumed MacTyre would need another day before returning and set myself to my own business. While Lord Cahir met with other clansmen to strengthen their loyalty, I repaired the fish trap on the Swilly. Rudd and I hauled in enough trout for a fresh and sweet supper. What a shame MacTyre would miss it, for he loved a good bit of trout, and loved catching them even more.

As dusk darkened to night, I warned Cahir not to expect his tobacco until the morrow, then I sought my pallet after a bit too much wine. I fell quickly into a liquid, syrup-like sleep, perhaps not restful, and yet even as I tried, I could not raise my head, as if a warm hand pressed down upon it. I contented myself with it until it seemed someone was laughing, a distant, smothered laugh—MacDavitt, always making a bit of fun at my expense—and then I was adrift again for there was a river, the waters tumbling over the rocks, flowing south instead of north, growing thicker and sticking to my shoes that then caught in the mud, dragging me down to where the water thickened more, sticky like tar and as black, and then the laughter silenced and my shoulder seared with pain, squeezed, wrenched and rudely hammered, and someone was crying in my ear. *Stoat, wake up Stoat*…and MacTyre's face was inches from my own, swollen and distorted, streaked with dirt and tears and…he jerked me up with his fists.

"Stoat…" MacTyre wiped the snot on his sleeve and wept, clenching my shirt and jerking my chest upright. In the dim light his puffed-up face had purpled. "They are all dead. All of them."

I was awake then, sure as if I'd slipped through a surface of ice, and he had not to speak it twice. "Outside," I said. We ran out to the court and to a far corner of the wall where no one could hear. "Catch your breath and tell me slowly."

MacTyre huffed, spit on the ground, and then squared his shoulders to face me. "I followed along the way toward Omagh. There were tracks and sign of them, I knew they were just ahead of me, but I came upon a stray horse, bridled but bare-backed. I kept riding and the horse fell in behind me. Before long I came upon another, standing still beside a ditch, bridle hanging to the ground. It was dark but I could soon see forms in the ditch. Bodies. *Bodies* in the ditch. MacDavitt's hair, bloodied. Sure it was him. I counted six, and no breath of life remaining. If anyone else was about, I neither saw nor heard, and no one came for me. I could do nothing alone, so I returned with all swiftness, the horses in tow."

"You've done well, and sure you're tired, but you'll hafta tek me to 'em. Go and have the lads prepare fresh horses and a wagon. And get yourself something to eat. We've got to bring them home at once."

"Stoat," he whispered, "we'll need more than one wagon."

My throat locked, and for an instant I wished I'd expire on the spot rather than be the one to deliver such news. I nodded, then rushed to Cahir's bedchamber and tapped on the door, knowing he'd be awake but not wanting to rouse Lady Maire if I could help it. She'd learn the truth soon enough. Cahir stepped out.

"MacTyre has just returned," I told him. "There has been a skirmish. Or mebbe an ambush of some kind."

Cahir stiffened. "Whatever it is, say it."

"MacDavitt and all who rode with him lay dead in a ditch near Omagh."

His face grayed and his lips parted as if he might vomit. He clenched his fists and gritted his teeth trying to gain control of his senses, yet his eyes watered.

"Are we…"

"Ready to fetch them. Yes. My lord, you need not go."

A flash of anger seared across his face. "I'll care for our men as they'd care for me. I'll bring them home with my own hands, to rest them in O'Doherty earth. Inishowen."

Cahir opened the bedchamber door. "Sionnach. Stay as you are. Stoat has come for me. McDavitt is killed. I must go to him." I heard a gasp, and then a cry, as if a full scream could not escape her throat. Cahir went to her and held her for a moment, and then we ran for the stables.

"MacTyre," Cahir said. "Was there anyone around, anyone else on the road you traveled?"

"None that I saw, sir. I'm sorry," and he began to weep. I put him in the first wagon. Tired and distraught as he was, we needed him to guide us to what he'd found. We picked up Rudd and ten others on the way out of the bawn. We would not be without plenty of well-armed men to protect our chief. Whether of age or not, he was our leader, and we knew not yet what we would face.

"Felim should be with us, but Carrickabraghy Castle is too far and there's no time," Cahir said. "I'll get a message to him as soon as we return and know more of what has happened."

These were the last words spoken by any of us for more than an hour, as the sun came up and the wind began to blow, the crows screeching fury across the sky. My body hollowed as if someone had cut me open with a shovel and scraped out my core. If I felt so, how would Cahir carry on, when MacDavitt was part father and part brother to him? I could not think of it and focused on each patch of ground that lay before us. The way grew unnaturally quiet as we came closer to Omagh, as if the whole world knew what had happened there and dared not so much as a breath to disturb the sacred rising of souls.

Not until the sun was high did Cahir break the silence with a question. "Who?" he asked, an edge upon his voice. "Who could have done such a thing?"

⟡

24

STOAT

Blood on the Ground

A man like McDavitt, so vigorous, so confident, so vast in experience that he'd assemble a solution before the rest of us had recognized a problem—to have one such as him on your side was a clear blessing from God. And so I had to wonder, where had things gone wrong? Who would rather him dead than alive?

I found no easy answer. It was easy to like MacDavitt, with his good looks, his bright smile, the long blond hair that made him look more English than Irish and therefore more welcomed in English homes and establishments. He was smart, his speech pleasing, but he was shrewd, and the English, like Docwra, may have questioned his true intentions. "It…it couldna have been Docwra, right? The two were on good terms?" I asked.

Cahir shook his head. "Not Docwra. Well, as may be, but I think unlikely. Docwra learns things from MacDavitt that he finds nowhere else. Why kill him? To what advantage?"

"Just so," I agreed. "Niall Garbh, then? MacDavitt had just visited him, and there's no doubt Niall envied him. Sure our man would've talked about the tobacco deal, his plans about where was going, and when. Might Niall have wanted MacDavitt out of the way, removing the last barrier to you and Inishowen? He's never made a secret of his desire for the land and MacDavitt said he was not trustworthy."

Cahir sighed. "All true, Stoat. I just don't know. Niall Garbh seems too careful for so wicked of an attack. He'd be more interested in a share of the tobacco profits. But, he might have offered MacDavitt's plans to some-one else. This was not a chance encounter, nor a battle, but a well-planned ambush. A hateful execution."

My chest tightened at the bare truth of it. "So tell me, what are you thinking?"

"Three things. First, it could be the Maguires or Cassidys of Fer-managh, who either oppose the tobacco business on their border, or won't have someone like MacDavitt taking the rewards from it," Cahir said.

"Aye, 'tis possible. Seems they might ha' negotiated first, being that the deal was not yet confirmed. What's the second thing?"

"It could have been rogue thieves returning from war. Desperate men. Trained fighters. Catching MacDavitt unaware."

"Rogue men who could best MacDavitt?" I shook my head.

"You're right. It would never happen."

"So then, what's left?"

Cahir paused, and then heaved a mighty breath. "You know what it is, and it pains me to say it."

"I'll say it, then. O'Neill."

Cahir nodded. "I sent 100 men against him on MacDavitt's ad-vice. The men didn't fight, but it still made us his enemies, and by now O'Neill himself must be an angry, desperate man."

"I canna think how O'Neill could know of MacDavitt's plans. He's still in hiding, and far from here, I'd wager."

"Sure he has spies," Cahir said, "and mebbe Niall is one."

"Only God knows," I said, my stomach twisting to a painful knot. "After Ballyshannon, I'd put nothing past him." A thought came to me that I almost did not speak, but then I had to. "Those men who attacked us at Glenconkeyne, disguised with the branches and mudded faces. Omagh is not so far that…they could have…been sent…"

"Aye."

The setting sun had turned the sky blood red before MacTyre sig-naled that we were near the location. He stood in the wagon, making one of his bird calls and waving toward the left. We slowed the horses so that we might study the surroundings. From my eyes, the place was nothing short of perfect for an ambush. We approached a curve in the road that was not really a road, but a heavily worn cattle path. Here the way narrowed, an arch of tree limbs just ahead, and on either side dense thickets that lined a narrow, shallow creek. Once we reached the curve, it was a clear trap, easily blocked both front and back, and thickets allowing cover for the killers. Cahir was right. They could not have been soldiers, for there was no honor in this work. They were assassins.

A thick cloud of flies swarmed, dispersing as we neared. Blood soaked the ground. Our men had been dragged from the pathway and heaved into the ditch, one on top of the other, like a pile of rubbish to be burned—a clear message of disrespect and savagery. At the far edge of the ditch beneath a low hanging limb, Cahir crouched. The blond hair could not be mistaken, nor the white clay pipe, shattered to pieces in the mud. God himself must have wept for the loss of such a beautiful and gifted creature.

Cahir and I lifted MacDavitt's body and placed it in the first wagon, crossing his arms upon his chest. He'd been shot twice, and all the men were similarly and fatally wounded. If they had returned fire we should never know, for their weapons had been taken. We stood by MacDavitt while the other men collected the rest of the bodies. MacTyre wept openly, his strength failing, and long before the terrible task was done, there remained not an eye nor a face among us not wet with grievous tears.

"Ought we ask in Omagh for any possible sightings or information, my lord?"

Cahir shook his head. "A time will coom for it. This moment I've no stomach for a village that ignores deadly gunfire and leaves six men to rot in a ditch. If anything, I should burn it all down, and none would blame me for it."

Then he fell silent, a procession of thoughts distorting his face, and when it had finished what remained of the boy was fully transformed into the man. "To burn would serve no good." Cahir said. "Better to handle that which is before us, lay our good men to rest, and bide our time until the truth be known."

"Exceedingly wise, my lord."

132

25

MAIRE

Silence

Cahir called me Sionnach. I knew it was intended as an endearment, but sometimes he used it to soften the blow of something that would follow. This time was mountains worse than any others, for without MacDavitt to love and guide us, we were naked and exposed, wee birds waiting in the nest while the rats closed in.

I was not like my mother in such a circumstance. I could not sit quietly in my chair, reading my prayers until the clouds shifted. While I waited for the men to return, I sent word of MacDavitt's death to Felim, urging that he and his family must come. When I informed Lady Eliza of the tragic event, she wept as if MacDavitt were her own son. She and her husband had loved him and trusted him with Cahir's fosterage. I sent word also to Lady Finola, knowing she'd loved and admired MacDavitt as well. Others were sure to learn of the tragedy soon enough. The news would spread rapidly without my help, and I had many great tasks before me.

I set the stone carvers to work first, making headstones and footstones for the dead. I arranged for the shrouded corpses to be buried on the sacred and ancient grounds at St. Mura's Church. Though it be a long way, mourners would walk the few miles from Burt Castle without complaint to pay their respects before the dead were interred. I notified the keeners who could ease the painful mourning of others with their songs and cries. Next, I hired the grave diggers who would face an arduous chore.

Along with the families of the men who had died with him, we could expect great numbers of people to attend MacDavitt's funeral. He was a giant among us, truth be told, and I'd not shame my husband by failing to provide the proper food and drink. I ordered pigs and capons to be slaughtered that we could feed the crowds of people who came to grieve. Rita set to work baking breads and pies, and Nonie gathered the vegetables and meats. I checked our supplies of drink.

I was making important decisions in Cahir's absence, but all with the intent to make the ceremony the best I could, and to lift the pressure from Cahir's shoulders. As well, I needed to amend for the times I was displeased with MacDavitt, and for my envy of the attention Cahir gave him.

Cahir and his men arrived the following midday. He sent the wagons into the stables where the women would start the cleansing and shrouding. When our eyes met, we both lost some of our strength. We hugged and cried, holding tight in the fear of terrible loss, both feeling broken without any means of repair. We were, at last, joined as a husband and wife should be, supporting each other through the best and the worst, and truly needing each other.

"You must rest," I said. "There is water in the basin in our bedchamber, food and drink on the table beside our bed, and clean clothes laid out for you for when you rise. I will manage everything else until then, have no worry."

He nodded and attempted a smile. His shoulders slumped with weariness, and he dragged his heavy feet up the stairs. Stoat came in behind him. I took his hand.

"Thank you, dear Stoat, my friend, for looking after Cahir. I'm aware of how much he means to you, and the help and protection you give him. I have no concern for his life when you are by his side. I also know the reliance you both had on our MacDavitt. I am sorry for the loss of such an extraordinary man. Please, by your bed there is food, clean clothing, and a soft pillow for your head. Rest, at least for a while."

He held me in his gaze, his eyes welling, surprising me for he never seemed to notice me at all. If anything, I thought he remained vexed by my insistence on bringing so many belongings from Gormanston.

"Dear Lady O'Doherty…"

"To you I am Lady Maire."

"Lady Maire, you are God's greatest gift to the O'Doherty household. If any be thanked may it be you. For your gracious self, I will protect him always. It is my honor."

The wake began almost immediately, for as soon as people learned of the deaths, they came, mostly on foot, to mourn, to offer help, to bring food, to take part in such a tragic event for the clan. Of the few funerals I'd attended so far in my life, this one was most solemn. People kept their silence, stunned by the terrible loss. Those who spoke only whispered, so not to disturb the fragile air that surrounded us. By late in the evening, enough ale had been swallowed so that the stories of MacDavitt and his mates began to emerge in quiet corners, or out among the horses. Cahir was not ready for such talk, and so he huddled with Stoat and Felim while the mourners carried on.

The funeral began late afternoon the following day, the setting of the sun symbolizing the passing of these men we would bury, and allowing the daytime for the many who walked to St. Mura's Church. All day the sky was mournful gray, the darkest clouds forming by mid-morning and blotting out any colors. I foolishly hoped those clouds would remain stable and hold back the rain.

At the end of a winding gravel path, our dead lay upon St. Mura's burial ground side by side near where their gravesites had been dug. The shrouds had been secured around them, looking bright white against the dark earth. Above us the sky seemed to descend, and the rain began in a gentle shower, forcing the women to don their scarves while the men held woolen caps in hand, dripping rainwater upon their shoes.

The priest began to speak, calmly acknowledging each man. He spoke of their families, of their service and bravery, of their sacrifice. My ears rang against the sounds and I heard not a word of it until he came to MacDavitt. "In him," the priest said, "our Lord planted a grand bit of humor, a navigating star of remarkable insight, a heart full of courage unsurpassed. He was a man of kindness and love, and at the same time a fierce and formidable warrior. He was rare among men, and we shall forever treasure the gift of him among us."

Standing beside me, Cahir turned his head away, but in that moment the clouds began to rumble, and the rain came down upon us. Cahir said something to Stoat, and the two of them gathered others. They were starting the interment, the priest giving the sign of the cross and the holy waters to each man in turn.

The rain slapped and pattered, turning the dirt to mud and drowning the voices to my ears. At the graves, Cahir dropped to his knees. He held each corpse's head in his hands and spoke to them words no one could hear, and then the other men gently lowered each to his place of rest. When he came to MacDavitt, Cahir touched his own forehead to MacDavitt's. So he remained and I knew he wept, but the rain concealed it. He stayed and stayed until at last the priest stood beside him and placed his hand on Cahir's head. "We now say farewell, and may you rest in peace," he said. And then as though a curtain came down upon us all, the rain surged and pummeled our heads and backs. The priest held Cahir's elbow until he rose to his feet, and then together they slowly left the graveside. Though the rain fell hard upon us, no one left the churchyard until Cahir, Felim, and the priest had passed through the gate.

When we returned to Burt, many of the mourners remained at the castle for days. By the time the last of them had trickled away, September had swept in on howling black rainstorms and bronze-edged sunsets. A brooding silence claimed Cahir and most of his days were spent deep in the woods, or fully engaged in some physical labor. He had called on Henry Docwra who condemned the massacre and MacDavitt's killing, but he offered no further information. Though Cahir longed to take revenge, he was left with his own thoughts and no clear place to lay the blame.

A few weeks later, Lady Finola returned to Burt, this time escorted by a score of her Scottish soldiers. She was dressed entirely in black, her face shrouded. Cahir and I welcomed her, but she would not speak until we brought her inside the castle. We seated her by the fire with a cup of warmed wine.

"I have received the worst news that ever I could know. I am notified that my son, my dearest son, my Red Hugh, has died in Valladolid. *Died!* He was twenty-nine years old. It is unspeakable. Unbearable. He died in his bed, and the dream that he upheld is gone to dust."

Cahir was on his feet, shocked and pacing. "What occurred? He was murdered? Shot, or poisoned?"

She shook her head. "I would have sworn it myself, that English spies, or even that greedy, heartless Niall Garbh had arranged a killing. But the letter I received from Matthew, my boy's own secretary, explained that some hideous worm infected his body, he knew not how, but once within it consumed Hugh's organs at a rapid pace, and my poor beloved son died in agony. Oh! I would rip it from his body and kill it myself had I been near, but now I wish only that I could hurl myself from a mountaintop and join him in Heaven. I do not have the courage to do it."

"I cannot believe it. He was my idol, I learned most of what I know from him, and from MacDavitt. I am bereft. I'm as hollow as a dried-up bone," Cahir said.

I wanted to hold him, to comfort him somehow, but I would only embarrass him should I even try. The most I could do was touch his hand. Lady Eliza joined us by the fire, and both of us hugged and kissed the grieving Finola. She wept, and then dried her eyes.

"And so," she turned again to Cahir, "I come to prepare you as best I can. My Hugh sired no sons to inherit his role. My second son, Rory, I've kept him in safety for this very reason, that if something should happen to Hugh he could be ready. And now he must emerge to become The O'Donnell, regardless of any claims Niall Garbh has made or will make. My Rory will be treated and addressed in the same way as O'Neill. It is the only means by which to protect our lands from the English. What now do we know of O'Neill?"

"He remains in hiding," Cahir said. "But there are rumors. He might have an agent negotiating surrender."

At that we were all silenced. Two of the greatest defenders of Ireland had fallen within a month's time. If O'Neill and O'Donnell surrender to the English, what would it mean for Donegal? What would it mean for Cahir and Inishowen?

138

26

CAHIR

The Documents

Though the geese had been killed and cleaned for Michaelmas, it was not the celebration it had been in years past. Such as it was, we divided the harvest for what we would eat, what we should store over winter, and what we could give to the suffering families.

Our traditions and holy celebrations meant nothing to Lord Deputy Mountjoy, who began his atrocious march north from Dublin, his soldiers scorching the earth to destroy crops and cattle, women, children, and entire families, leaving those who survived to starve. It was a cruel and cowardly tactic meant to force O'Neill out of hiding. Did O'Neill even care? I wondered. And yet his people would not betray him. How did he manage it?

Felim fed the pit fire with bark and oat straw while we pondered the situation. I was glad for his company. He'd been like a father and brother during my fosterage, especially during the years when MacDavitt was in Spain. Now he was my most trusted friend. He wasn't the thinker and schemer his elder brother had been, but I'd not find another warrior as fierce, nor another man as loyal.

The rumor we'd heard, that O'Neill had a long-time friend negotiating a surrender for him, was true. I had spies of my own, didn't I, confirming that while negotiations were taking place O'Neill was hiding at a retreat near Lough Neagh.

We learned also that Mountjoy would continue the burning and killing—his man Chichester leading the murderous charge—until terms of surrender were settled. He preferred his scorched earth tactic over a direct military attack on O'Neill. None would blame him, for sure an attack would unleash the fighting power of O'Donnell, O'Rourke, Maguire, and O'Sullivan Beare, who remained loyal to O'Neill. Even Felim's two younger brothers had joined his army.

"They are O'Doherty, and yet they serve O'Neill? That is a biting betrayal!" I said.

"O'Neill has more money than the Queen herself, and so he can pay them a wage," Felim said. "It's survival, isna? Plain as can be. When the time is right, they'll come to your side sure enough."

"I suppose, but my side feels rather bare at present," I said.

At Christmastime, Maire borrowed Stoat from my service to drive a wagon carrying herself and Nonie from village to farm. We had heaped the wagon full of small packages of oatmeal, butter and bread for the families of Inishowen, with hopes that these gifts might help fill the gaping hole of what should have been, when we were all meant to celebrate peace and plenty, good will, and the birth of Jesus Christ. How I wished He would return to us and mend things.

The fires carried on until February, and when they stopped, we knew an agreement must have been reached. It was weeks before news arrived from Mellifont, the Cistercian abbey near Drogheda where the secret negotiations had taken place. On the last day of March, O'Neill submitted to the English.

And, I wondered, why wouldn't he? When we learned the terms of his surrender it were like a sling of dung in our faces, those who fought with the English and sacrificed lives. O'Neill was fully pardoned. He would be titled the Earl of Tyrone as long as he discarded his "The O'Neill" clan title, as would the new lord Rory O'Donnell become Earl of Tir Conaill. Except for church lands, O'Neill would keep all of his properties as long as he spoke English instead of Irish and replaced Brehon law with English law. He could not employ an Irish bard, nor build a Catholic college on his land, but he was free to return to Ulster.

Had O'Neill somehow convinced Lord Mountjoy that the war

hadn't happened at all?

None of the spoils that the English had lavishly pledged would be coming to those of us who had fought for Docwra. No land, no plunder, no compensation for expenses, nor recognition for the many lives lost in service of the Queen. And yet, after the treaty was signed and O'Neill learned that Queen Elizabeth had died just prior to the negotiation, he'd fumed with arrogance that he'd been tricked, and would have received better terms from King James.

I fumed as well, that I had nothing of value to offer my own men who had served at Glenconkeyne, and still fresh in my memory were the soldiers we had buried there. Felim was equally vexed.

"The Englishman never sees the foulness of goin' back on 'is word, nor the hardship rained upon other men. He sees only how to get wat 'e wants, and cares not a feather more."

"As you say," I replied. "And so the eyes of the greedy adventurers, the men under Docwra's command who believed they were entitled to O'Neill's land, look to Inishowen as if it's free for the taking. I've seen them, on cavalry horses, goin' about on O'Doherty lands as if to measure out their new estates."

"God's wounds! Did you send your letter to the Lord Deputy?" Felim asked.

"Exactly as you said. I listed all the details of my patrimony as The O'Doherty, and requested his confirmation. And, he did in fact prepare a document confirming my ownership of the lands. I took the document to Docwra, asking that his men refrain from their desirous wanderings. He read it and scoffed. Mountjoy had merely scrawled something so that he'd be rid of me. The document is not valid without the King's seal upon it."

Felim's eyes widened, and his jaw dropped. "The scoundrel! He ought to have obtained the seal himself. It is his responsibility as administrator! He treats us all as imbeciles." He sat quietly for a moment, staring at his shoes and tugging sharply on his stiff, rust-colored beard. Then he shifted his gaze to me, sharp as a hawk.

"We shall play his game and win, lad. We shall request an audience with King James. You will introduce yourself not as The O'Doherty though we all know that's what you are. You will be Sir Cahir O'Doherty of Inishowen, owner by inheritance as the oldest son of Sir Sean Og O'Doherty. You will proudly ask directly for your patrimony, all of the lands and castles that are yours by law. He's a man who understands having to fight for what is due. His own mother was executed for treason, he was hounded by the Puritans, and yet with patience and resolve he has claimed the crown of England. And you shall have yours, seal and all."

142

27

MAIRE

For What is Due

Cahir found me at the garden wall among the swaying bluebells, his walk brisk, his face bright. His arms encircled my waist, and he swept me off my feet, kissed my lips and set me down again.

"Maire, my love. We are going to England to meet the King!"

"We are?" My heart leapt. Such a thing had never been considered before, as far as I knew.

"Yes, all of us. You, me, Mother, Felim, Stoat, and I don't know who else yet but we are going. I will need your help in a thousand ways. Will you?"

"Of course, I will help. What is this about?"

"I must meet the King in person, to make him aware of my father's good service to the crown. To assure him I perform the work of a man and leader, and I need the King's royal seal on all of our documents and deeds. It is the only way to stop Docwra's predators and the other English adventurers from claiming our land. They must be repelled, and I can hardly get this done soon enough."

He looked toward the castle. Several workers were busy at their tasks. From every direction came the sounds of it: chickens clucking and screeching to escape the ax, the voices of men calling to each other in the stables, the clinking and banging of the blacksmith's tools, and the lowing of cattle in the fields. "It is right and good," he said. "A meeting with the King shall restore us in faith, and lift all of us in stature. And as I speak of it, would our Viscount Gormanston send a letter to request it? Coming from a titled nobleman it will be taken quite seriously."

"I will write to my brother immediately. He is often full of himself and of no help to me. You remember how he behaved at the Nanny River, leaving us to deal with the mud by ourselves. But he could hardly turn down an opportunity to address the King."

"Might he stand with us on the day?"

"Oh, he must. Truly! To stand at the King's dais to introduce us? I'm sure he'll do it, peacock that he is."

Cahir laughed. "Excellent. He'll be notified of when the King will see us, and we shall arrange our travel. 'Tis a long journey, but we'll make the best of it. I'll see that you are more comfortable this time."

"Thank you. In the meantime," I said, "we'll require new clothes, all of us. I have nothing that would see me well in the King's presence, and you've quite outgrown your black leathers that were so alluring."

Cahir grinned at the memory, but the grin quickly fell to a frown when he glanced at his frayed shirt and worn-out breeks. "Aye, I s'pose it's true. Word has it King James has been generous toward his Irish and Scots-Irish nobles, but we'll not make it past the guards if we don't look wealthy and important. We must make a grand impression."

"You may leave that to me. Jenico will know what the men wear, and I'll write to a clothier for the latest in women's gowns. It will be expensive, even if Nonie and I do most of the sewing. The materials must be fine. Not just wool but linen, fustian, and possibly silk. Exotic feathers in your hat, ribbons and even pearls in my hair."

"Dear God in Heaven."

"I've heard there is a woman in Lifford who is quite the seamster. I shall find her. Oh! And a gift! We must have a gift for the King! What could it be?"

Cahir looked stunned.

"Oh, never mind, we'll will find something. Something splendid!"

"Bless you, Maire, and I'm a lucky man to have you at my side. It gives me great hope that we will turn things around and have the future we've dreamed about, not this constant struggle. We will be successful, will we not, Sionnach?"

"There's no doubt, because you are my clever Broc."

His eyes glinted with a playful light I'd not seen for months. Suddenly he took me into his arms, ran for the castle, and bounded up the stairs. People laughed as we passed but he ignored them and ran to our bedchamber where he plopped me upon our mattress. We giggled, and plucked eagerly at each other's clothes. My shift was tossed to the floor. We came together with such passion as if we'd at last been released from straps that held us apart, and in a sense it was so, for the severity of such grief over time had robbed us of all joy, lightness, and laughter, and the delicious craving from deep within that sparks physical love. I wrapped my legs around him as if never to let go and felt his hands grasping my hips with such desire to bind our bodies into one. I burned inside, as if molten light shot to my chest and thighs, to my fingertips and toes, and into to my head where a fever burned and then melted like butter in the sun. Droplets of sweat fell from his chin to my breasts. I rubbed them into my skin like a sorcerer's elixir.

We slept, and when we woke, he dressed and left me with a kiss and a smile. This time I knew. This time we had breached whatever barrier had kept us from conceiving. This time surely, I would take his seed. I longed to be fat with child.

146

✦

28

MAIRE

The King's Nod

We were summoned to attend the King in September at Hampton Court Palace where he and his courtiers had moved to avoid London's raging plague. We'd be three days to board a ship and sail from Culmore to Dublin. At Dublin, a few more days to get passage across the channel to Liverpool. From there, five days more by horse or coach over land to London, and then at least another day by river barge to Hampton Court. An arduous journey, certainly, but as long as it did not involve a Captain Seamus, I would be content.

I'd already begun, through letters and conversations with those who had traveled to London recently, to learn all I could about appearances and expectations for standing in the King's presence. The proper clothing was essential, for not only could a guard turn you away, but far worse, you might offend the King himself and ruin any chance for a happy outcome.

In the King's presence, Cahir would wear a white linen doublet, every inch of it embroidered with white silk thread. He would look sharp, wealthy, and bright to stand out from the courtiers who wore mostly black and gold. I'd worked on it day and night until I could do it no more. Jenico urged him to wear short trunk and hose because word had spread that the King admired a well-shaped leg. Cahir was more comfortable in the knee-length version with hose and a high-shank boot, heron feathers on his hat.

Felim's suit was rust colored with red ribbons. It was the color of mourning, but it also matched his beard and provided a striking look along with the striped kestrel feather on his hat.

My own jacket was sky blue, fitted to disguise a growing belly. All the other women wore darker shades of blue while Stoat and each of our escorts wore dark green doublets without livery until the King granted permission for something more distinct. The court of King James had discarded the tight, high hairdressing of Queen Elizabeth's time. I could wear long curls pulled back from my face, wispy tendrils at my forehead, and a braid in the back bearing the bluest magpie feathers.

We arrived two days before our scheduled audience, tired, tousled, and wet, but the King had provided lodgings at the sprawling palace, allowing us to restore ourselves and our finery. Cahir bloomed with excitement, and upon settling us all into our rooms he bounded off to explore with Jenico the vast grounds and gardens. I couldn't blame him, for neither of us had ever seen so enormous a palace with such a history and grandeur. They treated me tenderly and begged my company, but I was glad to see the door close behind them, wanting only to rest entirely alone. Nonie brought me food for which I was grateful, but even she was bid to let me be. Once alone, I examined the walls, the fine furnishings, and when the weariness claimed me I lay, tears streaming, the dream state almost enough to sooth me away.

On the day of our meeting, no detail could be overlooked, and I was proud of our procession—and the gift we carried—as we entered the King's Great Hall, vast in and of itself, richly decorated with colorful Flemish tapestries. Our escorts were allowed no further than this when the Yeomen of the Guard guided the family into the Great Watching Chamber. This room alone was as large as our Burt Castle, bright with white walls hung with more rich tapestries telling stories of Hercules and the conflict between virtue and vice. My eyes were drawn upward to the golden honeycomb panel that spanned the ceiling and displayed within each chamber the arms and badges of the highest-ranking nobles. We were to be humbled while awaiting our time.

Cahir warmed my hands in his. "Are you frightened?"

"No, not frightened, but amazed at the size of things, and the beauty. Gormanston is fine, but it is not a palace, and this is astonishing. If the purpose is to intimidate, that has been achieved," I said.

"I am impressed, sure enough," he said, "but I'll not be intimidated. I shan't allow it. I remember I am here not for myself but for my father's memory, for our family, for all the people of our clan. I canna fail in claiming full ownership. If plantation is what the King seeks for Ulster, he must know Inishowen is fully occupied and tilled. He'll need look elsewhere for the comers."

Felim and Lady Eliza stood by us, nodding in agreement. Cahir was ready. He was every bit a man of integrity and purpose. I put my own feelings aside to support him entirely. We were guided to a bench beside the entrance to the King's presence chamber, and we waited for more than an hour while others milled around the room, Jenico among them, creating a constant hum of low conversation while also waiting their turn. What deals and bargains were being made?

When at last our time was called, the Yeoman led us into the Presence Chamber heavily draped with silks and tapestries. We walked down the center of the room and halted halfway. We were meant to keep our eyes downcast as we bowed before the throne, but I could not help but glance at the grandeur of King James. He was indeed majestic, even at twenty paces away. Though he wore no crown, his dense, reddish thatch of hair was crown enough for me. His black cape fell evenly across his shoulders, and he wore a red fitted jerkin so richly embroidered with golden thread I could not imagine the work it required.

The King nodded, then lifted his hand. The Lord Steward said "Approach!" The guards stood tall, their pikes at either side of the aisle making clear the distance we must keep between ourselves and the King.

Observers seated on either side of the aisle whispered to each other as we passed. I shivered with anxiety, but Cahir stood tall, his footing wide, shoulders broad, hands clasped confidently at his hips. Felim stood by similarly, but he was unable to suppress his proud smile. Jenico stepped forward and bowed to the Lord Steward, who announced Viscount Gormanston. I felt so proud of my young brother, bowing before the King! He called forth each of us by name, starting with Sir Cahir O'Doherty, the good and rightful heir of Inishowen, Inch Island, and Elagh Castle, of the Province of Ulster, Ireland."

It all sounded so splendid. It might have been once, but never was it as I had expected. With the King's favor, perhaps our lands and castles might become as rich, abundant, and marvelous as Cahir envisioned, but I had put down my visions and would not gather them up again, not for a long time.

King James had large and searching eyes though the heavy lids made him appear tired. His mouth turned down at one corner, neither sad nor angry, but perhaps judgmental. I thought him a man of learning, and one who would recognize and not tolerate a lie.

"Sir Cahir. You may approach us at the dais," the King said. Cahir moved a few steps closer, just past the guards' pikes, and just before the King's carpet. He bowed most humbly, and kept his head lowered until permitted to rise and speak.

"Your Majestie, I and my family are deeply honored to be in your presence. We have brought to you a most unusual gift from our beloved Donegal. You may recall that several years ago, O'Doherty men in assistance to your garrison at Derry did capture a number of Spanish sailors who foolishly sailed into the mighty Lough Foyle. Of these men none survived, but a great man of our lineage did at that time seize and store something of great value. We present it to Your Majesty in the hope it shall bring you pleasure. It is a matched pair of bottles containing the finest aged wine from the vinyards of Spain."

"Ah," The King said. "We shall have a look at them and perhaps sample them this very night." He gestured for the Lord Steward to take them away.

The King need not know what I had learned weeks before, that the Irish had meant to rescue the Spanish, not capture them. Nor that the wines had been stolen from the English garrison. For this gift, our Felim had selected the bottles himself from his late brother's private collection.

Only after the gift was carried away did the King begin to question Cahir, who answered each clearly and respectfully, about the size and quantity of his lands, what crops were grown, and what livestock thrived. He described the events that led Sir Henry Docwra to recommend his knighting and stated he would fully come of age in one year and one half.

"We see you before us as an educated and capable young knight of our realm," the King said. "So we must wonder, why have you come to us?"

Cahir did not pause or dally, so brave and prepared was he. "Your Majestie, I wish only to be a good son and take up the work of my father, and perhaps improve on it for my own son to inherit someday. But, all of Ireland has been ravaged by war these past several years. I have done what I could to restore peace.

"Inishowen is a fertile land, but repeatedly it has been raided, robbed, and burned, food taken from the mouths of starving families, homes destroyed, precious livestock stolen or simply wasted, woodlands stripped, waterways ruined, fish stocks depleted. If this land can be cared for, protected and developed, it is fertile enough to feed all of Ulster, yea, if not all of Ireland. Food for your soldiers would be provided, it need not be stolen. And the farmers need not be killed for their harvest but let them share it willingly with the King's soldiers.

"I humbly ask only to have my own lands restored to me that are my patrimony, and that your Royal Seal upon it proves my ownership, and my loyalty to Your Majestie's service. This alone I ask, which will cost you nothing but will allow me to protect Inishowen for all of its highest and best uses."

I wanted to clap my hands in praise of my good husband though I knew I must remain silent. Our King could hardly reject such a humble request. But the King said nothing. He only nodded. His gaze, having fully examined Cahir, shifted to Jenico, who bowed dramatically with an extended leg, and then to Felim who swept his hat in a similar display, and on to Lady Eliza who performed a most delicate and graceful curtsey. Though I quickly focused on the carpet I knew he then settled his gaze squarely upon me. I could not look but I could feel it. My face grew hot, and a stroke of fear crossed my back along with it. I could be strong and rebellious at times, as my father would have said, but I was not the orator Cahir had turned out to be. I wanted no attention. I offered a deep curtsy. "Your Majestie," I said.

"You are this man's wife," the King said. "We shall hear your name."

"Yes, Your Majestie. I am Lady Maire O'Doherty."

"You may rise. You are a Preston, of noble birth and most welcomed. Viscount Gormanston's sister. We see the resemblance. Quite unmistakable."

"Your Majestie." I nodded and lowered my gaze.

"Something else is quite unmistakable," the King said, "and that is your countenance, like a canvas without *contornare*, without shape or emotion. I mean to say, where your husband's eyes sparkle, we see that yours give no light at all. The body stands, but the spirit reclines."

Shamed! My face burned and my chest thundered as I struggled to restrain my tears. I wished to bolt from his presence, but I knew it was not allowed. Cahir started toward me as did my brother, but the King held up his hand and every movement and sound was stilled.

"Be not offended. We say this not to be unkind, but to acknowledge what we see before us. Had we not known better, we might have thought you bewitched and sent you off to be cleansed. Instead, we recognize that you have suffered a great loss. We have seen such tortured eyes before. Have you not suffered so?"

It was hopeless. The tears spilled down my cheeks which flushed with humiliation. "I have, Your Majestie. Please forgive my…"

He raised his hand again. "Let there be no sorrow, and no apology, for we have quite troubled you without such intent. We may speak to you this way because our own beloved Queen Anne has suffered such a loss that the pain of it has stolen the light from her eyes and has stripped her face of the warmth and animation we so cherished. The bairn of our union expired before its time, and yet she birthed it still, and yet she longs to see its tiny face, and hear its infant cry. The only cry she hears is her own.

"Because of our Queen, we must share your grief and tell you that the bairn you carried was not ready for this world. God has taken it and holds it well in Eternity. The next child will be delivered unto you, and soon. It shall survive, healthy and strong, and it will bring you many blessings and great joy. Lord Steward, see that this gracious lady is treated with every possible kindness, that she receives any comfort she requires. She is an honored guest in our court. See also that Sir Cahir O'Doherty's papers are met, recorded, and given the Royal Seal, and that this family's return trip to London is by way of the Royal Barge."

Ten days before we left Burt Castle for our journey to London, everything had been prepared, and we looked forward to a joyful and useful adventure. I walked in a wood just beyond the castle wall when a sharp cramp seized my belly. I knew it was ominous, for it was like nothing I'd felt before. I waited, and when I could stand upright I returned to the castle. I hadn't reached the door before the cramp returned. It nearly sent me to my knees. I grabbed the stone wall and held fast, willing myself to resist it, praying that no one would find me there before the pain had passed. At last, if I crept slowly, I could make it to the stair. Then something trickled down my thigh.

I must have done something wrong. I shouldn't have walked so far. I climbed the stairs in agony until I reached our bedchamber and closed the door. I could not make a sound. It was my burden, my fault, my failure, and my guilt. No one could know. I stuffed the corner of a bedsheet into my mouth and bit down on it, writhing on the floor. It was my child, my greatest desire, and now my greatest sorrow to bear alone. A sharp pain, a heavy gush of blood, and something came away that was small and unrecognizable, and still I wanted it. My child. I had lost my first child. I wanted to die.

Cahir found me on the floor when dusk had fallen. I said nothing but he somehow understood. He held my hand until my weeping stopped.

"What can I do, Sionnach?"

"Please, tell no one. Go down to your supper as always. Tell them I'm resting and whisper to Nonie to bring me soap and water."

He kissed my forehead and was gone. In the morning when I woke, wildflowers were strewn across the bed. He served me warm honeyed wine.

After such a long journey, the anxiety around meeting King James, and the pain of grief lingering, the King's offer of transport on his Royal Barge was a kind and wonderful gift. The barge itself was lovely, gilded at the bow where the navigator stood, and brightly painted red along the gunwales. The wooden deck was well used but also clean and polished. At the stern was the captain, and the men of the King's Guard.

In the center stood a large tent made of fine gold-colored canvas bearing a red fringe. We all ducked beneath the fringe to find a bench. We were not the only passengers the King had so rewarded, and so the first two benches were occupied by courtiers. Our party required two benches also, close to where the captain shouted commands. Cahir, Felim, and Jenico took the first available bench, I, Lady Eliza and Nonie behind them, and the others further back or watching the river from the gunwales.

The Englishmen seated in front of us were quite elegant, their hats tall and feathered, their coats adorned with colored sashes and intricate embroidery in gold and silver threads. They were talking together amiably as we arrived, then silenced, offering simple nods as we were seated. As the barge began to move they seemed to relax and their conversation resumed. Fatigued as we were and not talking among ourselves, we took a bit of pleasure just listening.

The fellow on the right sat cross-legged, his elbow resting upon the back of the bench. He removed his hat for a scratch and then set it back in place. "This Mountjoy fellow. Heaven's sake. Riches are handed to him daily on a silver platter, and yet he's never satisfied. Some say if you'll join him for breakfast, best bring your pillow for you'll be long asleep before the meal meets his requirements."

The fellow on the left chuckled. He wore a similar hat but with a wide gold band around it. "He's done well for himself, you must admit. The Queen was crazy about him, and before she passed she seated him in the House of Commons, a man much younger than most."

"How d'you figure he gave this O'Neill fellow a full pardon after the carrying on he done in Ireland? Huge, bloody battles and all!" said the gentleman on the right.

"Well sir, he's made O'Neill and O'Donnell earls! That will surely teach them a lesson!" He laughed and shook his head. Mountjoy just took a liking to them, and King James favors O'Neill. Even invited him to the palace for a golf game."

"You joke!"

"Not at all. Anaways, seems Mountjoy can do no wrong. He joins the King's Privy Council soon, when all the while he sleeps openly with another man's wife."

"The King does not take offense? He's the one rewriting the Bible, is he not?"

"He turns a blind eye on his friends. Mountjoy not only sleeps with her, Lady Penelope. He's fathered five children on her and faces a massive legal battle! It's a vile scandal but it all rolls off him like water from a seal's back."

"Good God," the left man said.

"Say, have you heard of this fellow, Sir George Carey," the right man asked. "He's a true scoundrel. Serving as Lord Deputy in Dublin years ago, he drained the coffers to near bankruptcy. With Mountjoy's promotion, Carey's assigned to the position *again*, at least until the King chooses another. One could hope those gentlemen at Dublin lock the coffers away this time."

Cahir, Felim and I looked at each other with surprise. There was much to be learned from a bench on the Royal Barge.

29

MAIRE

The Queen's Strength

When at last we returned to Burt Castle, the stone walls seemed thicker and darker than I remembered, and the rooms smaller than before, as if those immense blocks had moved inward during our absence, pressing us tight. Still, it was home and I took my comfort where I could find it, often walking or riding a horse among the trees, or baking bread in the warm kitchen with Nonie and Rita. Sometimes the simplest things are best, the sounds and senses that conjure vague memories of a carefree, barefoot childhood.

Cahir, with his new sense of security and stature, made sure Sir Henry Docwra—and from there, also Docwra's men—knew of his meeting with the King and his official confirmation as owner of Inishowen lands. This done, he assigned men to mind his borders and fishing territories. Then, he turned his attention to his tenants and rents.

By the end of November, a letter came from Jenico, informing me that my sister Cat would soon be married to considerable advantage. Her betrothed was John Rochfort, whose family had lived in Ireland for centuries, with estates in Kildare, Meath, and Westmeath counties. The Rochfort men traditionally held careers in law and politics.

The arrangement reflected an excellent bit of negotiation by Jenico, although my sister had first attracted her man, and theirs was to be a love match. I was happy for her, of course I was. She wouldn't have to leave the region of her birth as I had. How very fortunate for her. But oh! In truth I was sick with envy! How I missed County Meath, the comforts of a manor house compared to a cold stone castle in a strange and war-torn land. This life was not what my father intended, of that I felt sure, but he'd focused more on a strong Catholic alliance than a pleasurable lifestyle.

I wallowed in ill humor for days and without shame. But then my ill humor turned to fear. Could I, entertaining my own unspoken disappointment, have created the barrier that prevented a safe and happy childbirth? The priest would quote scripture and tell me envy comes from the Devil and brings death. Was this my punishment for the sin of envy? But no, it could not have been, for I'd only just learned of Cat's marriage. I must pray happiness for her and let go of these feelings before I caused greater harm to myself and my husband.

I loved Cahir, truly. Since that painful night of loss, he'd become increasingly tender. Each day I'd swear he stood taller, his shoulders bursting with strength. He seemed more confident as well. His thinking was broad, complex, and forward, no longer centered on himself, his holdings, or even his father's ways. Within four months he would finally come of age, 18 years old, and assume the full power of his position. It was time then, wasn't it, for me to stop moping, stand strong beside him, firmly take up my position as wife and mother of the next O'Doherty generation. I should seize what contentment I could from that.

There were things I could do, though they could never be apparent. A woman's power flowed from caregiving, gentle persuasion, good food, wine, the seeding of ideas, softening a rigid mind through sensual diversion, shifting a mood from troubled to tantalized by whatever means she might devise. My mother would have blanched to hear me speak of such methods, but she'd used each of them herself. How else could she have survived so peacefully with my raging father?

Recalling the extreme pain I'd endured on that dreadful day, it was no pleasure to face another pregnancy, but it was my duty to produce an heir and I so longed for a little one in my arms. I was not the first woman to suffer such a difficulty. Other women had birthed healthy babies after a loss like mine. Queen Anne herself had suffered several. I should imagine her face before me when my birthing time came and take strength from her. It would be my plan, but my first order of business must be satisfied.

I must try something different, some helps that would make my joining with Cahir more pleasurable, and if we both felt so, wouldn't a happy birth logically follow? I pondered. What should I do?

I dared not consult with Lady Eliza. As kind as she was, her ways were traditional and out of fashion. If I chose a method not suggested by the priest, she would surely oppose it, but suggestions from the priests never exceeded prayer.

Come to think of it, what if prayer inspired a new idea? Wouldn't that be an answer? Wouldn't it be wrong to ignore it? What if, in addition to prayer, a potion of love could come to my aid?

I wrote to Lady Finola, a woman likely to use any means to achieve her goal; a woman who had the respect of nearly every other woman in Ulster, who was feared by every man, and was someone I could call my friend. At once I sent the letter, asking for advice that might improve my possibility of conceiving. I had only days to wait for my response, but come it did, carried by a swift rider directly to the steps of Burt Castle. Attached to her letter was a tiny glass vial wrapped in cloth. My hands trembled as I rushed up the stairs to privacy.

"Beautiful Lady Maire," she wrote. "God intends you to be the fertile mother of many children, of this I am certain. My dear, there is no shame in assisting God's plan by enhancing the joining with your husband. My experience is this: Heat is the fundamental element upon which you must rely. Let him eat hot foods and especially spiced meats. For a potion, you need only warm wine spiced with sweet pepper to rouse the sensation in the body and quicken his desire.

"In your bedchamber, let there be a vapor of warmed oil, ambergris and musk if you can find it, or use the perfume in the vial. Once you have him in your bed, apply to his parts this same oil, that his heat rises inside and out. Do this and you'll trouble only to remove him from your bed. For conception you will not have long to wait."

Just by reading her message my womb began to tingle. I opened the vial. The scent was sweet like the core of a rose, and a bit musky like the sweat of a horse—intense but not unpleasant. I paced the room, excited, restless, impatient for all that she'd described. I ran to the kitchen with instructions for Nonie and Rita to prepare a special supper only for Cahir and myself. I didn't tell what it was for. Let them imagine for themselves. They saw my excitement and did not fail to make something utterly delicious. When Cahir came in for supper, we dined alone in our bedchamber.

"What is this?" he asked.

"It is a hearty stew with some special flavorings just for us."

"It's quite different. What is in it?"

"The tenderest meat, of course. A bit of wine, I think, cinnamon, perhaps a pinch of pepper. Do you like it?" I asked sweetly.

"I do," he said, "but something is…unusual…a bit of…it warms. And something in our chamber, some scents…"

"Just a bit of perfume to make things nice. I'll take it away, will I?"

"Certainly not. I would have more. More of everything."

"Of course." I couldn't suppress my smile as I refilled his trencher and sprinkled his meat with salt. "I'll pour more wine."

"This may be the finest meal I've ever had, better even than at Hampton Court."

I nodded agreement. I stood by our table and shrugged off my robe, allowing it to flutter to the floor, revealing my undergarment of the finest gauze, hiding nothing of my anatomy. My skin rippled with pleasure. "Cahir?" I whispered.

He lifted his gaze from his plate to my breasts, then up to my eyes, then down again. He stood in an instant, shoving our table aside, a cup crashing to the floor as he wrapped me in his arms and carried me to our bed. I pushed his chest until he lay on his back, and then I administered the oil just as Finola had instructed. My goodness, I should have done this long ago. The act excited me beyond anything I'd felt before. He scooped his arm about my waist and flipped my body beneath his. My breath left my lungs, and I cared not if it ever returned.

I lost my envy for Cat's marriage, for how could it possibly exceed what Cahir and I had found? Even if we didn't immediately conceive, it could only be a matter of time. We slept in blissful peace.

We tip-toed down to breakfast, so late that all the others had gone, and what remained on the table were the hardened crusts of oat bread. We smeared them with fresh churned butter and ate as if it were the finest meal we'd ever known.

30

CAHIR

Intentions

Felim and I rode north toward the rain-washed uplands near the village of Carndonagh, where the cattle were feeding on rushes. We were but a stone's throw from Felim's castle, Carickabraghy. Many herdsmen were about, offering their opinions whether to move the beeves further east, or south to Inch Island for the winter. They seemed content as they were, but their food supply wouldn't last until spring. Soon the creaghting, the relocating, would begin.

Even as the days grew colder, the lands were starting to recover from the fires and molestation by the English soldiers. The call of gulls and freshening scents of the ocean added to the feeling that the earth could reclaim itself; that peace could again become normal. Yet, just to the east I spied a group of men who were similarly riding, seven or eight of them. They were well away, tiny figures to our eyes, moving northward along the horizon. Even from such distance I could see they were not of our clan. One dismounted, took to a knee perhaps to test the soil beneath him.

"D'you see them, Felim?" I asked.

"Aye, I do. We'll let them be, so."

"I don' think they are Docwra's men. They're not soldiers."

"Let's move on," Felim said. "Whoever they be, we canna stop them. No sense takin' up trouble before it's given."

"If we see them tomorrow, I'll count it as given," I said. A silence followed, as always it did when Felim had something to say. Unlike his brother who had never lacked for words, Felim took a pause to order to his thoughts before speaking. Sometimes it was only seconds, other times it could take a day or two. This time, only a few minutes, though I'd already grown impatient.

"Cahir," Felim said.

"Sure Felim, I'm still beside you. Speak your mind."

He cleared his throat, sounding like a hound's growl. "Do you recall the conversation we overheard while on the Royal Barge back to London?"

I sighed. "Aye, from those gents in their peacock clothing and high hats? We learned that two months ago the King had confirmed O'Neill's pardon, made Rory O'Donnell an earl, and promoted Lord Mountjoy to his Privy Council, even though the man got five children on another man's wife and suffers no consequence. How would I forget such a bounty of shameless news? Och, and one more, that Sir George Carey becomes Lord Deputy in Dublin—the greedy, skimming thief."

"Aye, we learn much with open ears," Felim said. "I think Sir George will warm the seat until the King makes his more permanent choice, but we'd best prepare for the worst."

"Haven't we already had the worst?"

Felim shook his head. "The King still fancies the plantation of Ireland with the English in his service, and his favored Scots. When the next Lord Deputy is named, 'tis unlikely to be a man of our preference, but one recommended by Mountjoy. Sir Arthur Chichester, I'd wager."

"Chichester? God's wounds! He'll burn the whole island," I said.

"He'll no' burn it. That's Mountjoy's way."

"Mountjoy may have suggested it, but Chichester and his men set the fires with vigor."

"Nah, lad. He'll be after land, buying parcels from desperate men around Belfast and Carrickfergus. Some say he's not for cattle as we'd expect but looks to divide the land into smaller bits to lease it, so he'll make the most money. He'll tek it all, bit by bit, and sweep it clean of Irish should he have the chance."

"He still fumes over his brother's killing at Carrickfergus. It's petty revenge and he'd have us all pay fer it, who never even knew the man."

Felim grunted. "'Tis worse than petty revenge. Some say the MacDonnells beheaded his brother, then used the man's head as a football. No one would soon forgive that. Damn brawling Scots. 'Tis no wonder he kills, but he is without discrimination, without conscience, without heart.

He kills man, woman, child, whatever is in his path. He is heartless. And he reeks of greed beyond any man I've yet encountered."

"Considering the English around these parts, that's a fierce measure. But, I have the King's seal, and I am knighted. Our land is protected," I said.

"Lad, the circumstance becomes complicated. The English doona understand, or mebbe they do, that the wealth of an Irish chief has never been in the quantity of land he owns. The land has always belonged to the clan. Our wealth is counted in the numbers of the beeves—the cattle. That's our value and trade."

"Yes. And so?"

"Nothing's changed by the King's seal, and yet everything has. The seal grants the land to you alone as owner, not the clan. Should you sell the land, or act in any way that forfeits to the crown, it's not one piece of it gone, but the whole, leaving our clansmen without a place or a claim."

"Such was never my intention. I've meant always to secure Inishowen and protect it from the greedy English vultures, not for myself but for us all. And I'll never forfeit."

"My sense is the men of our clan are uneasy about their future." Felim said. "Sometimes 'tis not what you do, but what they say you'll do, and we're overburdened with greedy vultures. We're wise to have English allies, and to avoid any troubles."

I shook my head, so certain was I that all was well. "It only means I'm overdue to complete the work at Elagh, confirming the seat of our clan. Let the men work with their hands and their backs to restore the castle proud and strong again, a sure statement that O'Doherty will always be Inishowen, and Inishowen O'Doherty."

"T'will be a fine statement, as you say—and good wages will speak the louder still." Felim nodded.

With the cattle moved and secured, and Felim at home with his family, I set to gathering materials and choosing craftsmen, not just to restore Elagh, but to enhance it, to make it grand as could be—a signal to the clan, yes, but also to the English that we were to be reckoned, rooted deeper than the greatest oak and forever immoveable.

I imagined the dining hall doubled in size for Maire to entertain guests. We'd have an enormous hearth, a buttery, library with portraits on the walls, and grand staircases on either end of the hall. Completing that would be a solar facing east for Maire to welcome each morning, and the nursery just above.

We could add more housing, expand the stables, the smithy, the armory. We'd have a wood yard, a vegetable garden, a cherry orchard, a fishpond, and anything else my lady desired. It would take years and much money, coming from cattle sales, from rents, crops, fisheries. I'd squeeze the money from anywhere I could to have my father's house returned to me, and I'd become the father.

31

STOAT

1605

Rejoicing

The news of Lady Maire's pregnancy spread like a great wave across the clan. At last, an heir would be born, a signal of continuation, of stability. The men, and myself most especially, were infused with a new sense of purpose at Elagh. The dining hall was brought to a swift and flawless finish. The wooden stairs at either end were sturdy and fine, and a wood carver's ivy pattern on the newel posts. All about and at every moment I heard hammering, sawing, scraping and shouts of order or need, and all were welcome to my ears for life would be again as it was meant.

Talk in the dining hall praised the future and the coming infant lord—for all assumed it would be male. In place of sad stories and wretchedness, there were tales of his O'Doherty bloodline, how great his bravery would be, and how by his birth alone he would restore the high status of O'Doherty clan from the days of my own grandfather.

Cahir didna mind that he was only a few months before coming of age himself, with years ahead of him as clan leader. For any event or vision that lifted the men's confidence, he was grateful and joined the chatter. He was thrilled at the thought of bein' a Da.

"What shall ye name him?" one of the lads called out.

"The child shall be named according to tradition. If a male, our first son then he must be named for my father, Sean Og. And if it's a daughter, she'll be named for Lady Maire's mother, Catherine," Cahir said.

Shouts rose from the men. "A son, he'll be!" "He must have a fierce nickname: Dragon master!" someone shouted. "Tarbh! The bull," called another. "He must be Grian, the sun!" called a third. "Wolf! MacTyre," came a fourth.

"Ah, that one's taken and well used as you all know! But these are all fine names to consider," Cahir said.

"Stoat!" someone shouted, and everyone laughed.

I stood at my bench, shaking my fist. "Ah, the lot of ye! He'd be fortunate, were he to learn the skills of Stoat. Few have managed it, so. Let 'im find his own, for sure this name's taken!"

"'Tis taken, beaten, twisted, dented and bent!" MacTyre shouted. I took it in good form, waving him off, and we all had a hearty laugh. I returned to my seat.

"Nah, Lady Maire and I will do the choosing," Cahir said, "but we must wait until we meet the little one, to make sure the name fits the face. Ye'll all be the first to hear it, and never you mind."

By St. Patrick's Day, the kitchen and cellars were finished as best we could with the materials we had. As the last nail was hammered, the news arrived that Sir Arthur Chichester had taken up his new position as Lord Deputy in Dublin. Of course, it was expected, and we'd all do well to avoid any troubles.

In April we celebrated Cahir's coming of age, and grand it was with a great bonfire in the bawn, much drinking of ale, lively music with the bodhran, fiddle, and flute, and the visits and tributes from all the dwellers of Inishowen.

Work continued at Elagh, especially on the bedchamber and nursery which were made ready by the first day of harvest and the last day of summer, just as Lady Maire was confined to await the birth. Hammers and saws were silenced, and only work on the grounds were permitted that Lady Maire should not be disturbed. In 10 days' time, the birthing commenced. Most of the men left the castle, cleared the bawn, and the midwives sent by Lady Finola arrived to join Lady Eliza and Nonie at Lady Maire's side.

Cahir stayed in the cellar drinking ale, pacing, and reading his books. I stayed nearby in the hall, should he look for me. I couldn't drink with him nor read, knowing the tragedies that often occurred in the birthing chamber. I fell to my knees and prayed while their sunny new bedchamber with the large windows was instead made dark as night. Black fabrics were fastened over window frames, all corners covered to block every splinter of light. Even the keyhole was covered so that nothing external, not even the air, could enter to disturb the sanctity of birth.

165

166

32

MAIRE

Herself

Candles lit each corner, a prayer said over each one, and the women whispered so as not to disturb or excite me. Around the room were stacks of linens, the swaddling bands, a pitcher of water, bottles and jars of medicines, a floor pallet to lay upon that I wouldn't soil the marriage bed, a chair from the dining table should I need it. Lady Eliza sat in a chair, her lips moving, prayer book in her lap. I'd seen my mother this way so many times and took comfort from it. How I wished she was in the room with us. She would say exactly the right thing to give me courage.

Why must something wanted so greatly, something so common among families, cause pain so monstrous that it threatens survival? My trembling hands wouldn't still; my lips, my legs, the same. My belly swelled so that it might burst open. Then I had my first true wave of pain, ensuring me that indeed I *would* burst open, but below, and slowly, with every wave that followed. I would've run, but I couldn't even stand without Nonie's help. I'd have screamed, but the midwife said I should save my strength, for the screaming would come much later.

There was no escape, and surely I would die as this progressed. Panic set in, leaving me only with prayer:

Heavenly Father,
Bless me with the courage and faith of Blessed Mary and forgive my sins. I did not always honor my father, nor ease my mother's troubles. I've often

been selfish and prideful, I've scorned my brother and sister, and I've spoken in unkind ways. I have doubted my husband, disliked the home he offered me. I swear from this day I will be a loving mother and a helpful wife. With all humility I beg you, preserve me from danger and shield this child I carry. Through Jesus Christ Our Lord,
Amen.

I sucked in breath. Hours passed. My stomach felt scoured while my belly was mountainous, pressed on all sides by an invisible but mighty force. With each moment it grew stronger, and I weaker. I forgot my terror and pleas to God, knowing only the agony of bones being pulled apart. I gripped the mattress and Lady Eliza's hand, clenched my teeth and shrieked with such violence that all the women braced my arms until a last, unspeakable wave forced a mass from my womb. I heard the precious cry.

"'Tis no' a lad, my lady," the midwife said, "but a fine lass she is, fair and well formed."

She lifted her, the domed forehead glistening, the hair in fine white wisps; cheeks and body smeared with blood, her tiny face more delicate than a rose petal, and fists like mushroom sprouts punching the air—a fighter from first breath. Something flooded from my breast to my shoulders and head, a fever that burned, a potion that cooled, and then more than a wanting but a needing to touch and hold this precious infant.

I cried, exhausted, impatient. Deprived while the midwife and Nonie bathed and swaddled my child. Lady Eliza's hand still sweated against mine, and outside the darkened door I heard Cahir and the priest who stood by to baptize her at once if she was born unwell.

The midwife held the infant that Cahir might see her face, our own daughter. My voice was weak but still I called out to him. "She is Catherine!" His tears glistened, and then at last they brought her to my arms, her dark eyes gazing into mine. Yes, she was mine, my Catherine. Catherine Anne!

Soon the afterbirth was gone. The midwives scrubbed me well before settling me into bed and took care of my daughter while I rested. I must have slept for hours. When I woke, they placed pillows at my back that I might sit up. I had one important task that could not wait. "Nonie," I said, "Fetch please some writing papers, the best you can find."

A first brief letter was dispatched to Finola, a birth announcement and gratitude for what she'd done for me. The second was to Jenico, now an uncle, and Cahir would have an heir. The third, written in my finest script once my hand had stopped shaking, was to King James himself and Queen Anne: gratitude to the King for his compassion and encouragement after noticing my sorrow; and to the Queen, the model of perseverance and love. Though she'd never met me, she was responsible for my success. I would forever praise her.

By December, our Catherine was three and a half months old, and blossoming bright as a primrose. Each morning, I lifted her from her crib and danced her around our bedchamber. Sometimes Cahir joined in until she gurgled with delight. So happy was I, that I took full credit for the perfect child I had delivered, and I forgot my prayer. Pride crept up beside me and I let it in. I tempted fate, didn't I, foolishly believing our daughter would always be the happiest child in all of Ireland, never to know troubles or fears.

33

MAIRE

A Murderous Plot

One winter day, Cahir and I lingered in bed as the early morning passed, watching our sweet Catherine wiggle her feet as she lay between us, sleeping and dreaming. "She is our treasure and our joy, Sionnach. We are so fortunate," Cahir said, "and she grows so quickly. Soon she'll be running and leaping. She'll need some friends to play with."

"And she will find them. Everyone will adore her. Maybe we shall make her a brother or a sister!"

Cahir laughed. "It's a good plan. My sister Rosa had her first child in June, a boy named Hugh that I've never seen. She married Red Hugh's younger brother Caffar. It's a pity we've not been able to meet for so long, so much trouble around us. Perhaps things have settled enough, and our children are not so distant in age that they couldn't play together. Do you think?"

"It would be joyful to see them together," I said.

"And I miss Rosa, anyway. She's clever. You might enjoy her companionship as well. With Elagh's dining hall being finished, might this be the time to plan a supper party?"

"Oh! Could we?" I said, surprised by my high-pitched voice. "It seems so long that we've toiled under a dark cloud. And we can invite those we wish to know better, like your Captain Hart at Culmore?"

"Yes. Hart and his wife Frances also have a son, young George."

"Goodness. We must make a day of it then, so the children can play. Once we've put them to sleep, the mothers and fathers may talk with one another."

Suddenly we were both roused by the excitement of having a gathering. He smiled and nodded. "I'll leave you to plan and offer help when you need it."

I was eager to start, ideas blossoming in my mind for the wonderful time we would have. How impressed everyone would be by the new Chief, Sir Cahir, his wife Lady Maire, and their beautiful child. We'd have an afternoon of games in the garden for the children. Horse racing for the men at dusk, the grand dinner in Elagh's splendid new hall and then music and dancing. We'd have beef, salmon, pheasant, capon pies, wines, and sweets of many kinds. It would even surpass events at Gormanston. Afterwards, no one should ever want to miss a supper at Elagh. My thoughts skipped about from rooms to musicians to the perfect silk gown. What color should it be?

And then as if in punishment, the very next day arrived a letter arrived from Jenico bringing startling news: Catholic conspirators in London had attempted to assassinate King James. Authorities received an anonymous letter of warning and searched the House of Lords. A man by the name of Guy Fawkes was discovered guarding thirty-six barrels of gunpowder that had been concealed in Westminster's undercroft, just beneath the House of Lords. The plan was to set off a great blast and consuming fire at the State Opening of Parliament when the King, his closest relatives, the Privy Council, and most of the Protestant aristocracy would be present. An anonymous letter revealed the plot—the Gunpowder Treason Plot, they called it—and thirteen men had been identified, some who were immediately killed upon discovery, and some arrested for treason and destined for execution. Jenico wrote,

"All of England is in uproar, the name Guy Fawkes to be heard everywhere, for he was the man in charge of the gunpowder. After his arrest,"Fawkes was tortured on order of the King.

"Sir Arthur Chichester, who has now assumed the position as Lord Deputy in Dublin, has received all of this news and in greater detail. His tolerance for Catholicism having always been thin, he now openly names it the single most serious threat to the monarchy and King James himself. I know not what he intends for Ireland, but there is talk of punishing and fining all recusants. As he owns an estate in Northern Antrim, he will likely be heavy handed in the region."

My thoughts of a supper vanished. I carried the letter to Cahir, whose brow lifted when he saw my hand trembling. He read in silence, allowing Stoat to peer over his shoulder. When he looked up at me, Stoat stepped back, his lips pursed.

"Maire," Cahir said, "If I didn't know Jenico's hand I would swear it was false. This tests my belief to its limit. Such an act, so brave yet so outrageous, puts us all in danger. The King is right to be angry, for his entire family was at risk, and all of his most trusted lords. I pray, will he remember it is thirteen men who were entirely responsible, and not every person of the Catholic faith."

He rubbed his jaw and the patch of beard still thickening. "We… we can't know what it will mean for us, for Gormanston, for Ireland. Not yet. Chichester will retaliate against Catholics in some way. He's only need-ed a reason. We must continue on the path we know, our heads held high, and do not waver. We are innocent of any crime, we stand strong as ever in support of the King. Pray you both for God's protection. And Stoat, get a message to Felim at once."

Cahir urged me to continue my plans for a party, though my joy for it was completely trampled. Preparing a guest list would only be a nightmare, for under the circumstances, would the mix of Catholic and Protestant guests result in conflict? Would our hope to grow friendships instead reveal enemies?

Sir Henry Docwra had recently married, and we had the new Bish-op Montgomery and wife at Raphoe. It would be lovely to make their acquaintance as both hold much power. But now? Could Anne Docwra and Susan Montgomery chat easily with Rosa O'Donnell and Maire O'Doherty? If the Gunpowder Plot came up—as surely it would—we'd be on the same side over the act, but wouldn't religion always divide us?

I didn't speak to Cahir about it, knowing how he wanted such gath-erings to confirm his title and build his standing. But each way I turned, the obstacles seemed ghastly impossible. I decided instead to employ his own special tactic: *promise, promise, delay, delay, delay.* Whenever he should ask I'd smile sweetly and claim that the plans were emerging nicely.

When a crate arrived from Jenico, I knew at once there could be no party and my delay tactics would no longer be needed.

174

THE NOBLEST SHARE OF EARTH

34

MAIRE

1606

A Box of Secrets

The crate from Gormanston was delivered by an old man pulling a wooden cart. He carried the crate to the castle door, Cahir gave him a coin, and then the man bid us thanks and farewell. We circled around the thing, wondering what might be inside. Though it was large enough to hold gifts for a newborn, as appropriate as that might be, my brother was not given to such a gesture and he had yet to take a wife who might manage it.

"No," I told Cahir, "such a crate from Jenico is a signal."

"A signal? For what? Why wouldn't he just write?"

"He's concealing bad news, I'd suppose. We shall see."

Stoat removed two wooden slats to reveal several gifts wrapped in gauze. Cahir opened the first, a tiny linen dressing gown for Catherine, with pretty lace at the neck. Then a knitted set of infant's stockings. I unwrapped some soaps, which led me to believe Jenico's housekeeper had packed the box. And then, at the bottom of the crate, a rectangular package that held a set of fine linen handkerchiefs. I carefully separated them until, as expected, a folded paper tumbled out.

"It must be news of unusual nature for him to send it this way." I handed the letter to Cahir, but he pushed it back.

"It is from your brother. Read it to us, will you?"

I nodded, a little nervous for what it might hold. "*My dearest sister,* he writes." Such an endearment confirmed it contained bad news.

"We have received news that Parliament in London, responding to the gunpowder plot against the king, has established the Popish Recusants Act, preventing Catholics from practicing law and medicine, and from acting as guardians or trustees. Magistrates may search private homes for weapons, and God only knows what else they will search for. A new oath of allegiance to the King will be enforced, and any recusant who doesn't take the Church of England sacrament at least once a year will be fined £60 or forfeit two-thirds of his estate. Appalling, yes.

"Our Lord Deputy in Dublin has decided the King's plan is too weak and has produced his own ideas for oppression. He calls them mandates. He summoned sixteen prominent Catholics in the Pale and mandated their attendance at worship in the Church of England. All disregarded his order—as they should—but Chichester fined and imprisoned them. Also appalling!"

I glanced at Cahir and Stoat. Both stared back at me, eyes wide with surprise. I shook my head and continued.

"A petition was filed against him, but he discovered the names of the instigators and imprisoned several of them. At this, even the London Privy Council was appalled, fearing—as they should—that these Old English leaders who command vast portions of Ireland could raise a rebellion to make O'Neill's war look like child's play.

"Chichester stands down and I have not, as of yet, fallen under his scrutiny. However, I know him, and he won't be told. He'll start it all again as soon as the Privy Council is suitably distracted. He wants power, and he wants his way.

"I am too near to Dublin to escape notice, but perhaps too low in the peerage to draw his interest. I feel certain it's the last time I'll be able to write unless by some kind of cipher. I believe we've embarked on a secret war, and we're all in a ship sailing backward.

Until next we may speak, I am,
Your beloved brother,
Jenico,
Viscount Gormanston"

"Goodness," I said. "What kind of arrogance this man Chichester has! It seems only a matter of time before Jenico is similarly treated."

"It's so, my love, but do not fear for Jenico, at least not yet. He has friends in the Pale, friends in Meath and relatives both in Meath and Dublin. He may feel alone as he writes, but he does have resources. We can also pray the Privy Council keeps Lord Deputy Chichester in his proper place."

"We ought to see, can we get him promoted," Stoat said, "like Lord Mountjoy. What better way to get him out of Ireland!"

"Aye, in truth," Cahir nodded.

I folded the letter. "I must hide this away somewhere," and I started toward the stairs.

"Maire, you'd best burn it. Your brother speaks his mind and it is well, but a written piece might one day be used against him," Cahir said.

"I'll take it," Stoat stepped toward the hearth and tossed it into the ready flames. As it burned, I prayed we'd heard the last of this Chichester.

178

35

CAHIR

The Oath

Months passed without word from my brother-in-law. Spring unfolded at Elagh in soft rains, with abundant bluebells, campion, dandelion and blackthorn blanketing the sloping hills that surrounded us. Lambing season was progressing well and we dined on mutton, mussels, salmon, and garden vegetables. On warmer days we threw the doors wide to welcome visitors. I swelled with pride to greet guests and travelers where I felt most at home, where my family and clan could thrive. I stood taller among the great stones and halls of my father.

But a pall still hovered over the land, a vague anticipation of danger and loss. Whispers and rumors were frequent, the threat of Catholic persecution simmering beneath the surface of everyday life. Yet I insisted we would not fret over something still distant. I peered up the River Foyle toward Derry and the garrison, believing my friendship with Sir Henry Docwra would protect us. And though I knew the possibility was remote, I dreamed that one day the garrison would close, and the fine and strategic location might once again belong to O'Doherty.

When spring turned to summer, a messenger arrived from Derry. Docwra, who so often behaved like a father to me, now summoned me to his presence at the garrison, not as a friend or ally, but as he might summon a suspected criminal for questioning. Not only me, but my wife, my lieutenants, and even my child.

This was the dreaded event of which Jenico had warned. Every man, woman, and child of the O'Doherty Clan would be summoned and required to speak the new Oath of Allegiance to the King. A refusal would be seen as an act of treason. Take the oath, Docwra wrote, or forfeit my patrimony.

We traveled to Derry the following day, wasting no time out of respect for my friend Docwra, and hoping we could together find an agreeable solution. I met him in his offices. His look was severe, and his attire dark and formal, ornamented with official bands and badges. After a rather cold greeting, he offered me a paper upon which was the King's Oath, in heavy black ink and stamped with red seals. Even at first glance, the oath was odious, shameful, and to be profoundly despised by those who loved the religion of our ancestors.

"The oath, as I read it, not only swears allegiance to the King, but also denies any power of the Pope to depose monarchs, even those whose greed and cruelty cause suffering for the people. It calls the Pope impious, heretical, damnable, and demands all persons to swear it so, even under threat of excommunication, and the Pope has no power to absolve us.

"Sir Henry," I pleaded, "sure you must understand what you are asking. These good people had nothing to do with a plot against the King, nor ever would, and they are loyal to the king as people of the O'Doherty Clan. There's no cause for making them deny and disrespect their own ancestors, nor to reject a deeply set way of living passed down through the ages. You could see that…"

Sir Henry's eyes narrowed. He behaved as if we were unwelcome strangers. "Sir Cahir, the oath comes not from my pen, nor is it for me to defend or reject. If you would serve the King, you must swear, or face prison or death. There is no other way."

I looked to Maire, tears filling her eyes.

"A moment, good sir, to speak with my wife?"

"Of course," Docwra said.

I, Maire, and the others among us gathered in the garrison yard. I placed my hand on Maire's shoulder and spoke to all. "We face a painful circumstance indeed. You all heard what the oath requires, and the penalties attached."

MacTyre was among us, and it brought no surprise that he should first speak. "We canna accept such an oath, we would be excommunicated at once!"

"We would not," I said. "And if we don't accept it, we will lose everything that is dear to us, or likely die. We must speak the words but maintain what is in our hearts. God our Father shall understand what befalls us and will protect us."

"If we do that—speak those words—we will be hated by everyone," MacTyre said. "By our own families, by our children, by Catholics and Protestants alike. They will call us hypocrites. They will shun us, and stone us, or worse."

Stoat stood off to the side. He didn't seem to take up MacTyre's view, yet he looked confused and cautious. If only Felim were here to help me lead them through this predicament.

"They will not, MacTyre, because each one of them will be called to do the same. And if anyone dares to call an O'Doherty a hypocrite I shall stab him in the eye. Listen to what is reasonable," I said, and paused until I had their full attention, as MacDavitt had often done. Think about the words contained in the oath, and why they first came about. The King fears for his life and that of his family. An oath to love, protect, and serve him is expected and commendable. But this oath was not written by the King. Of the seven affirmations the oath demands, only one requires loyalty to the King. All the rest are aimed at the Pope, as if he himself conceived the conspiracy, he himself planned the event. Of such crimes the Pope has not been accused.

"And yet, these affirmations are to strip powers from the Pope, and force from our lips words of hatred. I ask you all, when was it ever determined that one could control either love or hate in another? No person, no king, nor any clergyman can do so. I believe this oath comes not from the King, who is wise and kind. No, this oath stems from the harsh, bitter, and jealous minds of his bishops. They use the King's tragedy to their own advantage, an opportunity to steal Papal powers."

I looked about at their faces, some still confused, but others growing angry, aimed I hoped at the deceitful bishops. "Could it be that God will one day expose them? And that we may be among his brave instruments? To serve God, we must *stay alive*—we cannot serve him from the grave. Let us speak the words forced upon us, but know in our hearts they are false and not from the King. We have trudged through the bog before, and it brings salvation if we stay united, and keep a pious heart."

There were nods among some of the men, and I hoped my words had landed firmly. Maire remained tearful. I cupped her cheek and whispered to her ear. "Fear not, my love. God knows we do what we must for our children, and God is loving and forgiving, no matter the blasphemous words the oath holds. Trust me, we will be cleansed of it forthwith. I shall be first to speak these words to Sir Henry Docwra. They will be words only, and not my heart. I ask each of you to follow me."

Sir Henry stood beside a table upon which the written oath had been placed. For those of my clan who could not read, he or one of his officers would have to speak the words for them to repeat. It would not be me nor one of mine.

"Begin," he said.

I picked up the paper, aware of all the eyes upon me, and then very suddenly aware of a knot forming in the deepest center of my gut. "I, Sir Cahir O'Doherty, do truly and sincerely acknowledge, profess, testify, and declare in my conscience before God and the world, that our Sovereign Lord King James, is lawful and rightful King of this realm…"

I looked to Sir Henry. He looked down, his jowls dark, and would not meet my gaze.

"And that the Pope…neither of himself, nor by any authorities of the Church or See of Rome, have any power or authority to depose the King, or to dispose any of his Majesty's kingdoms, or dominions, or to authorize any foreign prince to invade or annoy him or his countries."

This so far did not discomfort me, for I would not see the King deposed, given his kind treatment of my wife and his confirmation of O'Doherty lands, Inishowen. And yet, Maire was trembling.

"I do swear, that notwithstanding any sentence of excommunication or deprivation, I will bear allegiance and true faith to his Majesty…"

The knot in my gut did now twist and burn. I learned right then that I did in fact fear excommunication, even though I'd sworn that the words had no true meaning.

"And I do further swear that I do from my heart abhor, detest as impious and heretical this damnable doctrine, that princes excommunicated by the pope may be deposed or murdered by their subjects or by any other whatsoever."

I spoke the words, Docwra still unable to meet my gaze, and several women among our people did openly weep. The words 'from my heart' were painful to speak and contradicted my promise that our hearts could be held separate—the only way to make this oath bearable.

And then I wondered, was there truly Catholic doctrine that encouraged the murder of princes? Had I ever known this? From my gut surged a rush of shame that burned my palms, my jaws, and filled me with confusion and doubt.

"And I do believe that the pope has no power to absolve me from this oath."

I righted myself then. 'The pope has no power.' I remembered my own words, that this oath was meant only to reduce the pope and in truth had nothing to do with the King or the safety of his family. I straightened my spine, signed my name at the top of a list. This statement would do nothing but damn the bishops for their deeds.

"Trust me, Maire. It is as I said," and passed the words to her. She rushed through them and signed her name, then passed the oath to Stoat, and he to others, that we all would do what we must. Many did speak it, yet some disappeared from our presence, fading into the land. When the last person had spoken, I would lead our people to a place of holy water near Saint Columba's well, where we could all pray, immerse ourselves in His presence, and regain peace.

But before such could happen, Sir Henry stopped me, having more news to impart.

"Sir Cahir," Docwra said, his voice remaining stern. "I have seen you grow from boy, to man, to leader, and respect you well. Though I do have love for Ireland, and the lands around Derry most especially, I have made the decision to return to England. My wife and I will board a ship within the fortnight. My differences with Lord Deputy Chichester cannot be mended. I have sold my position and holdings to Sir George Paulet. May you find him wise, and of fair nature."

I was stunned. There had been no hint or warning. "Sir Henry, your service has been exemplary. There can be no replacement, and you mustn't go before we can..."

He raised his hand for silence. "We cannot speak further, lad, I'm sorry. Guards, you will see them out."

Were we now nothing more than rubbish, to be swept away? I would have held a great banquet to honor him, but I wasn't even allowed to speak. We left his presence. The suddenness of his decision, the cold demeanor, and his refusal to speak of it left me uneasy.

Those who would, followed Maire and me to a holy well. Even to stand in such a sacred place had a powerful effect, but it was not enough, no not for any of us who said such offensive words. But time would bring its healing, too. Or so I did believe, and so I did hope.

36

MAIRE

A Hint of Betrayal

At dawn I took to my knees to pray, but the damage from what we'd done at Derry was painfully clear. Cahir had been strong, wise, and more the mature leader than ever I'd seen him. I was proud, truly, but the shame of speaking the oath had stolen the joy from those tender prayers. An anxious discomfort settled upon me like a great cold stone upon my chest until I could barely breathe. Perhaps I no longer deserved to breathe. Cahir's words were true. God did love us and did understand that we were forced to speak the oath if we would live to serve him, but the betrayal—to the Pope, to our religion, to our families? Their wrath was a poisoned mist settling upon us. Worst of all, I didn't know what to say to anyone, nor how to teach my daughter.

August arrived with just such a shadow across its sunlit fields, but we carried on, preparing to celebrate Catherine's first birthday when a tinker arrived at Elagh. It was not unusual, as such fellows and their families walked from village to village selling their wares or services. The fellow introduced himself as Manfri, promising to mend anything from a broken step, a torn sleeve, or a thrown horseshoe. He wore a long, dirty cloak, his gait uneven due to some injury, but his eyes were kind. In exchange for work he asked only a night's rest in the stable. Cahir eyed him with suspicion but allowed him to stay because Nonie had already brought things from the kitchen that needed repair.

"Stoat, you'll keep a watch on him, aye?" Cahir said.

The next morning, Manfri approached me in the garden when I was walking young Catherine among the fallen leaves. I held her hands to keep her from crawling in the dirt. Stoat walked the castle's outer wall, but Rudd watched us from the main gate, ready to quell any problem.

"Good morn, Lady O'Doherty. I wish ye well this fine day and ta thank ye for the night's sleep."

"A fine day to you, Manfri," I said, heaving Catherine to my hip. She was wary of strangers and whimpered but didn't cry. "You slept comfortably? And have broken your fast?"

"I am verra well, my lady. I wish not ta disturb, but ta offer ye a special gift, in gratitude, ye see, fer the comforts." He presented a small wooden jar sealed with wax. "'Tis a fine ointment used by all the ladies of Dublin to soothe their faces and hands. Sure ye will find it to yer likin'."

"A gift is not necessary," I said, but he pressed it into my palm.

"'Tis, my lady, and my pleasure ta gev. Made from the finest ingredients in County Meath."

County Meath. My family home. He looked into my eyes and I knew it was no jar of ointment. "I must try it at once. Thank you, Manfri." Holding Catherine with one hand, and the jar in the other, I walked calmly into the kitchen. "Nonie, could you please take Catherine for a bit, and send one of the lads for Cahir? I need to speak with him." As soon as I was beyond her hearing, I bolted up the stairs to our bedchamber.

I couldn't wait for Cahir. I found a sewing needle and I punched holes all around the sealing wax until it weakened, tilted, and came free. Beneath was a layer of sand, an edge of folded paper poking upward.

Cahir opened the door. "Did you ask for me?"

"Yes. Is Stoat behind you?" I held up the folded letter.

"Stoat!" he shouted down the stairs, and our man bounded up to join us and closed the door behind him.

I showed him the jar. "It's from Jenico. I'm sure of it. Manfri said it was an ointment, but it's my brother's form of cypher, in case Chichester's men are watching."

"Open it," Cahir said.

I smoothed the thick paper on my lap. There was no salutation or signature, the letters in unusual style, so that Jenico could deny the writing. Clever, our Jenico. I read:

"With shame and regret I inform you of the latest. We of Meath believe

we are being mistreated, misled, and betrayed by one of our own, who scarce seems to know from what source he stems.

"Our neighbor, Christopher St. Lawrence, who shall inherit his father's title, Baron Howth, hath betrayed both our fathers with his pride, greed, deceit, and self-importance. We've known of his erratic and quarrelsome behavior which lost him the position as governor of Monaghan. His wife Elizabeth left him last year and demands a large alimony. He is driven by burdensome debt.

"Despite his claim of being Protestant, he takes up the Catholic cause and has attended Mass. He has engaged with Irish nobility in the Pale and in the counties of Monaghan, Cavan, and Fermanagh. Among his contacts, O'Neill himself has been named.

"Some say he means to instigate a Spanish invasion, and yet we have heard he sails for London soon. The man wears multiple faces and turns toward any jingle of coin. We fear what mischief he shall stir.

"This by way of warning, I am yours."

"Cahir, I have met Sir Christopher only once, briefly, in my father's presence," I said. "His father thrashed his mother about like a mongrel, though he's quite ill now and could pass away soon with none to mourn him. But Sir Christopher's just like him and is sure to behave even worse once he assumes the title. It's little wonder that his wife left him and took his money."

Cahir nodded. "It's fair warning from Jenico, but there's naught we can do unless St. Lawrence should come here to involve us in something. If he would fill his pockets as an informer, he'll need a target wealthier and of higher standing than I. News of a Spanish invasion would make him rich in Dublin, but I'm doubtful he'll find evidence of such. If instead he can besmirch O'Neill and O'Donnell—who are enjoying their rich royal pardons and earldoms—there are some who would pay generously for any evidence of their treason. In the meantime, we'll have an eye out should he come to Inishowen, and send him on his way. We'll stay close to the castle and observe mass only at night, privately in our own chapel.

"Stoat, set a few more guards out to watch for intruders. Have a listen also for those who might speak against us or have words about the oath. I must know whom I can trust."

By October, Felim rejoined us at Elagh to help us move back to Burt Castle, smaller and easier to heat with one fire. The weather was unseasonably warm and I questioned whether we needed to move at all.

"Your point is well, Lady Maire," Felim said. "So mild is the earth, 'tis a sign from the Lord God that all is forgiven, and we may rejoice in the Yuletide. Just remember nature can be fickle and turn to ice on her whim. Best we prepare all the same."

And so we closed Elagh, and settled in at Burt once again. From October to December our weather remained mild, but by Christmas a great frost descended, a thick icy coat over every stretch of ground, killing cattle, and wild birds that fell to the ground, frozen by the cold and without food or water. In places, the frost was so thick a man could walk across the surface of a river. To some it was an omen of doom, fully attributed to the loathsome oath. Fevers and panic grew common among our people and brought deaths without apparent cause.

Weeks passed and conditions hardly improved, but a new rumor spread that shifted people's thoughts either toward greater fear, or hope. News came that the earls —O'Neill and O'Donnell—were meeting with the Old English, the Catholic families of ancient bloodlines who still commanded soldiers and stirred fear among the English nobles in London. These families were so infuriated by Chichester's mandates, fines and imprisonments, that war seemed imminent. It was only a rumor, nothing more. But soon that rumor was replaced by another, perhaps worse.

Sir George Paulet, the new governor of Derry, had taken up his position as commander of the English garrison. He was in no way like his predecessor, Henry Docwra. In the briefest span of time, he had gained the reputation of being arrogant, hateful to the Irish, and unskilled in military tactics. Paulet was said to be incompetent—entirely unfit for his assignment—and also cruel, thriving on the humiliation of his soldiers, and beating them daily.

"What else have you heard of him, Felim," Cahir asked.

"Little, except that he comes from Winchester. Mind you, that's the ancient Saxon city that drove the Jews out of England. He's no' likely ta favor those not of his kind, but I s'pose we ought to meet 'im before we judge 'im, so."

"Fair enough," Cahir said. "Then it's time we make the man's acquaintance."

My shoulders began to rise with tension. Why, I couldn't say, but something stirred my fear even worse than the warnings about St. Lawrence. "My lords," I said, "I shall pray the rumors be false."

37

STOAT

1607

Incivility

When the frost had subsided enough to allow safe travel, myself, Rudd, Felim, and Cahir, took the day's ride back to Elagh. In the morning, we crossed the River Foyle and rode the last stretch along the banks to the Derry garrison. Black smoke billowed above the smithy's corner, and the sounds grew louder of hammers banging, officers shouting, rifles firing in the training field and the cattle bellowing in their pens. At the gate, all other sounds were overtaken by the furious splash and tumble of the river beating against the garrison's jutting nose.

Unlike the open welcome under Docwra's governance, we were not allowed entry until the new governor himself came to decide whether we were worthy. We waited some time for the man to arrive. He stopped several meters distant and made us wait even longer until an officer identified us. He nodded that the gate be opened but kept his distance and his unfriendly countenance.

Cahir cocked his head at the man, for the usual procedure had been a welcome, a hearty grip, and the invitation into the garrison offices. Once there, he'd be offered wine or whiskey, and agreeable conversation. We all dismounted and waited for what was never to come.

"I say, what is your business here," Sir George called.

Cahir looked to Felim, but Felim shrugged and nodded for Cahirr to answer.

"Sir George, I am Sir Cahir O'Doherty of Inishowen. Beside me, Sir Felim MacDavitt of Carrichbraghy, and men of my clan, Stoat…that is Gearalt O'Doherty, and Rudd McGonigle. We have come in greeting, to welcome you as commander of the fine garrison of Derry."

I gazed around the palisade as Cahir spoke. Not a man turned in our direction, nor crossed the scraped dirt ground for a tool or a measure, nor stopped his activity, be it work, or no. Speech did not occur but for the occasional bark of orders. The men were red-faced, shivering, their clothing not fit against such biting cold, but no one, I gathered, wished to be singled out by this master. Those who could escape his notice scurried out of sight faster than a pack of rats.

This man Paulet took two steps forward and rudely examined Cahir from his hat down to his boots. I used the opportunity to examine the commander as well, for he was at least a head shorter than our Cahir, his wiry dark hair flecked with gray, and his face not scarred by weapons but surely lined and twisted by the arrogance of which he'd been accused.

"Well then," Paulet remarked, his voice tinged with contempt. "You are so-called 'The O'Doherty'? Of Inishowen, you say?" He scoffed. "Why, you are nothing but a boy, and hardly worthy of the land."

Cahir's face flushed red and his hand jerked toward the skean in his belt. "I beg your pardon, sir, but I am well of age, the leader of a proud and respected clan that has ruled Inishowen for 300 years. My age having little to do with it, I am knighted, and I hold the seals of King James himself. We have come out of respect, and do deserve the same from you."

"I hardly think so," Paulet sneered, "with the concoction of tainted blood running through your Irish veins. You descend only from outlaws, and have gained your position through bribery, theft, or murder as tends the Irish way of life. You are lower even than a cur, and far less worthy of trust from any Englishman. Be gone with you before I call my muskets."

The breath left my lungs. I stepped forward for sure a brawl was to start. Rudd reached for his blade, and Felim's hand grasped the hilt of his sword. Cahir kept a calmer head, though I knew not how, and raised his hand in a peaceful gesture.

"Sir George, you are mistaken. There is no call for hostility, nor any denigration of my line. I shall overlook it, your being new and unaccustomed to proper manners. Let us speak kindly in this new acquaintance, as surely we must both prosper from a friendly interaction. Inishowen has always been a cooperative supplier of goods to this garrison and would continue so, under friendly circumstances."

Cahir's calm response was so clever, I had to swallow my urge to laugh. Felim also raised a hand to his lips, but Paulet missed the chance to shift his course.

He marched several steps closer to Cahir, standing nearly face to face. "You would supply *me*? You would succor the men of *my* garrison? Do not imagine yourself worthy to scrape the dung from our boots."

"Sir!" Cahir took one step forward, but Paulet jumped back and swung his gloved hand across Cahir's cheek. Cahir reared backward but Felim caught him that he did not fall, and Rudd was beside him. I pulled my sword, but the vile rogue stomped away with surprising speed, and Felim called me back. Had I a pistol I'd have split Paulet's skull. Every face in the garrison now turned toward Cahir.

"Let us go. Let's get out of here. Now," Felim said, and in seconds we mounted and galloped from the garrison gates.

We rode most of the way back to Elagh in silence, none of us daring to speak until Cahir had the first word. He spoke not until we saw the wooded approach to Elagh's walls, and then at last he called out.

"Felim," he said. "How do we presently judge Sir George Paulet's character?"

Felim cleared his throat with a growl and spat upon the ground. "He is a scoundrel of the lowest measure, my lord. A maggot."

"A maggot, you say! My, that is low indeed. Rudd, what be your opinion?

"He is a maggot's excrement, sir. A rotted pile o' dung," Rudd said.

"Yes," Cahir nodded. "It is so! And your thoughts, Stoat?"

"My lord, he's a slimy, blind muck worm that feeds on maggot dung," I said.

"Well spoken, my friend. Thank you. I could not have framed it better. But listen to me, all of you. Lady Maire must never know what happened back there. She must never hear a word of it. Swear it."

"Cahir," Felim said. "You need no sworn statement from any of us, we're already sworn by faith and by blood to serve you forever, and so we shall. No one would ever speak of it."

After brief pause, Rudd said, "Unless MacTyre were here…"

We all burst into laughter, for that lad—God love him—could never keep a secret to save his own life.

"Truly," Felim continued, "we must think on this. What man behaves so? It was as if Paulet deliberately meant to provoke you. We must determine why, and find is there something afoot we've yet to discover? Nae matter what we find, never doubt that he'll live to regret this. Such foul treatment of any man, no less a man of stature, will not be left unanswered."

Upon return to Burt Castle, Cahir's first action of business was to cancel orders for provisions intended for the garrison. When Maire asked him why, he replied only that Paulet no longer required them. The garrison would take care of itself. She asked no more, but to me own mind, that was unlikely. Any other source of oats and meat would be more distant, more costly, and sure the London administration rarely provided enough to feed the garrisons outside the Pale. The cancellations would mean more raids of Inishowen by the hungry and cold-hearted English soldiers, and more loss and bloodshed for our own people. I hoped I was wrong.

38

STOAT

As Rumors Fly

In spring we packed the household at Burt again and returned to Elagh. The warmer sun lured forth the fragrant flowers that made the castle so inviting, but something was different about it this time. A current—running beneath the ground, I supposed—caused a faint and disturbing vibration, invisible but present enough to tighten the skin upon my bones, across my brow, within my belly. Everyone seemed aware of it, or were they? Did it only seem they were as troubled? Was I alone in sensing that at any moment our lives could be altered, as if the ground could give way and all of us would slip into darkness? But I couldna put a finger on it, nor put words to this disturbance. I couldna talk about it, so, and for the present could only find calm amid the busyness of work.

We attended to Elagh's upper floors and interior chambers until every nail had been struck, and the rooms were finished to Lady Maire's instruction and delight. By June, a third letter arrived from Viscount Gormanston, this time in a gift box delivered by a lone messenger. Inside the box was a fine writing instrument, the gift of a very special quill, its hollow stem cleverly concealing a single page tightly rolled.

Lady Maire carefully worked the page out and flattened it upon Cahir's writing desk. "It is quite dense in small script. Jenico says rumors gush from Dublin making it difficult to know what is true. George St. Lawrence, Christopher's cousin, was arrested for treason and is being questioned. Christopher himself may have betrayed him.

"As well, Christopher's father, Baron Howth, lies on his death bed and Christopher will inherit his title within days. Once he can call himself 'Baron Howth' his self-importance will swell to vast proportions.

"Gossip we've heard already," Cahir said.

"But then this," she continued. "The Irish Council Chamber, those men in Dublin who advise the Lord Deputy, received an anonymous letter claiming a revolt is being planned by the Old English recusants and the Gaelic Irish of the north and west."

Cahir scoffed. "Well, I've heard nothing of it!" He slammed his fist on the desk. "This is foolishness," he said. "I've heard nothing of the kind, there is no activity of this nature. If such a letter exists, Christopher probably wrote it himself and sent it to stir fears so he can make money as a false informant. Sure he'll do anything to serve himself, regardless of its effect on others."

"Wait," Lady Maire said. "Jenico says both O'Neill and O'Donnell have been named, with Christopher claiming that together they had discussed an alliance with the Old English."

Cahir paused, and then shook his head. "It is madness. Even if they had considered such an alliance, why in Heaven's name would O'Neill and O'Donnell discuss it with St. Lawrence? The man is clearly unstable. Everyone is angry about Chichester's mandates, and the King's oath, of course, but so many men died at Kinsale, and we are all still trying to recover. O'Neill is profoundly fortunate to still have his head. He has the King's favor, and what a mighty advantage that is. Why would he risk everything to incite another war? Why would he risk Chichester's return to have us all in fire and famine again?"

"I don't know," Lady Maire said. "There's nothing more."

She seemed to tremble, and I couldna blame her. The thought of Chichester's return could stir my gut as well, but Cahir was truly bothered.

"We can't go on with this kind of uncertainty hovering over our heads like a bitter storm," Cahir sighed as if exhausted. "I mean to find out for myself what is afoot instead of listening to rumors. Felim and I need to sell some beeves to cover my expenses at Elagh. It may take a bit of time, but we'll start preparations by contacting our agents to arrange the sale, and then we'll begin the drive to Dublin. Once there, we'll have time to see for ourselves what information we can gather. We'll speak to our friends who can sort the truths and offer some assurance."

That night I tossed upon my cot with questions swirling in my head. Could we trust anyone in Dublin, even Jenico, for the truth? Couldn't those men in Dublin recognize a liar and schemer when they spoke with someone like St. Lawrence? The last thing Inishowen could bear was Chichester's return. Could we somehow conjure a solution like MacDavitt used to do, that seemed to serve every need?

MacDavitt. By God, we needed him now. I thought on it until the fatigue began to claim even my anxious mind. I drifted, recalling afternoons with Cahir, swimming from the shore of Ballyshannon through the warm waters, the castle tall but getting smaller as the current took us beyond Assaroe toward the sea. The sky grew dark, yet ahead of us MacDavitt swam with powerful strokes, and then I realized I swam alone, Cahir having fallen behind, and above me the bow of a great ship bobbed upon the swells. Red Hugh was on the deck grasping to heave MacDavitt aboard, but my arms were sluggish, and I couldn't gain on the ship. Red Hugh laughed, his chin jutting toward the sky, mocking me as the ship made way, leaving me behind. The great vessel did not turn west to sail for Spain, but east.

196

39

CAHIR

Dublin

In early August, our agents in Dublin confirmed the sale of Inishowen beeves for a good profit. Sure they were the finest beeves to be had, fattened on the rich fields at Buncrana, or so we said. To be honest, the unusual winter frost destroyed much of their grazing and took some weight off them, though we did our best with the foddering.

We quickly made our preparations for the drive south to the Dublin Market. I'd never attended it before, but Felim was a veteran of the journey and would lead us across the 160 miles that lay between us and Dublin's northwest quarter. Aside from Felim and I on horseback, I had twenty men and several boys on foot minding the cattle with goad sticks, and forty men standing guard at Elagh until our return.

We managed about ten miles each day, often slowed by damaged pathways. From the harsh winter and wet summer, there remained pits and gorges that could break a leg, bogs ready to trap and swallow a stray, and frost-burned meadow grasses scattered in patches, and the patches thin. Still, the beeves needed to eat and drink all along the way. We paid local farmers when we crossed their fields. The farmers welcomed the coin and offered us bread and milk.

When we reached Gormanston, we still had three days of travel to Dublin, and August had turned to September, but Jenico gave us a generous welcome, grazing for the beeves, and good campground for the men. Felim and I dined and slept in the castle, comforts for which we were most grateful, and then we departed early the next morn. On the last day of travel a dust cloud hovered over what was surely the cattle market, and the drovers shouted with joy. It meant dry ground, rest, ale, and a warm cot for sleeping.

The beeves were gathered into a large pen for inspection. We held firm to our price and received it, and by evening we were celebrating in a nearby alehouse. I couldna help but recall the day I'd met Maire, her disappointment in my traditional clothing, and how MacDavitt had found the solution, as always he had done.

"Aye," Felim nodded. "My brother is sorely missed. If I could ha' found his killer I'd ha' shredded him to bits."

We clapped each other's shoulders and drank to MacDavitt's honor. Before I could swallow a young lad grabbed me by the elbow.

"Sir! You are The O'Doherty?"

"I am, lad, what is it?"

"Viscount Gormanston sent me to find you." He handed me a folded message small enough to fit in his palm. I offered a coin, he gave me a bow and ran off. The message was so brief I read it in a glance: *Brother, Return to Gormanston, not to linger in Dublin. There is news.*

With words so few, I wondered if the news be bad or good, but sure it was bad. Good news can always wait.

We paid the drovers and lads half their wages for their work on the drive, and the balance would follow when they arrived at Elagh. Should I pay it all, they'd spend it and mayhap never make it home. I assigned two men to lead the return trip—Felim and I leaving for Gormanston at dawn.

We rode all day, imagining the worst, stopping only for brief rests and to water the horses. Jenico was waiting on the front court steps when we arrived in the darkening twilight. In the library he had glasses of whiskey ready.

"What is it, brother? My concern is extreme. Is Maire safe?"

"I'm sure she is, it should not have affected her. Not yet." Jenico said, rubbing the back of his neck. "The news is this: Just days ago, a French ship sailed up Lough Swilly and arrived at Rathmullen. It collected Hugh O'Neill, Rory O'Donnell, their wives, and I don't know all of the others yet, but it seems close to a hundred passengers who boarded along with them. The ship sailed east. The destination could be France, Flanders, or even Spain. I'm confident it isn't London."

I shook my head. "That can't be. It must be a rumor. O'Neill has been pardoned, both he and O'Donnell are made earls. Why would they leave, abandon their lands, abandon Donegal? It makes no sense."

"When…How did you learn this?" Felim asked.

Jenico stiffened his spine. "Well? How do you think? We must all have our spies and the sharing of information among friends. I learned of it just yesterday."

Felim leaned toward him, an elbow on his knee. "You have great confidence in it?"

"Absolute," Jenico replied. "I sent the warnings, didn't I? Christopher—Baron Howth—he may have played into it, spreading his tales and trying to be on both sides of things, filling Lord Deputy Chichester's head with lies and doubts. He is half-wild."

"I must…I must get home. To Maire. To Inishowen. There will be confusion," I said, to no answer.

"Word has it that O'Neill was summoned to London." Jenico said. "With all of Howth's interference, O'Neill may have believed King James intended his arrest. Maybe it was true. I just don't know."

"My…" Felim began, cleared his throat, and started again. "My younger brothers, Sean and Eamann. They were working for O'Neill. Were they on the ship?"

Jenico shrugged. "I couldn't know, I have no list, but were I to wager I'd say yes. I am sorry. I hope I'm mistaken."

"I must get home. We've got to get home," I said. "Maire will be frightened and…"

"Slow down, lad," Felim pressed his hand on my arm. "We ought think on it a bit. We shouldna travel at night anahow. Lady Maire has Stoat watching over her and you left Elagh well-guarded." He turned to Jenico. "If ye'll have us ta stay tonight, we'll go with clearer eyes in the dawn. Spend a little time sortin' through this news before then."

"You're welcome to stay. A wise choice, I s'pose, but I've no more information than what I've told. It feels as if the earth beneath us shakes, if the greatest powers of the north have abandoned Ireland."

"Honestly, Felim," I said, "d'you believe any of us will sleep?"

Jenico refilled my whiskey glass.

We started out even before dawn, yet at each stop we made on the journey home, we heard more rumors of the earls' departure, each one wilder than the last. How quickly they spread! First, that the earls alone had left Ulster, abandoning their families, and leaving all for the taking by the tinkers, robbers, and villains of any sort.

Further on, we heard that all members of the great clans, O'Neill, O'Donnell, O'Cahan, MacSweeney, and even O'Doherty, had abandoned their lands, leaving all the towns and villages at the mercy of the plundering English garrisons.

By the time we reached Dungannon, the rumors turned violent. In an alehouse we heard men shaming the earls of Ulster, leaving wives and children to be dragged from their beds, beaten, ravished, and murdered, homes ransacked and burned. Felim insisted these were only rumors, but it didn't stop the terror searing beneath my skin.

"Remember," Felim said, "these are fools who aim to make themselves seem important. They canna know more than we by settin' at table swilling their ale. Only a few days have passed. We've seen no messengers carrying news to Dublin. More likely there be a veil of shock and confusion that stills any action. Tomorrow we'll sort what needs must when the devil drives."

By the time we reached Strabane, I began to believe Felim. The village seemed quiet, men and women going about their business in what seemed a usual manor. No homes had been burned, no bodies lay by the road, no one came at us begging relief. My fears for the safety of Maire and Catherine waned, though I was no less eager to get home to them. In place of those fears remained a bundle of endless questions.

40

STOAT

Alone

From the highest tower at Elagh I saw Cahir and Felim coming over the hill. I rushed out to meet them at the outer gate. They looked wearier than ever I'd seen them, but they clapped their arms around me and begged to hear what news I had to tell them. "Lady Maire waits in the court. Ye'll wish to speak wi' her before we talk, aye?"

Cahir shook his head. "Lady Maire will be with us for all of it. There'll be no keepin' her away."

"No sir," I said, and shouted for the lads in the stable to handle the weary horses. In seconds my lady was in Cahir's arms, and there followed a hug and kiss for Felim too. We hurried into the hall for comfort and privacy. She poured the whiskey at once, and a dram for herself so, as we settled down to talk.

"'Tis a joy to my eyes to see each of you and the fine bones of Elagh," Cahir said. "I can't tell you the horrible rumors we heard on the trails, but here you are safe, and Catherine?"

"She's as bright as the north star. She sleeps, but when she wakes she'll be yours," Lady Maire said.

Cahir nodded, "Thanks be to God. Stoat, I can bear it no longer. Tell everything you've learned."

I nodded, rarely finding myself in such a position, and this one had me uneasy. "Mind you, most o' what I tell is hearsay, but from fair sources and not the lads chattering in the ale house."

"Just tell," my master said.

"The ship that came to Rathmullen was sent by the Archduke of Flanders. I know little about him except that he became aware of O'Neill's situation here, perhaps by a letter from O'Neill himself, and he meant to rescue both of the earls whom he considers his Catholic allies in Ireland. A month ago, or thereabouts, O'Neill had a visit from a friar, a messenger for the Archduke, who believed Rory O'Donnell was to be arrested in London for treason."

"Why? On what evidence?" Cahir asked.

"I know nothing more about it. Only that the friar warned O'Neill and O'Donnell not to go to London, but instead to prepare for a journey. A ship would come for them."

Cahir's eyes flashed wide. "Wait now. You are saying they knew of this a month ago? And we were never told? Never had an inkling that something was amiss? The Archduke's spies knew O'Donnell was to be arrested, and we did not?"

Felim gripped Cahir's shoulder. "*Cuinas.* Calm down. Let him speak. He's not to blame for anything, he's to help us." Cahir glanced at Felim as if he'd lost all his senses. I carried on.

"I've no' discovered the ship's destination, so mebbe they didna know it even when they left Lough Swilly, but I did hear there were men watching from the village as people boarded that ship—Paulet's spies, I'd s'pose—so it's possible that Chichester is getting this information even as you are."

Cahir's face then drained of his reddened rage. "Chichester. He'll think our driving the beeves to Dublin was nothing but a ruse to draw his attention while the two earls slipped away. *Blessed God of Peace*, I hope I'm wrong. Continue. Who was with them?"

I heaved a sigh, easing some anxiety. "I know few names of the many souls who boarded, except it were O'Neill, his wife, children, secretaries and servants, chaplains. The same for O'Donnell except he sent his wife, Lady Bridget, to her family in Maynooth. She's heavy with child and probably couldna' endure a long, rocky voyage. Sir Felim, I do believe both of your brothers, Sean and Eamonn, were aboard."

Felim caught his breath and looked away. "Yes. They were with O'Neill. Sean left his wife behind, at Carrickabraghy."

Cahir turned slowly toward Felim, and stood up from his chair. "You knew? Your brothers were leaving Ireland on a ship with O'Neill, and you knew?"

"I did," Felim said, his head still bent, his voice gruff. "They are my brothers. I was sworn to them to keep my silence. No one knew when the ship would come. But the plan between us was always that I would stay. I would never leave your side."

Cahir shook his head in disbelief. "But, why was I not to know? Just weeks ago when we left Derry, you said all were sworn to me, from the time I was inaugurated. Now you have withheld from me, lied to me. Betrayed me."

I looked to Lady Maire, who had remained silent all this time, but she was weeping.

"It is no betrayal, lad," Felim said. "I am sworn always to support you and protect you. I am here as always I have been. I am also bound to me own brothers, you see. They broke a confidence in telling me, and begged I keep my silence for their sake. I did what I could in good faith to them, and to you."

Cahir fell back into his chair. "How did you do it?" His voice fell softly. "How did you spend these weeks with me, knowing you withheld such a secret? Knowing what it would mean to me?"

Felim was weeping just as Lady Maire and looked into Cahir's eyes. "With more pain than you can imagine," he said.

The hall fell silent, but I had more to tell. "My Lord," I turned to Cahir, "your sister Rosa was there, and departed with the O'Donnells, with her husband Caffar and their son. I am sorry."

Cahir stood up and gazed around the hall, his hands upon his hips. "Let me see now. How fare my circumstances today? I stand in Elagh Castle. My nearest neighbor is George Paulet, the most crude and arrogant man ever to cross Irish soil, and his garrison riddled with fear. To the south, no longer lies the great Dungannon and the invincible Hugh O'Neill, the famous Earl of Tyrone. Gone. To my west lay Burt Castle and Buncrana Stronghold, my flank no longer protected by O'Donnell and MacSweeney, nor nurtured by my sweet sister. They have all gone. To the north, Carrick-abraghy Castle, home of my beloved mentor and foster brother who lies to me and withholds information of vital importance. He must hurry home to take care of his brother's abandoned wife.

"To the northeast lies Culmore, now an English garrison that blocks my river, ruins my commerce, and steals my fish. Then we come round to O'Cahan, an all-but-finished clan that spent their energy, money and power fighting O'Neill over lands the English already assume as their own. Then we come back around to Elagh, for which I have just sold hundreds of beeves to pay for the expense of improvements. And, from here forward I must worry each morning, will this be the day the English realize the weakness of O'Doherty Clan, invade our Inishowen, and then gladly sweep us all into the sea?"

His words so sharp, his spirit so tormented as if ready to shatter, none of us facing him had the courage to speak or move.

Just then Nonie came down from the nursery bringing Catherine to see her father, but it was too late. He stormed out of Elagh without a backward glance, and into the deepest woods. He didn't return until nightfall, and then went up to his bed without a word to anyone. I slept by his door that night, feeling foolish and weak that I found no words to console him. Felim would know what to do. Felim would find an answer to restore him. Somehow, and soon, I hoped.

41

STOAT

Behavior of a Man

Felim left for home the following morning. Carrickabraghy was more than a day's ride from Elagh, time enough and distance for the two men to settle and heal.

It was time, anaways, to move from Elagh back to Burt Castle for the winter. Once we'd packed, moved, and resettled, I managed the last of those tasks while Cahir immersed himself in physical labor. There was still work to be done at Buncrana, and so by late October he'd organized a crew of workers to travel by boat to Tory Island, off Donegal's northwest coast, where timber was still in abundance. He felt a bit exposed in his own land—the departures from Rathmullen, the spies, the betrayal he suffered—and so instead of leaving Burt protected by the usual twenty men, he ordered forty to stand guard with me in charge, as he had when he was in Dublin. I was glad for it.

Within a few days, rumors reached my ears that Cahir's travels and wood gathering had not gone unnoticed, but Paulet's spies had seen him and had made themselves seem important to their commander by exaggerating and distorting Cahirs activities. One of the spies had reported back to Derry that Cahir and his men were building an outpost on the island to shelter Spanish invaders. Another insisted that Cahir was gathering his men in open rebellion.

Three days later, Paulet himself arrived at Burt Castle with a party of ten men.

I watched them approach our outer gate and alerted Lady Maire.

"You need not fear, my lady. We outnumber him by far and will send him running."

"I'm not afraid, Stoat. How dare he even come near our home. Where is he? I shall have a word for him myself!"

"Best, Lady Maire, to address him from the safety of our tower."

"If you say," she replied. Offended as she was, I struggled to keep up with her as she climbed the winding stone steps. From the parapet she glared at the man and shouted down upon his head. "Sir! Commander Paulet. I am Lady Maire O'Doherty, mistress of this castle. Why do you come to my home with armed men? Why do you disturb us here? My Lord Cahir O'Doherty is away, at work on our private lands. You have no business here."

Paulet didna even have the courtesy to address her by her proper title. "Your husband is in open rebellion against the crown. We shall take possession of this castle immediately as it is forfeit. Your husband is a trai-tor," Paulet shouted back.

"You are a fool, sir. I suggest you turn about. My husband is a knight of the King's realm, a loyal subject of King James, and we are in communication with His Majesty as well as our Lord Deputy. This is my home. This is my land, mine and my husband's. You have disturbed our peace for no reason, and I shall make sure your superiors are informed of your pitiful transgression. Again, you have no business here."

God love her, Lady Maire's voice rang out and showered down on Paulet and his men as if they were boys out of school. I gestured to our men and all made their presence known: forty helmets, forty guns well aimed.

Paulet retreated, and wisely so, but within a week we discovered he'd done his damage anyway. He'd sent a letter to Chichester, claiming Cahir occupied Tory Island and had mobilized 300 men. And yet our own spies reported Paulet had made not a single effort to secure his garrisons against an attack, nor had he put any of his soldiers on alert. Is that the behavior of a man facing rebellion?

Upon returning home Cahir was so furious he could barely speak. He rode to Carrickabraghy to consult with Felim before taking any action. As the result, he wrote a letter, first to Paulet.

The following day Cahir received a reply from Paulet, which he read aloud to Lady Maire and me, his face reddening, his hand shaking with rage.

'He says my writings are *'like my dealings, the one very disloyal, the other very false'* and that not until yesterday did he believe *'the reports of my disloyal going into armor.'''* Into armor? What can he be talking about? He writes, *'you with your legion of priests and friars late sent from Spain are discovered well enough'.* It is senseless. Lies upon lies. He carries on and on like a mad man!"

"You see it as it is," Lady Maire said. "Do you not think others will recognize the language as serving his own interests and that his statements are not factual?"

"Sweet Maire, you see the best in people. I think others have no interest in truth and will use whatever they might find to serve their own interests. This is fodder for such men. I must see that the truth gets to where it needs be."

Cahir wrote to the Lord Deputy, proclaiming his innocence. At the same time, Paulet continued to pepper Chichester's desk with foul lies and accusations to make himself seem like the important hero, when in fact he was a dirty rogue.

"Stoat," Cahir said, "I canna allow Paulet to continue. With his lies he'll destroy my reputation, my household, and my position. He'd arrest me today if he could find a way to take Inishowen for himself. He's a muck worm, among so many others. I've no choice but to present myself in Dublin to ask for Chichester's assistance. Perhaps he will see that Paulet's harassment is stopped. I am knighted, I have met the King and gained his favor. I have done nothing wrong. I must stand up for myself and my family."

"Aye, and I am at your side, sir." We rode together, the two of us, back across the many miles to Dublin Castle. We didna have Felim's company, and within a short time of our arrival, how I wished we'd had. Lord Deputy Chichester's face was hard as stone. He silenced Cahir within minutes, cutting short the explanation of Paulet's behavior and cruel methods.

"You are a foolish boy," Chichester said, "and I'd be a foolish man to entertain any complaint or report from your lips, especially in criticism of a garrison commander. His credibility shall always outweigh yours. If I must hear more of this, know that your word will never be enough. I shall require assurances to dispel the suspicion that surrounds you. To hear of this again I shall require independent assurances of your good behavior."

Cahir stepped back. "My Lord, I am formally knighted by your predecessor and Sir Henry Docwra. I have no complaints against my behavior, I have committed no wrongs. My word is as trustworthy as any nobleman's."

"Your word has no credibility at all where you now stand, and I tire of your whining. Guards!" Chichester shouted, and immediately we heard the thunder of heavy boots and the clang of pikes coming toward us, and quickly they grabbed Cahir's arms, lifted him off his feet, and dragged him toward a dark hallway.

"Go to Gormanston," Cahir said to me as the guards pulled him away. "By assurances, Chichester means money. Go to Viscount Gormanston for help."

"And get word to Lady Maire, will I?"

"No! No. She and Catherine are safe. Let us not frighten her."

At Gormanston, the Viscount recognized me from our first visit, and welcomed me into his library, but his kind smile fell when I told him what had happened. He stood and began to pace.

"It is despicable. Paulet should not be allowed to set foot on Inishowen, and never to threaten my sister! It's an act to alarm us all, and we must oppose it with equal vigor. Warm yourself by the hearth while I dress for the journey, and we will collect Cahir at once."

I waited half an hour until the Viscount returned in his fine clothing trimmed with badges of Gormanston honor. His appearance as a Peer of the Realm would remind Chichester to be careful of whom he offended, and to properly respect his office. He was right to do so, as it happened.

Back at Dublin Castle by late afternoon, the Viscount went at once to Chichester's presence. I was not permitted to attend and had to wait outside the door. A quarter hour later the Viscount emerged, his color making clear the tenor of the discussion, and rather than smiling my lord's teeth did grind.

"Come," he said. "The guard will take us to Cahir."

We crossed the open court—under much scrutiny from castle guards and dwellers—to the Bermingham Tower where prisoners were kept, and the guard led us up the first level of stairs. My master was in a small, white-washed room with one window that overlooked the west wall. He had one chair on which he sat, and behind him a single cot on which to sleep. Cahir offered his chair but instead the Viscount leaned against the stone window ledge. I waited by the door, knowing the guard was just on the opposite side.

"Jenico, you are good to come, my brother. I wish I had not the occasion to ask you," Cahir said.

The Viscount nodded. "You did the right thing, in presenting yourself to Chichester. It's not your fault he is mad with greed and sick with fear and anger toward Catholics. Were it not for my rank he might have arrested me as well. He doesn't seem to need a valid reason. I don't think he believes all of Paulet's accusations, but it presents an opportunity, does it not, to squeeze money out of a Catholic without fining him and enraging the old English landholders a bit more. I'll make sure they all know of this foolishness anyway."

"Did he speak of assurances on my good behavior, even though I've done nothing wrong?"

Jenico scoffed. "Believe me, he was almost giddy. Do you know what he wants? From two men of English nobility and good reputation, he'll have 500 gold coins each. And from you, he'll require £1,000. A thousand! I think I actually blushed! It is completely outrageous."

Cahir jumped up from his chair and paced the floor like an animal wild for escape. "'Twould take me five years to raise it! He cannot be serious! He wants to keep me here until I die. No man should have that kind of power and no man should treat another as such who has done nothing to deserve it. I have a wife, a child. I've served him better in every way a good citizen should so do. My God! Jenico, my head is sure to burst! What…what in the world…what in Heaven's name should I do?"

Jenico sat in the chair since Cahir could no longer sit at all. "Calm yourself, friend. It's a terrible thing but we'll not let him beat us. We'll find a way around him somehow. But for now, my advice would be to pay what he wants…"

Cahir gasped, his eyes wide enough to let his eyeballs jump from their sockets.

"Wait, hear me out. Chichester thinks he can do this because he's Lord Deputy and there is no one to stop him. As long as you are imprisoned, he's in complete control. The first thing we must do is get you out. We'll pay him. It will take me a few days to call on the right people who will help, but we'll pay him and work out the debts later. As soon as you are back in Donegal the story will be spread—to the London council; to the Irish privy council, to all the Old English landholders in the Pale, and across all four provinces. Everyone will know of his greed and excess. I don't know what will come of it but at the least it will draw attention to his activities and weaken his power."

"That, to me, would be a worthy accomplishment. Other than staying quiet and out of sight to prevent any more rumors, what would you suggest I do?"

"The moment you are freed, go home to Maire and Catherine. Reassure your men. And start surrounding yourself with powerful friends, Catholic or no. Men of power will be critical against this adversary."

Cahir nodded. "I am ever in your debt, Jenico. Without you I would be lost, truly. You're the best of brothers, the finest of friends," Cahir said. The two men gripped hands and embraced.

"Speak not to Chichester until I return," Jenico said. "Don't give him an opportunity to trap you in something."

"Aye. Thank you. Stoat, you may send a message to Lady Maire, but tell her only we are with Jenico and our return will be delayed."

42

CAHIR

The Council

Upon my return from Dublin, Maire was curious about the result of my conversation with the Lord Deputy. "What did he say about Paulet? And why were you delayed so long coming home?" she asked.

To tell the truth would only raise more her concerns for her. She'd been angry enough at Paulet's visit. I decided to soften the blow.

"Chichester was not fully convinced about my innocence, Sionnach, but nor was he convinced by Paulet's lies. So he fined me a bit, and I did have to borrow from Jenico for I hadn't brought enough money on the trip. I will cover the cost through business dealings and restore it to Jenico soon. All will be well. For now, let us turn our attention to something better. Christmas is not long from us, and we should make some plans, aye?

Her brows were furrowed, but she seemed to accept my story and allowed herself the distraction. Together, Maire and I began preparations for the traditional Christmas gathering at Burt, which had always involved feasting, music, dancing, and games.

Our numbers would be fewer than the year before, so many of our friends and relatives having sailed with O'Neill and O'Donnell. Of those travelers, rumors came from many sources. We'd heard the ship had carried them to Flanders, and they all lived under the support of the Archduke, and that the ship had next gone to Italy where they were welcomed and entertained. They seemed to be having a grand adventure, though I had learned from one of my spies that O'Neill had already contacted his agent for money.

While Maire organized the meals and entertainments, I spread word that we'd have a traditional clan council meeting—gathering all of Inishowen's leaders, the men who remained loyal to me, stalwart men who loved Inishowen as I did, who shared our history, and who would speak with honesty. I wanted to hear what others had to say about our changing circumstances, particularly the things Paulet was doing in the King's name.

I wrote first to Felim. I was wrong to remain angry with him when he'd stayed by my side and had been loyal to me even as his beloved brothers were departing. He held his tongue, and I couldn't blame him for it. The fact is that I needed him—his wisdom, his experience, his loyalty, and his steady, calm, thoughtful approach to any circumstance. In truth, I needed MacDavitt, but Felim was the next best man.

After Felim, the most important leaders were the MacAilin family, three brothers who lived and farmed in the Gleneely area of Inishowen's northeast corner. They were brave and agile warriors and intensely loyal to Clan O'Doherty.

On the day of the gathering, Rudd and MacTyre built a roaring fire in a clearing surrounded by dense woods. By the time I called our council into order, more than forty men joined us, each of whom could gather hundreds of warriors if the need arose.

We gave thanks at first for the continuing productivity of Inishowen lands. Harvest had been lower than in past years, but still it would sustain us. For this we cheered and gulped our ale. But it didn't take long for the tone to shift to discontent. I refused to raise the topic myself but gave Felim a nod when the men began to complain about Paulet.

"He allows his men to trample our crops and take our sheep as if they owned them. His officers trot about on cavalry horses as if to survey and measure our lands for their profits," one of the MacAilins said. "They seem to believe the King owns everything from Burt to Malin Head, and we are naught but lowly laborers to be ignored."

"Aye!" his brother said. "Each day I pray His Majesty will realize they serve no purpose here, and he will reassign them to some distant island where they might yet earn their pay."

"And Paulet!" the third MacAilin brother began. "He's no business running a garrison. He knows nothing of his position, he ought be driving a tinker's wagon, selling cheap wares. His men despise him, for he is cruel without cause."

I nodded, having felt the lash of that myself. I stood, offering open hands to the men before me. "What shall we consider as our course of action? I've appealed to the Lord Deputy, but it landed me in prison and cost me dearly in fines. If I wrote letters to the King, Chichester would deny my complaints as Catholic treachery, and turn his wrath upon us for even greater abuse."

Felim stood to speak, and like many older men he chose his words carefully and spoke slowly, that no one could mistake. "I fear the Lord Deputy uses persecution and fines to pay for the lands he does secretly amass near Carrickfergus—lands he leases to former soldiers for atrocious fees. His greed grows like the fat man devouring beef. His holdings creep silently from east to west, closer and closer to Inishowen—a deadly disease spreading—and with O'Neill gone, none stand in his way. We all know the treasure that is Inishowen. Paulet is a troubling distraction, but I believe Chichester is the true enemy, who will not stop until what's ours is his."

"We must fight him!" someone shouted, and cheers soared over the roar of the fire. "Fight! Fight for Inishowen! Fight for Clan O'Doherty!"

"Fight," I said, "but never die. We must fight wisely if we are to survive and save Inishowen. I pray the earls will soon return with the power of Spain behind them, but until they do, we must win every battle. Too many men have been lost in these years past, from war, famine, fire, and brutality. We lose no more."

The men around the fire shouted agreements and a new battle cry, "Fight and never die! Fight and never die!

"And so," Felim stood, raising his hands to quiet the men. For his age and wisdom he was highly respected, and soon all voices stilled for his words. "We are as one in the belief we must fight for Inishowen as no other course is left to us. We are united. If we would fight, our needs are many, and most importantly we cannot fight alone. We need allies who will support us as brothers in victory. There is much thought and work ahead, which falls to The O'Doherty and myself. We will need time, but we have many friends. We must leave this council tonight without decisions but with much to consider. Until we are brought together again, what has been spoken here, must remain here."

I raised my fist to the heavens. "*Ár nDuthchas!*" I shouted the clan's famous motto, confirming our blood connections. The men echoed back to me with voices fierce and loud, our shared commitment to pass to the next generation what was once bestowed on us.

Allies we needed. Allies, we had always counted many. And so, allies we would find.

43

STOAT

1608

Plans and Promises

With early spring came heavy rains, delaying our return to Elagh and canceling some of the projects Cahir had planned for Burt and Buncrana. Restless, he walked around the castle yard, letting the rain soak his hair, his clothing, his shoes. Yet he walked even as little Catherine stood by a window, pointed at her father and giggled. Lady Maire begged him to come in and warm himself by the fire. She tempted him with food and spirits, but he only nodded and kept walking.

"Something distracts him, Stoat. Won't you go and bring him in?" she asked.

"My lady, I have tried but he only turns me away."

She sighed. "Whatever it is, I suppose it will pass. Come, Catherine, let's leave your Da to himself."

When the days grew warmer, Cahir's walks moved closer to the castle, sometimes his daughter's hand in his as he pointed out the flowers and ferns, the bees that hummed above them, and the lizards and squirrels that fed beneath them. He walked taller than before, his gaze more upward than down. And when the grounds were firm enough we moved east to Elagh. Here he was more relaxed, larger somehow. He spoke fondly of days when he'd been Catherine's age and older, romping around the castle yard before he was fostered to the MacDavitts.

On our first night, we celebrated with a grand supper in the hall, and Cahir gladly welcomed neighbors and the families that made up our household. As the hour grew late and guests returned to their own lodgings, he held Catherine close and stroked her fine hair as she drifted into slumber.

"Sionnach," he said softly. Now that we're home again, and many of our problems are now behind us, what would you think about arranging a gathering—one like you've mentioned before, to invite people we'd like to know better. Captain Hart and his wife, Bishop Montgomery and his. And you've never met my sister Peg. She's an O'Hanlon and lives halfway between Elagh and Dublin. If she and her husband could come, I believe you will like her much."

"Oh, my good Broc, you do see me sometimes. Yes, of course, I would love to meet your sister, and to have a house full. We need to gather people to us, and let the children play together. I imagine we'll have many. Sure we are not the only ones looking for some enjoyable outing. When should we do it?"

"Presently, I've some business with Felim in the north. I would see to that first, and you could be planning while I'm away. I suppose mid-April would serve well?"

"It would be lovely, the warmer weather, flowers blooming, the lambing season well underway. It's so much fun for children." She kissed him and he grasped her hand, kissing her fingers.

"It's settled then. Stoat, I'll need you with me at Felim's. We'll leave the day after tomorrow. Assign the castle guards for while we're away, will you?"

"I will, sir. And any others to escort?"

"No. We go alone. We are perfectly safe and best we keep things simple," Cahir said.

We left Elagh before the sun climbed over the hills below Derry. The ride was pleasant enough, the weather fair, but my master spoke not a word until we passed Kilmackelvenny, well away from the eyes and ears most likely to raise a question, and from there a straight route north to Carrick-abraghy.

"Is there news, Stoat? Any new rumors being passed?

"Good sir, had I news it would reach your ear long before you had to ask. I've heard nothing. Does something worry you?"

Cahir huffed. "Much worries me, my friend, but I need a veil of darkness and silence around us. Our only true advantage is there. What we face is formidable. You will know all of it soon."

218

44

STOAT

A Noble Purpose

Two days of steady travel brought us to Carrickabraghy without complication or obstacle. We entered the castle gate to find men from all parts of our precious Inishowen, their mounts settled in the stalls. All counted, this meeting included more than half of those at the Christmas council, leaders at the highest level who would find or make the advantages; who trained and led others in arms, whose skill in battle was worthy of legend.

Once the greetings had been said, we assembled in the hall and no time was wasted. Felim, as elder and host, began.

"Good lads, we all know why we are here, and it's a noble purpose. The noblest. Ye'll recall from our last gathering, we acknowledged and agreed the situation with the English has grown intolerable. Our boundaries are ignored. Our leaders, all of wisdom and ancient heritage, are treated without reverence. Our women are seen like fruit, free to be plucked from any tree, or murdered like helpless animals.

"We are force-sworn to English law, yet the English see fit to change or twist it according to their whims. Let the English make any false claim against an Irishman, be he of high status or low, our man must make a defense, and if he lacks words to disprove the claim he's imprisoned, and women, too, leaving his home and belongings bare against pillage and burn. So it happens in war times, and so it splinters our peace.

"We're not heard when we cry foul. Cahir himself has applied for a court position in London, whereby he'd have more sway o'er the English criminals, but we've had no reply. Sir George Paulet does nothing and thereby encourages the crimes and abuses. Lord Deputy Chichester's only response is to imprison our chief, and then rob him to the core, calling it a legal fine.

"We'll have no more of it. United, we will fight. Aye, we are small against the English who have holds in every corner of our island. But we shall be wise, use their own weaknesses against them, and in the end, they shall be forced to reckon with O'Doherty, to acknowledge our rights and boundaries. Let them call it rebellion. In truth it is survival. They will not listen? Then let them hear the ring of our swords! The blast of our cannons. The screams of their own soldiers. The thunder raining down upon them! We'll fight and never die!"

The men roared and shook their fists, and then Cahir stood to speak. As they cheered him forth, all would see as I did from the back of the gathering, Cahir rising on a new level of power. It filled his shoulders, sculpted the hard stone of his cheekbones, broadened his arms with strength like oak, his back and thighs equally burgeoned, his hands large and bristling. All boyishness had slipped away, leaving in its place the frame of Sean Og himself, but adding to that Cahir's own ferocity, a lion waking and hungry. It stirred my blood near to boiling.

"Good men of Clan O'Doherty, our advantages may be few, but together we are mighty. We know before setting out that this man Paulet will stumble over his own arrogance. Already his lack of military capability is apparent, and his leadership nonexistent.

"Beyond that, in my years in the service of Sir Henry Docwra at the Derry Garrison I learned its weaknesses. I know where weapons and powder are stored. I know the schedules and routines of the garrison itself, and where they are lacking in skills.

"To succeed, our plan must overwhelm their expectations. It will involve a ruse, a surprise attack, maneuvering to draw the English where we want them, to spread them thin, and terrorize them to defeat. We shall address each point of it today, and your experience and ideas are much needed, that we overlook nothing, misjudge nothing, use every advantage, and protect our own."

Gruff voices shouted as one, "*Ar nDuthchas!* Fight and never die!"

Then the hand-drawn maps were spread across the trestle table, broad and muscular hands flattening the inked mountains, fields and loughs, and marking with charcoal the locations of greatest O'Doherty strength. By minute and hour the empty spaces were filled with forts, battle points, strategic locations for skirmish, and Buncrana's designation as our headquarters, it being the most central fortress.

Preferred pathways were assigned for the movement of men and arms. Voices were hushed in places, and coarse with disagreement in others, until concurrence was met. I knew every plan, and every alternative plan if the first would be foiled. I knew as well where I was meant to be once the fighting commenced: always beside my master, Cahir.

After three days we started our journey home. I had only one misgiving as we left the gates of Carrickabraghy, and sure Cahir himself had the same: Lady Maire.

45

STOAT

The Fragile Alliance

The first morning upon returning home, Cahir was to address his highest priority with Lady Maire. Together they ate their breakfast at the big trestle table. I had eaten a quick bit in the kitchen where Nonie had fixed my clabber and bread. Afterwards I stood guard in my usual place by the main door. My lady had just pushed her bowl aside and was sorting her writing papers.

"I've been thinking, my love," Cahir began, "about the gathering we've been planning. I've just come from Buncrana. It is beyond beautiful this spring. The grounds are carpeted with bluebells, the yellow primrose as well, and white flowered vines climbing the towers. It would be a charming setting for our guests."

Lady Maire shook her head and sighed. "Oh, Cahir. I am just writing a letter to Queen Anne. I've had word that she's lost a child. She gave birth to a daughter, named Sofia after her mother, but the infant died the very next day. The Queen must be in pieces. I can hardly think about a party when…"

"Oh, sweet Maire, you are right. A terrible thing to happen. Your letter will comfort her, and we must address the King, it being his loss also. This is of great importance and Stoat can see that your letter is taken to the carriers in haste."

"Yes, certainly," Maire said. "I feel so sad for her."

"Indeed. But let's not let it postpone our plans for the supper, aye?

The weather being so poor recently, we must take advantage of the fair season. We don't know when we'll have a better time, and I think it's important we make a show of it."

"Well, I…" she sighed again. "Are you sure it is proper, while the royal couple grieves?"

"It will be of no consequence to them, far away in London, and as I say, we must acknowledge this as gift from Heaven, it being so long since we've seen even a single blossom. It's an event much needed. It will be good for business."

"But, Buncrana? I've already started with some of the decorations here, and I…Well, won't it be more of a burden to move?"

"You must trust me, Maire. Wait until you see the work we've done there. It is quite comfortable and convenient. I know it comes as a surprise, but will you honor me with this change of plan?"

"Goodness, you seem to have your mind set on it. If you're so convinced, then of course we can go to Buncrana," she said.

"I'll make sure it is well handled. We can transfer everything we need to Buncrana with no extra work for you, and I think you'll be delighted when you see it. Catherine has never seen the keep, and she could climb on the stairs to her heart's content. And it's not far from Burt, which we could use for extra lodging if needed."

"Yes, yes. You've convinced me. Now go, so I can finish my letter!"

Cahir kissed her smartly and heaved free his tightened breath. "Good then. What do you think of the 18th? Would that give you enough time to prepare?"

"You've been thinking a lot about this! I'm glad. Yes, the 18th will be perfect."

"Splendid. Stoat, will you help organize the move?" Cahir asked, his brow lifted and a half smile upon his lips

"My Lord." I nodded.

"Now, Sionnach, I'm overdue on my responsibility to check in with the governor at Lifford. Tomorrow I'll meet with him, and then up to Culmore to invite Captain Hart, his wife and children, to join us on the afternoon of the 18th."

"Yes! And I have much to do as well. Thank you, my love. It is a blessing to have something fun to plan and prepare."

Cahir didn't mention the true purpose of his journey, to meet Niall Garbh O'Donnell and secure his support for the rebellion. Niall had achieved his lifelong goal to be The O'Donnell, leader of the famous and formidable clan. But he assumed the title when Rory O'Donnell sailed away with Hugh O'Neill. Who was to stop him then? Nevertheless, he was now the overlord of O'Doherty Clan, and Cahir was obliged to inform him of our plans.

We arrived late morning at Castlefinn, seated on the Finn estuary, a tributary of the Foyle River, where Felim joined us. The castle was surrounded by stone walls five feet thick, and all around was good, level ground, the beeves grazing in contentment as far as we could see.

"He's as fierce a warrior as any of us be destined to meet," Felim said, "but he's less gifted in strategy, diplomacy, or…I shall say…honesty. Mind what you say that could shackle us, should he tek another side."

Cahir gave a firm nod, but I recognized his confident posturing and pride. He was to meet the only Irishman remaining in Ulster who was of higher station than he. He intended to make an impression.

Niall's servants opened the doors and led us through a hall to where he sat, in a grand chair by a large many-paned window facing the sun. He wore a heavy claret-colored robe over his woolens, and canvas slippers on his feet. The gray of his hair now dominated the black. His long face seemed even longer with a jutting chin and wispy beard. His eyes were dark, small, and sharp like the hawk.

Felim started to introduce Cahir, but Niall waved him off. "Sit, all of ye, and let the lad speak for 'imself."

Cahir stood proudly. "Sir, you knew my father, Sean Og O'Doherty; Felim, my foster brother, and also The MacDavitt, rest his soul. I am knighted, Sir Cahir O'Doherty, the confirmed leader of O'Doherty clan. Sure you are aware of the growing conflict and strife among our people. We've reached the limit of tolerance for the overstepping English, the disrespect, the false accusations and imprisonments, and the abuse and cruelty to our people. We must make our stand clear. I've come to inform you that a rising is forthcoming. We ask for your full support in this. We cannot succeed without your firm stand beside us and behind us."

Niall Garbh leaned his head back against his chair, and one corner of his lip lifted in a partial grin. "And so you would turn against those who have knighted you."

"Sir Niall, I wouldn't do so had they not first turned on me and shown no respect for the honor bestowed. We, Clan O'Doherty, believe we are without choice. The English will slowly pick away at us until there is nothing left."

Niall gave a solid nod. "Aye, it is their favorite tactic. Less costly, you understand." He scratched the back of his neck and peered out the window. "Do you see all of those cattle there? They are mine. I took them from that weakling Rory when they gave him the earldom. I had advised the bastards. I brought them valuable information. I fought under their flag and sacrificed good men who fell in their battles. The earldom was always mine. But they feared me too much, I was too strong for them, and too wise, so they put a lesser man in the seat who they meant to control. See where that got them. So, I took every last beeve Rory had. All his wealth, mine in a single sweep. What could he do about it? I have an army of followers. Not he. And now he's gone."

"We acknowledge your position, Sir, and hope you'll agree, the time has come to take what is ours." Cahir began to tell Niall in general the plan of attack, the plan to overcome Paulet, to take Derry, to use Irish forts to divide the English and demolish theirs. Felim began to shift and grumble. Cahir was revealing more than he should, as if in pride for his own leadership, and the cleverness of his men. Niall urged him on.

"Of course, of course. And well done! You must move forward with this in haste before anything is discovered. I will indeed support the cause. So much that I will send a company of men to your side to increase your number and intimidate the English. And I'll promise you this: The exact minute you have taken the garrison at Derry, send word by a messenger on the swiftest horse, and I will activate attacks against the garrisons at Lifford, Donegal, and Ballyshannon. We shall clear them all from Ulster, and rule on our own terms as ever we should."

He called for his servant to bring wine, and we toasted to victory. We toasted to Cahir and to Felim who would lead the attack. We toasted to the strength of Inishowen, and to the return of right and proper Irish control of Ulster.

The three of us left Castlefinn uplifted, hopeful, excited by Niall's support, but there was also caution. The excitement waned as we returned, Felim to Buncrana, and I and my master to Elagh. Once we completed our move to Buncrana, it would become our headquarters for war.

Everything was in place and in motion according to plan. That night the moon rose from the sea like the upturned cup of a golden chalice, so bright and fierce that it drove off mist and cloud, yet it descended quickly of its own weight until a great field of black trees claimed its light.

46

MAIRE

Supper in Springtime

Of all the castles that belonged to Cahir, I was least familiar with Buncrana, and to host a gathering in an unfamiliar place seemed to invite trouble. But Cahir kept his word, and I had no burden from the move except for my own personal needs and Catherine's. When we arrived, even before I entered the castle, he showed me the endless sea of bluebells that moved in gentle waves beneath the soft breeze, as far as I could see in every direction. Cahir was right, our guests would be enchanted. They would be stunned by its beauty.

On the opposite side of the castle the Crana River reflected the clouds above and flowed like rich cream poured over ribbons of blue. Whatever concerns I may have had, I discarded. The obvious theme for our supper was in keeping with the flowers and the river. My gown was the perfect hue, as was Lady Eliza's being just a shade lighter. Catherine's dress was the lightest baby blue, so that I could find her if she lost herself among the darker blossoms.

Cahir seemed unusually consumed by his business arrangements. Several men came to see him, I presumed to discuss the lambing progress, and the movement of our cattle. He was steeped in a new kind of confidence. Yet he did not neglect me on our first night there. He held me close, whispered in my ear of how proud he was of me, how he could hardly wait to show me and our daughter to our guests.

"Let's dispense tonight with oils or special treatments. I need only to touch you, hold you, and I am filled with love for you. I'm near to bursting, I am. This night, you are an angel and I am a giant!"

He swept me into his arms and bit me gently on the neck, an act both alarming and exciting. From there he moved his way down and down, with sucks and bites that awakened my skin and started a fire in my belly. Then he rolled over, laughing, and lifted me above him in such a way I could have split into two, my body burning and trembling, but only wanting more, loving his attention. And then something rose inside me, like the volcano I'd heard of but never seen, until together we collapsed, sweating beneath the window on a cold spring night. I was blessed, truly, to be so loved by a man I loved so deeply.

The next two days were cluttered with tasks. We caught each other's glances from across the room or across the court, smiling and blushing as if we were new lovers kept apart but ever hungering for the touch of the other. Our nights were tender and passionate, more than I dreamed possible, and yet something stirred fear within me. I didn't deserve such love, and yet here it was, and what if I should lose it? What if Paulet stirs things up again and Chichester comes? So foolish, to waste time worrying over something unknown that might never happen. And yet an uneasy feeling rose and fell like the tide.

On the day our guests were to arrive, I was nervous, and I swore to myself I would not blurt out my thoughts as I had at the Gormanston supper. Then the memory came to me, the story Cahir had told me about the wishing stone in Buncrana's churchyard. Perhaps a wish was just the thing to dispel my anxiety. I hurried into the yard and searched the walls for the cup-like hole Cahir had mentioned. I quickly found it, though it was partly hidden behind a great alder tree. According to the legend, I needed to stand a few paces away, reach toward the wishing stone, close my eyes and make a wish. Then with eyes still closed I should move toward the stone so that my fist presses into the stone cup. If I succeed, my wish would come true! I closed my eyes.

"Dear wishing stone," I said out loud. "I wish that our party will be wonderful for everyone, that we'll make new friends, that I curb my tongue no matter what I hear, and that more of these happy gatherings will follow." I realized that was four wishes instead of one, but perhaps the stone was generous, and I was short on time. I squeezed my eyelids closed, reached toward the stone and approached it. I was sure I was almost upon it when I stumbled over a jutting root of the alder and soiled the hem of my new gown. Then Rita called for me and there was no time to try again.

In the kitchen, Rita glittered with sweat as she worked so near to the ovens, but the scent of fresh bread filled the great hall and had my mouth watering. We'd have fresh bread, pies, and sweet cakes. Then Nonie showed me the catch that had just been brought in from our river traps. We would feast on sea trout and salmon.

The dining room was draped with garlands made from green vines and bluebells, and the lanterns were all filled with new wax candles, a mad expense for a special occasion. The side table was crowded with wines brought by our brother-in-law, Eochy O'Hanlon. With his arrival I finally met Cahir's sister Mairead, older by one year, and everyone called her Peg. She was nearly as tall as Cahir and with similar coarse ginger hair. We took each other's hands as we met, and I knew we'd become friends.

Our villagers arrived, and then the MacAilins, and then Bishop Montgomery with his wife Susan and their daughter of about 10 years, Jane. The Bishop was most kind, though his balding head, long face, and heavy black beard made him seem severe. Rumors had it that he'd fought Hugh O'Neill relentlessly to win back what he considered were church lands.

Cahir's friend, Captain Henry Hart arrived with his wife Frances and their four-year-old son George, who was a good playmate for Catherine. The children were enchanted by the bluebells, leaping like rabbits from the cabbage patch to the raspberry bushes, all in a great blue sea of flowers.

We parents laughed and let them play while Lady Eliza's harpist entranced us with shimmering music, like water over smooth stones, and the men shared jovial stores of hunting in the hills. We nearly fell into a trance before we were all called to the table, stacked high with breads, fruits, and meat pies, while the children were taken to a playroom for their supper.

Our meal was well received, and all of my anxiety melted like the candle wax. Most of us had finished eating, and some of the guests had already headed home when I found myself merry and drowsy with wine, chatting easily with Peg and Frances at our table. Cahir invited Captain Hart into the buttery just next to us, to taste a special sherry.

Several minutes later, I heard a shout. It startled me, but I glanced around the table and no one else seemed to have noticed. I continued conversation, but then came again the shout. Two voices, Cahir and Henry Hart. "You will end my career, so why should I not just die?" Captain Hart said. Everyone at the table heard those words. Frances's face paled.

"Please excuse me." I pushed back from the table, my hand trembling. I entered the buttery. "What is this? Why are you arguing?" And before they could answer I realized Captain Hart was held by two of our clansmen, one who bound the captain's hands, while Cahir stood like a stone wall between Hart and the door.

"The Captain is angry because we, Clan O'Doherty, will take Culmore Garrison this night, and he and his wife will help us do it. His son George will remain in our custody, to make sure that they do as we require," Cahir said.

Captain Hart was red-faced with rage, but he didn't speak.

"Cahir, you cannot do this," I pleaded. "The English will kill us all. We'll lose everything! Stop it now and I'm sure we can sort things out. You can apologize for this terrible mistake. Please, Cahir." He did not even acknowledge my words.

"If they refuse to do as we have asked, their son will die. There is no other way," Cahir said.

His voice was one I'd never heard, sharp-edged, determined, without feeling. The hot blood of my heart shot into my face and I burned with anger and humiliation. "Stop it, Cahir. Please," but I might as well have been in another house, another town, another country.

I turned back through the door to the dining room. All our guests were standing, looks of horror on their faces. "Frances. There's been mistake, Cahir does not mean it," and before anyone could react the hall was filled with Cahir's men. Cahir stepped out of the buttery.

"No one will leave Buncrana," he said. "We rise against the greed and brutality of the English. We rise to claim our lands and our heritage. Tonight we take back what is ours."

Mrs. Hart she began to scream and cry, and I along with her, still begging Cahir to stop. He roared.

"If I hear one more word from either of you, I'll hurl you both out yon window. Hear me!" Then he turned back to the captain. "So what is your choice, Hart? Do as we say, and you shall live. Refuse and you will die, you along with your family."

Hart looked to his weeping wife; his own face streaked with tears. "We will live. But you will regret what you've done."

"I will not. Take them," Cahir said to his men, and then, for a moment we were alone.

I stood before my husband as I'd never done before, my heart thundering. "Why did you not tell me? All the loving, the planning together, and all along this was in your mind?"

"It is clan business, Maire."

"Am I not of the clan? Am I not Lady O'Doherty?"

"The council made the decisions."

I sucked in my breath. "The council. And you are the head of the council. A council of fools."

"Don't say that."

"My father must have despised me to utter hell, to shackle me to a man who lies and schemes behind my back, putting me and our daughter in mortal danger; to condemn me to a land of endless war, cruelty and deprivation, a land even its own leaders have seen fit to abandon, yet I am trapped and no way out. He must have despised me and wished me worse than dead, for that's what he's achieved."

Cahir reached out. "No! Maire, I had no… I had no choice. You must…

"I must nothing. I warned you long ago never to say that again. You always have a choice. And now I choose—that you must never speak to me again. I thought you loved me, but this is not love."

"It is," he said. "For you, for our family. For Inishowen. We *must* survive."

47

STOAT

Culmore and Derry

From the alcove, I heard each piercing word between Maire and Cahir. From such a blow, I feared the love between them could never be restored. Only if we were to be entirely successful could Cahir convince Lady Maire to recant. But there was no time even to think. I belonged at Cahir's side, and we departed at once for Culmore, with Captain and Mrs. Hart, and a company of 100 well-armed and helmeted O'Doherty soldiers. All the others at Buncrana, including the Harts' son George, would remain there under armed guards.

We traveled in silence. The clouded sky that blocked the starlight and concealed us better until we reached our meeting place by 11:00 that night. All of our soldiers had taken their assigned positions, and the next part of our plan unfolded.

Cahir, I, and several other men accompanied Mrs. Hart toward the garrison gate. She walked before us, knowing we held her husband and son who'd be killed if she didn't do as she'd been instructed. She called to the soldiers inside the gate.

"Hello, hello! Please! I am Mrs. Henry Hart. Your Captain Hart, he has fallen from his horse a few miles behind us. We think he has broken his arm. I've come for help. Please, can you help me?" She wept, making her appeal more credible.

The guards recognized her, for they swung open the gates and two came out to Mrs. Hart. Seconds later, men on horseback swept past intending to rescue their wounded captain, only to be overtaken while the rest of our company swarmed into the garrison.

Our soldiers captured the guards and pulled others from their beds, all of them cursing and howling as we locked them in the cellar and gathered their weapons and stores. Soon Mrs. Hart, the men who helped her, Captain Hart, and the soldiers who rode out for him, all had been collected and locked in the cellar, to remain there under guard until new orders came.

"You need not fear for your lives. I seek not blood," Cahir shouted, "but respect for O'Doherty Clan, and return of what is ours."

Cahir then sent a messenger to Buncrana: "See that our men bring young George Hart back to his mother at Culmore. Be sure he's not harmed."

While our guards held the cellar and the garrison itself, the rest of us were far from finished with our plan. Derry Garrison lay a short distance away and had to be taken before any warning could reach them.

Cahir and Felim led the way until we arrived at the hill near Derry just after 1:00 in the morning. All remained quiet, and because of Paulet's arrogance, no guards were at duty in the watchtowers. Joining us were the MacLochlainns, the MacAilins, and many others. Cahir divided our force in two and led the first attack upon the lower side of the garrison, where the weapons, gun powder, and supplies were stored. All were taken quickly for our camp, and Cahir took control without bloodshed. "It is not blood that I seek!" he told them.

But the second half of our force was not so forgiving. Felim led the attack on the upper side built into the hill. From our position, Cahir and I heard the shouts and gunfire, and after a time flames began to leap from the timbers and wooden houses Felim's party had set afire. Before the fire had spread very far, Felim returned in triumph. They had broken down a door, rousing Sir George Paulet from his bed. Paulet escaped to another house. "The dirty coward," Felim said. "Screamin' fer his life, he fell at the feet o' two soldiers who charged out with swords to defend him, and they followed him straight to hell."

In the town of Derry, the flames climbed, reflected more brightly by the clouds above, and awakening all of the inhabitants. Cahir sent guards to make sure our ancient Church of Colm Cille was not harmed. The following day, with both garrisons firmly in Irish hands, our men took time to rest, and Cahir sent me on a special assignment.

"Stoat, we both know Burt is the safest castle in all of Inishowen, is she not?"

"She's impenetrable, our most defendable castle, sure we saw to it."

"We did. That's why I want you to return to Buncrana. Take from here the bishop's wife, Susan Montgomery, and the other English women to be our hostages. Collect Lady Maire, Catherine, my mother, sister Peg, and all the women and children we left there, remove all of them to Burt. Once you've done, watch over them a bit, make them safe, alert me if there is trouble. Take as many men as you need to defend the castle and protect them. No one enters, and no one departs unless upon my orders. When you're satisfied, you know our plans. You know where I'll be."

"Aye, My Lord, but was I not meant to watch over you, sir?"

He smiled. "So you were, and so you shall, friend. But this first. I'll be in your debt."

"No sir, you never shall."

236

48

MAIRE

Prisoner of Burt

Clouds like sandstone pressed down upon us all, heavy, immoveable, relentlessly threatening a storm but never releasing it. We were crowded into Burt Castle, cattle to the slaughter, for none of us expected to survive what was happening.

I watched with a bitter taste in my mouth while Stoat checked every woman and child. Had anyone been injured? Did each person find a place to rest? Had everyone been given food? Water? How much did we have in store? He stationed guards all around the bawn and in the high towers, ready to defend if—when—the English should come. While the guards chose their positions and arranged their weapons and supplies, we looked about warily for any sign of threat. Seeing none, we had no illusion it wasn't forthcoming.

"Stoat," I said, standing beside him on the east tower where Cahir had first brought me years before. "Burt has this lovely view, in all directions. That's what makes it safe, isn't it, because you can see the enemy coming from a great distance. You have time to prepare."

"That's right, Lady Maire, and expel them before harm is done."

"And so, in truth, even if we know from where an attack is coming, the view won't help us get reinforcements or ammunition unless someone can get to our ally's camp."

"Our positions ha' been carefully planned, and Burt is well supplied." Stoat stood tall and rigid, facing the direction our largest cannon was aimed, east from whence the English would come.

"Where is Cahir?"

"I canna say, my lady. He could be anawheres. He may send word."

"But you already know. Tell me."

Stoat sighed. "He needs you here, that's all I can tell. I'll not break my word. If help is needed, best send a lad to Buncrana. Is there something?"

I looked away. "I need my husband back. I need this to all go away. I need you to tell me this has just been a terrible dream, and quite soon it will be over."

"I can only tell you this: An army of honorable and loyal men sees something more valuable in this than dreams. Cahir will come to you when he can. Soon."

Before dawn the next morning, Stoat departed, leaving in his place an officer simply known as MacDavitt. What an honor for him, perhaps, to be addressed in the same way as his clan's most legendary and admired leader. It comforted me in a way, though most of the women among us would not find comfort in any direction.

For days I walked among them while Nonie took care of my Catherine. I tried to soothe these women who were now prisoners. I was still the lady of the house, though I was every bit as much a prisoner as they. To some of them I was the enemy.

"How shamed you must be, Lady Maire," Susan Montgomery spoke in her sharp, superior tone. "Your husband marches off on this absurd venture, forcing good people to act against their will, imprisoning all of us. We are likely to starve and die if we are not killed first by our own English guns. My husband is a bishop. A bishop! And you walk about, your head high when you ought be on your knees begging God's forgiveness."

My backed stiffened. Most of the women near us gasped. Others jeered. A few of them even laughed. I turned to look upon her, thick like an oak, top heavy, her hair tightly bound beneath her white cap and her ruddy pink face interrupted by black, bead-like eyes. How I hated her.

"Mrs. Montgomery. You are a rather substantial woman," I said, and someone giggled. "Beside you I may seem small, but I am strong. I am the daughter of an English Viscount. A Preston! I married into an ancient and noble bloodline. A family of wealth, tradition, honor. A family revered for its hospitality." I paused and gestured for Nonie to take Catherine into the kitchen, because this next bit was coming like a plunging blade.

"I've quite lost patience in hospitality for you. Speak not of my husband for he is brave beyond your understanding. If I hear a single word from your disrespectful lips, I will heave you myself from the highest tower of this castle, and dust off my hands when I hear you splatter the stones."

The woman's face lost color. She spoke to me no more, but the whispers among the others were ceaseless, and I heard the cries of the children whether they made sounds or did not.

I fumed for days, helpless and with no clear target upon which to spew my growing anger. The month of May marched on as surely as the English army. I begged God to let me die rather than endure the torturous waiting.

240

49

STOAT

Glenveagh Forest

I found Cahir's camp easily enough near the town of Letterkenny. He'd left an obvious trail, meant to draw the English away from our castles to a place where we'd have more cover, more routes of escape, more chances to surprise and attack. The camp was to move twenty miles northwest, to new headquarters at Doe Castle.

"Those local lads," Cahir shook his head and laughed. "Hearing that Derry and Culmore were in Irish hands, they ran to Doe—held by the English, ye see—and shouted that the wolves were thick in the wood after their horses and beeves. The English ran out after the wolves, and our men just walked into the castle and closed the gates. The English, thus expelled, and had to walk all the way to Lifford." He laughed again. "Doe is ours just at the moment we need it."

The following day we marched until nightfall without stopping, when our spies reported small boats arriving at Fanad, a village at the northwest corner of Lough Swilly. We were rising for a skirmish in case it were English comin', but after a short while the spies returned with good news. The passengers in the boats were friends, not foe, our Lord Felim MacDavitt leading them. Cahir scratched his head a bit, but sent an escort to bring them quickly to Doe. Felim had been charged with holding Culmore garrison for us, and their arrival meant that Culmore was lost.

We hardly slept that night, wondering what news Felim would

bring. Cahir paced the floor more than an hour in a fit of anxious confusion. By dawn the weary travelers crowded into our once spacious camp, now was bursting at her seams with hungry men.

"Felim," Cahir welcomed him with a hearty hug, but it was short-lived, his eyes bright as if on fire. "What are you doing here? Could you not send word? What has happened?"

"Aye, it was for the best to move out," he said.

"I counted on you to hold Culmore. You were well supplied for it." Anger rang clear in his voice.

"The English set up for a siege just east of the garrison. With their cannons, we'd not ha' held up against them for long."

"But Felim, we knew they would do that. It was accounted for in our plan! You had enough men, enough weapons, supplies to hold out for a month. You could have shredded them! At least held out long enough to weaken them."

"You didna see it fer yourself. We burned the garrison as we left and there's the end to it. It will be long before Culmore will serve them again."

Cahir heaved a great sigh and looked out over the blue waters of Sheephaven Bay lapping at the castle's east side. "They will repair it, Felim. It's what they do. They'll probably use the people of Inishowen for slave labor. And you know what happens next? Now that they have their hold on Culmore? They have full access to Lough Foyle and the sea, for shipments of provisions and weapons, nothing to interfere. Once that's set up, they'll march north along the coast. Red Castle will fall. Then Green Castle. Then White Castle. Malin Head. Inishowen is taken, because we've no means to defend it. Don't you see?"

"They have no boats, Cahir."

"What need they with boats when they have ships, Felim. Truly! What need?"

Felim sat on a log, brooding, looking older than he ever had and I ached for him, but Cahir was right in his assessment. Retaking Inishowen now would require nothing short of a miracle.

"The Lord Deputy has put a price on our heads—£200 for me, £500 for you. Bills are being posted everywhere," Felim said.

"So, you feared betrayal. It means nothing. It was only a matter of time before he would do it. The men of Inishowen are loyal," Cahir said.

"Aye, I s'pose, but not so much the men of Connacht, the men of

East Ulster."

"And did you not realize a rising would risk our lives? Felim. When you and MacDavitt sent me off to learn under Docwra, I gathered every bit of knowledge that none of us ever had before. You should've stayed at Culmore. You should've trusted, because I knew our plan would've worked."

Cahir shook his head as the last of Felim's men settled into the castle bawn. "Well, the English will know about Doe Castle by now, and they'll come for us. We've got to move again. We've got to shift. Niall Garbh said he had a place for us should we need it. Settle your men, Felim, and wait for my return. Stoat, come with me, to see what Niall Garbh has to offer."

"You'll trust him again?" Felim asked.

"Where else can we turn?" Cahir said.

He sent a messenger to Niall, arranging a meeting in a safe, wooded location we had used once before. At dawn the following day we rode there on our fastest horses and cloaked ourselves beneath the brush. Niall arrived a few hours later.

"It's all arranged," he told us. "Just ten miles from Doe, if you follow this map you'll find a wild glen, dense with birches and oaks."

Across the ground he spread a hand-drawn map of the Glenveagh Forest. "So dense is this forest, it will shield you like a magic veil. He might stand just an arm's distance away from yourself, and yet he'd never see you at all," he said. More streaks of gray crossed his scalp than I'd noticed before, yet he seemed pleased as a child with a clever new toy.

"Follow this map strictly. The camp is carved into the forest so perfectly it can conceal a company of men as sure as the den conceals the fox. Aye, do they come for you, the art of the skirmish will terrify, harm, and reduce them with little risk to your own. Trust me in this," Niall Garbh said. "When you choose, you can march west and in fishhook fashion, swing south and back east again, to draw them in a merry circle away from Inishowen. But ye'd best get going. The English do search and their spies are aplenty."

"What assurances have you for us, aye?" Cahir asked. "Not to say I don't trust you, but you could give the English the same information and sure they'd pay plenty for it. How can we be sure it's our interests you're looking after?"

"I just gave you my best fox hole, lad. It is some sacrifice for me, but if it will ease your mind a bit, I'll send twenty of my own men to shore up your company. Does that settle you down?"

"Aye, sir. In one week, have them here."

A week later we had settled into the glen that was as Niall Garbh had described, but his men did not join us for another two days, and just ten of them, not twenty as promised. Only days later did a messenger arrive from Niall Garbh himself:

"An attack is imminent, and men enough to overwhelm. The English know your location and will burn you out. I have supplied them with three guides instructed to lead them off your path, but such diversion won't last, and they'll have you trapped. You must move out swiftly."

We prepared once again to march at midnight. Should the English arrive by morning they'd find only the bones and remains of our meal. We would be long gone on the march already planned. An uneasiness crept up my spine as we left the glen. So quickly we would be found? Was Niall playing some kind of game with us?

Cahir read my mind by the look on my face. "He's having a laugh, aye? Playing both sides of the table. Putting our men at risk while he plays his fiddle and dangles his bait. I wonder, has he offered us up in exchange for Inishowen. It's what he's always wanted. I'm the fool to have ever trusted him. Should I see him again I'll cut his throat."

I was eager for that moment. We marched as planned, attacking English strongholds, taking beeves for our sustenance as we moved, and taking down those who had turned traitor to our cause. We were powerful. We were victorious. We turned to ashes the English garrison at Armagh. The English searched recklessly for us, but we never marched in a straight line as they did, so they couldn't determine our route nor meet our speed.

We gained followers and supporters as we marched toward Dungannon, and rested sure our O'Doherty castles stood firm. We were far from Burt and Buncrana. What a joy it would be to arrive home again in triumph.

After a few days our spies reported that the English were onto Niall Garbh, and angry to find our camp deserted. They had put him in shackles. This time the laugh was ours.

50

MAIRE

Siege of Burt Castle

In late May, the celebratory fires of Beltane did not burn. Instead, the distant black smoke spoke of family homes reduced to ash, precious fruits of the harvest lost, and valuable livestock wasted. We ought to have been gathering the lettuce and cabbages, boiling mutton stew, savoring the first crab and lobster from the sea. Instead, we were clustered in Burt, our clothing filthy, our teeth aching, our temperaments in ruins. Our bellies held only the stale remains of last year's stores and the deer shot and butchered by our guards.

When Buncrana was attacked, we needed no telling. We heard the distant cannon and saw the smoke rising when they put the castle to fire. All of us wailed in terror except for the soldiers loading their guns, and even them—many being so young and inexperienced—were wide-eyed with fear. I couldn't comfort poor Catherine, who screamed in response to the others though she knew not what was coming. Soon the men and women who'd fled Buncrana rushed to Burt for refuge. Did they not realize Burt Castle would be next?

Within a week, MacDavitt saw the English coming from the northeast lowlands, filling the green surfaces with the brown, black and gray of their garments, resembling a mudslide surging relentlessly forward. The next day, a party of cavalry approached and fired shots against the castle's outer walls. The leader, sitting tall on his mount, advanced fearlessly. "I am Sir Oliver Lambert," he shouted. "I demand the surrender of this castle at once, in the name of King James our sovereign."

A shot rang out from our high tower, striking Sir Oliver in the shoulder. He fell to the ground, his men quickly coming to his aid. The English retreated, our soldiers cheered, but we were left with no illusions of safety. They would come for us again and in greater force.

There was little more we could do to prepare. We attempted to protect our food and water supply and send the women and children to the cellar to be out of harm's way. We blocked the doors and windows with tables and chairs, and made sure all supplies and ammunition would be ready and quickly at hand. After that we could only argue. The men insisting it was their duty to stand against the attackers; the women insisting it would be better to beg their mercy, thereby saving lives.

"This is all an absurd waste of time, don't you see?" Susan Montgomery said. "You cannot possibly hold out against the English army. You'll get us all killed if you don't surrender. Fools! It is useless even to try."

"You were not invited to speak, Mrs. Montgomery. Kindly hold your tongue," I said, turning to MacDavitt. "Where do you think our lord Cahir could be? Do you think he is coming? Should we hold strong until he can relieve us?"

"I've no word, Lady Maire, I only know we must do our duty as assigned until further notice. There's been none. It would be cowardice to surrender. It would be a negligent act, a mutiny."

"It would be wise!" Mrs. Montgomery shouted.

I grabbed her by the thick of her arm and shoved her against the wall. "Be silent or I will lock you in the dungeon, and do not doubt for a second that we have one ready for you."

She sank to the stone floor, her mouth left open in shock. I cared not a whit for what she thought. "Do what you must, MacDavitt. I trust you, but please keep me informed as you go, and keep an eye out for any sign of Lord Cahir."

"Yes, of course, my lady."

A week later Peg and I walked the northwest tower. We not only saw the English coming but heard them, like thunder rumbling beneath the ground. The number of soldiers had at least doubled, and they'd brought with them cannon and other artillery. I gazed across the field and felt the land beneath us quake. My gut seized and I wanted to vomit, but I refused to show such weakness. I pressed my trembling hands against my throat. Only Peg would know my heart.

"He is not coming," I whispered to her ear.

"My brother?" She grasped my shoulders so tightly I thought her fingers would break. "Pray, sweet Maire. *Pray hard.* For him, for help, and failing that, for strength."

As they approached, the English army pounded our walls with shot, and then their commander demanded surrender.

MacDavitt stepped forward on the east tower. He could not still his hands, but his voice held strong. "We hold this castle for Sir Cahir O'Doherty. Each of us will sacrifice his life in defense of this fort and all within it. To surrender will mean death at your hands. Spare us, and our Lord will hang us as traitors. Do your worst! We will hold out to the end."

Peg and I ran down the spiral stairs to the ground floor, while above us the Irish showered upon the English the most hateful shouts, curses, unspeakable threats, and wild, terrifying, guttural screams that frightened me to the marrow. With great clack and clatter the English sent the first shower of musket balls into the face of Burt Castle. Our men returned fire with more fierce screeching to fluster and baffle the enemy. The English pushed the cannon forward, the great wooden wheels creaking up the hill.

"Peg," I said. "Please check on Catherine for me. And I believe there is a Mr. Dooding down there somewhere. He has studied English law and might be able to help us. If you find him, send him up."

Some of the women followed Dooding into the hall, including Susan Montgomery. "Make them surrender! We must surrender," she screamed. I continued up the tower stairs, pulling Dooding by the wrist.

"See if you can negotiate a surrender that spares everyone's lives, Mr. Dooding. See what you can do," I said.

Dooding looked uneasy, but he nodded, and after MacDavitt waved a small white flag for a temporary truce, he raised a timid, shaky voice to the English commander. "I am George Dooding, solicitor for the O'Doherty family. The Irish offer to surrender, but we shall require terms meeting these three conditions. First, there must be a jointure for Lady Maire O'Doherty and child. Second, all goods and properties belonging to the inhabitants shall be respected. And third, all lives within Burt Castle will be spared." Dooding nodded in gentlemanly fashion and took a step back from the battlement.

In response, the English said nothing but pushed their big cannon nearer to our wall. Suddenly my rage surfaced. I stomped up the east tower to the top, my shawl billowing in the wind, and glared down upon the commander and his men. "If you dare to put a breach in the wall of Burt Castle, you'll quickly find the bishop's wife stuffed in that hole. And then I say, *fire away!*"

The Irish soldiers cheered, and some of the English laughed. Susan Montgomery charged up the tower steps and screamed down upon the soldiers. "You must ignore such a wicked suggestion. *I am* the bishop's wife!" she cried. "You will suffer under the Devil himself if I am harmed!"

The commander scoffed. "The King's honor for which we fight is far more important than the life of any woman."

The troublesome lady screamed and cried and ran back down to the cellar, seeking comfort from anyone who would still listen to her. By the end of the day, I reached an agreement with the commander. "Allow us one more night in the castle, unthreatened by your guns. One more night in peace within our home, and then with tomorrow's dawning we shall surrender, one and all."

Sir Oliver likely longed for a night's rest for himself and his men. He nodded agreement and with a wave of his hand, set a number of guards around the castle perimeter and sent the rest of his soldiers back to their camp.

How I prayed that night, and wondered, and hoped. Could it be possible that Cahir was close to us? That he might arrive in the night, attack the English, and set us free? Or maybe he would skirmish at their edges and draw them away from Burt that we might then escape? A thin ribbon of hope floated across my mind that Cahir was already surrounding the castle and the English camp, setting up his battle plan, ensuring our safety and freedom. I felt his hand gentlly brush across my hair, his breath warm upon my lips. We could forgive each other our hateful words. We could get back what we'd once had among the bluebells.

"See Da?" my sweet Catherine asked. I pulled her to my lap and hugged her.

"At this minute, he is riding Asher across the great meadow. We will pray hard, won't we? That your father comes to us in the night, and we will cry for joy when we see his face. Pray with all your heart," I said, though she was too young to understand. "See him in your precious dreams."

I slept little, alert to every lonely cry of a wolf, every high-pitched call of the long-eared owl. I wished I could hear the soothing rhythm of the ocean or even the wind in the trees, but the night was deathly still, and with each hour that passed the truth cut deeper into my soul.

He was not coming.

As the first light broke the darkness, I gathered into the great hall everyone who had served myself and Cahir these past few years. With Catherine clinging at my neck, I bowed my head to them in respect. "My friends, today will be difficult, more so than any of us have experienced. No matter what happens, nor what is done or said, you must all stand proud for our clan, for Inishowen, and for your own strength these past days. Do not give them the satisfaction of your fear. Stand tall and show them your best."

In moments the dawn filled the sky. I pushed the English women to the front and we opened the battered castle doors. Sir Oliver and several of his men were waiting just outside. Sir Oliver did not dismount from his horse, nor bid us good morning. "The prisoners from Derry shall be returned to their homes," he said. "Lady Montgomery, we have arranged a personal escort to return you immediately to the Bishop at Raphoe." She puffed out her breast like a rooster and dared a haughty glance back at me.

The rest of us waited while these orders were carried out, clenching our fear between our teeth until Sir Oliver addressed us. "Lady Maire O'Doherty, Lady Eliza O'Doherty, and all the rest of you in their company, are now prisoners of the English army. You shall all be transported by ship to Dublin Castle, where you shall be held for questioning. You will be escorted by my soldiers to meet the ship at Rathmullen. You depart immediately."

I, Catherine, Lady Eliza, Peg, Nonie, Rita, Mr. Dooding, MacDavitt, and a few of his men were shoved aboard two small boats taken from our own sheds, that carried us across the Crana river and around Inch Island to the ship, *Tramontane*, bobbing at Rathmullen's wharf. Too weary even to be frightened, we boarded the ship as prisoners and huddled together in the stinking hold below deck. What became of the other soldiers who had defended Burt Castle, we were not to know. If yet they lived, I hoped they would get word to Cahir.

51

STOAT

Kilmacrennan

As June became July, our fish-hook march ended in west Donegal. It had been successful, in that our contacts and support had grown, and our enemies in those regions to the south were few. For all that, we also knew the English had laid ruin to much of Inishowen, and their presence had hindered our spies. We'd received little news, and I feared some of our men had been captured or killed. We held in good faith the reason we'd not heard from MacDavitt, there being no need to report the safety of Burt Castle. As we crossed the fields near Woodlands Grove, we glimpsed the ship *Tramontane* just leaving the mouth of Lough Swilly.

"How I wish our attempt to board her had been successful," Cahir said. "So often the weather works against us. If we could have captured the shipment of munitions, we'd have gained a fierce advantage for the next battle. I wonder if they return to Dublin empty or carry away their spoils."

One thing we had learned from our spies was that the English had pressed Irish soldiers, specifically from a branch of the O'Neills, to help them retake Doe Castle. We were surprised they hadn't already captured it during our southward march when we couldn't defend the castle, but sometimes English operations are slow. With the ship away, they'd have to march north from Letterkenny to reach Doe. This gave us a mighty advantage to cut them off from their path northward and attack when they were weary and weak.

While our men pitched camp just west of Kilmacrennan, Cahir,

Felim, and I searched for the most advantageous location from which to strike. We discovered a dense stretch of marsh along the route the English would have to take. Recent rains had ruined the ground for artillery and only soldiers on foot would get through. Considering the depth of mud, even their march would be slowed. We set about cutting discreet marks upon trees at the highest points from which our soldiers could fire muskets down upon the English heads.

Confident of our position, we began gathering the guns and powder, swords and skeans, and heavy doublets of light and dark brown that would blend into the colors of the marsh. I made sure we had our iron helmets, especially important for our men in the marsh, their heads being the only targets that might show above the tall grasses. With the advance work done, we retreated to the camp to rest.

"We have word the English muster at Letterkenny," Cahir said. "I'd wager they'll begin the march at dawn. Our timing is good. I've also had news that the English released Niall Garbh and sent him home to Castlefin. He once promised us a company of men. He owes us and he knows it. With some of our men sick, and others injured, sure I wouldn't have minded that company to strengthen our force."

"Again, you would trust him?" Felim said.

Cahir scoffed. "Not at all. Sure it's to his benefit if we hold Doe. It's O'Donnell and MacSweeney country, a big part of his dominion. But he'd expose us as quick as I could blink to gain an edge with the English. We can win this without him. Let's be in position well before mid-morning."

In the pre-dawn darkness, we moved with cat-like stealth toward our positions. Despite the struggle of walking through marsh, our men—700 of them—settled low into the wet, mushy ground, arranged their pikes, muskets, ammunition, and disappeared into the tall, spiky grasses. Our best shooters climbed the trees and loaded their weapons. As the sun rose, my breast filled with pride for these men. Though I knew where they were hidden, I myself was not able to see them.

Felim and his men were positioned at the west edge of the marsh, while Cahir and I chose the highest point on the east edge, next to a leaning oak. Cahir used the tree for cover, while I stayed low, MacTyre beside me, and Rudd next to him.

"Cahir, stay down. Don't forget to fasten your helmet," I said.

"Aye, Stoat. Settle now. I'll have an eye for the English. Most likely the scouts will see them first, but I've an inkling some could come up from behind. Sure I'll see them right enough to alert the lads."

Minute by minute the sky grew brighter, and still I could not see our men among the marsh unless they moved about. I was growing more excited. This battle was sure to be a legendary victory, so well planned and positioned were we. Our men at Doe Castle were prepared to hold off a siege, but with prowess and a bit of luck they'd never have to.

By the angle of the sun, I figured it was mid-morning or a bit past before we heard sounds of an approaching army still a fair distance away, but tension was rising in the air, and in my own shoulders. Cahir was well hidden, but he was anxious as well, and often poked his head into view.

"My Lord, the English are coming. Can you see them yet? And put on your helmet."

"Why d'ye keep sayin' that to him," MacTyre asked. "Yer like a worried old marm!"

Cahir spoke quiet and low. "I'll put it on when they come into the glen. Just now I need a full view. Keep the men in position."

MacTyre began to fiddle with his musket, making rattling noises sure to give us away.

"Cut it out, MacTyre."

"I have to, Stoat. It's jammed."

"Already? What ha' ye done to it? I canna see."

"Here, lemme have it," Rudd said.

The English were closer, I could hear them talking. Our men at the front had been warned to hold fire until they could see the soldiers before them, making sure they were in range, but sure they felt the same as I, as if someone poured cold water down my back. They English were coming. We'd surprise them all right—and blast them all from the earth!

The sun was full ablaze when I saw them through the marsh. I hoped the sun blinded them, but Cahir was out of position. "My Lord, take cover!"

"Stand firm, Stoat," Cahir said. "I'm covered."

"Bleedin' piece o' shite, this weapon!" MacTyre complained.

"Shut up, blockhead!" Rudd hissed.

Shots exploded from the front line of our marsh, the English suddenly shouting, some screaming and running, trying desperately for cover, but the cover was ours. In minutes they were flat on the ground, returning fire, shooting blindly into the marsh at our hidden soldiers. Rudd fired, then MacTyre. I turned to Cahir. He'd moved from behind the tree for a better view of the battle.

"My Lord, your helmet! Get down!"

"Stand firm lads! *Ar nDuthchas! Ar nDuthchas! Pound them straight to Hell!*" Cahir shouted.

A volley screamed across the marsh and I saw Cahir's jaw snap upward, then his body fell to a heap like a wet sack of stones.

"Cahir! My Lord! *Get up!*" I panicked. Oh Lord Jesus help us, GET UP CAHIR! I leaped out to reach him though I knew by the pain in my gut that he was dead, his skull opened and spilling blood, his face blank and limp, his body awkward and still. I tried for one foolish second to lift him to his feet, as if I could make him all right, but another volley roared past my ears and I screamed for help. Never could I leave his body to the enemy's hate and cruelty. Rudd and MacTyre tried to reach me and the shooting paused for a moment, the men below us in confusion. What had happened? What had suddenly shifted? And the word spread like a savage tornado screaming across the marsh: *Cahir O'Doherty is dead.*

Once the English realized, their voices roared and their volleys doubled, wasting the marsh around them. Our men bolted, dropped their muskets and ran in every direction, many of them falling as soon as they left their cover. MacTyre and Rudd tugged me away, and Felim behind us tried to collect Cahir's body, dragging it as he crawled through the battered, muddy ground, but then the artillery engaged from high ground, flattening the marsh grass and hills to a sickening sea of mud and blood. Felim had to release Cahir and run.

As MacTyre and Rudd dragged me away, I searched frantically behind me for Cahir's face. I saw only the upturned helmet, the bloodied ginger hair, and the torn yellow sleeve of his undershirt.

52

MAIRE

Dublin Castle

I couldn't breathe. My heart pounded and my chest ached as if leather straps pulled ever tighter around me. Had something happened to seize my heart? Was something in the air causing me to feel so? Yet I struggled. Peg tried to calm me, rubbing my back as I leaned forward, trying to find relief. When at last I could draw the air more comfortably, I realized indeed how filthy and fetid were our surroundings. For days we sweated and nearly starved in the hold of the English ship, but the call of the seagulls told me we'd soon reach the docks at Dublin.

Upon arrival we were marched from the dock and through the gates of Dublin Castle, the crowds jeering as if we were criminals. Rough hands shoved me and the others into Bermingham tower where most prisoners were kept. The dim stone rooms were already crowded, with no place for me and Catherine to sit. The small shafts high on the wall let in little light, and we followed the beam as it moved across the floor, having nothing better to do. Catherine's belly rumbled. I begged the guard for water for the poor girl. "She's only three years old! Please? She doesn't understand what is happening."

"Nothing happens until the Lord Deputy has inspected the prisoners," the guard said.

"Well then, why don't you bring him?"

He slammed his half pike against the wooden door that held us in, and we were forced to wait in growing discomfort.

Hours later I heard the heavy boots of the guard approaching, and then he announced, "The Honorable Lord Deputy of Ireland, Sir Arthur Chichester."

At last Chichester had arrived, and with one look at him I wished he hadn't. He stepped in front of the doorway but remained at least a foot distant as if we were all diseased. We must have smelled so, but after such treatment, it was his own fault, not ours. I noticed first his high forehead and thinning brownish hair above. Then the falling ruff at his neck. Between his dark mustache and wiry beard, his lips were thin and frowning. But his eyes? They were flat, black, and revealed as much emotion as a blot of ink on an old brick floor.

"Lord Deputy, sir, I am Lady Maire O…"

"Step back," the guard said.

"Bailiff, your list," Chichester said.

"Yes, sir," the bailiff began. "Lady O'Doherty."

"I am here."

"Say nothing!" the bailiff said, and placed a mark by my name.

"Lady O'Hanlon."

"Peg!" I blurted but was ignored.

"Lady Elizabeth O'Doherty. "

"Catherine O'Doherty."

"Nonie McCarthy."

"Rita Coyle."

"We must question Lady O'Hanlon first," Chichester said. "Who are these two?"

"They are servants of the O'Doherty family. They are cooks," the bailiff replied.

"Send them to work in our kitchens."

"Yes sir," the bailiff answered.

"And where are the men?"

"Just up the stairs, sir."

The Lord Deputy turned away.

"Oh, my Lord Deputy, please. A moment?" I begged. "My daughter needs water, and I must get word to my husband. He will not know where we are. Could there be a way that I might send…"

Chichester turned on his heel to face me, a half grin rising on those thin lips. "You wish to send a message? You wish to speak to O'Doherty, do you? Well then, Lady O'Doherty, he is closer than you may imagine, just across the courtyard there. Speak to your heart's content. *Do.* Tell all."

He gestured toward the small square window. Peg looked out and then jumped in front of it. "Get away, Maire. You can't look. It's a trick, that's all. A cruel trick. Turn away."

I should have listened, but I resisted. No Preston used the word *can't.* I gently pushed Peg aside, though she'd begun to cry. At the far end of the castle, upon the gate facing Dublin town, was a small, rounded shape upon a spike, rising above the wooden posts. It could have been a head. That's what these English liked to do with their criminals, hang severed heads in grotesque fashion as a warning to others. It could have been anyone's head. There was something on the shape, though. It could only be hair, so I was right, it was a prisoner killed. But then a gust of wind caused the hair to lift, and revealed a flash of ginger. It came to me as if someone had turned a page in a book and pressed it before my eyes. Broc. *Broc.* Suddenly from my belly a heat surged uncontrollably upward through my chest, squeezing through the tightness of my neck, and then flooding violently into my face. From there it erupted, a terrible venom, a hellish roar. I wretched in vile pain from my empty stomach. My thoughts dissolved. My legs collapsed beneath me.

I fell on the cold stone floor where I lay and cried for hours, faintly aware that Catherine clung to my arm and Peg stroked my back. Lady Eliza cried too, sitting on a wooden stool, her hands to her face, and head in her lap. When I found the strength to crawl, it was to her. "Eliza, I'm so sorry. You have lost your beautiful son. And I have lost my loving husband. My love."

"We are bereft," she said, her voice just a whisper.

"My heart is in pieces, and I am forever shamed. My last words to him were that he should never speak to me again. I was angry. *Stupid.* I didn't mean it. I never wanted…"

"You couldn't have known that it…" she broke into tears. "Couldn't have known he would fall."

My gut twisted yet again. "My foolish, unwanted wish. I'd cut my own tongue if I could take those words back. Can you ever forgive me?"

"You must forgive yourself, dear. Cahir forgave you immediately, I cannot doubt it," she said. "But the English brutes who did this cruel thing to him I shall never forgive."

"Nor I. But it means…his body so destroyed…that we cannot meet in Heaven." My tears burst forth anew.

Elizabeth shook her head, her eyes wide and black with fury. She pulled me to her and lifted my face from her lap. "You listen to me. I don't care what the churchmen have said, for *fear* is their only offering. Our Cahir lived without fear. Our Cahir was beautiful, strong, and wise. Do you think for one moment that God would create such a creature and not want him by his side when his mortal life was through? Cahir was lifted to Heaven the moment he breathed his last. Know this as I do. You and I will meet him there when our times come, and don't you ever doubt it."

It was the most loving and comforting thing she could have said. It didn't stop my weeping, but it did restore my hope.

Had we only the English to rely on, surely we'd all have died from thirst and starvation, but Nonie managed to bring us water, soup, and bread. We went for it, eager as dogs after the wretched thirst and hunger we had suffered. Catherine regained some color in her cheeks though she was weak and confused. Eliza was also weakened, but somehow the hatred for our English captors stiffened our resolve to survive.

Peg was the first to be called out for questioning. She was arrested—not for anything she had done, but because she was an O'Hanlon by marriage. Her husband was a loyalist but he'd led a revolt in Armagh after the English had swindled his father and taken some of his lands. He was marked as part of Cahir's rebellion, and he was glad for it. The interrogators soon realized Peg had been with us at the time, the women held captive at Burt, and could not have been involved in her husband's scheme. She was returned to us, shaken, but not so much that she couldn't give me a wink.

That they questioned Lady Eliza who could barely stand simply demonstrated their lack of conscience. She could give them nothing but proud and loving memories of her son, and his love for Inishowen. In each case, the answer was the same. She too had been captive at Burt Castle with no means of participating in a rebellion. We had all been captives. Didn't they understand?

When my turn came, I was taken directly to Chichester himself. I would not show fear. I would not give him such satisfaction.

"When did you begin your plan for this rebellion?"

"Sir, I planned nothing but a dinner party."

"It was a ruse. Admit it. You and your traitorous husband tricked good English people into helping unleash your murderous attack."

"Sir, there was no ruse. People simply came to dinner. No one was attacked. No one was killed."

"You lie and scheme like every other Irish creature."

"I am English, sir."

"You are guilty. This is not the last time we will talk. I will get your confession. I will discover every sordid detail, and any of you who had the slightest part in it will hang."

Several days later, Jenico at last arrived at Dublin Castle from Gormanston. And with him was my dear friend and protector, Stoat, his body thin, his eyes rimmed red. He fell to his knees before me, though the enclosure of our chamber kept us apart. I myself was trembling.

"How did you get here?" I asked. "How did you escape the English? Inishowen? You must tell me everything, and start with what happened to Cahir. I must know. *Please.*"

"My lady, it pains me so. 'Twas at Kilmacrennan where we'd set a fine trap for the English. We should have destroyed them all. But we'd barely begun when Cahir stepped from behind a tree to encourage the men. One blast from an English musket and he fell. It was finished. We were all finished. Many died with him, and the place will ever be a bloody scar upon the earth.

"Those who survived scattered. After hiding in the north for weeks with Rudd and MacTyre, we separated. They returned to their homes, and I moved by night to find my way to Lady Finola. For many years she's had a home near Kilmacrennan. She welcomed and restored me. I told her I wished to tell you about Cahir before anyone else, she gave me a fast horse that I might hurry to your side, but I was too late. The cruel English."

"Yes," I said. "The cruel English."

"Stoat has told me every detail," Jenico said, "I don't believe Cahir's rising ever had a chance of success, but I understand why he did it, why his men demanded it. His was a shocking and unavoidable fate. You must also know that Felim has since been arrested, among twenty-five others. I fear their executions will be slated even before they'll be brought to trial."

I started to cry again, there was nothing for it, so great a part of our lives was Felim, as had been his brother MacDavitt. Hadn't there been enough deaths without having to execute good men? But no, they had to make a spectacle of it. Oh, if I could be a queen even for a day, I'd put every greedy and violent person on a ship to nowhere.

"I shall begin negotiations with the Lord Deputy for your freedom," Jenico said, "but know you he is a big cat with several mice at play. The separation will take time."

In fact, it required eighty days to unwrap Chichester's oily fingers from around us. He had no proof against us, only harsh words from people who knew nothing but wanted to feel important. Only when we'd become a nuisance and an expense did he finally release us, and still I had to march into the kitchens and take Nonie and Rita by the hands, making sure he could not keep them as his slaves.

From the day he showed us Cahir's head on the spike, I had begun to nurture a special hatred for Sir Arthur Chichester. My restored freedom renewed my spirit and stirred my desire to truly understand this enemy. I began writing letters to everyone I knew who'd had dealings with him. I wished to learn about his deeds, his associates, and his intentions.

53

MAIRE

County Meath

Nonie was delighted to return to the Gormanston Castle kitchen, and to show its finer features to Rita. Less happy was Jenico's cook, Arden, who had thought of the kitchen as her own for years. The softening element was young Theo, a handsome chef's apprentice hired for his particular skill in cooking meats. The three women doted on the lad, and I enjoyed the first good meal I'd had in months. I only wished some others could have shared the pleasure. To stand at the kitchen door and face the parlor where Cahir and I first talked was to recall the joyfulness of Christmas, but then it quickly faded to the opposite—my sorrow over such a loss, the painful loneliness without him, and always the bitter regret over things said and not said, and things I could have done differently.

Upon our release at Dublin, Peg returned to her home in Armagh to join her husband who would soon be sent to the Swedish Army as punishment for his part in the rebellion. Lady Eliza accompanied her most of the way, then hired an escort to take her back to Inishowen where she meant to live among her cousins.

Catherine had embraced Gormanston's charms completely, climbing the stairs, tumbling upon the beds in each room, and then running down the stairs again to romp through the garden. I prayed it would be long before she'd understand the loss of her father.

Jenico, my dear brother who had rescued us all from that prison, had much on his mind. He sent wide-eyed, meaningful looks across the breakfast table, hoping for an opening in which to speak so that I would listen. I'd avoided it for days. I knew what was coming. Though I disliked it, this morn I allowed the smallest of nods.

"Had Cahir succeeded," Jenico began, "it might have changed by great measure how people thought, how lands would be handled, how religions would be accepted or tolerated. His was a grand but impossible dream, God love him. But my standing in the peerage, and my fortune by way of partnerships and trade, have been compromised. Lord Deputy Chichester charged me and Sir Thomas Fitzwilliams heavily for our sureties concerning Cahir's good behavior—financially calamitous for both of us. It shall only get worse. Our issue, not just for me but for your future as well, and Catherine's, is to make serious changes before the wolves sense greater weakness.

"We must find ways to distance ourselves from anything related to a rebellion, and sadly to the O'Doherty clan. I see the pain on your face even as I say it, but in your heart, you know the truth of it. You wouldn't be accepted by any family here, nor be acknowledged by any society, nor would Catherine be accepted to any schools. She would be teased and ridiculed, and I dare say other children would throw rocks at her even though they had no understanding of why. In the end, you would both live in loneliness and poverty.

"What I'm saying, Maire, is…"

"Yes. I know. It is a sharp sword to my heart. But I accept your advice and I acknowledge the truth of it. I must remarry. Change my name. I must give my darling girl a promising start in life. I cannot linger in deep mourning. I must tear apart my past life, and hers, to rebuild them in good light. Through new names, new lives, and new connections, we can also disconnect your position from any lasting stain.

"Our father and our mother," Jenico said, "—we must do it for them and their memory. You do understand, we owe them that much. However, I have what I hope will be good news to your ears."

"Have you? Good news is most welcome. Tell me," I said.

"There is a man of your acquaintance from several years ago. He has settled here in County Meath, a barrister of good income, of pleasing looks, of good humor. He owns a spacious house not far away, with a garden and a fishpond. If it is not too soon for me to say, having learned of your circumstance, already he has asked for your hand."

"Goodness! He must think I am wealthy."

Jenico shook his head. "He is fully aware of your circumstance. He is not troubled by it."

"His name?"

"Anthony Warren, the son of William Warren, of Warrenstown. William had some business dealings with Cahir's father, Sean Og, several years past."

"I do recall the name, but it has been so long ago. And I must say at this moment, to consider another man and another marriage, it causes my stomach to burn."

"I am sorry, good sister. Truly, I am. Cahir was a brother to me, after all. But at the same time, I must ask, because we must all carry on. Will you consider it?"

"Of course. Yes, I will. But please understand I have some things to do first. Some situations that must be made right. Accounts to be settled. Allow me a month, that I may set things, and myself, in proper order before he and I should meet again? It is hardly an appropriate grieving period, as mother would've said, but the circumstance is unusual. In a month's time I will be able to present myself in a better light."

He nodded. "I shall speak to him. In the meantime, is there some way I might help with these situations?"

"Wait a moment. Did you say he is a barrister? Mister Warren is a barrister?"

"He is. And a good one."

"Ah. Perhaps we could meet much sooner then. One or two situations I must resolve could benefit from a legal perspective."

"I'm sure he'd be delighted to help.

"Thank you. You might not expect so, but I learned some useful information while wasting away in prison. I'll need the time to gather a bit more, and then I'd like to consult with him briefly."

"I shall arrange it."

"Already you've done so much to help, but after that, one more thing. I will need Stoat, and some good horses that will carry us swiftly and safely to Inishowen and back again. I must speak with some people there."

"Consider it done, sister. But no fancy coach for you this time." Jenico grinned.

54

STOAT

Mongavlin Castle

The autumn winds swept through the glens by the time Lady Maire found me in Gormanston's stables. I had spent my days working there, keeping myself busy, my hands constantly in motion whether grooming the horses, shoveling the dung, raking hay, cleaning the tack, or hauling the water. Work was comforting. Work gave me purpose.

I expected she would come to me one day. I'd seen her in a vision, walking across a broad open field that gently dipped from hill to valley, the tall grasses turned gold and swaying in the wind, a fine castle just footsteps from a flowing river with high stone towers to mind the river's traffic. At first it seemed a vision of our beloved Buncrana, but in truth it more closely resembled Mongavlin Castle, on the bank of the River Foyle. I tried to hold the vision, but like all such transitory things it did not last.

When she came, she hugged me and I was somehow renewed. Whatever she desired, I would provide, no matter the cost.

"Stoat, my good friend. I am in need of a tremendous favor. Will you take me back to Inishowen?" she asked. "It will be a hard thing to endure, filled with memories both lovely and painful, but we will not stay long. I need help to travel out of sight. I trust only you."

"I am ever your servant, Lady Maire. You must know that."

"Thank you. It's just that I've no wish to be seen by people there. I couldn't bear to speak to anyone except the few I must meet. You've always been masterful at moving in shadow. Can you help me in this way, if we leave tomorrow?"

I bowed my head in complete submission. "I'll fix up our packs straight away."

"We go to Mongavlin Castle. It's abandoned, but clean and fair."

"I know it well. Lady Finola lived there when Lord Cahir and I were to take Derry Garrison. Niall Garbh had cast her out because he wanted to store all his plunder there, the greedy old fool. But Cahir had no intention of giving Niall anything taken from Derry, for he'd done nothing to earn it. Cahir cast him out and put Lady Finola back where she belonged. He was grand, he was, our Cahir." I smiled at the memory. It brought a tear to Lady Maire's eye, but sometimes 'tis a comfort to hear stories of loved ones. It keeps them alive.

"Lady Finola still possesses the castle though she can no longer live there. It's a safe meeting place. I have written to her and a few others who will join us."

"Whomever we should collect, and whatever else you require, we'll gather all as we go, aye?"

"Truly you are a gift from God, Stoat."

I was pleased that Nonie joined us on the journey, leaving young Catherine in the care of Rita and Jenico's cooks. We left before dawn, avoiding other travelers. We passed Newry on the second day and stopped next at Armagh to collect Lady Peg well before the ship for Sweden would arrive to carry her and her husband into exile. Dungannon Village was not far after that, and we turned west to collect Lady Eliza at Letterkenny.

I saw myself as their humble servant, protector, or executer, as it might fit the occasion. The ways were rugged, and keeping out of sight sometimes impossible, but we kept moving. We arrived at Mongavlin on a cold but sunny afternoon, no one in sight, the slope of the land and sway-ing grasses just as I'd seen in my vision. Then, one by one those we had collected followed Lady Maire down the hill and through the great cas-tle door. A spark shot up my spine. Something most unusual, something mighty and monumental was about to happen. What role I would play? I followed them inside.

Lady Finola had already arrived and greeted us warmly, her beauty as diverting as always. After stowing the horses, I got a blazing fire going in the hearth while she offered everyone wine and good brown bread. There were wooden chairs around a small table, but little else for comfort. I took my natural position, guarding the door, and Lady Maire proceeded to her purpose. They were a council, the five of them, more determined than anyone might imagine, and to my eyes, powerful.

"Please, sit with me. You are all dear and loving friends," Lady Maire said, and the women gathered at the table, clasping hands to form a ring. "We've endured the most terrible times, and unspeakable losses."

"You most of all," Peg said.

"I'm not sure that's so, but I do know that at this moment my grief is so fierce it moves me to action. We face the worst of injustices—to be heaped upon us by those who have already taken everything. While our circumstances are hellish in nature, these men of power conspire even further—as if *their* intentions are the only right and natural course of progress. You all know. You all have the same searing frustration inside. It is unacceptable that these criminals shall succeed and profit from their crimes. And they are crimes. Atrocities! There is nothing noble about burning madly the lands they themselves wish to own, starving and murdering women and children as if for sport, and then decorating themselves as heroes.

Finola groaned loudly. "So true!" she said. "So true."

"I also know that each one of us has knowledge, and courage, and powers so rarely used they are quite unrecognized by the men in our world, except for our good friend Stoat. These gifts are our weapons, exceeding by far the power of the pike or the musket ball," Lady Maire continued. "We have learned in silence. We have seen things we were expected to ignore, but we ignore nothing, and forget nothing. Our memory is sharper than the sword.

"We will make sure we ourselves are not ignored, by getting the attention of the right people, whether they give it willingly or no. And to them we will deliver truths unbearable. Truths that force them to act if for nothing more than their own survival. Lady Finola, do you have writing papers with you? And quill an ink?"

"I do, Lady Maire. I do."

"Wonderful. Then we shall start our list."

"A list?" Lady Eliza asked.

"Yes. We have just one chance. We must go at this with great care, making sure nothing is missed, and that our approach is like a battle plan, but better. We will create our own way, something they've never seen before and cannot control. We must succeed. We *shall* succeed, brilliantly."

"At the top of our list must be Niall Garbh," Lady Finola said. "He has been a source of trouble and woe to me since I first married The O'Donnell. All my sons are dead now, and much blood is on his hands, so much of it caused by his greed and arrogance. He certainly urged our Cahir in his rising, hoping to enrich himself from it, and I'm sure he meant to take Inishowen. I shall write to the King's Privy Council. They will know the things he has done while pretending to be loyal to the crown. It will be well received, for they have already tired of his lies and demands."

"Yes," Lady Maire said. "I will help in any way you need, and we must secure a trusted messenger who can get your letter into the proper hands."

"I can help with that, As I did for Lord Cahir," I said.

"Thank you, Stoat. Yes, I remember. Second on our list, I think, should be what happened at Armagh, and our good brother O'Hanlon. We can't have him sent to the brutish Swedes after he supported Cahir as he did," Lady Maire said.

Peg nodded. "My husband's father has become weak of mind, and Lord Chichester takes advantage," Peg said. "His plan for the Armagh plantation will force all of our people off more than half of the land. It would displace so many relatives and families. His father was told he must agree or go to prison. For the crime of defending his own father, my Eochy's exile has already been confirmed, the ship on its way. My husband must go, and I with him. May God damn Chichester forever!"

Lady Maire shook her head. "It is not too late. You are here with us, and so something can be done. We must make sure the ship to Sweden is delayed or see that you and Eochy board the ship bound for Flanders by mistake. Stoat, do you perhaps have acquaintances on the wharfs?"

"Of course, my lady. I'm quite sure such *mistakes* happen every day. I'll see to it back in Dublin."

"Thank you, dear friend. Then we come to number three on our list: Buncrana. For Cahir's memory, this ancestral castle must be saved. The English have occupied Burt Castle, and beautiful Elagh as well, but I wish to know about Buncrana, what remains of it. I hear already it has been leased to someone. I wonder, who is this man? Does he have a wife? What are his plans? My lovely and trusted friend, Nonie, you have been at my side so many years. I must ask this tremendous favor, one that I hope you'll not mind. Might you go there, pretending to seek a position, and gather such information? I should go myself but if I'm seen it could raise alarm and perhaps spoil some of our plans.

"My lady, 'tis no trouble at all, but my pleasure to do so. I'm quite curious about Buncrana as well. I will learn all I can," Nonie said.

"Stoat, will you take her? And come back to me quickly?"

I nodded once again, though I did so love our Buncrana and feared what we might find.

"That brings me to number four," Maire said, "which shreds our hearts like a cat's claw. Lady Eliza, can you tell it, or shall I?"

Eliza was already weeping, the silver streaks marking her pale cheeks. "I will tell it," she said. "I *need* to tell it. When Cahir started his rising, he protected his younger brothers, too young to fight in battle. He sent them away to a safe place with foster families who gave them great love and education. But Sir Arthur Chichester, most foul among the creatures on God's good Earth, sent his vultures to track the boys down, that they could not later make hereditary claim for O'Doherty Clan and Inishowen. He meant to execute them or ship them away to be slaves. He captured my boy Rory, questioned him most cruelly, and then put him in the English army, though he is just a child. I heard a single rumor, that Rory escaped to Austria, but there's been nothing more. I know not if he lives or has died.

"My youngest, Sean, remains in hiding where he will not be found until we can scrape the scum of Chichester from this land. Sean is our hope, *our future*. He is the bloodline that will restore the House of O'Doherty. Pray you all that Chichester is blinded to all our children; that he feels God's wrath in his gut; that he never reaps the wealth he desires; and, that he shall never know the joy of his own children."

Everyone at the table wept, and I meself had to blot my cheeks with my sleeve. I looked to Maire, whose face was red, swollen, and wet with tears. I knew her gladness that Catherine was a girl who would not pose a threat to Chichester. At the same time, I wondered as I often did, why Englishmen who had lived under Queen Mary and Queen Elizabeth, still assumed women were powerless and inferior.

After a moment, Lady Maire regained her composure and spoke with a strength even greater than before. "We must all be prepared at any time to protect young Sean," she said, "and should any rumor start about him it must be dispelled at once. There *is* no Sean until he faces no threat."

She straightened her back and hardened her face with determination. "The last on our list, number five, is Lord Deputy Chichester himself." She looked at each of us in turn, for all had experienced some interaction with him and knew his nature. This would be the most difficult task of all. "His treatment of my husband will never be forgotten. I must confront him, for he owes an extraordinary debt. Should he live a thousand lifetimes he could never repay it. But he will pay heavily. This task I must do, and alone. I cannot endanger any of you, should my plan go awry."

"I will go," I shouted. "Let him die upon my sword. It is my job, is it not?"

"No. Not this time, Stoat. There's something else I must ask of you, and there is no task of greater importance, not even Chichester. We must speak of it privately."

"I am always at your service, my lady. Whatever the task, I shall do it, without question," I said. "I await your instructions."

Lady Finola scoffed. "Dear Maire. You are fierce and you are valiant. No one at this table believes you could ever fail. You will scold Sir Chichester down to a boy in his swaddlings. But you cannot, you *must* not do it alone. He holds no reverence for a woman and you'd never get through the gate. You shall need an army, ferocious with guns and blades, and smart in the ways of war. It's the only thing this man truly understands. As God provides, I just happen to have one available." She revealed a wicked grin. "You shall be escorted by my Scotsmen."

"Your Scotsmen?" Lady Maire asked. "I thought you no longer maintained your Scottish guards."

"You are right, but they served me well right here at Mongavlin Castle, and they so admired the place, that they have settled here, more than 100 of them. They are Campbells, all, and they've surrounded this castle with fine homes they built themselves. Often, I believe, they are bored by the quiet life and would welcome an opportunity to use their well-honed skills. Besides, they've despised Lord Chichester since first he arrived at Carrickfergus. How many do you need? Remember this will be a show of strength but also for your safety."

"Ten!" I shouted, knowing Lady Maire was likely to request only one or two.

"She shall have them," Lady Finola declared. "Lady Maire, you will arrive at Dublin Castle unnoticed, as if on a windstorm, and suddenly Chichester shall be surrounded by the biggest, tallest, and fiercest warriors of all. And let him believe you command these, and 100 more waiting just

around the bend. Demand what you will. Accept no terms. When your requirements are fulfilled, just such a windstorm shall lift you up and deliver
you away.

55

MAIRE

Crimes and Settlements

My Scottish escorts brought a piercing reminder of my first encounter with Cahir, for they all wore long yellow tunics, linens most likely dyed in urine. Instead of a leather jerkin or cloak, they wore thick, heavy furs of bear, wolf and sheep. The men were all soldiers of frightful size and the furs made them look monstrous, but it was late winter when we arrived in Dublin and I envied the warmth of those furs compared to my own woolens.

We remained outside of Dublin's wall and rested our horses in a farmer's barn while we put our plan into action. My first step was to call on my baker, Rita, who was most happy to assist me. Together we gathered the yellowish mushrooms that thrived beneath Gormanston's oaks and beech trees—the ones my mother had warned me never to touch. When dried, ground, and added to the dough, they introduced a nut-like flavor to fresh baked bread. Having worked in Chichester's kitchens before, Rita wasn't questioned when she baked and delivered her baskets full of loaves. The bread was not so heavily poisoned as to kill the castle guards, but the number of men fit and able to deter us would be considerably reduced.

Next, while two of our Scots distracted the guards at the main gate, we circled around to the west side and crossed a ditch to the postern gate. Here a guard was on his knees wretching onto the flagstones. One of our Scots knocked him out with the hilt of his sword. From there, we quickly darted past the Parliamentary Hall before us, turning right toward the kitchen garden, and then left into the Lord Deputy's house where another guard fell by the same treatment.

We would not kill on this venture, for it would make us no better than Chichester. I was frightened to the bone, but nothing was going to stop us, and no one was going to kill me with these Scots at my back. I remembered the day I watched Lady Finola from my bedchamber window, sitting straight and tall on her horse, her head held high with her Scots aligned on both sides of her. These men were devoted to her, and here they were to serve and protect me. I puffed myself up like a queen.

"Guards!" I called, a signal not only to send the Scots to their positions but also to alert the Lord Deputy of our presence. Two guards came for us, but quickly met with the flat of the Scotsmen's broadswords and were shoved like sacks into a storage closet.

When no one else came but a young servant boy, I addressed him. "I am Lady Maire O'Doherty. I require at once an audience with the Lord Deputy. He will wish to see me."

The boy was shaking in his shoes. "You…you must leave at once," he said.

My leading soldier, Gilmat, showered the boy with a great blast of official-sounding speech, loud, sharp, urgent, and tangled so thick with accent it defied understanding. Two others from my escort surged forward and pressed the boy against the wall. "Lord Chichester!" Gilmat bellowed. The boy pointed the direction. Gilmat smiled and nodded. "My lady. Shall we carry on?"

"Sir," I said, and led the way through the castle residence to the Lord Deputy's private study at the end of a dim hall. Two armed guards at the door shouldered their muskets but before they could aim the Scots were upon them and knocked them out. We barged into the office. Chichester cowered behind the door, his face purpled with rage when he saw me.

"Oh, there you are, sir," I said, and within seconds Gilmat and his mate Hamish had jerked Chichester forward, spun him around and tied his arms to his chair. His eyes were wide, astonished, and beaming with hate. In my white mourning dress, I must have looked like a tiny angel between two yellow leviathans. I was quite enjoying the moment. "Lord Deputy Chichester," I said. "It's time we had a talk."

"Lady O'Doherty, you dare to restrain me! My guards shall kill you in seconds."

"Oh dear," I replied, as calmly as I could manage. "I'm afraid I have a great deal of business with you, sir, and your guards are quite indisposed. Best we talk first, and then I'll leave without commotion."

"I've no intention of…" Chichester began, but my soldiers moved a step closer, revealing their weapons. "You'll burn for this," he said.

"No sir," I said calmly. "I won't. Now then. I've been looking into your deeds from the past and of late. Goodness, what a trail you leave. Your first crime as a young man was to rob the Queen's purveyor. The Queen's! So bold for one so young. And certainly foolish, for it did not go well. To avoid going to prison you had to escape, and how convenient! Just across the English Channel was Ireland, and a government already well populated with English thieves. Sure you felt right at home. Certainly you found your opportunities.

Your next move into criminal behavior was a bit of boyish fun, joining Sir Francis Drake's ship, unlawfully stealing treasures from the Spanish. Piracy, you know, and outlawed by the Queen. You even captained your own ship until Drake died and you and your lads shoved him overboard in a lead coffin. A terrible demise. Does your darling wife Lettice know of your rogue adventures on the seas? Or her father, perhaps?"

He tried to rise from his chair, but Hamish pushed him down.

"You decided a murderous piracy might not be so lucrative after all, but it wasn't until your brother was killed at Carrickfergus that you truly released your demon, killing every being in sight without distinction or conscience. In Belfast and in Dublin, you found a full stable of thieves, liars, and greedy manipulators holding high positions. Lord Mountjoy found his perfect henchman in you, who wouldn't mind killing women and children as if they were rats, and burning vast lands to create famines, and all the while your lord never soiled a finger.

When Mountjoy returned to London, the charming nobles of Dublin's high government welcomed you graciously, for you were of their own breed. And you could stay as long as you wished if you'd accept the least rewarding and most demanding government position as Lord Deputy. But goodness! You transformed your job into a vast goldmine with easy diggings. If the pirates of the world had known your profitable schemes, they'd never have launched a ship."

"You know nothing," Chichester said.

"On the contrary. I know everything. Test me if you must, but it will cost." Gilmat and Hamish pressed a bit closer to Chichester.

"Your next act of treachery came as if on a silver platter, isn't that so? The Catholics did you a grand favor with their gunpowder plot in London, so much so, there were rumors that the whole plot was invented by Protestants so to manipulate the King. But you! You independently created the mandates. A brilliant means to easily pick the pockets of men in the peerage with your well-staged raging and hefty, juicy fines. If a man of wealth and good standing, his family rooted in Ireland for centuries and providing continuous service and loyalty to the crown, should refuse to attend a Protestant worship, you could ruin him with the single stroke of your pen. If anyone complained, you'd simply pop him into prison before he had the chance to alert the King. I certainly know what that feels like. Let the Privy Council shake its fist, you were happily out of reach."

"Enough! I've no need to listen to a woman. I'll have you back in prison and in chains!" he said.

I gave him a dramatic shrug. "Actually, I'm not quite finished, and it seems your guards may be some time in responding." I waved my hand to Gilmat, who spoke a word and the soldier opened the chamber door to reveal the line of Scottish soldiers with weapons drawn, waiting for action. Chichester's face paled.

"We'll finish our conversation, shall we? I know all about your properties at Carrickfergus, Antrim, Armagh, Belfast, and some of them so vast that you'd be hanged at once if the King had even the slightest notion of their size. You've connected with land-grabbing thieves even greater than yourself, and you take a healthy bite of each parcel they collect. Best of all, no one can complain because you granted yourself the power to preside over all of Ireland's land transactions. You know what is being bought or sold, where and when large parcels become available, and each transaction crosses through your sticky, greedy hands. The Devil himself must admire you! But then also, God is watching.

"Having kept me in prison for eighty days—a young widow who has committed no crime—you prevented me from filing for any inheritance of my husband's properties on behalf of myself and our child. You made your claim for the whole of Inishowen before anyone else knew it might be available, and you took all the fishing rights that go with it, infringing even on the rights of your own neighbor, Sir Randall MacDonnell. My God, your greed knows no end. You are despicable."

"And you, Lady, are nothing."

"Ah yes, that is truly the way you think. You—the master of stealing, lying, falsifying documents, scorched earth destruction, famine, disease, the murder of helpless women, the killing of infants. If I am nothing, you are the Devil's vomit. The fires of hell will be far too good for you."

He scoffed. "Let me be."

"Did you know, Sir Chichester, that since my marriage to Cahir I have been in frequent correspondence with King James and his lovely wife, Queen Anne? He was most kind to me after I lost my first child. The Queen had experienced the same tragedy just before me, and another most recently. Such an event is far more painful than any torture you could design. But I have learned, simply by a visit to the church, that you and your wife have also lost a child. Another tragedy and I'm sorry for you. It is good to show compassion for the misfortunes of others, don't you agree, and to maintain good communication?

"I am certain also, that after our close correspondence about our children, His Majesty would not wish to see myself and my daughter homeless and without income. In fact, I think it best that I go to him directly, explain our situation, and weep at his feet as I request both the land and a pension."

"But first, I am not at all sure King James is aware of the vastness and productive value of our Inishowen. Goodness, I have been remiss in keeping him informed of such things. Surely, he would want a part of this abundance for the Crown—at least the lovely coast at Malin Head, and the mouth of the River Foyle for his ships. He'd be especially concerned that he's not been kept abreast of this by your friend, the Earl of Salisbury. How could someone so high in the King's council withhold such valuable information from His Majestie? I should inform the King at once."

"Enough!" Chichester shouted.

"But sir, this is only the fourth thing on my list. There is much more to discuss."

"What do you want?"

I gasped. "At last, your ears have opened! My requests are quite simple and you may dispense with them this very day. First, you will return to Viscount Gormanston and Sir Thomas Fitzwilliams the £500 each that you stole from them by way of outrageous and falsely devised fines against my husband. The monies were never contributed to the government coffer but instead were used by you personally to purchase more land. I have proof of this and do not doubt it. I will take back the money today in gold coin please.

"And second, in compensation for the loss of my home and properties, I will require and annual pension of £105, starting today, for my lifetime and to transfer to my children upon my death. I will require this on paper, written in your hand and with the Lord Deputy's official seal upon it as well as the King's. I will not be cheated or fooled by the falsehood performed for my husband years ago.

"Argue with me and the pension doubles. Refuse me, and the King will know the details of every single one of your cheats, your concealments, and your crimes. Harm me, and there is another at ready who will step exactly into my place and carry on. You will never be secure."

Chichester's face was dark, his eyes searing, and his mouth locked in a grimace. "A woman should not be such as you," he said.

I nodded in agreement. "There'd have been no need for it, if not for a man such as you," I replied.

The Scotsmen stood by while I watched him count the money, establish my pension and its terms, then sign and apply the seals. When I had what I needed in hand, I and my Scotsmen departed quickly through the postern gate, gathered our horses and disappeared into the land. It would take weeks for Chichester to muster any troops against us, and he was wise enough to know things would not end well if he did. As long as King James lived, I and mine would be protected, but evermore I would keep a great distance between myself and Sir Arthur Chichester.

56

MAIRE

Treasures

By late February the weather remained quite cool, and yet the grounds were nearly as green as summer, well-watered by the frequent showers. My mind was often distracted, divided, and then scattered among the many fears and sorrows I had experienced. Walking in the woods was the only thing that soothed me if only for a brief time. I walked before breakfast and then joined Jenico at the table where he enjoyed his eggs and rashers. My own appetite remained poor, but he talked a lot, knowing silence at the table fed my loneliness.

"I received a message from my agent in London yesterday," he said. "Would you like to know what he said?"

"Of course. Are you teasing me?

He chuckled and pulled the paper from his shirt and smoothed it beside his plate. "It seems that the men at The Tower have been busy. In their custody is a fellow by the name of Niall Garbh O'Donnell, from Donegal. Are you familiar with him?"

"I know him only by reputation," I said. "It is not a good one. Though he's been a man of some wealth and importance, he is not well liked."

"So it seems. He has been imprisoned in the Tower of London. They are questioning him about his role in the rebellion. Informants claim he instigated the entire affair, urging your Cahir to raise the fight, and then plotting ways to help him fail, in hopes of acquiring Inishowen."

"From what I've learned," I said, "he did much more than hope."

"Well, he may be able to buy his way out of troubles, but failing that he will likely be a permanent resident in the tower."

"What a pity for him." I closed my eyes and said a silent prayer of gratitude for Lady Finola.

"It is most quiet around Gormanston without Catherine's laughter, but you were wise to send her to school. She's a bright girl, and she will settle.

"I miss her with each breath."

"I have received another letter that I think might interest you. It is from Mister Warren."

"Is it?"

"He wishes to call on you. His home is quite near. If you are willing, he would like to come to Gormanston tomorrow afternoon."

For the first time in many months my eyes did not fill with tears. I had begun to accept my losses, for truly there was no other choice. "Have him come for midday dinner, then. I'll see what your cooks have to offer."

"I'll send a note."

Mr. Warren arrived at noon the following day. Jenico greeted him at the door, and I waited by the staircase. I'd put away my mourning dress, and savored the feel of my old favorite blue, left in a closet by my sister. It was loose on my frame, for I'd lost much weight, but a quick tuck in the back made it presentable. Anthony was taller than I had realized. I liked the strength of his jaw and the sparkle of mirth in his eyes.

"How lovely to see you again," I said. He bowed and kissed my hand. Over a light meal of fruits, cheese and chicken, we engaged in small talk. The weather, last year's fair harvest at Meath, Jenico's new horse. Afterwards he invited me for a walk in the garden.

"It's a bit scant this season, but in a few weeks it will bloom with great color," I said. "The flowers always remind me of my mother, she loved them so."

We were alone together for the first time, but Jenico couldn't help but spy from the parlor window.

"I trust your business dealings have been concluded to your liking and benefit?" he asked.

"Most perfectly," I said. "It's of tremendous value to have the proper information and guidance when needed." I offered a modest glance and touched the back of his hand."

"Perhaps you'll allow me to dance with you at the spring party."

"That would be lovely. I appreciate your willingness to go slow, to allow the course of our relationship to build naturally, like the flow of a river. But goodness, spring seems such a long time away, doesn't it?"

"It does," he said, and yet it's much closer than it feels.

"My brother tells me you have a garden, and a fishpond as well."

Anthony smiled brightly, the lines on his face revealing his good humor. He glanced toward the windows from which Jenico was peering. "Would you like to see it?"

"I believe I would."

We walked casually toward the stable where his carriage was stored. When we had escaped Jenico's view, he grabbed my hand and we ran the rest of the way like wayward children. We laughed, climbing into his carriage, and along the way shared our childhood experiences of life in County Meath. When we arrived at his two-story house, I admired the wide entrance, large windows, and a view of the river.

"I have named it Willow Court, after a garden my father admired in Cornwall."

"*Willow Court.* A nice, inviting name." I said.

We walked along the winding path of his garden to find the fishpond, lovely but void of fish because of cold weather and hungry birds.

"Would you care to go inside the house?"

"It's most improper. Jenico would have a fit."

"Well, it would be warmer inside. Would you like to go anyway? We'd not be entirely alone. There are servants to greet you. Besides, you already know my intentions, Lady Maire. My only purpose is to convince you that they are good. I shall make no advances until I can be certain they would be welcomed."

"Please just call me Maire."

He led me through a beautifully furnished gathering room, a large and sparkling kitchen with two cooks, a library much like the one at Gormanston, and a music room with colorful drapes that delighted me. Then he guided me through a hall toward a bright sitting room.

"There's something here I wish to show you. A few weeks ago I visited a cabinet maker's shop in Dublin. I was looking for a new piece to add to the library when I stumbled upon something most unusual. I thought you might like to see it."

He pointed toward a large storage chest set against the wall. It was a storage chest with a domed lid. A lid decorated with leather ornaments shaped like flowers. I went to it, my hands shaking. My heart began to quicken. Could it be the very wedding chest my mother had given me so many years ago? Impossible! Was it the exact same that was stolen from me, and that Cahir had promised to return? "Where did you find this chest? In a cabinet maker's shop, you say?"

"He told me he'd bought it from a sea captain. It was in poor condition, but it was an unusual piece so he decided to restore it himself, for sale. When I saw it, it just occurred to me that you might like it. I don't know why. Open it."

I knelt beside it. The dome looked almost as it had when I first saw it. I lifted the lid carefully and found inside the chest's walls and floor completely lined with royal blue velvet. I gasped and ran my fingers upon the glorious fabric. "It is beautiful. Absolutely beautiful."

"Maire," he said softly. "I'm so glad it pleases you. Please accept it as my gift. And if you will, there's just one thing more. If you'll give me the tremendous honor of becoming my wife, I will fill that chest with treasure upon treasure, anything your tender heart desires."

His words so familiar set my skin to tingling. How could it be? I was receiving a message, most certainly, and one that was not to be ignored. I nodded, mostly to myself, slightly confused as if I'd just awakened from a dream, but also wondering how to acknowledge the kindness of this extraordinary man. "I don't know by what miracle all this has come about, but you have restored something in me. The chest is magnificent. Thank you."

"And your answer? You needn't give it now, but may I assume you will think on it?"

I smiled. "I shall think, and dream, and wonder, is this my path for discovery. I shall not make you wait very long."

I gazed through the glittering window. I was a little nervous for what lay ahead, but sure I could manage it.

57

GEEP

1616

Leaving Buncrana

A veil of gray mist settled upon the river, drifted over the trees and cloaked the sun, all but the strongest golden rays. The changing color shifted Fia's mood and disturbed her attention to our story. I paused. "What troubles you, my sweet? Are you over-tired?"

She shook her head, her gaze fixed upon her shoes. "I'm not tired, but I am sad. I thought this was a happy love story about Maire and Cahir, but there have been many problems, and so many people have died. Is love not happiness?"

I sighed. "Dear girl. Love is most definitely happiness. A person who walks this earth and finds love is most fortunate indeed. It doesna mean there will be no obstacles or tragedies in life, but love can soften the pain of it. Love can comfort you in ways unexpected, settle you when all you want to do is run, and when troubles rise love gives you strength."

"Do you have people you love?"

"Och, they are all gone, but let me assure you, love comes in all sorts of grand ways. Sure you know them already. You love your Uncle Vaughn, aye? And you love to ride horses?"

"I do." She nodded.

"Okay, so, there are different kinds of love. Brothers and sisters, cousins and friends, places, like Inishowen, or music, or art. Mostly those will bring you joy."

"But when people die the joy goes away."

"Well, it does, lass, for a while, but you needn't worry about it for a long time. And when someone you love dies, the memory of them returns the joy for as long as you wish."

"Memories make me sad."

"What's 'at? You're far too young to have sad memories."

"I don't really know what they mean. I just remember having people around me all the time, and then they were all gone."

"God's wounds! You shouldna have to suffer such. When you're older you'll have many memories and can choose which to dwell on, be it a sorrowful one, something that brings laughter, or a beautiful one, like your wedding."

She looked out over the river flowing swiftly past. "I don't think that's true, Geep. If you could choose, why would you stay at this old castle keep, and say you will die here because of something that happened long ago? If you can choose something better to dwell on, why wouldn't you?"

I scoffed. Did she have a bow and arrow, her aim would be deadly. "I am old and useless, Fia. Such a man has only time for regrets."

She huffed back at me and shook her head like a mother whose child misbehaves.

"So, you know the whole story now. What did you think of Lady Maire?" I asked her.

"I loved her. I think she could be the one you mentioned at the beginning, both a warrior and a schemer in a single soul. She did it all."

"Sure she turned things about, aye?"

"What happened to her?"

"She made a good life for herself, she did."

About then we heard coach wheels rattling up the carriageway. Fia jumped up, smoothed her gown, and waited for the horses to come around the curve and into view. A skinny young coachman jumped from the back and leaped toward us, ready to open the door the instant the carriage stopped. Fia bounced on her toes and then turned back toward me and held out her hand. "Please come with me, Geep? Please?"

I tucked my head between my knees that I neither had to see her face nor watch her go away. The sweetest child that ever God had made. It was time to let her go, and time to face my own wretched fate.

"Geep, you cannot stay. It is too lonely. If I've learned anything from your story, it's that bad things happen, but good things carry on. Isn't that right?"

I supposed it was, but how could *I* go on? Who would carry the shame of Cahir's death? The loss of Buncrana? Of Inishowen? Didn't someone have to?"

"Geep!" she cried, but I couldna answer. It was not my fate to go with her. Not what I deserved.

Then in frustration she stomped her foot on the stones. "STOAT!" she shouted.

My head jerked up at the sound, and our eyes met. We both knew she had me now. She knew my secret. She knew exactly who I was and all of my sorrows.

"Please come. I need you," she said, "and I will never sleep another night if you stay here.'

She deserved far better, but I supposed it was true. I had been the most constant person in her young life. It would be cruel to take from her what little stability she had, to send her off alone, uncertain of what awaited her. I conceded to her victory, pushed away from the castle wall that had held me for so long. I stood on creaky knees, took her hand, and turned for one last look at Buncrana's keep and Captain Vaughn's sprawling house. Two women were hugging by the big oak door. One of them was lovely Nonie, carrying two fat traveling satchels. She smiled when she saw me and passed the sachels to the young coachman.

"I hoped I would find you here. Help me into the coach, will you?" And once seated she patted the bench, for me join her there.

I looked across the meadow to the River Crana flowing on and on behind the old castle, always moving, always changing, always the same. As lovely as it was, never could it compare with Nonie's big brown eyes.

Fia sat directly across from me, and just as the wheels of the coach heaved into motion, the young coachman pounded the roof above us and shouted, "*To Willow Court!*" Then the lass gave my sleeve an urgent tug.

"So, Geep, tell me now," she said. "When Cahir and Maire were getting to know each other, they shared nicknames. Cahir called Maire Sionnach, after the foxes of Meath. And then, Maire named Cahir Broc, because he behaved like a badger. But what about Catherine? Didn't they ever give her special name?

"Ah, didn't I tell you? They did, sure enough," I nodded. "She was the deer. They called her *Fia*."

EPILOGUE

In the end, Lady Maire and her daughter Catherine did survive. Lady Maire received the financial settlement she requested, and in time she remarried. Further details on young Catherine's later life could not be found.

The O'Doherty Clan survives also, and in many forms including the author's ancestral name, Daughtrey. The O'Doherty Heritage website claims there are more than 300 anglicizations of the surname which, in the original Irish, is *Ó Dochartaigh*. The clan welcomes all to celebrate its continuity with a reunion held at five-year intervals on the Inishowen homelands. To learn more, visit the website:

https://www.odohertyheritage.org

Lord Deputy Arthur Chichester concluded Cahir's rebellion with harsh executions and emerged from his position in Dublin and as owner of the largest landed estate in the Ulster province. In 1606 he married Lettice Perrot who gave birth to a son, Arthur. The child died in infancy. Chichester died in London in 1625. Having no other children, his estate passed to his brother.

288

SUGGESTED READING

That Audacious Traitor
Brian Bonner
Salesian Press Trust Limited

The Plantation of Ulster
Philip Robinson
Ulster Historical Foundation

Inishowen
Paintings and Stories from the land of Eoghan
Ros Harvey, Sean Beattie, Martin Lynch

Making Ireland English
The Irish Aristocracy in the Seventeenth Century
Jane Ohlmeyer
Yale University Press

290

ABOUT THE AUTHOR

The Noblest Share of Earth is Nancy Blanton's fifth novel set in 17th century Ireland. Each of her books has won literary awards from state, national, and/or international organizations. All are available from her website or online booksellers. Her blog, *My Lady's Closet*, focuses on writing, books, historical fiction, research, and travel. She is also co-founder of a writers' co-op, Amelia Indie Authors, Amelia Island, Florida.

Nancy is a Florida native with degrees in journalism and mass communication. Her interest in and love for Ireland stem from her father and grandmother, as well as her own unforgettable experiences, and friends she has made on the Emerald Isle.

www.nancyblanton.com

www.facebook.com/NancyBlanton.author

blantonn17c / Instagram

If you've enjoyed this book, please consider leaving a positive review on Amazon.com, barnesandnoble.com, bookshop.org, Goodreads, or any of your favorite booksellers or social sharing sites.

Thank you!